Devona Fayana is a  dreamy and steamy lo heart's most ardent des reflects the beauty of t delights in painting the enjoys a lovely afternoon tea, a as strolling through rose gardens while listening to Lana Del Rey.

Ardent

DEVONA FAYANA

Copyright 2024 © by Devona Fayana

The moral right of the author has been asserted.

All characters and events in this publication, other than those clearly in the public domain, are fictitious, and any resemblance to real persons, living or dead, is purely coincidental.

All rights reserved. No part of this publication may be reproduced, stored in a retrieval system, or transmitted in any form or by any means, without the prior permission in writing of the copyright owner, nor be otherwise circulated in any form of binding or cover other than that in which it is published and without a similar condition including this condition being imposed on the subsequent purchaser.

ISBN - 9798874307257 (Paperback)

Cover Design and Illustration by Vanessa Hulcom

For Rayarna.
My best friend, my angel, my rock.

Content Warnings

This love story contains sexual content, mild violence and topics that may be sensitive to some readers. It is my hope that I've handled these topics with care. For a detailed list, please visit *devonafayana.com/books*.

1. Carmel

I never thought that I would come close to death by the hands of a man that I love. For they say that a father's heart should overflow with fervent love for his children, but I can't comprehend why my own father tried to kill me.

He says that he loves me, yet how he shows love tends to leave me battered. The toxicity of his soul has inevitably marked me with the most tender bruises, permanently scarring the innermost roots of my heart. I am broken, and I'm not quite sure what it will take for me to find myself again. For there is a heaviness weighing down on me, and every time I try to shake it off, it only fights back with more vigor.

This battle with sorrow has gone on for years now. It comes and goes in waves. But it also lingers in and around every crevice of my existence. I yearn to lust for life, but why is it that I often find myself so familiarly acquainted with pain?

"Natalia," he whispers from behind.

I lift my eyes from my lap, gazing at the sea before me through my blurred film of tears. It's truly a mesmerizing sight. A rich harmony of peach, lilac and violet adorn the canvas of the heavens. The twilight sky marks my favorite time of day, for the serene waters whisper the softest melody throughout the quietness of the beach.

With every ounce of strength within me, I am trying to gather the capacity to tame my bundle of nerves, yet his presence weighs upon me with an immense amount of pressure that feels utterly impossible to flee from. I am doing my absolute best to remain calm in this moment, but anxiety will not permit.

"You're just like your mother," he mutters under his breath. "Weak, and fucking emotional. Natalia, look at me when I'm talking to you."

He is so close behind me now that I can feel it, but I simply cannot bring myself to look back at him at all. My soul wouldn't dare, for I don't want to give him another excuse to hurt me again. Through which, I keep my eyes fixed upon the sea, zip-lipped and petrified, inhaling the humid air as I ponder on whether to run or remain.

My heart feels detached to numbness, as though it's pounding so rapidly against the walls of my chest that it brings me to no longer feel anything anymore. I am desperate, yearning for some space to breathe, but it's hard when someone's presence alone is indescribably suffocating.

"Leave me, please." I quiver over my shoulder.

He remains motionless and says not a word. Yet I can still feel the stain of his fingers locked like a clasp around my neck. His lethal hold seeped so deeply through the delicate layers of my skin, so violently to the extent that every nerve in my throat feels paralyzed with the magnitude of my heartache. Makeup may cover these marks, but no amount of his apologies will heal the scars.

Bravely, I attempt to open my mouth in order to tell him to step away, but words refuse to release from my lips. My skin prickles, my heart stings. Because I have come to the realization that who I am, and what I do for him, will truly never be enough in his sight. It hurts to feel as though you have to win the approval of someone you love. But honestly, my soul has grown absolutely exhausted to keep fighting for something that should be given freely.

"Natty, my love!" Julieta, my sister, suddenly calls out from somewhere in the distance.

I peer in the direction of her call to find her speeding gracefully toward me across the grains of sand. Her dark brown waves dance effortlessly through the air as she flies swiftly in my direction. Dressed beautifully in white, her sun-kissed skin gleams golden like the natural highlights in her hair. She truly does resemble an angel, glowing and floating so briskly across the beach on the way to rescue me. In fact, she is my angel, really. My most cherished friend whom I'm quite sure was given to me as a gift from heaven.

I rise from the sand to meet her, leaping wholeheartedly into her warm embrace. The safety of her presence brings me to weep with immense relief as I bury my face into her curls. It's as though my soul is enveloped within a deep sense of peace as I bask in her coconut vanilla scent, which ushers me right back to vivid memories of our late mother.

"Oh my sweet Natty, we got your message. Diego and I came as soon as we could. Please tell me the matter." I then sense her looking aside to finally acknowledge our father, but no words are exchanged. "Did you tell him, dearest?"

I search into her hazel doe eyes that reflect such earnest concern. "Julieta, I—"

"Would someone care to tell me what's going on here?" Diego, my elder brother, suddenly appears from behind as his commanding voice ushers absolute stillness upon the beach.

He draws near, wrapping his ginormous arm around me ever so gently while his eyes remain fiercely fixed upon our father.

Diego is incredibly tall. Around six foot three, tan and athletically built. But I guess that can't be much of a surprise when one is an athlete turned law enforcement officer.

My father's eyes are burning so intensely upon my skin. Therefore, I remain silent. I wait patiently for him to speak and tell my siblings the truth, but that silence only becomes magnified between us. Through which, I look up at my brother in uneasy anticipation, watching his jaw clench tight as he irritably runs his hand through his hair.

He asks, "What happened, Nat?"

My father huffs. "Nothing happened, Diego." Instantaneously, everyone's attention shoots in his direction. "I have made my decision. Natalia is staying here. No damn discussions."

Julieta's quiet sigh swells with a hint of despair. "Please papá, you cannot say that. It is not your choice to decide what Natalia wants to do—"

"I am responsible for her, Julieta. Do not tell me how to be a father to my own child," he snaps, causing Julieta to shudder beside me. Diego's arm around me hardens like stone as a result of it. My father's focus then glowers toward me again, but I still can't bring myself to meet his eyes just yet. "Natalia Garcia, mark my words. You will come to regret this foolish decision."

A humorless chuckle leaves Diego, before his authoritative voice takes over the beach once more. "And tell me why she should trust you after all the hell that you put us all through?"

"Diego," Julieta whispers gently, always known for being the peacemaker.

Diego's distress evidently rises as he releases a troubled sigh. "Nat, what did we tell you about going to see him alone? You know what he's like."

"I just wanted to say goodbye," I tell him, struggling to swallow the fist of pins stuck in my throat. "But I never thought he would've…"

The words struggle to get out of me as my eyes soak upon seeing Diego's increasing vexed state. And just like that, it all flashes before me when he leaps toward our father's direction with the fiercest aggression that sparks an overwhelming level of anxiety within me.

"What did you do this time?" Diego asks him, though not a finger is laid on my father. But being in the presence of Diego's direct anger is enough for anyone to tremble on the floor in fear.

I glimpse at my father as he scowls at Diego with his eyes narrowed in the most arrogant-like demeanor.

"Get out of my sight," he tells him. "You're a disappointment to me. You all are."

We all remain still, watching our father walk away until Diego speaks up again. "I'm sure mom would say the same to you, if she were still here," he shouts toward our father's direction.

Instantly, my father freezes with his back still facing toward us.

"Yeah, you heard me," Diego presses, "always walking away, like the pathetic excuse of a father that you are. If you ever hurt Natalia again—"

"Come," he mutters, finally turning around with the most frightening smirk on his face. "What will you do, Diego? Cry hysterically under your bed, just like you did when I beat the fucking crap out of your goddamn mother?"

Julieta's hand rips out of mine as she speeds her way in between them. "Stop it, papá! Diego was only a child. We all were. How could you possibly say that?"

My father's monstrous eyes glue on to me again. So quickly, I look elsewhere.

"Natalia, you need me. Your head is in the clouds if you think that you can survive in the real world without me. Let alone make it as an artist! What the hell gave you the confidence to believe otherwise? You lack the skill and determination to succeed in a highly competitive industry like this. You will fail miserably in London. Do you really think I want that for you, as your father? Life is not the dreamland that you think it is. How many times have I been telling you, all of you, that I know this from personal experience? You're so damn hard of hearing, you know that?

When things don't work out the way you expected, Natalia, don't expect me to pick up the damn pieces. I may have accumulated wealth, but I worked damn hard for my money. I fought tooth and nail to bring us here to the United States as a family. I struggled to be where I am today, so that you would not have to struggle as I did when I was your age! But because of your foolish disobedience, it's time for you to learn what it means to struggle too. Those who don't hear, must feel. I refuse to see your face again. You are all an embarrassment to me, and undoubtedly, my greatest regret."

He stands there for one last second before departing from the scene. I just watch him, absolutely stunned while my heart bleeds with the poison of doubt and disbelief. Before I know it, he's then out of sight. I let out a sigh of relief as I head closer toward my siblings.

Diego wraps his arms around us, and in silence we dwell in complete shock and utter heartache.

I regret ever saying goodbye to my father. You think that some people would change or have the decency of exchanging goodbyes on good terms, but he really is something else.

For so long I have yearned to see the brighter picture of what my soul has always desired for my relationship with him to look like. But eventually, reality kicks in, and not every family always gets a happy ever after.

There is a serene sense of security that I always found in the strong arms of my brother. Lovingly enwrapped within his firm embrace, I begin to wonder what life would have truly looked like if our father was emotionally available in our childhood. He was a monster before my mother died, and he is still a monster today. They say a tiger never changes its stripes, but I can see how my mother's death has drowned his heart deeply with indescribable grief. With four children to raise on his own, I can comprehend that he underwent a large amount of pressure to deal with.

I have distant memories of him constantly working. Always in meetings, forever spending hours on the phone, busy making business deal after business deal. It's a difficult thing to accept that he wasn't the available father that my siblings and I needed. When I lost my mother at the age of five, I did not lose one parent, but two.

For as long as I can remember, I have ached to belong, because it's as though I had become an orphan so young. My siblings are all I've ever had. They are the only source of true love that I have ever experienced, and that's why it has been so hard for me to make the choice to study a fine art master's degree in one of London's most prestigious universities.

I'm carrying a sense of guilt about this decision to move, because I'm kind of afraid that I'm slowly turning into my father. For his idea of love is career progression and striving toward financial success while neglecting his family in the process. He has always managed to prosper within multiple business ventures, and he obtained a magnitude of financial security, grand material wealth, and impressive properties throughout various countries. But there is something deep within me that I desire more than that. Love, an ardent love. For years I had wished for my father to delight in making memories, as much as he did earning money. But now I desire to live my life freely with passion and to enjoy it by pursuing my dreams, rather than being bound to my father's wishes and doing whatever pleases him.

I'm determined to experience so much more than that now, for I know that there is an abundance of wealth that one could obtain, the kind of wealth that is not merely all about riches. I want to create, and I want to love. I dream of being free. To truly know what it means to live, and not just survive, that I may finally break out of the frustrating limitations that have been restricted on me for so long.

2. Mother, Dreamer

My mother committed suicide for reasons that I truly wouldn't dare to speak on. But in my lowest and darkest of moments, I can't help but wonder if I also share that ultimate destiny. I'm constantly afraid, crippled by such suffocating anxiety as I try to keep my head above the waters, navigating through the boisterous waves that life throws violently in my direction. There are good days and bad days, but with all my heart I am holding on to the possibilities of a greater change.

Shortly after our father departs from the beach, Julieta, Diego and I dwell quietly in tranquility beside the shore. As moments pass, I fall in admiration of the sky transitioning from twilight pinks to midnight blues, becoming beautifully encrusted with an abundance of stars that reflect gloriously upon the sea like scattered jewels.

I look toward the sea, beholding the glory of the horizon and drifting into a daydream, wondering what tomorrow will hold for me as my last precious day here in Carmel-by-the-sea.

Suddenly, Diego lifts me out of my daydream.

"I think we should call Maria," he randomly suggests, proceeding to take out his phone.

Instantly, I panic. "No! Can we not?"

He studies me, perplexed. "Why not, Nat?"

"Oh, Diego. Dearest, don't be so oblivious," Julieta says, letting out a giggle.

Swiftly, Diego looks at me and then to Julieta.

"Huh, have I missed something?" he asks, now pausing abruptly to roll his eyes. "Look, I know that you girls don't always get along. But come on, Nat. She's our sister. You've gotta tell her about it eventually."

His dazzling hazel eyes stare deeply into mine with the gravest conviction. My brother is always benevolent at heart. Ever since our mother passed away, he has truly become the glue of our family. He holds us together. Without him, I'm not sure where we would be.

"Fine. Call her," I reply, in surrender.

Upon my agreement, his eyes smile at me in delight before he presses the video call button and rotates the phone landscape in order to fit us all into the screen. My heart speeds up as dread begins to torment me with pricking anxiety with each second the phone rings.

"Well well well, am I surprised to see you three altogether," Maria's monotone voice moans, glum in tone. Her expression, bleak.

She's on video-call from her laptop, the device that she spends ninety nine percent of her time on. Her makeup, as always, is immaculate. Flawless and filter-like, adorned with her signature red lip and pretty lash extensions. Her stunning jet black hair shines like gloss. Bone straight without a strand out of place. Naturally, she is brunette with the softest honey highlights just like the rest of us. However, I must admit that her new hair suits her quite beautifully.

"We are truly delighted to see you, my love," Julieta politely begins.

"How's it going in New York?" Diego asks eagerly, leaning closer to the screen.

"Fine," she responds, bluntly.

Her eyes aren't on us, but rather something else on her screen. She seems kind of distracted, and I'm not entirely sure what to make of it.

"Hello Natalia," she murmurs.

"Hey."

Diego clears his throat. "Actually, we called to see how you were. But Nat's also got some news that she wants to share with you."

Instantly, I catch the intense stare of disapproval from Julieta to Diego.

"What is it now?" Maria mumbles.

I take a deep breath, softly exhaling all of my

anxiety as I prepare to speak. "Well, I'm moving to London tomorrow in order to study fine art. I thought that it would be best for me to start a new chapter over there. Sorry that I didn't have a chance to tell you sooner."

Before I even finished the sentence, I already prepared to defend myself. Because her expression transforms right before our eyes, from blank, to absolutely exasperated.

"Wait. Tell me that you're joking," she mutters, with utter reproach. "Natalia, are you really that insane? Why the hell would you—"

"Alright, give it a rest Maria," Diego interrupts.

"No, I am not insane," I reply, despite my voice shaking. "I have dreams of my own, Maria! I understand that it may not be an honored career path compared to yours and Diego's. Neither am I a homemaker like Jules, but that doesn't mean that what I want is not valuable or important."

"Have you not learned your lesson from mamá? Look where she ended up! There is absolutely no logic in choosing the path of a starving artist. You're wasting your time! You will fail—"

"Maria, there's no need for that, sweetie. Natalia is going to London, and we will support her." Julieta's angelic voice soothes the tension for a mere moment.

"You know what, I don't even know why I'm shocked, because knowing Natalia, I should've expected her to do something as ridiculous as this.

Chasing childish dreams that just simply will not happen. Don't tell me that you've walked out on papá as well? Because I know that he would never agree to this."

"Man, that's enough." Diego's impatience grows more evident. "Stop it with the complaining, Maria. I would've expected you to be more supportive, at least."

Maria shrugs her shoulders without a care in the world. "Don't say I didn't warn you. After everything that papá has built for us, you decide to leave for something as stupid as this? We all know exactly why mamá did what she did. Yet still, Natalia, you remain ridiculously blinded by fantasy. It's fucking pathetic."

Instantly, she hangs up, leaving us all utterly speechless at once. Relieved, I let out a sigh. But the depths of my heart fail to withhold the mighty waterworks from my eyes.

Am I truly making the wrong choice?

"Come here." Diego sighs, holding me tight and steadfast within his arms. "I'm sorry, Nat. It was a mistake to call her."

I'm too distraught to respond. For the last thing I ever want is for any member of my family to be disappointed and deeply ashamed of me. I love them, dearly. Though I also know that there is no point in trying to force anyone to see the same vision as I do. So as hard as it is, I'm learning let it go. I'm coming to the realization that I owe nobody an explanation of what I desire for my own life. And I comprehend that everyone is different. There is no journey, nor one path of life that could ever replicate another. Through which, I am truly earnest to just take a leap of faith and try. For I would rather take the risk and follow my heart, than not make any effort at all.

There's a part of me that can see why my father found my decision difficult to grasp. For indeed, he worked tremendously hard to move from Spain to the United States. And from poverty, he diligently worked his way up to prosperity. I am forever grateful. I always will be. Before I was even born, my family settled in this exceedingly beautiful paradise called Carmel-by-the-sea. I must admit that growing up here has been wonderful. There's barely ever a dull day there. The stunning sun, the majestic sea that I love so deeply, and even the amazing people here are truly delightful. I adore the oceans of blessings that my father has worked so hard to give us. But as I have grown older, my heart has longed to experience so much more beyond what I'm familiar with.

I am itching to go beyond the borders and pursue the wildest dreams of my heart, and I know that it may seem silly to some, but I am certain, deep down, that I can no longer keep living a lie by pretending to be someone that I'm not. Through which, I refuse to watch the rest of my life pass by, while limited to the expectations of others.

***

The early evening sun glistens with luminous glory, lavishing its love upon my bronzed skin. My mermaid waves glow radiant like locks of gold underneath the sunlight. Diego and Julieta are sitting at the front of Diego's convertible. Their conversation is wholesome and sweet, filled with utter laughter and bliss. I know I will miss this. The thick air of California hugging onto my skin, while the scent of salt, coconut and sunscreen breezes over me whenever I pass by the beach. I take one last look at the sea, which blissfully saturates my soul in great wonderment of its beauty. After all these years, I still find myself captivated by the glory of it.

As Diego zooms toward the airport, my spirit whirls about so many emotions. This is actually happening. I'm embarking on this new season, a chapter of my life that is marked with a greater level of uncertainty. From Carmel to London. It'll be a new culture, a new city. Finally, I'll be stepping out of familiarity. I may not know of a soul that dwells in London, but I am eager to flourish within this new land that I am due to be planted in.

"Natty, dearest. We're here, my love!" Julieta sings, rejoicing with excitement as the car parks up.

"You ready, Nat?" Diego asks, turning around to see how I'm doing once he clicks off his seatbelt.

Sheer nervousness grips onto my vocal cords. "Yeah, I am certainly ready!" I tell them.

Diego rushes outside with haste, and like the gentlemen he is, he opens the doors for us.

For the last time, I look around to soak in all of paradise before I prepare to enter the airport. Then all at once, I hear a loud car door slam to my right.

Swiftly approaching us is my father, casually dressed in all black. He is wearing sunglasses tinted so dark that I can barely make out the expression on his face.

In fear and uneasiness, I step closer to Diego. Instantaneously, my father comes to an abrupt halt a few feet away from us without a word.

"Father," I breathe, anxiously. "How did you know when I would be leaving?"

He shrugs, gesturing toward me and says, "You told me yesterday. I can't just let you leave without saying goodbye."

"Umm, I guess."

He hesitates. "I know that I haven't been the best father. I've made my mistakes, Natalia. But we all have our demons." He then pauses, gripping his brows together. "I'm sorry."

Diego wraps his arm around me firmly for comfort. I understand that he is trying his best to ease my troubled heart, but deep down, I know that if I told him the darkest details of last night, then things certainly would have turned out different. Yet, I didn't. I told him that it was nothing, and I assured him that I was overreacting, for I have come to the decision to forgive my father. This family is too precious to me. Too fragile and too delicate to break once more. To be honest, I'm convinced that the events of last night were probably my fault anyway. It was just a mistake. It must've been.

"It's alright, I forgive you," I assure him.

His arms spread open ever so stiffly, and step by step, he draws nearer.

Diego instantly takes a step before me. "Don't come any closer," he tells our father.

"It's okay, Dee," I whisper.

Diego's sharp jaw ticks with irritation before moving out of our father's way. Reluctantly, I receive his cold embrace, only to be heavily saturated within an overwhelming scent of tobacco. A habit of his that I thought he had finally quit.

"I love you," he tells me, taking off his glasses.

It's that cold look in his eyes, and that empty tone of his voice that truly frightens me to the core. And as hard as I'm trying to flee from this country to escape him, I have the most certain feeling that last night was not be the last time that I would experience that side of him. There's something in the air that tells me that he'll do it again. Regardless of whether I dwell across the oceans of the earth, the heaviness of his presence will always find a way to haunt me.

3. Rose Garden

London is indescribably glorious in late August. It is as picturesque and dreamy as literature and movies make it out to be. My first few weeks here have been such bliss, it almost feels like the most wondrous dream. Even in this moment, as I take a pleasant stroll through the Hyde Park Rose Garden, I can't help but admire the fragrant florals as I bask in the mellow sunlight.

There are a few pretty pictures that I manage to capture of the roses for some art references. Although suddenly, out of nowhere, my phone begins to bleep within my purse. Once I take it out, my whole world instantly stops, for it's as though everything around me comes to a halt all at once.

Elian: Pick up the goddamn phone, Natalia. If you continue to ignore me, I will come to London and fucking get you myself. I know where you live.

Wait, what on earth is my father talking about?

I cannot even gather the thoughts right now to fully comprehend what is going on at present. My entire body is trembling with a dreadful chill of anxiety as I read over the message several times, for I can't simply understand how he is possibly aware of such information.

I am hoping with all of my heart that he isn't telling the truth, but there is a part of me that is convinced that it was probably Maria who spilled the details about where I'm currently residing. I don't comprehend why she would even do such a thing. Truthfully, I don't want to respond to my father at all. Though I'm afraid that the longer I keep my distance, the more aggressive he will become. Words cannot fully describe the magnitude of fear that I carry because of him. It breaks my heart, deeply. For all I truly desire is separation and serenity. He's toxic. Sickening, brutal. It's all too overwhelming for me.

Me: I'm sorry, I can't speak to you right now.

As quickly as ever, I put my phone away with shaky hands, only to hear it instantly bleep once again.

Elian: Do not let me come over there tomorrow and drag you back here myself. I fucking mean it, Natalia. If I am allowing you to stay overseas, I require you to keep in contact with me. No damn excuses. Expect a call within ten minutes.

Honestly, I don't have the energy to deal with him at present. Neither can I seem to gather any capacity at all to respond to his message. It's exhausting, constantly trying to fight back in such a battle that you know you will only end up failing.

When it comes to my father, I'm learning to never oppose him. He always gets his way. Yet words fail to fully express how much he really drains me. Quite frankly, it's frightening. Especially with Diego not being around.

Taking deep breaths, I take the time to calm down as I dwell upon a beautiful little bench that is adorned exquisitely with an arch of climbing red roses, perfectly situated underneath the cool shade. The calm glory of the garden is so pretty and divine that it inspires me to begin drawing in my sketchbook. Yet upon aiming to create a quick impression of an isolated rose on the floor right next to me, a huge white malamute charges in my direction and proceeds to sniff away at it.

"Cleo!" Dominance marks the owner's deep voice not far away. "Come here, sweet girl."

"Ah, not to worry," I assure him, fixing my gaze upon how stunning this animal is. My hands sink through the malamute's dense and fluffy white fur as she barks at me with a greeting. "She's so pretty, and she's not hurting anyone."

The owner is now chuckling nearby beside me. In the corner of my sight, I capture his muscular arms handsomely enriched with a deep honey complexion. His hands, stained with what looks like small smears of colorful paint that resembles the prettiness of a rainbow.

"I'm so sorry, I don't mean to keep you. She's just too irresistible!" I giggle.

I look up to finally meet his lovely eyes that shine like emeralds. They brighten and smile as the apples of his cheeks rise in delight, flushing with a fair shade of scarlet.

"Indeed, she is," he responds, beaming. "She gets too excited when I take her here with me for work, especially during the summer."

This man glows so radiantly, he's utterly angelic. Tall, slender, and ethereal-looking. Every inch of his torso peaks through his sage green shirt, looking gloriously defined like the finest of sculptures. His fresh chocolate curls are pulled back into a messy man bun, with a few strands framing his face so beautifully. It almost feels impossible to detach my focus away from his gorgeous green gems of eyes. He smiles, then I smile.

"Wow, you work here at the rose garden? How wonderful, that sounds like an absolute dream to me! What kind of work do you do?" I ask him.

His face lights up in soft amusement. "Forgive me, I should clarify that I'm an artist. Occasionally, I come here to paint, depending on the weather. Other days, I tend to work in my studio."

"Oh my goodness, I'm an artist too!" I squeal.

"Well, I'm not a professional artist yet. Though, I wish to be very soon. I have desired it for as long as I can remember."

A gentle glow radiates across his face as he kneels beside Cleo, joining me to pamper her with some love. The sudden wave of his scent flows over me with refreshment and allure. Woody and invigorating. Like cedarwood and bergamot, with a hint of lemongrass.

"That sounds excellent. What's your medium?"

"I work with acrylic paints," I respond, trying to hide my grin, but I can't. Sometimes it's impossible to hide your happiness, regardless of how hard you try to conceal it. "How about you?"

"Oils," he responds, revealing the sweetest dimples that I have ever seen.

"I just adore painting flowers. Sometimes I sketch them too."

"That's brilliant! What is it that you have there?" he asks tenderly, gesturing sweetly toward my sketchbook. "May I?"

Hesitantly, I decide to show him my artwork. I then follow his gaze as it floats ever so joyously throughout the pages, and the reaction on his face instantly ushers a spark of hope within my heart.

His eyes travel from the sketchbook to mine. "May I ask your name?"

"Natalia," I reply, feeling something uninvited within the pit of my stomach, like a billion little butterflies fluttering around inside.

"You're unreservedly remarkable, Natalia," he tells me. "I hope that you will seriously consider going forward with this professionally."

He awaits my response, but words refuse to jump from the surface of my tongue. Yet he gives me one last smile before his attention draws back to my sketchbook again.

As he continues to flick through, I honestly feel as though my heart is swelling up with an overwhelming pleasure and sense of pride for my work that I have never felt before, so much to the point where it's almost as though I have literally forgotten how to speak.

"You're so kind, truly," I whisper. "Thank you so much. Sorry, I didn't get your name?"

"Gideon," he responds, warmly.

"Gideon, thank you for being so sweet. To be truthful with you, I am surprised when I receive such compliments. I guess I've always been too hard on myself, especially when it comes to my work."

His gentle eyes reveal the most sincere empathy. "We tend to be our greatest critics, don't we?"

"Yeah, but you know what's also worse? When you pour yourself out into something that you so strongly adore, only for people to just crush it with their harsh words." I sigh, trying to not let my trauma overcome me.

An awkward silence lifts within the air, yet there is something about the look that he gives me that somehow submerges me into a haven of serenity.

"Natalia," he breathes. "People often belittle what they themselves do not comprehend."

"I guess so. But it hurts to know that your passion and life's work can seem so worthless and insignificant through the lens of many others."

He pauses. "I am not aware of the cause as to why you may be hard on yourself. However, I do know that validation can't come from people. It's easier said than done, I'm aware of that, but believe me when I tell you, Natalia, that you must recognize the beauty in who you are and the work that you produce. Because once you acquire that, nobody can take that away from you."

"Wow, it sounds like you're really speaking from experience."

His gaze falls low. "Yes, I am."

"I'd really love to see your work one day. I bet your art is wonderful too! Truly, it's great to meet an artist here. Only recently I just moved here to study. I'm not from here, you see."

He chuckles. "Yes, I gathered that. What part of the United States are you from?"

"I'm from a small beach city called Carmel-by-the-sea. It's within the state of California, not many people have heard of it before."

"That's quite interesting. Unfortunately, I have not had the pleasure in visiting there."

I smile to myself, thinking that he has the poshest British accent that I've ever heard.

"It is lovely there."

"Then what brings you here to London?"

"Freedom," I whisper. "Dreams, adventure and new beginnings, I suppose."

Suddenly he rises, placing Cleo back on a leash. "That sounds brilliant. I'm pleased for you," he replies. Then awkwardly, he points over his shoulder toward an easel in the distance. "It was a pleasure meeting you, Natalia, but I need to get back to work. I don't feel quite comfortable leaving my belongings there unattended for too long."

I glance at the stunning landscape painting that sits contently upon the easel, which wondrously reflects the splendor of Hyde Park.

"Oh, that's alright! No worries!" I tell him.

Once I stand up from the bench, I force my lips to zip shut in order to silence myself from gasping. For it is truly unbelievable how massively his body towers over me. Possibly a couple of inches shorter than Diego. But regardless, he's actually like a gentle giant. I've never come across someone like this man before, ever.

"You are welcome to take a look, if that is something you feel comfortable with," he says.

My teeth clamp on my tongue with nerves at the thought of it, yet there's also a part of me that would adore to get to know more about Gideon and his work.

"Awww, of course! I'd love to—"

But out of nowhere, my phone begins buzzing non-stop through the layers of my purse once again.

I quickly apologize to Gideon, only to see my father calling. For heaven's sake, I can't ignore him this time. I'm so deeply afraid of what could happen if I do.

"Well..." I ponder on what to do, absolutely indecisive on whether I should stay or leave. "What I meant to say was... that's so sweet of you to offer, Gideon. I wish I could, but I can't on this occasion, sadly. I'm ever so sorry. I have to rush off to get some things done."

Gideon blinks ever so slowly, partnered with the most charming and serene expression. "Of course. Take care of yourself, Natalia. I hope that you get everything you want out of London. You seem like you are deserving of the world, and more."

"Aww, umm thank you," I whisper. "You too, Gideon. Take care of yourself."

As we begin to depart on separate paths, I wave him goodbye before ultimately coming to a stop again. "Oh and Gideon?" I call out.

Immediately, he turns around, seemingly surprised at my call. His bright eyes grab mine, and within an instant, I'm surged into the greatest wave of tranquility once more.

"I'm so glad that I met you," I tell him.

His eyes shine with genuine felicity as he shoots me another smile with a wave, and as I breeze my way through the floral archways, my mind can't help but dwell on him. It kind of seems like an answered prayer. An encounter of encouragement that my soul deeply needed. Everything about him seems so pure, ethereal and divine. The way he speaks, the way he moves. Such poise and grace that flows with every word he says. I understand that the thought of him being an angel is absurd, but I'm genuinely so encouraged by our chance meeting that it almost feels heaven sent.

Sometimes I like to think of my mother watching over me from heaven, helping me out or guiding me wherever she can. And if those supernatural occurrences are indeed possible, then without a doubt, I believe that encounter could have been divine.

I'll never forget this day, even though I know that I will probably never meet him again anyway. It was probably a coincidence, I keep telling myself. So I shake it off, and proceed to make haste to return my father's call.

4. *Serendipity*

Summertime cools down gracefully into the crisp of fall. It's a much beloved season here in England. Pumpkin spice and cozy nights, cinnamon candles and boots begin to make their appearance.

As I journey through the city, dried auburn and amber leaves break away from their branches, flowing lightly through the chill of the musky air. The art exhibition that I'm heading to today is now just a stone's throw away. It's within a prestigious art gallery that stands prettily with classic European architecture. It's so beautifully captivating, yet my heart suddenly begins to bleed with the sting of distress upon hearing my phone beginning to ring.

I already know exactly who it is.

"Yes, father?"

"I have a surprise for you."

"A surprise?" I breathe, trying my best to sound excited so that he doesn't get offended.

He chuckles, darkly. "I arrived at Heathrow Airport early this morning. Currently in central London as we speak."

My heart drops.

"W-w-what?"

"Come on, Natalia. I would have expected you to be more enthusiastic than that."

"What are you doing here?" I ask him, unable to mute the fear in my voice.

"I have meetings here in London over the next couple of days. Share me your current location."

"No. I... I don't feel comfortable doing that."

"Are you being disobedient with me?"

Oh god.

I bite my lip to absolute numbness, completely at loss for words to say. "Sorry father," I respond, shakily. "What I meant to say was... I'm out at the moment. I think it would be best if we postpone for a later date."

"Out where? Be specific."

"Umm, an art exhibition."

"Just send me your goddamn location, Natalia. Don't fuck around with my time."

"But why?"

"Do it, and I'll meet you there."

Tears begin to well from the cracks of my soul in utter silence, for I fully comprehend that there's no way for me to get out of this mess. I'd rather deal with him now, rather than have to face the darker consequences later.

Once I forward my location and end the call, I try my best to recompose myself as I enter the building. The white walls are beautifully decorated with masterpieces by several artists, instantly uplifting my spirit as admirers and collectors from all walks of life fill the gallery. Pictures are being taken, artworks are being discussed, and the sound of laughter and conversation travel throughout the hall with liveliness and splendor. However, I suddenly come across a particular piece that somehow sparks a memory within me. Vivid enough to make me feel as though I can jump into it and find myself in an enchanting garden. I'm absolutely in love with it. Stepping closer, I search for the name of the artist, which reads: 'Rose Garden by Gideon Knight'.

Am I dreaming right now?

The more dwell on it, the more I refuse to believe it. I stare at his name, then I rub my eyes and walk away, only to come back and check it again.

I can't believe it.

Once I turn around, I am surprised by the sight of him before me. He is truly impossible to miss. For his radiance is truly captivating enough to immediately pull all of my attention, reigning tall with great stature, towering about the art lovers that surround him. He is absolutely otherworldly, with jade stone eyes that instantly grab mine, seemingly as though he has just read my mind.

"Natalia." He sounds delighted. "It's a pleasure to see you this evening. How are you?"

His hair is back in one again today, with defined ringlets framing his sculpted face. I've never seen someone whose honey bronze complexion glows as beautifully as his. Truly, like the smoothest caramel you'd ever see. When I smile, he smiles back, and he looks through me with such sincere and caring eyes that overflow with tranquility. They say that eyes are like windows to the soul. I never knew what that meant until I met him.

"Gideon, what a delight! Oh, please forgive me, I'm ever so sorry if you think that I may be stalking you. I honestly had no idea that you'd be here. I promise you!"

"No need to apologize," he assures, tenderly. "I am very pleased to see you here this evening."

"I'm quite sure that this was the beautiful painting that you were creating in Hyde Park?"

"Yes, indeed."

"Aww, how incredibly lucky I am to actually see the end result! I admire your work, Gideon. It's beautiful."

"Thank you," he responds with a smile, seeming hesitant about something in deep thought.

"What's the matter?" I ask him.

A fair shade of red spreads subtly across his golden cheeks. "Natalia, I kind of hoped for this to happen."

"For what to happen?" I press, lightly.

"I was hoping to see you again."

"You were?"

"Yes." He beams, though appearing nervous. "It would be a pleasure to have the opportunity to get to know you, Natalia. Also, if you need any assistance with finding an agent or with starting up as a professional artist, I am more than happy to help. My agent, Angelina Collins, is brilliant. She would appreciate your work. I can introduce you to her right now, if that's something that you would be comfortable with."

I just stare at him in utter awe, blinking the wetness away from my eyes. "Oh my goodness. Really? Yes, of course I'd be happy to meet her! This honestly means the absolute world to me."

Gideon's smooth pink lips spread softly into a grin. "Brilliant. Do you have a social media page that we can show her?"

"Absolutely, I do!"

I happily tell him my details and he follows me instantly, scrolling through my pictures of artwork that appear to impress him exceedingly with great delight.

"Natalia!"

Oh no.

My father's voice disturbs the gallery once again. "Natalia, where are you?" he shouts out.

A veil of shame wraps about me as the heaviest silence spreads between Gideon and I.

"I'm ever so sorry," I apologize, completely

unable to meet Gideon's eyes due to the severity of my embarrassment.

"Hey," he whispers, softly with care. "It's no problem at all—"

"Natalia." My father huffs, finally locating me. "You didn't answer when I called you. Are you deaf all of a sudden now?"

"No, father..." My voice squeaks. "I'm sorry."

He gestures to Gideon in the most rude and irritable manner. "Who is this kid? Is this the reason why you aren't returning my damn calls?"

A let out a quiet breath. "Father, I'd like to introduce you to Gideon Knight. One of the artists whose work is part of this exhibition. Gideon, this is—"

"Hold on, what the hell do you want with my daughter?" he directs to Gideon.

"It's not like that," I quickly clarify, extremely uncomfortable now.

Gideon's brows instantly grip together before his expression softens quickly again. "Sir, I've seen your daughter's work, and it's brilliant. Natalia and I were speaking about introducing her to an agent. She's extremely talented."

"Sir?" My father barks a laugh, then looks at me and says, "I like this one."

Gideon is looking at me as though he can read my distress. "Natalia—"

"Come along now," my father interrupts, guiding me away with his arm. "We're leaving."

"Wait! Can I please just have a few moments to finish my conversation with Gideon?" I beg him. "I only just got here!"

"No. Say goodbye to your friend."

Heat rushes to the surface of my cheeks. "I really have to go, Gideon. I'm ever so sorry," I whisper, closest to tears I've ever been without letting them drip.

Gideon gazes at me with the sweetest sense of compassion, staring deeply into my eyes as though he is reading the story that is spread all over my heart. It's deeply comforting, yet heartbreaking to me all at once.

"Sir," he directs to my father. "I must emphasize that this would be a beneficial opportunity for Natalia. An agent can open great doors for her professional career. Please, allow me the pleasure of introducing her to my agent. I assure you, it shouldn't take too much of your time."

"Oh come on, we all know that she's not going to make it," my father mutters. "I'd appreciate it, young man, if you stopped wasting my daughter's time. It's people such as yourself that sell her false hopes and dreams, yet I'm gonna be the one who will be left to deal with her disappointment. Now, here's a favor you can do for me, leave her be."

There's an expression upon Gideon's face that I've never seen before. A perplexed look of disappointment of some sort, mixed with irritation and a quiet vexed state that I can so easily discern.

"Sorry, but I'm going to have to disagree with you there—"

"It's okay, Gideon," I say quietly. "My father and I should get going."

My father places his hand over my arm, and it brings me to shudder. "There's my obedient girl. Now, come along. I'm taking you out for dinner tonight. Goodbye, young man."

"Bye, Gideon," I breathe, forcing a smile, though deep down all I want to do is breakdown and cry.

I don't look at Gideon as I leave. I don't even attempt to listen out for his response, for I know it will just break me. How awful I feel for missing out on such an opportunity to meet an agent. It hurts. I despise my father so deeply. Why can't he just let me live and let me be? For heaven's sake, I can't keep going on like this. I feel as though I'm going to have to tell Diego, but even then, I am afraid that his reaction will make matters worse. I guess that all I can do is be quiet and let my father have his way. For I feel as though that's the only way that I have a chance in remaining safe.

Immediately after having dinner with my father, I convinced him to allow me to take the tube back home by myself. Thankfully, he let me, due to a random date that he's got planned coming up anyway. He always seems to be so unpredictable, it's ridiculous.

I try my best to find rest within the stillness of the air, standing on the little balcony of my studio apartment, admiring the roads that illuminate with a magnitude of bright lights and red buses.

My mother always used to make me the perfect cup of hot chocolate whenever I felt scared or afraid due to my father's rage. It brings my soul to calm, I guess. Through which, I make one just before heading to bed, delighting in the whipped cream and marshmallows that melts on my tastebuds. I close my eyes and think of her, wishing that she'd return and never did what she did. There are times when I blame myself for not being a good enough reason for her to want to stay, but as I've grown older, my heart cannot help but think that her pain must have been so immense, there was nothing that my siblings and I could have done to save her or bring change.

Once I bury myself underneath the sheets, a myriad of thoughts rush to the surface of my heart, and waves of anxiety crash through my mind, because I don't want to be frightened of my father, and I also don't want to worry about my future. Yet even though I have no knowledge at all of what the future could possibly hold for me, I know what I want. I'm just not quite sure if the plan will come to pass. I dread the day, if it comes, when I hear my father say I told you so.

The pressure is a lot. I feel as though there is no room at all to fail nor make any mistakes in this pivotal season of my life. This time is imperative for me to focus, yet I'm tired of the reproach and the many other opinions that I keep coming across in this life. The discouraging narrative surrounding artists and other creatives, not having a chance of obtaining success within this corporate-driven world. I'm tired of being despised and overlooked, just for the passion that burns deeply within my heart. This path that I have chosen seems like just a silly venture to many, and I feel as though I am constantly swimming against the tide, doing the complete opposite of what the world tells me to do, but I'm determined to try my best.

    I close my eyes and drift off to sleep with visions of Gideon. Vivid flashbacks of him in the rose garden, whose own portrait is a masterpiece. I wonder about the details of his life. His story, and his journey an artist. For it's like whenever he speaks, I am heard and understood with such caring intensity, and the sweetness of his fruitful soul has a way of drawing an abundance of hope into my heart.

    I'm beginning to see that I not only admire Gideon's work, but there also seems to be a bubble of affection for him that is rising within me, and it can't help but keep growing in deep adoration of him every time that we meet. For the more I dwell on him, the more truth is rising through the cracks of my soul. Unveiling the reality that I do, indeed, desire to see him again. But it's too late now. I wonder whether we will cross paths again at all, or whether destiny has given up all chances with me.

5. Knightsbridge

There's a man outside whose gaze remains fervently unwavering from me as I sit by a window inside a coffee shop. It's officially the holiday season, and the rainy city of London is embellished with a mighty sea of colorful Christmas lights throughout so beautifully. Yet there's something about this man whose eyes can't help but attach themselves onto mine. I sense a deep desire of lust burning over my skin through the intensity of eyes, soaking in every part of me as he stands proud in a suit that looks like it's worth more than someone's annual income.

Once moments pass, I sneak a glance at him leaning against the streetlight, lighting a cigarette ever so smoothly underneath the drizzle of rain. I'm utterly captivated. For there is something strikingly fierce about him, as though a dark demeanor consumes his very spirit.

He's different, marked immaculately with sharp features that look as though he was carved by the hands of God himself, handsomely enwrapped with a golden tan that glows deeply with a gorgeous complexion that convinces me that he could possibly be from the Mediterranean.

I've never seen hair as dark as his, utterly black like a raven. It's gleaming like ink from the light layers of rain, but something about the aura of this man suddenly shifts to something rather disturbing. He appears almost furious actually, now pacing back and forth with slow and steady steps that exudes a sense of unsettling dread.

There's a phone in his hand, and he seems to be rather troubled as he converses with whoever is on the other side of the line. Unexpectedly, he then ends the call sooner than I anticipated, and when he does, he enters the coffee shop that I'm in.

Instantly, it's like almost everything about the energy shifts, like a heaviness weighing down from the ceiling as heads turn and silence floods throughout the building.

I peek at him in the corner of my eye, and notice that there are people speaking with him in the queue. Someone asks for a photo. Another person takes out a notebook and pen. He signs, and I feel myself frown.

Who on earth is this man?

I can't help but stare at him while he continues with photographs, trying to flip through my mind if

I can recall him from somewhere, but I can't. Then all at once, his eyes snatch mine, and the sharpest grey gaze cuts right through me, bringing me to look away immediately.

I decide to distract myself by scrolling through the endless job listings which seem to fail to capture my interest. Since my father left London, he has decided to no longer support me financially, and that's perfectly okay, because I no longer wish to depend on him anyway.

I take a sip of my gingerbread latte, delighting in the tase of spice and whipped cream that blesses my tastebuds, but deep down, I truly can't help but wonder who that man really is.

Showers of hail cover Knightsbridge while the gloom of thunder and lightning dominates the sky outside the coffee shop.

"Excuse me." A deep and husky voice ripples right under my skin from behind me.

I shift my chair, thinking that someone must be wanting to pass by, but there's silence. Rather, I turn to find the affluent looking gentleman that I was admiring not long ago.

"Oh," I breathe, nervously. "May I help you?"

His dark brows knit together as distress begins to taint his handsome face. "Yes," he mutters, pulling out a chair in order to sit next me.

I wait for him to expand, but after moments pass, I can see that he isn't willing to give anything away just yet. Instead, he continues to study me with intimidating ice grey eyes, which usher the coldest of shivers right through me.

"Look, I do not mean to pry." There's a hint of Italian in his accent. "But I happened to notice that you are currently looking for work, am I correct?"

"Ummm, yes," I respond, while catching his focus fixing upon my laptop which remains open on the job website.

"Tell me what kind of work that you're looking for," he commands, leaning back on his chair.

"Why does that matter to you?"

His striking eyes narrow toward mine, almost as though he is glaring at me like I'm some sort of fool.

"Seriously, who are you?" I press.

"Excuse me?"

"Was it my father who set you up to do this?"

"I don't know who the fuck your father is."

"Well, would you care to tell me what my job search has to do with you? You're not a spy, are you?"

He stares at me without a word, locking his jaw shut with what looks like sheer irritation taking over him.

"Well?" I ask him.

His eyes quickly scan me up and down in quite a rude countenance. "You need to watch your tone with me."

"W-w-what tone?" I whisper, in a shudder.

He leans forward, giving me a taste of his rich oud and musk scent. "Tell me what makes you think that I'm a secret agent. I am intrigued to get a glimpse of understanding of what is going on in that little head of yours."

"You know what... forget I said anything. Please excuse me, I need to return to my search."

I turn back to my laptop and force myself to fade him from my memory, but his presence feels like the darkest cloud. An indescribable weight of pressure that cannot be so easily ignored.

"So..." He sighs, loudly enough to quickly steer my attention right toward him again. "You are just going to pretend that I am not here? You're quite a little feisty one, aren't you?"

"I beg your pardon?"

He shrugs with the most pissed off expression upon his face. "I have asked you a question, yet you choose to ignore me."

"And I asked you what my job search has to do with you," I snap, refusing to shift my gaze from his, regardless of how much this man intimidates me.

His harsh eyes flicker up and down as they travel over me. "If you knew who I was, you wouldn't dare speak to me in such an unacceptable manner."

"I'm done with this conversation."

"I didn't dismiss you."

Immediately, I get up and grab my things.

"Wait," he commands, bringing me to an immediate halt. "You haven't heard my proposal."

I glance at his gleaming Audemars Piguet watch. "Proposal?" I ask.

"Fifty thousand to be my PA. However, you will need to persuade me that you're worthy of this position during an interview first."

I clutch my bag tighter. "Stop messing around, it's not funny. I don't believe you."

"You doubt my wealth?"

"I doubt *you*."

"Tell me why."

"Because…" Stupidly, I lose my trail of thought as he rises from the table, for this man radiates an absolute strength that would rival superman himself.

Hesitantly, I lift my chin up high in order to meet his eyes with confidence. He's ever so slightly taller than Diego, but his presence is heavy and abnormally thick with a sense of uneasiness. I am unsure whether I will be able to get my head around it. He is utterly breathtaking. Though, not in a butterflies and roses type of way. He takes my breath away as though he carries an ability to paralyze my soul into fight or flight. I'm beginning to panic, trying to flip through thoughts of what to say next.

"Umm," I continue, "I honestly don't know you. You just appear out of nowhere—"

"Then allow me to give you the opportunity to

show you to my office. It's not far from here, we will converse about the details there."

I hold his intense eyes, not knowing whether to go with him or whether to keep pressing on with what seems like an endless job search.

I really don't want to waste his time, or mine.

"I'm sorry, but I just don't trust you. I mean, you've just popped up out of the blue and started asking me questions."

His cold grey eyes swiftly roll in agitation before they swoop down into mine. "Look, I own a company with thousands of employees working under me. Many of which are currently working at the Knightsbridge headquarters right now."

"Then explain to me why you're so desperate for a personal assistant?"

"My current assistant handed in his resignation this morning. As busy as I am, I will need to be in Dubai over the next few weeks to handle some matters. Ideally, it would be preferable to hire a new assistant to commence working under me in the new year. I do not have the time to go through a series of interviews right now, but I saw you, and thought to give you an opportunity since you are already engaged in looking for work."

His phone begins buzzing away, but he acts as though it is non-existent as I take a moment to think.

"To be perfectly honest with you, I think that you are wasting your time when you could be searching elsewhere. It's quite clear that you seem irritated with me. Besides, I am a student. Full-time work isn't for me. I would only be able to work a few days a week."

He pauses for a second. "It'll do for now."

I take a good look at him as I ponder on the thought. His olive complexion glows like gold leaf against the white shirt that he's wearing, and the black suit is pressed to utter perfection. He looks expensive. He smells expensive. Truly looking most affluent than anyone I've ever laid eyes on in my life. Everything about him looks polished and rich in every sense, yet there's that dark demeanor upon him that cannot be shaken. It's uncomfortable. I am hoping that if I do end up working for him, it will get easier to handle with time.

"Fine... I'll go, just so we can talk about it."

"Perfect." His lips press together in the most insincere smile. "Follow me."

Within the blink of an eye, he storms out. And as quick as I can, I rush behind him and try to keep up.

Thank God it's no longer raining.

"Tell me your name," he orders, now lighting a cigarette as we speed through the sidewalk.

"Natalia," I reply. "Umm, and yours?"

He quickly glances down to meet my eyes for a brief second before exhaling a cloud of smoke.

"Francesco Giordano," he responds, irritably.

"Hmmm, from what I saw back there, I'm gathering that you're famous or something? Is it terrible of me that I've never heard of you before?"

For a brief moment, I catch a glimpse of the corner of his lips turn up ever so slightly. "Trust me, that's a good thing."

6. Thunder

Upon entering Francesco's elegant establishment, the most beautiful blonde lady that I have ever seen swiftly darts into his office with a sense of annoyance about her. She looks like Barbie and Snow White in one. For her complexion is as fair as snow, with the clearest skin that I've ever laid eyes on. Her waist-long hair flows with a stunning body of soft waves. Light makeup adorns her radiant face, and her burgundy-colored suit fits perfectly on her slim figure. There's honestly not a flaw about her, yet I can see that there's some sort of message behind a smirk upon her face as she prettily strides toward Francesco's desk. Although, the moment she notices me, her face drops all amusement.

"Daisy," Francesco greets her, firmly.

Her eyes are just as fierce as his, yet they're so uncomfortably glued on him. But it's so obvious, I can tell, that her thoughts are fixed all over me. She has the weirdest expression on her face. One that looks as though she's smiling, but there's something deep within her that seems rather troubled.

"Francesco," she replies, in the same sharp manner.

"Natalia, I'd like to introduce you to Daisy Smith, the chief operating officer of my company."

"Pleasure," she mumbles, glancing at me up and down with clear disgust before shaking my hand. She then directs her attention toward Francesco once more. "Is this one of the new cleaning ladies?" she asks him.

Excuse me?

Francesco's jaw stiffens shut. "No."

Daisy glares at me with her sapphire eyes.

"Then what is she here for, Francesco?"

"The PA position."

"You cannot be serious," she mutters through her teeth, folding her arms within an irritable manner.

"I can't recall asking for your opinion," he tells her.

She stands taller in her heels and cuts her eye at me with the most uncomfortable sense of arrogance ever. "I'd like to be present for the interview," she tells him.

"You are needed elsewhere," he responds, evidently unbothered as he types away like thunder on his keyboard. "Leave us, Daisy. I'll handle this."

She stares at him with widened eyes that overflow with a magnitude of horror and distress all at once. "Fine!" she mutters, strutting back out in her heels, slamming the door behind her.

"Apologies," he murmurs quietly, still juggling with whatever he is doing on the computer screen.

I take a deep breath. "It's okay."

Suddenly, all noise stops.

"I'm intrigued, Natalia," he breathes, leaning upon his chair while drinking in the sight of me.

There's something sultry about the way he looks at me. Fire and desire, with a heavy barrier that surrounds him. The charisma that he carries is indescribable. Potent with a divine power and authority that can't help but grow on me.

"Intrigued about what?" I ask, a bit too softly.

He fights a smile.

"Tell me a bit about yourself. Make it brief."

"Well, umm... I'm from the United States."

"Wow." He murmurs, clearly unimpressed. "I never would have guessed that."

I laugh out loud at his sarcasm, but then I realize that it was inappropriate. He's actually waiting for a response.

Wait, has the interview started already?

"Umm," I whisper, noticing that he now has a notebook in his hand with a pen in the other. Oh gosh, he's taking notes. "Well, I used to assist my father in his business. He owns a several restaurants around the world. Mainly in Spain."

"Interesting," he murmurs.

"But most recently, I haven't had that much work experience as I devoted to help my sister with childcare after she gave birth to her third child. She's working on starting a dressmaking business from home, you see. Gosh, I'm ever so sorry... is that inappropriate?"

He pauses. "No."

I clear my throat. "I moved here not long ago in order to study art. My dream has always been to live in London and pursue my ambition to become an artist."

His gaze locks quietly with mine.

"And how is that going for you?"

"Not too bad," I whisper.

"Expand for me."

"I mean, as beautiful as London is, I must say that the living costs are quite high here."

His eyes sail from my eyes to my lips, allowing a stretch of stillness to fill the space between us before blinking his focus back to his notes again.

He asks me for my university schedule. I tell him, and then he proceeds to ask me further several questions that I have had absolutely no time at all to prepare for.

He then asks me, "What are your plans once you graduate?"

"I don't know," I reply, digging my nails into the palm of my hands, absolutely petrified at the thought of my future.

He briefly rolls his eyes. So quickly that I was lucky enough to catch it. "Alright." He sighs. "You do not know whether you will remain in London or not?"

"No," I whisper. "As I said before, it's terribly expensive to live here... especially all on your own. Of course, I'd absolutely adore staying here if I am able. We'll just have to see what the future holds."

His grey eyes examine me. "I am going to give you a probationary period, and we'll take it from there. Are you comfortable with traveling?"

"I'm more than happy to travel. However, it's important for me to ensure that this job will not interfere with my studies. So please, don't expect me to drop everything for the sake of this role. I'm more than happy to look for work elsewhere if this will be burdensome to you."

His patience is clearly waning. "When did I ever mention it being burdensome?"

"You didn't, but I can see that you're a very busy man. Because of that, you may need someone to attend to your needs more often than I have the freedom to do so."

I feel my heart thumping so rapidly.
Did I really just say all that?
There's a subtle smirk on his face. Why?

"Natalia," he breathes, with flat amusement. "I don't need you to worry about me and my business matters."

"But I do, don't I? If I'm going to end up as

your personal assistant."

"You're quite cheeky, aren't you?"

He carries power behind his words, snatching mine away from my lips which inevitably releases a huge wave of quiet unease throughout the room.

"Look," he begins again. "Let me get the paperwork ready for you to sign."

As quickly as ever, he types away with speed on his computer, and instantaneously, the printer starts.

With swiftness, he places the contract and a pen in front of me. "Seventy thousand, beginning in January."

"Seventy?" I unintentionally gasp, looking up at him. "You said fifty thousand, not seventy!"

His eyes become marked with a subtle emotion that I have never seen in his eyes all afternoon. "Natalia, I will not allow you to struggle while working for me."

"Wow, umm. Thank you so much," I whisper. "This honestly feels like the most wonderful dream. Please, pinch me! This can't be real."

His brows pull together. "Pinch you?"

"Yes!"

An amused breath quickly escapes him. "That's not necessary, Natalia."

I laugh it off as a serene air lifts through the atmosphere. Then once all of the paperwork is finally completed, I thank him once again and arise to get my things together.

There's a pressing on me that stains from his gaze, and ever so briefly, I catch him staring at me before he detaches his eyes elsewhere.

He clears his throat. "You don't have to commute far, do you?" he asks.

"Not too far, thankfully! My apartment is in Maida Vale," I respond, heading toward the exit door. "The underground is super convenient, isn't it?"

"Wait," he breathes. "Let me take you home."

I laugh in unbelief, but that quickly fades away once I realize that he genuinely means it.

"Francesco," I whisper, "I'm pretty sure that you had a long day. It's fine."

"I will call my driver to take you."

"Oh no, please. You don't have to do that! I'm more than fine taking the underground," I assure him, but then I realize that it's too late.

"Peter," he orders sternly on the phone. "The next destination will be Maida Vale. Yes, for Natalia Garcia. Get her home safe."

Upon hanging up, he breezes past me without a word and leads me out, and once we make our way toward the exit, I am greeted by an older gentleman who is dressed rather smartly. His hair is blond with flecks of grey peeking through. He holds the door open for me while Francesco returns the greeting and introduces us to one another.

Peter appears to be rather pleasant. Much friendlier than anyone else that I have come across in this company so far. So I step in, and make myself comfortable. Francesco shuts the door for me once I'm settled inside, and immediately after, Peter rolls down my window.

"Natalia," Francesco begins, "do not trouble yourself to take public transport on your first day. I will come and collect you myself." He says it with a look so serious and decided that I have to think twice about persuading him otherwise.

"Francesco... I promise that it's perfectly alright. I understand that you're a busy man. Please don't trouble yourself because of me."

"I want to," he clarifies.

"Fine," I whisper, in surrender.

"I will be in touch nearer the time."

Before I even gather the words to respond, he's already striding back into the enormous building again. I watch him, stunned. Admiring how smoothly he walks with such masculine poise and grace. I'm then thrust back into reality as Peter asks me for the address, and before I know it, we zoom off onto the streets.

Is this really happening?

My eyes peek up at the dazzling city lights that sparkle amongst the darkness of the sky. I honestly can't help but dwell upon the events that have just taken place today. How crazy it truly is for my whole life to change within just a matter of hours. I cannot contain my happiness! My excitement is exploding through the roof at this point. Through which, I clutch my phone tightly within my hands, eager to call Julieta and Diego with the good news once I arrive home.

7. South Kensington

Gideon got in touch with me over the weekend to ask if I'd be interested in meeting for lunch, as well as coming alongside him during a meeting at a gallery in South Kensington. It was truly the most delightful surprise. I totally forgot that he even had my social media details. Thanks to him, I've finally been blessed with the opportunity to be introduced to several professionals in the industry today, including Angelina, his agent, who hopefully may represent me one day.

After the meeting, Gideon has a conversation with one of the gallery assistants while I take a further look at the artworks that are displayed throughout.

Angelina makes her exit clearly known as she shares her goodbyes with a booming voice that echoes throughout the gallery. She then grins at me with a nod in the most animated way, now speeding off to catch up with further scheduled meetings. My eyes follow her path in amusement as she trots through the white hallway toward the exit. But then suddenly, I notice a pair of familiar eyes staring at me.

Francesco.

He is with one of the gallery assistants, and they both seem to be admiring one of the pieces of artwork. It appears as though the lady is aiming to sell him that particular piece, yet strangely, his eyes are entirely fixated on me.

Is he expecting me to say hello or something?

"How did you find the meeting?" Gideon suddenly asks me from behind, bringing me to jump out of my skin.

"Oh goodness, you scared me!"

"Hey," he whispers. "What's the matter? What are you staring at?"

It's as though I lose all trace of ability to speak as my sight trickles toward Francesco's direction again. He's looking as elegant and handsome as when I first saw him. So strikingly refined in the sexiest grey tailored suit. It's clear that he works out, for his body reigns massively well-built. Strong, and god-like. Exuding masculinity with such power, it's extremely attractive to me.

"That's my boss," I reply in a whisper, snapping out of it as I look back at Gideon.

"That's Francesco Giordano?"

"Yes, the man I was telling you about earlier," I respond, quickly licking my lips as they dry with anxiety.

Oh gosh, where is my lipgloss.

"He is heading this way," Gideon says, glancing straight over my head.

"Wait! What?"

"Miss Garcia." The familiar, husky voice grips tight every cell of my being.

I turn to greet him, and thankfully, he doesn't look as angry as he did the other day. But still, there's an intimidating air that surrounds him, and it feels strange to experience it once again.

"Francesco, hey!" I smile, but all he does is raise an eyebrow. "What are you doing here? I thought that you were supposed to be in Dubai."

"Unfortunately, my meetings overseas have had to be rescheduled to next week. However, I could ask you the same question."

I let out a laugh. But the moment I do, I realize that it's inappropriate, once again. "Umm... I'm an artist, remember? This is my friend, Gideon. He has an art exhibition coming up here soon."

"Pleasure to meet you." Gideon exposes his hand to shake Francesco's, but there is no exchange.

Francesco glares at Gideon. "Friend?"

What's that supposed to mean?

Suddenly, the gallery assistant rushes back to Francesco's side. "One hundred thousand, sir."

"I'll take it," he replies.

Her eyes then light up as if to say thank you. "Bear with us one moment, Mr Giordano. We will get the paperwork ready!"

"Yes, of course."

I wasn't aware that Francesco invested in art. To be honest, it only makes me even more attracted to him.

Once the gallery assistant leaves the scene, we're all left in an awkward position again. Gideon's urge to escape through the nearest exit is itching right through me, and Francesco's presence is just too overwhelming.

"Wow," I breathe, trying to lighten up the air. "I never knew that you were quite the collector!"

"You don't know me, Miss Garcia."

His words cut me sharp. "I…"

"Hey listen, Francesco, it was nice meeting you," Gideon interrupts, "but Natalia and I should get going."

"Wait," Francesco commands, ceasing us from all movement. "Remind me, what is your name?"

Gideon pauses for a second. "Gideon Knight."

Francesco's brows crinkle together. "I have never heard of you."

Silence.

"But I'm sure that you have a few pieces on display here now, don't you, Gideon?" I speak up, nervously. "Why don't you show Francesco while he is waiting for the paperwork."

Gideon is looking at me with displeasure, but I

truly can't let him leave just yet. Especially knowing that Francesco doesn't realize the exceptional talent of the wonderful artist that he's speaking to.

"Natalia, your boss is quite capable of looking around the gallery himself," Gideon responds.

"Actually, you know what, I want to see them again anyway. Come, show us please!" I beg. "You want to see them too, don't you Francesco?"

Francesco smiles unusually softly as he looks at me, but that softness instantly evaporates the moment that his eyes catch on to Gideon. "If it makes you feel better, then yes. I will take a look at it, briefly."

"How wonderful!" I say, clearing the air upon leading the way. Without delay, they both follow, and I show Francesco to my favorite piece of Gideon's that is here currently hanging in the gallery. It's a textured oil painting of a beautiful little cottage in the countryside, nearby pretty pink flowers.

"It's utterly beautiful, Gideon," I mention. "It's so dreamy, isn't it?" I press, as my eyes briefly lock with Francesco's.

"Certainly," he replies.

His agreement is actually a refreshing surprise. Though, I can't tell whether he's actually being genuine or sarcastic. I peek toward Gideon's direction, and he looks as irritated as ever.

The gallery assistant randomly pops up again beside Francesco. "Mr Giordano, we are ready for you now. Please accept our apologies for the delay."

Francesco acknowledges her, and then points briefly to Gideon's painting. "I'll take this one too."

"Oh my goodness!" I blurt, before covering my lips.

He's fighting a smile again.

"Good heavens, sir!" The assistant happily rejoices. "Someone is feeling quite festive today!"

Francesco shoots me a blank look before he walks off with the assistant. "Yes," I hear him murmur. "I sure am."

8. Selfish

It's the second week of December, and I decide to spend the course of the morning in bed. I've been sketching some pretty flowers that Gideon sweetly blessed me with the other day. White, huge and beautiful fresh roses. It was such a lovely gift from him. They're so heavenly, bringing such a fabulous floral scent into my modest apartment. It adds such delicate femininity that this outdated apartment needs.

Lightning is quick to capture my attention outside the window. Once again, it's a rainy day today, showering so heavily with bricks. Those weighty hailstones keep knocking so vigorously against the windows that I'm afraid that they may shatter. Though unexpectedly, my phone begins to ring. I pick it up assuming it's Diego, since he calls me most mornings.

"Dee Dee! I miss you."

"Natalia."

"Francesco!" I breathe, startled at the sudden sound of his voice. "Oh! Forgive me. I thought you were—"

"Save it," he interrupts. "I need you to come into the office, immediately."

"Oh… Whatever for?"

"There are a number of matters that we need to discuss, regarding your schedule."

"My goodness, that sounds quite worrying! Should I be concerned about this?"

There's a pause before he speaks. "Arrive as soon as you can, Natalia. I'll be waiting."

I knock on his office door, and he opens it without delay, blessing me with the rich fragrance of oud that beautifully exudes from him. He looks utterly dashing today, dressed in a classic white shirt with neat navy blue pants. I can't help but be reminded of those charming gentlemen from the old Hollywood movies. Truly, Francesco is the absolute epitome of refinement and masculinity. But there's something in his eyes that look wild in this moment, with dilated pupils as he sets his eyes on me. In fact, they're so large right now that I can barely see the grey in his eyes. Why?

"I came as soon as I can!" I tell him, while trying to catch a breath. "Gosh, I ran here from the underground station!"

He gives me one look. "That wasn't necessary."

"But you said to come as soon as!"

"Yes, you are correct." The corner of his lips twitch. "However, I did not anticipate that you would comply so soon."

"Why is that?"

"Please, sit down."

"What's going on?" I ask, while taking a seat.

"Natalia," he breathes. "You look..."

"Umm, I look what?"

He clears his throat. "Cold."

Stupidly, I can't help but burst out giggling at his response.

"Sorry," I apologize, failing terribly to compose myself. "You're not making sense. How on earth do I look cold? I'm absolutely boiling from running to make it here to you on time!"

I can't stop laughing, and Francesco is seriously not impressed. His sharp cold eyes irritably roll about the room before they attach themselves to me again.

"Why did you call me here, Francesco?"

He pauses. "Come with me, Natalia."

"I beg your pardon?"

"Assist me on my trip to Dubai."

"I can't do that."

"Why not?"

"Because I honestly don't see the point of me going with you right now. I thought that you didn't need me to assist you until the new year?"

"Yes, you are correct. However, I…"

"You what?" I hold in my giggles.

He's being so serious.

Why can't I stop laughing?

"You are welcome to assist me, Natalia." His jaw presses shut. "If you'd like."

"Hmm. Let me think about that… Will there be any other employees coming along too?"

His brows tug together. "Tell me, why is that your concern?"

Because I want to be alone with you.

"Because I haven't had any training."

"I can make arrangements."

I think about it for a long while. A bit too long, actually. It's just that I've always desired to travel, especially to Dubai. But then I think of Julieta, and how desperately she's longing to see me sometime during the holidays. My heart sinks to disappoint her, so I'd rather let this opportunity go on this occasion.

"I'm sorry, Francesco." I sigh, with deep regret. "I can't, sadly. I promised my family that I'd visit them soon. It's such a shame because I've always desired to visit Dubai. I feel so bad for not being able to go!"

"Don't be," he breathes. "There are future trips scheduled over the next few months."

"Wow, really?"

"Yes," he responds, gifting me with a rare smile.

"Gosh, I was so scared when you called."

He seems intrigued. "Tell me why?"

"I'm afraid of letting you down. I need this job more than anything right now. I can't fail at this. I'm such a failure, and I'm so tired of failing, you know?" I hear my voice beginning to crackle, so I swallow the numbness away from my throat.

"Remind me how old you are."

"Twenty-four."

"And a failure?" He exhales, studying me with narrowing eyes. "Fucking hell, Natalia. Your life has not even started."

"Well, how old are you?" I ask out of curiosity. "And no, I haven't bothered to do research about you."

He rewards me with a brief laugh. "Thirty-four."

I rise to get a glass of water across the office, and though I'm not looking, I feel his gaze pressing on me with such indescribable intensity that I feel it crawling under my skin.

"Would you like a glass?" I ask.

"No."

"Thank you so much for investing in Gideon's work," I say, now watching him fully occupied as he taps away on his phone. "That was so lovely of you!"

His eyes fire up at me and back down to the screen. "Pleasure."

Once I finish refreshing myself with a drink, I make my way to the chair to gather my things.

"Shall I leave now? I'm guessing that you'll be quite busy for the rest of the day. I don't want to disturb any more of your time."

"Natalia, you are not a disturbance to me," he clarifies, now putting his phone away. His gaze is still locked on me, so steady and unshifting.

"I... I'm not?"

My cheeks steam uncontrollably as I remain the center of his attention. He's quiet, now looking at me as though he's thinking deeply on something, though I can't for the life of me read out what that is.

"Oh goodness, your stare can be so direct, Mr Giordano. What are you thinking about, anyway?"

There's a sparkle in his eye, but then he quickly blinks it away before his dark gaze returns again.

"If I told you what I am thinking, you would think that I've lost my mind."

I breathe softly through my mouth, releasing all the air and anxious little butterflies that are overflowing from within me. "Try me," I whisper.

He pauses. "I think, Natalia, that you are undoubtedly the most beautiful woman that I have set my eyes on, and I cannot ascertain what effect that will have on my work."

"What? Are you serious, or is this a joke? Though, I would never think you to be a humorous person."

He gives me this blank look that shows that there's no amusement to what has been said at all.

Those intimidating eyes grip the depths of my soul at the core, and it causes my legs to feel like they've been numbed with ice. It's honestly too much at this point that I have to take a seat.

"I cannot afford any distractions, certainly not now. It's not your fault, it's me. I've fucked up," he tells me.

"Yes." I tremble, lost for words. "Absolutely, you truly have."

Immediately, I grab my purse and head quickly toward the exit.

"Natalia..." he calls, and his voice pulls my body like a string. I turn around to give him one last look, and he's standing ten feet away from me with his gaze tainted with lust.

Deep down, I feel lust for him too, but I don't let it overcome me.

"What, Francesco? You're basically telling me that you're letting me go, and you know how much I needed this job! What on earth could you possibly want from me now?"

He turns around to swiftly write something down, then he reaches out the small piece of paper toward me. "Here, please take it."

Drawing nearer, I take a quick peek at it, only to see that it's a hefty cheque of seventy thousand pounds.

"No way, I'm not taking it!"
"Just take it, Natalia."

"No! Money is meant to be earned, Francesco. I'm not another painted canvas that you can just throw money at! Why on earth did you even hire me in the first place?"

He sighs, vexedly. "I had no attraction to you then."

"Wait. Are you calling me ugly?"

"For fuck's sake, Natalia."

"Explain yourself! Francesco, you're not making any sense."

His jaw stiffens so sharp that it could cut me. "Look, I've met many gorgeous women in my life. But I've never come across anyone like you. Your authenticity... it fucks with me."

"I... I don't know what to say."

"There is no need for you to say anything," he breathes, now closing the gap between us.

I look right up in the direction of the ceiling in order to meet his eyes. "Francesco..."

"Please," he presses, placing the cheque in front of me. "Take it, Natalia. I know that you need it, and I apologize for wasting your time."

Why on earth is he like this?

"Francesco, just let me work for you."

He leans in, so near that I can feel his huge body pressing lightly against mine. "Natalia, how can I possibly concentrate... with you around?"

I stare into his eyes as he holds mine, yielding to my lustful desires as our lips almost draw near to meet.

He takes a step back.

"Shit," he breathes, amused.

I huff. "What in the world was that for?"

"We can't do this, Natalia."

"But Francesco, I need this job…"

He shrugs, unbothered. "Look elsewhere."

"Are there not any other departments here that I can work in? Please say yes."

"No." He sighs, clearly losing patience with me. "Look, I have offered you a cheque, take it or leave it."

I stare at the cheque, and it's tempting. But I wholeheartedly believe that if I take it, I will lose some sort of dignity that I'm not willing to slip away. I barely know this man! I'm not inclined to just take seventy thousand out of his hand just like that.

"Well, would you allow me to work through the probation, at least? Just until I figure out what to do next," I suggest.

For a moment he thinks about it, but then he cuts his eye and walks away behind the desk.

I groan at his unresponsiveness. "I can't believe that you're firing me before I've even had my first day!"

"I'm not firing you, Natalia. I'm protecting you."

"Protecting me from what?"

"From *this*, whatever the fuck this is."

"But Francesco—"

"You don't deserve this."

"I don't deserve what?"

"A boss who wants you for selfish intentions. It's not right, Natalia. Neither is it professional. This cannot be happening in my company. Now please, take your cheque and leave."

"Ugh! I don't want your damn cheque, I want you!"

His eyes squint as though convinced he's heard incorrectly. "Excuse me?"

"No, sorry!" I squeal in horror. "That came out wrong. What I meant to say was… it's not merely about the cheque, Francesco. I mean, of course I desire this job, but I've also grown so fond of you. It would be a shame for us to depart like this on bad terms. Please, don't send me away."

His eyes soften a notch. "What exactly do you mean by this?"

"I don't even know. Just don't let me go like this, please. You say that you've felt drawn to me. Well, I feel drawn to you too. Though you can be grumpy as ever, I admire that about you. Because you're you, and you're not a people pleaser, unlike myself."

"You are a people pleaser?"

"Yes, and I'm not proud of it."

Still standing, he leans against the desk and stares me at me with desire in his eyes.

"Come here," he whispers. And when I comply, he asks, "What happened to your boyfriend?"

"I don't have a boyfriend."

"Don't lie to me."

"I'm not lying!"

"Then tell me, who was that boy that you were with at the gallery?"

"Gideon? I told you, he's just a friend."

Francesco doesn't look convinced. "Alright."

"I'm telling the truth, I promise!"

"Have you seen the way he looks at you?"

I shake my head, lacking full awareness as to how Gideon looks at me. I understand that he's sweet and endearing, because he has so much love to share with others, including myself. So I don't really get what Francesco is trying to say. I always saw Gideon as loving and sweet to everyone.

"Francesco, he's truly a nice person. Very friendly and supportive, in fact. Why do you care anyway?"

"It's important for me to know."

"But why?"

"God, Natalia." He fights a chuckle. "What am I ever going to do with you?"

9. Emeralds

Gideon has invited me out for a meal this evening. Something totally unexpected, once again, but an irresistible invitation that I eagerly delighted to accept.

His gaze stains gently upon me as our dinner arrives. The apples of my cheeks are literally baking with fire throughout the whole time that I'm with him. For his eyes are like lasers, blazing right through me. They dazzle like jade. So warm, and enthralling. What I admire about Gideon is that his countenance is always undoubtedly inviting. He's so open and welcoming to the point where I honestly feel like we've known each other all our lives.

"You know, I'm still wondering why our destinies are so closely intertwined with each other. I still wonder all this time the reason as to why we crossed paths twice," I mention.

His lips stretch bashfully into a smile. "Would you not have it this way?"

"Well, these kinds of things don't usually happen to me. But I'm truly glad that I have met you."

"What do you mean by that?" he asks gently. "Things such as?"

"Good things," I clarify.

"And what caused you to be convinced of this belief?"

"People. Perhaps certain members of my family in particular. It's difficult when you've been brought up in a family where there is so much brokenness and despair present. I almost feel like if you're around people long enough, you're at risk of adopting their mindset."

"Nat," he whispers, ever so softly. "Regarding your father—"

"I don't want to talk about him."

He stares at me quietly with such care, as though he comprehends every word, thought and feeling without me having to expand any further.

"Forgive me," he breathes, clearing his throat. "It was concerning... seeing you treated that way. Your father's limited beliefs about your dreams are not a reflection of your abilities, Natalia. I hope that you are aware of that."

I sniffle, breaking eye contact with him. "It's hard to believe that, Gideon. All my life I've been told what I can't do. It's like I have constantly been told about how much of a failure that I am, so it's hard to just let go completely of his opinion, do you know what I mean? This isn't easy for me."

I never expected my heart to pour out like oil so vulnerably, but there's something in my soul that keeps pulling closer to him. Like magnets, drawn to each other. He makes me feel something. Something indescribable. I truly wonder if he feels the same.

"One person's opinion about you doesn't reflect the world's. There are people out there, Natalia, that would very much appreciate your work. I do. You're remarkable."

"Thanks," I whisper, holding back the tears. "But to be truthful with you, Gideon, I can't help but wonder if you're just being kind to me out of pity."

"You can't expect to receive the support from others if you don't believe in yourself. Trust me, I've been there."

"You have?"

He sighs. "Indeed. Believe me when I tell you that you're talented."

"Gideon, I'd love to learn more about your journey as an artist. Your words of wisdom capture my heart in a way that I find so inspiring."

He smiles, serenely. "Thanks, Nat."

"What are you hiding?"

"Erm… I'm not hiding anything, Natalia. Why would you ask that?" he asks, slightly amused.

"I feel as though I'm naturally inclined to be so

open with you, yet you remain such a mystery to me."

He chuckles. "Is that a bad thing?"

"No," I clarify. "But the less I know about you, the more I'm becoming convinced that you're not real. Gideon, you're so perfect that it's frightening. You always say the right things, it's as though you have no flaw in you at all."

"We all have weaknesses... including me. I've made mistakes in life, plenty. There is also trauma and grief that I have also found myself acquainted with. You're not alone in your suffering, Nat. Even though there will be some days where it may feel like it."

"But you never show it with me... I know that we haven't known each other long, but I can't help but see that you're so different to anyone that I've ever known. You carry such an angelic heart, fortified with a sort of incomparable strength and enwrapped with such wisdom that I find absolutely admirable."

His gaze holds mine for a little while, before sighing quietly with a subtle look of sorrow in his eyes. "Natalia..."

"I mean it," I whisper.

"We all handle trauma differently, Nat. Though you do know that you're not alone, don't you?" he asks, gently. "You're never alone in your struggles, Natalia. I assure you."

"It feels that way sometimes, and I don't ever

want to be a burden to you by bombarding you with all of my heartaches."

"That's not the case with me," he replies, softly.

"Really?"

"Natalia, the way I feel about you—"

Out of nowhere, the waitress arrives and asks if we would like a refill on our drinks. Politely, we decline, and upon her departure my mind suddenly becomes blank.

"Sorry, what were you going to say?" I ask him.

His eyes soften over me with such warmth that toasts me within the sweetest affection. "Damn, I can't remember," he says, with a small smile and blushed cheeks. "You're beautiful, Natalia. It's not nice to see you doubt your value, especially in my life."

I've never come across a man as graceful as Gideon before. The kindest gentleman that I know who exudes such patience, thoughtfulness and understanding, who feeds into my faith for my dreams, rather than intensify my doubt by belittling me.

I feel such stirring within the depths of my being, steadily springing waters of refreshment to the deepest barren places of my soul. Gideon's words are like medicine, immersing healing and replenishment of hope into places that I never knew I needed.

"Do you believe in destiny?" I ask him.

He leans back against his chair, gazing at me in

deep thought. "No, but then I met you."

What does he mean by that?

My cheeks tingle upon pondering on what to say, failing to hide my bliss that overflows from his sweet spirit to mine.

His emerald eyes are still smiling. "How are your studies?" he continues. "I trust that all is going well?"

"Yeah, actually. It's going very well, thank you. I decided to focus on florals and landscapes for this module, but I really need some inspiration. Do you know of any places around London that you can recommend for me to get some references?"

"That sounds brilliant. I have a few printed landscape references available in my studio. You are more than welcome to visit one day and take what you need."

"Wow, thanks Gideon! I'd love to. Did you previously study art too, or are you self-taught?"

"No," he responds softly, clearing his throat. "I didn't have a choice to study, unfortunately."

"Aww, I'm sorry to hear that. Why not?"

"My childhood was complex. I had it pretty rough. As a result, I have had responsibilities to attend to ever since."

"I'm so sorry to hear that your childhood has been so hard on you too."

He then opens his mouth as though to speak, but then he shuts it once more.

"Gideon—"

"Natalia—"

We both speak at once, bringing the fullness of my soul to feel as though it's fluttering to intensity, peaking to overwhelm.

"Sorry, Nat," he breathes, tenderly. "What were you going to say?"

"I... I can't even remember now. I hate when that happens."

He chuckles. "I'm sure that it will return to your remembrance."

"You're so sweet and supportive to me, I hope that you know that it means the absolute world. I appreciate you."

"You deserve nothing less than that, Natalia."

I stare at him, speechless. Utterly lost with words to say. I'm truly so blessed to have him in my life. I know that if I speak another word, tears will overflow from my eyes like the most abundant waterfall. Therefore, I remain silent, and proceed to finish what is left of my meal.

I thank Gideon for a lovely dinner as we leave the restaurant in the early evening. The sky has transformed to a mesmerizing color of a solid royal blue, almost reminding me of a Van Gogh painting. The streetlights of Leicester Square are scattered throughout, beautifully lit with a warm yellow hue upon the sidewalks. It almost makes me feel as though I'm in an old Hollywood romance scene. Gideon's support has made me feel as though I am the main character of my life again. Finally, I am receiving the confidence that I need to take control of my own life and pursue my dreams. There's a part of me that still believes that he is indeed a gift sent from heaven, and I am wholeheartedly glad that tonight happened.

"Do you need to go somewhere now?" I ask him, marveling at the cold cloud of air that rushes out of my mouth.

He smiles at me, then looks toward something ahead. "Natalia, have you visited Trafalgar Square by any chance?"

"No, I haven't." I admit, though I have heard of it many times before. "Why?"

"Would you care to see it? It's only two minutes or so from here. I can take you there if that is something you'd like. I... I don't wish to depart from you, just yet."

As he says it, we move closer together, and his hand accidentally brushes gently against mine.

"Aww, umm... of course, Gideon. I'd love to."

"Brilliant," he responds, with another cute smile. But I'm shivering, absolutely freezing from the cold weather. I regret not wearing appropriate outerwear, yet I notice Gideon's gaze scanning over me, appearing concerned as he looks worryingly into my eyes. "Are you cold?"

"No," I lie. "Actually, just a little bit."

Almost immediately, he takes off his coat without hesitation. And in the most gentle manner, he then places it over me and begins to wrap me up in his scarf. I bite my cheek as I toast in his manly scent.

Is this really happening?

His hands briefly touch my neck as he carefully handles my hair, and it brings me to shiver once more. Though not due to the cold, but because his unexpected touch feels powered by some sort of electric, rushing right under my skin like the strongest of currents. It's something that I've never felt before with him.

I laugh at the thought of this. "Gideon, are you sure about this? You'll be freezing! You don't have to do this. I don't want you getting unwell."

He rubs the top of my arms to warm me up. "I care about you more," he replies.

I just stare into his eyes, stolen for words. He chuckles to himself, giving me a sight of those gorgeous dimples again.

I follow him as he leads the way. Few minutes later, we find ourselves in a huge plaza. There's a large and glorious cream colored building with enormous pillars that stand so proudly before the entrance. There are also sculptures within the plaza that are absolutely breathtaking. Gideon then leads me to a beautiful fountain, and he sits down upon the edge. Still standing, I gape in great awe as I immerse the beauty of my surroundings.

"That building is the National Gallery. I'm sure that you would like it there," he tells me, gesturing toward the gorgeous ivory building with exquisite architecture.

I head closer toward the heavenly fountain to join him on the edge. "It's so stunning."

"Indeed, it is," he agrees, gazing at me.

"Gideon…"

He looks at me attentively with welcoming eyes. "Yes?"

"If you could make a wish, what could it be?"

He smiles softly before looking up toward the full moon. I lose myself within his beauty, so deeply enough to capture the moon dazzling iridescent through the reflection of his olive eyes.

"Though I comprehend that it's impossible, I would wish to go back to a certain time of my life. Just for a short moment."

"Really, why?"

A blanket of sadness covers his eyes. "There are people that I have loved… and unfortunately, lost."

"Me too," I whisper, trying to hold back the tears as I think of my mother. "Who did you lose?"

He holds my trembling hand, calming me still. "My parents," he replies.

I pause, reflecting on whether I heard that correctly.

"I'm terribly sorry for your loss. I know what it's like to lose a parent. I can't even imagine how hard it must be to lose two."

I feel my body naturally leaning closer toward him, more intimate than I have ever been with him before, as though his heart is pulling me in deeper to intertwine with his.

"I'm sorry that you had to experience that," he says sorrowfully, just as my tears drip. His thumb then moves quick enough to catch them and wipe them away ever so tenderly. "Would you like to talk about it?"

"I can't," I breathe, failing to meet his eyes.

"That's alright," he whispers, sweetly. "There's no pressure."

My emotions suddenly take over, giving me no choice but to let out a silent river of tears as I bury my face into my hands. It's embarrassing. He probably thinks that I'm emotionally unstable or something of the sort. I want to get up and leave, because every time I think of my mother so much sorrow overwhelms me, regardless of how long it's been since I lost her.

With such steady carefulness, I feel his presence drawing nearer. He wraps his arm gently over me, and I'm not sure whether to draw back. But I feel safe. I feel safe enough to release the distress that's been bottling up for so long within me. I feel serene to the point where I feel comfortable to face these emotions in his presence. So I let myself rest, saturating fully within his serene spirit. For I am tired of being strong, yet I am also tired of being weak. Honestly, I feel like an orphan, completely lost without my mother here, and not truly understanding what it means to have a father. I'm an alien to love. The majority of my childhood felt empty with the sense of deep longing for belonging. I have searched far and wide for the void in my heart to be replenished, only to experience heartbreak in the hands of the men that I trusted.

I am afraid. Afraid of the idea of love. And despite it all, I feel my heart warming up to Gideon. I don't know what to do. Whether to push, or whether to pull. Yet here I find myself in the arms of an angel, who destiny has ushered onto my path. It's otherworldly. His divine ability to truly break down the walls of defense that I have so long built around my perimeter of my heart. The warmth of his kindness and affection has melted the deepest areas of my soul that have been so hardened like rock. I don't know whether to be disappointed in myself, because for so many years of my life, I have avoided vulnerability. Though today, everything has changed. How can one day, and one man, have so much power to change the course of my destiny?

I feel somewhat ashamed for crying in front of Gideon. For as the years have passed by, my father toughened me up to the point where I became incapable of truly feeling and expressing my emotions openly. But there's something about Gideon that makes me feel again. His sweetness overrides the sour and bitter taste that my father had stained upon my heart. It's as though his presence alone is surging me with the strength and the courage to feel something again. To not run away from the things that I carry within my heart. So now I'm left to wonder what my future would obtain for me.

I wonder whether I will truly make it as an artist, or whether I'm going fail. I wonder whether I will have to return to Carmel. And then I wonder about Gideon. This man who has so quickly captured and opened up my heart to a magnitude of possibilities regarding my dreams.

Deep down, after tonight I can't help but wonder whether, if truly, our destinies would eventually align and be in favor of us.

10. Sweetheart

In many cases, if you were to ask a single woman within her early twenties what her plans are for a Saturday night, she would most likely tell you that she's either going on a girls night out, or on a cute date. Like all weekends, I'm doing neither. It's strange, really. Scrolling endlessly on social media gives you the opportunity to see old friends and acquaintances live out what seems like the ideal lifestyle for those in their twenties, but I've always loved living within my own little world. Like now, I'm curled up in bed with a piping hot chocolate and a pretty clothbound edition of *Little Women* in my hand. This is my perfect way of spending a Saturday night. Though sometimes, I can't help but wonder if I'm ever missing out.

Suddenly, my phone rings, causing me to jump out of my bed as though I've just encountered a terrifying ghost. I'm hoping with all of my heart that this will not be my father. I haven't heard from him in a while.

"Hello?" I breathe in panic, pressing my phone against my ear without even checking the name first.

"Where are you?" Francesco's heavy voice sends waves of chills through me.

"Francesco, I think you've called the wrong person! It's me—"

"Natalia, yes. I am aware."

"Then please inform me why on earth you need to know where I am on a Saturday night?"

"I have something here for you."

"What?" My pulse quickens. "Can it not wait for the new year, when I'm due to start?"

"No," he replies, bluntly. "I have a flight to catch within a matter of hours."

"You're not making sense."

"Tell me where you are, Natalia."

I hear urgency within the words he utters, and it's something that I've never experienced with him before. I don't understand this. I don't comprehend him. His unpredictability, it tears right through me.

"Francesco, I'm at home in bed. If it's not urgent then I think it's best to wait until I see you at work. But then again… Ugh." I groan. "Can you tell me what it is first? I want to see if it's worth getting out of bed for."

"That's not possible."

"Why?"

"Because that would ruin the surprise."

He's gripped my interest now.

"Wow, you have a surprise... for me? Are you truly being serious with me Francesco, or is this a joke?"

"Why would you ask such a question?"

"I mean, I don't understand. I never thought that you would be the type of boss to hand out random surprises to his employees."

Silence hits. "May I drop by, briefly?"

"Umm... sure," I whisper, running my fingers through my waves to scrunch my curls into an anxious fist.

I can't believe that I've agreed to this.

"I'll be there shortly."

"Wait, don't you need my address?"

"I already have it."

Before I can even open my mouth, he hangs up so abruptly, leaving me with nothing but a heart full of nerves, and such little time.

Immediately after the phone call, I begin speed polishing my apartment as soon as I can. Not that it is dirty or anything in the first place, but if you saw the state of it then you would understand why I feel uncomfortable inviting someone as established as Francesco here. Unfortunately, this is all I can afford within a city so expensive as London. I'm hoping that maybe once I've settled in this job for a while, I will be able to find somewhere a bit more modern and better suited for me.

There's a knock on the door. I hurry toward it, and crack it open a little. The longer that I can keep Francesco outside of my apartment, the better. But just looking at him right now takes my breath away. He stands there, looking at me with an unearthly glory that captures every sense of desire within me. He's dressed handsomely in a white shirt with dark grey pants, and those colors suit him wonderfully. Maybe because it makes his sharp grey eyes stand out so beautifully. Or maybe it's because the outfit against his golden skin that makes him look like he's just stepped out of a classic Italian movie.

"Hey," I whisper, feeling the frosty cold air flow harshly through the slim door gap.

It would be better if he could stay outside to be honest, especially because I just remembered that I'm wearing nothing but my tiny night chemise that seems rather inappropriate.

Why on earth did I not remember to change?

"Natalia, good evening," he greets me, more gently than usual. Suddenly, he then clears his throat before his usual dominant voice reappears. "I apologize for this meeting being arranged at the last minute."

"Meeting?" I giggle.

Time stops for a moment, and his eyes soften on me before he speaks again. "May I come in?"

"Umm, sure."

The moment that he enters the apartment is the moment that I feel the whole weight of the universe come crushing down on me. I quickly tell him to make himself comfortable, before I desperately dig through my wardrobe to search for something to cover me. But to my misfortune, I realize that I've thrown everything in the laundry earlier this morning.

I feel so stupid right now.

I feel his eyes sailing all over me, pulsing right underneath my skin to utter intensity. There's this overwhelming feeling that I'm battling with at present, absolute shame and embarrassment for not only what I'm wearing, but also due to allowing him into such a small, outdated and uncomfortable apartment. Honestly. Francesco is so huge that his head almost bumped upon the ceiling as he walked in. It's overwhelming. I feel as though I can barely breathe with him in here. His presence takes up so much room.

Desperate for fresh air, I crack open the window to gain some refreshment.

"Would you like a drink or anything?" I ask, trying to avoid seeing the look in his eyes.

"No, I am not planning on staying—"

"Okay, I'm so sorry about this," I say abruptly, now turning to face him to finally meet his narrowing gaze. "I'm so embarrassed!"

He stares at me. "Embarrassed about what?"

"This!" I gesture into the air at my run-down apartment. Then upon sitting on the couch, I cover my face with both hands to shield myself from seeing the look on his face. "It feels stupid having you here. I wasn't prepared, I'm sorry."

His heavy footsteps draw nearer, pressing louder upon the creaking old floorboards that seem so close to shattering. The couch then sinks beside me, and I feel his presence so near that I can almost feel his aura masking thickly over my skin.

"Natalia," he breathes, husky and heavy with conviction. "There is no need for an apology."

"But I bet it's so different to what you're used to," I reply. "I'm sure that this environment is so foreign to you, isn't it?"

"On the contrary."

"What, really?"

"Look, I wanted to give you something as a token of my appreciation," he says, now handing me what appears to be a professionally wrapped present in black wrapping paper, adorned with black ribbon. "Merry Christmas."

"Oh Francesco, I don't deserve this."

His brows twitch.

"I mean... I'm just not used to anyone outside of my siblings take the time out to surprise me like this, you know? Francesco, what's going on?"

"With what?" he asks calmly.

"With you... with us?"

He releases a quiet, humorless laugh. "I've often

wondered that. Especially since we... erm..."

"Since we what?" I whisper.

His eyes shoot toward me, studying my face as though he's admiring a canvas that's adorned to a masterpiece. "Never mind," he breathes softly, cutting his gaze away from mine. My heart feels empty as he dismisses it, for it feels as though I was kind of anticipating him to say something else. He then inhales and exhales, now rising from the couch. "Will you be alright here?"

"What do you mean by that?"

"During the Christmas break. Your family are in the United States, am I correct?"

"Yeah, they are. I will be visiting them for a few days toward the new year, but for Christmas, I'll be staying here."

"You won't feel lonely, will you?"

"Oh, no. I don't celebrate Christmas anymore, so I shouldn't feel too bad spending it alone."

The finest wrinkles appear between his brows. "You don't celebrate it... anymore? Tell me, why is that?"

Because I found my mother dead on Christmas Day.

"I just grew out of it, I guess."

He pauses. "If I were here, I would have—"

"You would have what?"

Another moment of silence. This time, it's long enough to make me want to pull closer to him. Therefore, I lift up from the couch, and attempt to sit nearer. When I do, he freezes with piercing eyes that remain stuck on me, looking as though they're flooding with wonder.

"Don't leave just yet," I whisper. "Stay. Let me make you a lovely hot chocolate before you leave. Besides, I haven't even opened my present yet!"

He releases a husky chuckle. "A hot chocolate?"

"Yep." I nod. "It looks like you need it!"

His brows furrow briefly, and the corners of his lips turn up softly. "Do I now?"

"Yes, you won't regret it!" I tell him.

A subtle light begins to shine within his eyes. "Thank you, Natalia. That would be nice."

While I create the most wonderful hot chocolate for Francesco, I ask him what time his flight is to Dubai.

"In several hours," he tells me.

"I'm guessing that Peter is outside?"

"You guess correctly."

"Aww, you should invite him in so that he can have a hot chocolate too! The poor guy must be so lonely!"

He chuckles. "I'm sure that Peter will be just fine, Natalia."

Whenever I get those lucky glimpses of his handsome smile, without fail I have a tendency to feel every hair on my skin lift up with goosebumps. Honestly, I've never felt such a strong wanting for a man like this before. Neither have I experienced the unending sparkling sensation of sensual desire what feels like warm honey, oozing from his soul to mine, saturating every inch of my body with sugar coated butterflies that makes me feel absolutely fuzzy inside.

I want him. I want Francesco, so badly.

As I hand the hot chocolate to him, he thanks me, and his fingers brush gently against mine as he receives the cup. I sit there, watching him with hopeful anticipation of his reaction once he takes the first sip.

"This is delicious, Natalia. Thank you very much," he says, licking the whipped cream from his lips.

"Yay! I'm so happy that you like it! Now, let's get back to this present, shall we?"

I shake it first, trying to listen out for any clues. It thuds, and I have no idea what it could possibly be. So carefully, I open it, tearing through the expensive wrapping paper which then reveals a thick, dark book.

Pride and Prejudice, Second Edition.

"Oh, my goodness! How did you remember?" I squeal, realizing that he was listening attentively during the interview when he asked what I did in my spare time. "A second edition? Francesco, these are literally impossible to find! How on earth did you..."

A joyful smile spreads so beautifully across his face. "Merry Christmas, Natalia—"

Lost for words, all I do is leap toward him with

a hug. I squeeze him tight with all the gratitude in the world. Though immediately, I quickly come to realize that I've stupidly crossed the line as I feel his body stiffening underneath me.

"Oh god, I'm so sorry!" I shriek, releasing him. "I crossed the line, didn't I? That was wrong of me."

"No." He clears his throat, and readjusts his unbuttoned collar. "It's fine on this occasion. I expected that you would be pleased with it."

"Are you sure this wasn't a mistake... giving me this gift of such great value?"

"You're worth it."

"I am?" I press, wanting him to expand further.

He gives me this sexy side eye before he takes another sip of his hot chocolate. "You know how I feel about you."

"Actually, I don't? Tell me."

"It can't be possible that you have already forgotten our conversation that took place earlier this week."

"Francesco..." I giggle. "You told me that you're attracted to me, but you didn't share with me the details about how you feel. In fact, you often act as though you can't feel anything at all. You're always so uptight and reserved. It's as though you have some kind of barrier around you, and it's clear that you barely let anyone in. Why?"

His jaw locks tight as his eyes refuse to shift from mine. "Circumstances through life have altered me in ways that cannot be reversed."

"You're broken?"

"Aren't we all?"

"In different ways, I guess, but you…"

His glorious eyes search deep within my soul, totally unwavering, seemingly expectant for me to keep going.

"But I what?" he presses.

"You're different," I whisper. "I feel it and I see it every time that I'm around you. You put on this mask of strength for the world because everyone expects you to be okay. But I see it, Francesco. Your humanity, your heart. Underneath the appearance, behind all the wealth and the worldly success, I see you. I know that you long for rest and for love, just as much as anyone else. You're not superman, you know. Even though you may look like him, you will always be you. And as grumpy as you appear to be, I know that you're deep down a sweetheart, really."

He leaves me with nothing, but silence.

"Natalia," he eventually whispers.

He seems lost for words, but then all at once, he robs mine away the moment he traces the edge of my bottom lip with his thumb. He attaches his gaze onto them, and I'm fighting the urge to lean in. There's a part of me that expects him to move his hand away, but he doesn't. Rather, he simply rests his palm so tenderly against my cheek, cradling my face as his gaze searches through mine.

"I have to go," he says, gently.

Instantly, his phone buzzes.

"Okay," I whisper, feeling my heart sinking to see him leave so soon.

His eyes linger on me for a while longer, before he then gets up and heads toward the front door. I follow him out, but then he turns back once more.

"Thank you for this," he breathes.

"For what?" I ask.

"Everything."

"Umm... Francesco, I've done nothing!"

He opens the door. "You don't realize how beautiful you are, do you?"

My tongue sizzles numb with what feels like pins and needles. For long few seconds, I'm left utterly speechless.

"Have a safe trip," I whisper. I then reach up to kiss just above his jaw, feeling the apples of his cheek rise subtly in delight.

"Take good care of yourself, Natalia."

"You too, Francesco."

And just like that, he disappears quickly into the distance, leaving his lingering scent of oud and love that saturates my home.

11. Vincent

Gideon gazes deeply into my eyes as he places a loose strand of my hair behind my ear. "Why is Vincent Van Gogh your favorite artist?" he asks me.

"Well, although I'm in love with Claude Monet too, Vincent has such a special place in my heart because I feel that he carried a courageous spirit," I tell him. "Such bravery to swim against the tide, despite life not truly unfolding the way he would have liked."

"Agreed," he breathes, stepping closer to me. His eyes glue onto my lips, bringing my whole world to cease spinning, despite us being in the midst of the National Gallery. "What is your favorite piece of his?"

"Almond Blossom."

He smiles. "You're quite a fan of flowers."

"I adore them," I whisper, teary-eyed.

"Talk to me, Nat. What's the matter?"

"Mamá painted flowers too. She was an artist with such strong passion. Yet her heart's desire tended to intimidate my father."

His eyes overflow with care. "How so?"

I sigh, breaking his gaze as I soak in the artwork before me. "My father has quite a narcissistic spirit. Everything has to revolve around him. Mamá had other things that she delighted in beyond just being a wife and mother. She carried such a creative soul with a zest for life... until he became violent."

"Violent?"

"Yes," I whisper.

"Natalia..."

I press a tear away with the back of my hand. "He's been violent with me too before. For some odd reason he despises me the most out of all my siblings. It anguishes my soul to pieces, because I simply can't comprehend why. Gideon, it breaks my heart. It's my fault, isn't it?"

He closes his eyes in such sorrowful defeat. "You don't deserve this, Nat. None of this is your fault," he assures me. Yet deep down, there's a part of me that can't believe it.

I hold his gaze as he cradles my face in his hands. "All I've ever wanted was to make him proud. But regardless of what I do, it's as though he is never pleased."

"You can't please people who require you to fit in the mold of what they believe you should be,"

Gideon breathes softly. "You'd never be free."

"But neither am I free now, Gideon. My whole world revolves around attending to my father's needs whenever he calls me. Even though I have traveled across the oceans of the earth, he haunts me. He follows me constantly wherever I go, and his lingering disbelief concerning my dreams weighs me down so much with an indescribable amount of doubt."

"We're going to have to take one day at a time, Nat. But please know that you are not alone. I'm here, if and when you need me. I apologize once more for what you've had to experience."

I sigh, releasing bubble of sorrow that blocks my throat to numbness. "It's nothing compared to what you've been through, Gideon."

"It's not healthy to compare my experiences to yours, Nat. We've spoken about this."

"But it's true. What you told me today... I never expected it. To hear all that you've gone through is overwhelmingly heartbreaking to me. Your sisters and grandmother are so blessed to have you look after them after what happened with your parents. I understand that you've always envisioned your life to turn out differently, but the sacrifice you've taken to care and provide for your family is so honorable, Gideon. You're the most honorable man that I have ever had the pleasure in knowing. Your mom and dad would be so proud."

He quickly blinks away the sadness in his eyes.

"It's important for me to care for my family," he replies. "There's nothing that I care more about than their safety and well-being… including yours, Nat."

My lips part, deeply in shock with a quietness in spirit that feels at rest within his serene embrace.

"Gideon, you're the sweetest. I'm really not used to meeting people like you. Barely have I ever been treated as sweet and as lovely as you take care of this broken soul of mine."

"When will you see that you're worth it? You deserve nothing less than respect and care."

"Gideon…" I whisper.

"I mean it," he tells me.

He tenderly takes hold of my hand and raises it to his lips for a kiss. He tells me that I'm beautiful. Talented, in many ways. I then thank him, doing my best to believe in what he says.

We continue to journey together throughout the rest of the gallery. And wholeheartedly, I feel at home in the presence Gideon. He's an absolute angel, who carries such a potent sense of peace that my heart constantly yearns to belong.

He holds me gently by the hand, and at first, I'm startled at how unexpected it is. Yet still, I'm learning to yield to my heart's desires, despite my fears and concerns of uncertainty. Through which, I overcome it. Interweaving my hand, and my heart, with his.

12. Honey

Gideon and I take the most refreshing evening stroll across Westminster Bridge after such an amazing day. After the gallery, we passed by the art store, then he showed me all of the lovely places in London that I've always wanted to see. We also went to his studio, and he blessed me with some art references that I deeply needed. He's a provider in every way, pulling my heart to fall deeper and stronger for him. But honestly, it's beginning to hurt, because the last thing I want is to ruin the special friendship that Gideon and I have.

The sky is painted onyx, decorated with faint stars here and there. The splendor of the River Thames is absolutely mesmerizing, and as I peer over the edge of the bridge, the streams of water glisten beautifully iridescent with reflection of the full moon. Gideon's body heat sends waves of warmth to mine as he stands close beside me. He looks enraptured. Those emerald eyes gleam full of wonderment, saturating in the pretty surroundings.

"Thank you for the most wonderful day," I say. "I will never forget it, Gideon. Truly, it's been one of the greatest and happiest days of my life! How did you feel about today?"

"Natalia, seeing you happy is enough for me."

His hand glides through the loose strand of my hair, resting it tenderly behind my ear again. After today, I've noticed that it's one of his favorite things to do. His touch grows electrifying. It's like thousands of peony petals blooming from within my heart.

My skin tickles with longing as his thumb travels along my jaw, now coming to a halt at the tip of my chin. I rise above my shyness in order to finally look into his eyes, and he's gazing at me with an alluring delight, burning so lovingly deep from within that I can feel it. His focus slides down from my eyes to my lips, and I lift taller like a ballerina in order to reach his mouth for a kiss. But annoyingly, a discomfort switches on within my heart. A sense of some sort, knowing deep down that this is wrong. So I let go, and take a step back, right before our lips have the opportunity to meet.

"I'm sorry." I sigh, a bit too harshly as I steer my eyes toward the river. "Gideon, I don't know if us growing closer together is a wise choice for us to make."

"Natalia," he whispers gently in the distance. "I'm afraid that I can't comprehend why?"

There's a tone in his voice that sounds different, as though it is tainted with a sorrowful and almost frustrated disappointment. Hearing it almost causes me to lose my words altogether, for I'm honestly so disappointed in myself for disappointing people. It feels like I can't get anything right. But at the same time, I feel as though I'm beginning to understand that regardless of the choices I make, not everyone is going to agree with them. For as much as I have grown up to become a people pleaser, I'm coming to a time in my life where I am reaching my absolute breaking point. First my father, and now Gideon. Two individuals that are really important to me. It hurts letting down someone you love. But how far must one go in neglecting their own heart and convictions?

I cannot tell whether it is fear or caution that is withholding me from wanting to get closer to Gideon. All I know, is that as much as my heart admires him, I am afraid that it will only damage the beautiful relationship that we have now if we go any further, and that frightens me.

I have no choice but to tell him the truth.

"Gideon, I don't even know if I will ever be capable of love," I admit, so close to tears at this point.

I see the rims of his eyes darkening red, though not a tear is shed at all.

He takes a deep breath. "Natalia, you are the embodiment of love. I need you to be transparent with me here. What makes you think that we can't give this a chance?"

I let the tears fall, but the windy weather over Westminster Bridge quickly dries them off my face. Gideon draws nearer, but I step back. We're standing right beside the Big Ben. The London Eye is glistening bright, and the city is beaming with an abundance of lights, but all I see is him. He's magnified in my sight, my soul, and now my life, and what breaks me is that I can see the hurt in his eyes. It's as though with every word I say, his sorrow only grows more potent.

"You know what, I genuinely think that this is all a mistake," I whisper, now meeting his eyes.

His eyes slowly shut while his brows knit close together. "Natalia, don't do this. Please."

"I must."

"Why, Nat?"

My blood begins to boil further in frustration. "I already told you, Gideon. For goodness sake, look at me! I am too broken, too damaged to give you what your soul deserves. I'm scared that our friendship will be ruined if we take things further. I can't lose you! Truly... I couldn't bear to lose you, Gee."

"Natalia." He sighs, coming closer. Ever so sweetly, he holds face in his hands. They feel warm, just like his heart. "I need you to listen closely to what I am telling you. I am not going anywhere, I promise. As long as I am welcome in your life, I will remain devoted to you. If you want to take things slow, we can. There's no pressure."

I can't even see his face clearly. Not with this heavy film of tears covering my eyes. I just see his honey bronze skin and bright green eyes, softening with each moment that passes by.

"I... I need time," I whisper with a trembling voice. "Gideon, I don't want to disappoint you." I let my face fall into his chest as I cry. "I don't want us to go so far, only for you to resent me in the end. They all do, everyone resents me."

"Who is everyone, Nat?"

"My father."

I feel his arms embrace me firmer. "Natalia—"

"He told me that nobody will ever love me like he does, that nobody would ever want me. He said I'm unlovable, a disgrace... Gee, I don't want to you to see that in me too. It is better if we keep our distance."

"Natalia, *he* is the one with the issues, not you. Believe me when I tell you this—"

"But what could honestly bring him to hate me so much?"

"Unfortunately, that is only something he would know. We may not find out the reason. But I need you to be assured, Nat, that you are not who he says you are. You're far from it."

"You really think so?"

"Yes," he whispers. "I will tell you what I think of you, Natalia. I think that you are an amazing and remarkable woman with a golden heart. You are courageous and capable. A master of art, but you do not realize it yet. Your future is so bright, Nat. You just can't see it yet."

I almost break down in his arms, because truly, that is one of the kindest and most loving things that anyone has ever said to me in my entire life.

Gideon continues to bring comfort to my heart, and I'm slowly beginning to feel much more at peace again. His care means so much to me, I just hope that my brokenness isn't too much of a burden to him.

"I'm tired, Gee. In every possible way at this point," I whisper. "Is there anywhere we can sit for a while?"

"Would you like me to take you back home?"

"Not yet, I just want to be here a little while longer with you."

There's a glimmer in his eye as he smiles before leading me somewhere quiet to sit. He's walking beside me, and I take a quick glance at his free hand. It's tempting. My heart wants to hold him, but there's a battle going on within me. For my mind tells me that I just desire to keep Gideon as a friend, yet my heart screams that him and I could be so much more. It's difficult. Yet, I overcome the doubt anyway, and reach gently for his hand. He freezes for a millisecond in surprise, but soon after, he settles down again. He tenderly squeezes me for assurance, ushering calmness to my heart. Then I follow his footsteps as he takes me some place new, looking forward to resting peacefully in tranquility together underneath the full moon.

13. First Love

The first Monday of the new year welcomes London with a fresh blanket of snow. Crisp air and darkened peach skies with congested roads that are filled with commuters from all walks of life.

It's been merely two days since I returned back to London from Carmel. Thankfully, my father was out of the country during my short stay at Julieta's. It was really lovely being with my family again.

Upon my arrival back to London, Francesco has been adamant about picking me up this morning for reasons my heart can't make out.

Just before his estimated arrival, Gideon has been so kind to visit me with a warm breakfast as he prepares to leave for the Cotswolds to check in on his family today. I've never known someone as caring and compassionate as him.

"That's him, isn't it?" Gideon asks me, while peeking over the balcony. "I fail to comprehend the reason as to why he deems it necessary to pick you up. You're more than capable of going to work on your own."

I'm picking up a hint of irritation in his voice.

"One moment," I quickly tell him, polishing my makeup after finishing breakfast. "Try not to worry about it. I'm sure that all is well, Gee."

"It's not," he murmurs, quietly. "I'm not quite sure if I trust his intentions, Nat."

"Why? Are you saying that you don't think I'm worthy of having such a well-paid job?"

"Of course not. What I'm saying is that you're a very beautiful woman."

"I think you're exaggerating there."

His eyes meet mine. "Don't you realize the amount of attention that you get when you're out in public? You're very captivating, Nat. I'm quite sure that he can also see that."

I sigh, brushing off his opinion while I swiftly join him on the balcony. But just as I do, my phone begins to ring.

"Hello? Dee, now isn't the best time—"

"Good morning, Miss Garcia," Francesco's husky voice responds. Super deep, intimidating and utterly powerful, all at once.

"Oh, forgive me! I didn't realize... Good morning, Francesco," I breathe nervously, leaning over the balcony to see him outside leaning casually against the car.

He stands high and strong in a nude suit with a white shirt, perfectly contrasting with his tan complexion and strikingly dark features. It doesn't take long for him to notice me checking him out. Instantly, a sexy smirk appears on his face.

"I'll be down in a few moments," I tell him.

"I'll be waiting."

"Okay," I whisper.

Suddenly, Gideon draws nearer, and almost immediately there's something about Francesco's expression that darkens, which brings me to utter dread.

"Is everything alright?" Gideon asks.

"Yeah, of course," I tell him, hanging up and breaking my gaze with Francesco.

As quickly as I can, I gather my things.

"Have a good day," he tells me.

"Text me," I remind him.

"You'll do great today."

I kiss him on the cheek as he opens the door for me. After locking it, we make our way to the exit.

"Let me know when you're in the Cotswolds safely, please. Don't forget!"

He smiles. "Will do, and hey, don't be nervous. Today is going to be a good day. You're capable of anything, Nat. Remember that."

I thank him upon exiting the building, and Francesco's face instantly transitions from stern to vexed at the sight of us. I watch his eyes fixed on

Gideon, and my eyes dart worryingly between them, until clumsily, I slip on some ice right before reaching him at the car.

"Natalia, we're late," Francesco mutters, grabbing me by my arm just in time to prevent me from falling.

Gideon's body tenses up beside me as though he's going to say something, so I speak first. "Okay, I'm sorry. Let's go."

"Hold on... Are you alright, Nat?" Gideon asks me, with concern in his eyes.

"Of course, Gee. Honestly, I'm okay."

Tense glances between Gideon and Francesco immediately start to avalanche into intensity. At this point, my patience is thinning immensely as they're beginning to make me feel uncomfortable now.

"Is everything alright?" I ask, overwhelmed with worry. "You both don't know each other, do you?"

"No." Francesco's jaw ticks. "I don't know this boy, at all." His face then scrunches in frustration, rolling his eyes as he angrily opens the car door. "Are you ready Natalia? We have work to do."

"Yeah, I'm ready," I reply, taking a quick glance at Gideon who is looking at me with weary eyes.

"I'll see you soon," he breathes. "Please call me if there are any problems."

As I step into the car, I hear Francesco respond in a stern manner, "She'll be fine with me."

Abruptly, he then shuts my door and strides over to his side. Instantly once his door slams shut, Peter speeds off into the road. Gideon's soft eyes remained locked with mine as I watch him fade into the distance.

"Your man is a friendly little fellow isn't he," Francesco randomly murmurs under his breath, gazing outside his window with his fingers clenched around his chin.

My eyes can't help but stare at him in disbelief, yet his fierce gaze suddenly fires back at me without an utterance at all.

"He's not my man, I've told you that before."

For brief moment, I'm sure that his face softens for a second, but then he quickly puts up his guard firmly again. "From what I saw back there, it seems to me that he thinks otherwise."

His gaze is too direct. It makes me feel like a flame of fire that can never be put out. So I stare outside the window, looking at the pretty city that is covered with snowflakes, but there's something about what he just said that I can't let go.

"My relationship with Gideon isn't really any of your business, is it?"

He doesn't respond.

All I feel is the weight of his daunting attention still pressing entirely on me, but I can't bear to look back at him. Words cannot fully express how intimidating Francesco Giordano can be to me.

Suddenly, his phone begins to bell, and he answers it without delay. I just sit there, listening to him discuss random business matters on the phone for what honestly seems like forever, for the uncomfortable air that he always carries finds a way to keep me on edge.

In my mind, all I can dwell on is whether I am making the right choices. Not merely regarding working for Francesco, but also with how my friendship with Gideon seems to be progressing.

The ride is dragging through the congested roads, and one phone call seems to always follow another. So throughout the ride to Knightsbridge, I dwell awkwardly in silence. Twiddling my thumbs and tuning out the constant, dominant voice in the background, keeping my heart steadfast on the classical music through the speakers.

14. Comprehension

Francesco's eyes slide across my body as I take my outwear off. I pretend that I don't see, and rather walk toward the corner of his office to hang my things. Yet still, remaining the center of his gaze is one of the most amorous experiences that one could be overcome with. It possesses me with a sort of wanting to keep lingering on as the core of his desire. And I feel it, deep down, that it's scorching right through me, tumbling down every wall of pride and bringing me to acknowledge that I actually delight in seeing his eyes drink in every curve of my body with a carnal desire.

"So," I breathe airily. "How was Dubai?"

"Tolerable."

"Okay. Umm, what will I be doing today?"

He stands still in front of his desk, tall and utterly statuesque. The way he is looking at me resembles a very frightening statue, as though he's sculpted by Michelangelo himself. God-like, firm and unmoving, with eyes that refuse to shift.

"Sit down," he commands.

I walk toward the chair and sit down right in front of him. Every fibre of my being feels like I am morphing rapidly between fire and ice. It's his unpredictability, and I don't know where to look. I feel nervous and overwhelmed with every second that he stares at me.

I honestly don't know how I'll get through the day.

"Look at me," he whispers.

Shyly, I comply, and for the first time in a long while, he doesn't look pissed off with me.

"Natalia, I thought that today would be an ideal day for us to become better acquainted with one another. However, there are a few crucial meetings that I must attend to throughout the course of the morning. In the meantime, Daisy and her assistant, Darlene, will be carrying out your training."

"Oh, that's a shame."

His brows string together. "Expand for me."

"I just thought that I would be with you today."

Briefly, his brows rise to furrow. A perplexed expression then appears upon his handsome face, nodding slightly forward as though to restrain himself from smirking. "Do you want to be with me, Natalia?" he asks, flirtatiously.

He knows exactly what he's doing.

I feel stupid. My cheeks are sizzling to numbness as he robs me of the ability to find any words to respond.

Suddenly, the office door knocks. Francesco orders whoever it is to enter, and Daisy quickly zooms in, strutting with her head held high as her heels clap against the ground. Her blonde, blow-dried hair breezes beautifully through the air as she places a large chunk of papers on Francesco's desk. Soon after, another lady follows behind her. She's much shorter, around my height, and already appears to be as joyous as sunshine. Radiant with a smile, she greets us as politely as ever. Her rich complexion glows bronze against her suit, and her stunning curls are styled prettily in a bun. I am welcomed by her with such warmth. Yet Daisy on the other hand, doesn't acknowledge me at all.

Francesco has his guard up again.

"Natalia, you have previously met Daisy before the holidays," he says, loud and clearly in his stern manager voice while breezing through the pile of papers.

"Yes," I respond with a smile. Though the smile becomes instantly erased with one look from her.

She just stares at me without words.

Her focus is glued upon my dress, as though there's something seriously bothering her. I'm not quite sure what Daisy's problem is, but it's honestly starting to make me feel extremely uncomfortable. I'd like to mention it, but I've already made such a big, ridiculous fuss on my first day.

Francesco's impatience switches from Daisy to Darlene. "Darlene, this is Natalia Garcia, my new PA. I hear that you are an excellent assistant to Daisy. I trust that you will guide and take care of Natalia accordingly going forward."

"Of course! Will do, Mr Giordano. Welcome to the company, Natalia! Also forgive me, but I have to say that you both are matching colors today," she mentions with a giggle, pointing at Francesco and I.

Daisy's sapphire eyes squint at me.

If looks could kill.

"You forget, Natalia, that this is a professional establishment. Not a speed dating event," Daisy's voice raises sharply. She raises one of her perfectly arched eyebrows, then crosses her arms, and takes one step forward in my direction. "Have you forgotten the guidelines, Miss Garcia?"

"Leave her be." Francesco steps in, with a serious command that refuses to be questioned.

What on earth is she talking about?

I believe that I am dressed rather appropriately today. I'm quite sure that if I didn't, Gideon would have absolutely mentioned something to me about it. Wouldn't he?

Daisy is still glaring at me.

Darlene then sits next to me and flips through some paperwork. I watch Francesco discreetly as he walks toward Daisy and guides her to the corner of the office. I glance at them here and there. Their conversation is quiet, almost like silent whispering. But their body language, Daisy's in particular, looks absolutely unsettling. It's so odd that I frown at the sight of it. Though unexpectedly, she then catches me looking in their direction. She freezes, and I freeze, forcing myself depart my focus elsewhere and begin a surface-level conversation with Darlene.

The last few hours of training with Daisy and Darlene has dragged immensely. I think that I am getting the hang of things, but when someone clearly dislikes you, you honestly just want to remove yourself from the situation. In this instance, I cannot, and hour by hour, I'm counting down the minutes until lunchtime.

"You've made a mistake coming here," Daisy whispers to me, with such a furious look on her face that it's almost as though I can notice the heat of fire filling her eyes.

I'm now in her office as Francesco is still busy attending to his meetings. Something in my heart tells me that she's probably right at this point. My eyes steer toward Darlene, who is sitting far across the room, but she's too busy fulfilling tasks to notice what's going on.

I turn toward Daisy, who smells strong with a flowery scent. "Why do you think this is a mistake, Daisy?"

"It's Ms Smith, to you," she corrects, looking

genuinely upset. "Look, little madam, I don't know what Francesco's deal is here, but I know him well enough to know that he's not taking you seriously. Neither can I. You're too much of a risk, and I cannot allow you to jeopardize our business."

"I don't understand. How am I a risk? What have I ever done to you? I'm willing to work my hardest in this company! This is only my first day, and you haven't given me a chance. What is your problem?" I mutter through my teeth, though not loud enough for Darlene to hear.

Daisy looks down at me with the most repulsed look and calls out, "Darlene?"

"Yes, Ms Smith."

"Take over from here, I'm taking an early lunch. You can handle the rest of the training, can't you?"

"Absolutely. Yes, of course, Ms Smith." Darlene replies, nodding enthusiastically. "Enjoy your—"

The door slams shut, leaving Darlene and I in complete and utter silence. Instantly, my eyes zip toward Darlene, but it appears as though that this behavior is something that she is used to. Though now that Daisy has left, I feel like I can release a huge sigh of relief. Hopefully the day will go quicker now that I don't have to do training with her again. It's been a long day already, and it's not even one in the afternoon yet. Honestly, I just want to go back home. I'm so ready for this day to finally be over and done with.

***

Darlene says that she usually meets her husband out in Knightsbridge for lunch. But before she left, she showed me to the employee cafeteria and wished me luck for the rest of my first day. I thanked her, because she's been so kind. Though as I now search for a seat in the sea of crowds, I almost regret not going outside to coffee shop for lunch instead. I feel like I'm back at high school again. Those times when everyone is in cliques, staring and wondering which group you belong in. It's uncomfortable. Through which, I clutch tightly on to my bag of lunch after paying, and swiftly speed toward the main entrance.

However, as stupid and clumsy as I am, I trip on something that I fail to see, and someone behind me grabs me by my arm unnecessarily tight

"Ouch!" I squeal, shoving my arm out of their tough grip. I then look up, only to see Francesco's face hardened with concern.

"Do you normally fall this frequently?"

"No." I huff, stepping away from him, but then remember to thank him afterward just before walking away. "Thank you, though."

"Wait. Come here," he says, locking his jaw with a gaze bounces up and down over me.

Colleagues from all around are watching us as they pass by. Francesco looks so out of place in the midst of them all. I can't quite put my finger on it. Everything about him seems so different, and so enriched. I admire that about him.

"No. *You*, come here," I reply.

I understand that he is my boss, but I'm tired of being commanded with what to do by the managers here like I'm a puppy. Besides, it's my lunchtime.

Francesco looks genuinely confused at my response. "Excuse me?"

I give him that look. The look that tells him I can tell that he's heard me. I glance at the clock. There's only forty-five minutes left of my peaceful lunch, and he's wasting it.

Proudly, he takes steady steps toward me with his head held high, as though he's styling it out, hoping that nobody will notice what just happened.

I can't take him seriously at the moment.

"It's my break, what do you want?"

He sighs a sigh of disappointment. "Where are you spending your break?"

My attention fixes on the busy cafeteria once more. "Good question. I don't know."

"Come with me."

"If you're going to have lunch in a management room, then I'm really not interested in going. I'd prefer to go somewhere more peaceful, and free of judgment."

He exhales a sharp breath. "Natalia, I work around the clock. I don't take lunch. However, I know a place where we can go."

"We?"

As quick as lightning, he rolls his eyes and strides toward the elevator. "Follow me."

And because I have no other options that I can think of right now, I catch up behind him, wondering where he has in mind.

Francesco presses the highest level on the elevator.
"Where are we going?" I ask him.
He leans casually against the elevator wall, staring at me with alluring eyes as his hands rest in his pockets. "Patience, Natalia," he whispers.
I bite my cheek as they flush with heat, and I'm doing my best to keep my focus on the doors in front of me, but the weight of his presence is too overwhelming. The most beautiful words in existence cannot sum up how Francesco makes me feel when I am the entire focus of his attention. Gideon makes me feel warmth, but Francesco makes me feel as though I've been positioned right under scorching heat. My heart weakens, and my mind melts. He is standing so far, yet he feels so near. Every word that he says, and every look that he gives me crawls so deeply underneath my skin with craving. There's a part of me that wants to hate this feeling, but the longer I'm around him, the greater my yearning of desire grows intolerable.

I'm seriously going crazy, aren't I?

The elevator doors finally swing open, and once we step outside, we walk up a staircase toward a random sky lounge. It's modern and sophisticated with luxurious cream couches, white marble tables and outdoor heating.

"Wow!" I marvel, taking in the breathtaking view of the city. "It's so magical here!"

Francesco shoots me a rare smile before he leans forward upon the railing to light a cigarette. "Take a seat. Make yourself welcome."

I lie sitting up on the couch and warm up by the heating. "Thanks! Does anyone else know about this place? I'm surprised nobody else is up here."

He exhales smoke as though he's releasing a build up of stress within him. "No." Then glancing back at me for a split second, he looks back at the city and says, "This area is reserved for my use only."

"So you really don't mind me coming here in the future?"

"I am authorizing you to come here, yes."

"Francesco... are you okay?"

He stiffens for a moment, then exhales smoke again.

"Francesco."

He's ignoring me.

I don't know why I even bother with him sometimes in the first place. His rudeness is beginning to irritate me, actually. Through which, I leave him to it while proceeding to eat some lunch.

Though suddenly, he turns toward me. Straight faced, but clearly bothered. And after chucking the cigarette away at the nearest disposal, he draws near to sit on the couch right beside me.

"Natalia, what makes you think that you can

ask me personal questions?" he asks, pissed.

I'm lost for words. I stutter, not knowing where to begin. Irritably, he looks elsewhere, and it is within this exact moment that I officially lose my appetite.

"You're not eating?" he asks.

"Nope," I whisper, staring into the sky. "I've lost my appetite."

"That makes two of us," he mumbles.

My eyes attach onto him again, and he's already watching me with a cold look. "I wish you that would stop acting inconsistent and just talk to me, for goodness sake."

"And I wish that you would remember who you are speaking to, Natalia."

"How can two work together if one is troubled? Francesco, I can tell something is bothering you. You weren't like this back at my apartment... something is wrong, what's the matter? As I said before, it seems as though you're not free to disclose your feelings so it's like you bottle it up, which I can tell has a tendency to result in your frustration leaking out into your behavior toward others. I don't like it."

"You don't know anything about me."

"I don't need to know anything about you to be able see right through you."

His phone begins to bell, but he acts as though it is non-existent.

"Tell me, what do you see?"

"Well, I see a man who has obtained so much success that he probably just feels lonely at the top all on his own. I see restlessness. I see frustration. I see stress. You walk as though the weight of the world is heavy upon your shoulders, all the time. I see it in your eyes, but today, I can hear it so much in your voice."

"Are you a psychic or something?"

"No!" I sigh. "I'm just someone that's going through pain too. It's not difficult to sense someone who is carrying pain in silence. You feel it, like magnets."

"What happened to you?"

"I won't tell you everything, but I will tell you the main thing, which started everything. And that is, I lost someone. When I lost that person, I lost myself, way before I even had the chance to grow up and discover who I was meant to be."

He remains still.

"My life has never been the same since," I add, clearing my throat, pushing the tears back. "It was my fault too. I've been blamed for her death. And no, I didn't murder anyone, but one doesn't always have to be physically involved to contribute to a tragedy, do they?"

There's a long silence within the air, which brings me to look elsewhere. I feel his gaze simmering through my veins as I mentally count the clouds in the sky.

"I comprehend that," he whispers deeply, almost with a broken voice stained with the darkest heartache.

Out of nowhere, the sound of rushing footsteps roars over the staircase.

"Mr Giordano, sir!" the colleague calls out, breathlessly. Once he notices me, my presence somehow causes him to look at Francesco and I in the most perplexed and gravest of looks.

"Proceed, Louis," Francesco responds, sharply, immediately snapping him back to earth.

"Sorry to be a disturbance, sir," his voice shakes, "but something urgent has surfaced."

Francesco glances at his watch and rises from the couch without delay. He then straightens out his polished suit, and stops to acknowledge at me. "You know the way back, don't you?" he asks, unusually gently.

"Yes," I whisper, admiring the fact that his voice sounds so much softer than normal.

"Meet me at my office when you're done."

He's long gone before I can say anything.

Why does he have a habit of doing that?

I can't help but feel the loss of his presence. It's like going from hot to cold, from summer sunshine to winter snow, and from heaviness to emptiness, all in a mere moment. And though he's not particularly the most comfortable to be around, I can feel that there is something peculiar that he carries, and it keeps clinging me closer no matter how much I try to convince myself otherwise. I cannot understand it, but I hope that the more that I come to know him, the greater I will grow in comprehension.

15. Lover of Literature

I knock on the door to Francesco's office, surprised to hear soft classical music vibrating through the other side. I hear him calling me to enter, and once I do, I recognize the song that is playing through his speakers. *Clair De Lune.*

He is sitting at his desk, typing away with quickness on the keyboard. He doesn't even look at me, nor acknowledge my presence at all. So I just sit down in my usual spot, waiting with silent anticipation in the comfy seat opposite his desk.

"I adore *Clair De Lune*," I think aloud, fixing my attention upon the beautiful scenery out the remarkable floor to ceiling windows.

"Is that so?" he replies flatly, still multitasking.

"I'm surprised that you're a classical person. Who is your favorite composer?"

The noisy keyboard stops, which brings all my

focus back to him. He then leans back on his chair, with his chin lifted slightly as he examines me.

"You share your opinions quite boldly, don't you?"

"Umm... I'm only trying to make conversation with you. It's so awkward otherwise! Plus, I'm quite sure that it was only this morning that you mentioned that you'd like us to become better acquainted with each other. Anyway, what's wrong with me asking you simple questions? It's not like I'm asking for your medical history."

He fights a smile, then rises from his chair to steadily step around his desk to pause right in front of me. "I have other plans," he tells me.

"Plans?"

"Tell me, what are you doing tonight?" he asks, leaning casually against the desk.

"Well, I haven't made any plans yet. Other than just relax at home and read a book, I guess. As always. I'm not one to go out much, but why do you ask, is something the matter? I won't need to stay behind for work, will I?"

"Good," he responds, pressing his lips into a fine line. "We're going out for dinner."

"Oh, is this like a work meal where a group of colleagues get together? Darlene didn't mention anything about this earlier. Where are we all going?"

"No," he clarifies. "Natalia, I want to dine with you this evening at The Shard. Just you and I."

"Isn't The Shard one of the tallest buildings in London? Francesco, what is your reasoning behind this?"

"I want to dine with you, Natalia," he confirms bluntly, now walking away toward a glass table to pour himself a drink.

"Hmmm, I'm not sure how to feel about this. I guess if it was a group thing then it would be fine. But just you and I... it's a bit strange. Do you not think?"

He glances over his shoulder to look at me from the table. "No."

"Francesco, if being more acquainted with me is something that you desire, then you must remember that you have me all to yourself right now, during actual work hours. What makes it so different if we were to be here in a restaurant, compared to here in your office?"

I hear him sigh impatiently in the distance, followed by the sharp noise of his glass hitting against the table. He then turns around and steps slowly toward me, with eye contact so strong I cannot dare to detach myself from.

"Natalia, let me make this clear to you. I want you to myself, alone. Somewhere that we can be without distraction."

"Why?" I whisper.

"These endless questions," he breathes, now smirking. "You overthink quite frequently, don't you?"

"Yes," I breathe. "Very much so."

A softness clouds over his eyes. "Don't."

I glance way up high to take a peek at Francesco in the corner of my eyes as we walk together swiftly toward the exit. He's a giant in every sense. Exuding allure with power and glory through every move that he makes. Hundreds of eyes follow us as Peter awaits us outside beside the car. He opens the door, and I slide in. Francesco shuts the door for me, and my heart is shaking into pieces. I just hope that I'm able to get myself together again.

He holds so much power over me, it's ungodly.

I do my best to compose myself, despite my mix of nervousness and lust intertwining all at once.

The car zooms off through the sparkling city as pretty snowflakes continue to fall lightly from the sky. It's dark outside, with only the dazzling lights upon the streets and cars to brighten my view. I peek once more at Francesco, who strangely, doesn't have a phone in his hand. Instead, he is leaning on the door, staring outside the window as though he is engaged in deep thought.

"Hey, what are you thinking?" I ask him.

His eyes fall to his lap before they crawling across the seat toward me. "Nothing."

I give him a smile, but he doesn't smile back. In the corner of my sight, I feel his gaze penetrating my skin. Not my face, but my legs. For a mere second I catch those fire-filled eyes flow from my thighs all the way down to my ankles. And in this moment, everything about our proximity begins to feel stuffy. It's too overwhelming for me, so I crack the window.

"You alright?" he murmurs.

"Yes."

I hear him chuckle. "Natalia, it's cold."

"Sorry, I think I'm just burning up a little."

A concerned look spreads across his face as he sits up toward me. "Are you unwell?"

"I'm just feeling quite warm that's all."

His brows crease, forming a little v shape upon his forehead as he lays the back of his hand against my face.

"You seem well," he says, quietly. "Would you prefer to be taken home?"

I'm beginning to overthink again, for my heart races so uncontrollably into a million directions as his hand glides carefully from my cheek to my jaw, now cradling my face ever so tenderly in his hand.

I truly don't understand why this is happening.

I do not understand why I am liking it either.

"No." I croak, clearing my throat. "I want to be with you. I mean, have dinner with you."

Francesco's gaze falls from mine, fastening upon my mouth. His lips then barely part, before lifting up to grab my eyes once again. Without notice, he releases his hand from my face, and I mourn instantly at the loss. His touch is otherworldly. Igniting a craving inside of me for more. Because as much as I'm confused by it all, I want him to do it again.

I can't really contain my excitement being here in this fascinating restaurant. It's so pretty! Absolutely captivating. There's a perfect wide view of the breadth of the city that illuminates brightly with an abundance of lights.

The restaurant itself, however, is super dark and dimly lit. There are little tea light candles placed prettily around the tables, it's beautifully romantic. Yet I can't help but wonder if it's appropriate for a business relationship.

What is this really about, and why are we here?

There's part of me that feels like I just keep lying to myself, to be honest with you. For there's a part of me that is in deep denial of believing that someone like Francesco could actually be interested in someone like me.

We order dinner and drink wine. For a while, I've noticed that since our arrival at The Shard, Francesco seems unusually entertained whenever he looks at me. It's the growing brilliance within his eyes, and that's something that I'm not used to seeing in him.

"You seem different now that work is over," I tell him. "You seem free, and kind of happy."

His smile doesn't disappear, but it softens. "I sometimes forget that you've only just moved here. Your reactions to the things here are priceless."

"You know, I've always wanted to live here since I was a child. It's literally my dream place to live, I adore it. I've always desired to see more of the world! But look at this glorious view of the city... Francesco, you truly do take me to such stunning views of London."

He takes a sip of his red wine and seals my attention with his gaze. "I can take you to see so much more than this."

I bite my cheek as I hold back a smile. "Where would you take me?"

"Anywhere you want. Tell me, and it's yours."

My body steams with desire at the way he's looking at me. I often wonder if he does this to me on purpose.

"You have a very beautiful accent," I mention. "What part of Italy are you from?"

"Pienza, Tuscany."

"Oh, how wonderful!"

"Tell me about where you're from. I want to know."

"I'm from a beach city called Carmel-by-the-sea. It's within the state of California. It's sunny, vibrant and very beautiful! You could say that I used to be a beach babe, always hanging out at the beach. Surfing was one of my hobbies, but I wanted something more."

"What did you feel was missing, exactly?"

"Hmmm. Fulfillment, I guess. I lived in Carmel my whole life, although my siblings were born in

Spain. As much as I love it back home, I've always wanted to immerse myself in a different culture and a whole new environment. But what about you, what enticed you to leave such a beautiful place like Italy for London?"

He pauses. "I didn't have a choice."

"Oh! What do you mean by... you didn't have a choice?"

His jaw clamps shut as he stares into the distance outside the skyline view. "This particular company was founded in Italy by my father, Luigi Giordano. He arranged plans to move and expand to the UK, then the US. However, there came a time when he wasn't able to continue working. From then, it was down to me to keep the business running."

"Wow, that's so interesting. I'm really sorry that your father can no longer work. How is he now?"

"Dead," he responds, bluntly, without any glimpse of emotion.

My heart stings.

I can't tell whether he's in pain, anger or denial.

"I'm so sorry, Francesco."

"Don't be," he breathes, staring at me with the darkest of looks. "Because I'm not."

What does he mean by that?

Before I know it, the waitress arrives with our dinner. We thank her, but then all of a sudden she appears quite hesitant to leave.

"Can I help you?" Francesco asks her.

Redness peeks through her olive skin. "I know who you are, and I respect your privacy, sir, but the ladies at the table in the far corner would like a photograph taken with you, if you don't mind. If not, please don't worry. I can tell them that you would just like to relax this evening. They just requested me to ask you, that's all."

I peek over to the table in the corner. It's a group of around five women who look around their mid to late twenties. Grins spread across their faces as they giggle amongst themselves while staring at Francesco.

My stomach twists.

Truthfully, they are all so beautiful. I really don't understand what Francesco is seeing in me. I feel sick. All of a sudden, I don't feel like eating anymore.

"Of course," he responds to her, with a tight smile. He then looks at me and asks, "Do you mind?"

"Of course not," I lie.

How could I, though? He's Francesco Giordano, with or without me. I have no right at all to be jealous.

The whole restaurant ceases in activity the moment he stands up. Wherever he moves, eyes follow. Noise quietens, and everyone seems to become fixated solely upon him. He moves like the moon in the sky, dominating the night, outshining all those who surround him. The ladies seem exceedingly impressed. Happy and delighted. Taking picture after picture, with group shots and an unnecessary amount of videos being taken. Yet there's something about Francesco that appears different to how he normally is at work. There is indeed a still a grumpy and heavy aura that consumes him, but he doesn't seem as uptight and irritable as per usual. He seems freer, and that's how I like him to be.

"My apologies," he breathes, returning to his seat.

I smile but I don't say anything, because I'm feeling quite speechless and overwhelmed at the moment. So I take a bite of my dinner and before sipping on some ice cold water.

"Francesco," I begin, a little nervously. "Why have I not heard of you?"

"That's a good thing," he murmurs.

"How is it a good thing? I think it shows how disconnected to the world I must be."

"I like it, Natalia."

I know that I'm blushing. I feel bare. He knows how to hold eye contact, and he's never the one to break it.

His gaze toward me is always so lustful and direct. It feels as though he has some sort of superman ability to see through under my skin.

"Why do you like it?" I ask, out of curiosity.

"I value authenticity."

I beam at the compliment. "Is that why you

chose me to be your personal assistant?"

His eyes smile, but his lips don't. "Maybe."

"If you're such a busy man, what do you do in your spare time?"

"Wouldn't you like to know." A gorgeous smirk appears before he takes another sip of wine.

"Well, something that I do know is that you're a lover of literature, like me! I've seen your admirable little library in the office. Do you ever read poetry? I adore it!"

He chuckles humorlessly. "Who knew that the day would come when I would be speaking to someone about poetry."

"Oh, so you do read poetry?" I'm honestly so impressed that I'm beginning to get excited.

"Tell me your favorite poem," he commands.

"It has to be *Sonnet 18*, by William Shakespeare. I find the first few lines especially to be incredibly beautiful. I believe it goes something like—"

Suddenly, he begins to recite the first few lines perfectly and flawlessly breathtaking that it brings my lips to part. He then stops speaking, and for the first time in forever, he genuinely laughs.

The way he recites the poem takes my breath away for too long of a moment. He sounds so romantic, so Italian. For a second there I felt as though I was in my own little romance flick!

"Francesco, you really know Shakespeare?"

"I do not know much."

"Seems like you know enough to me!"

I'm feeling so happy being with him right now. I'm wholeheartedly enjoying myself this evening because I feel at peace with everything around me. But then shockingly, he suddenly takes me by surprise. For with carefulness, he brushes his thumb over my wrist so effortlessly with affection.

"Look, Natalia," he breathes.

"Oh gosh. What is it?"

"I'll be visiting Italy in April. Come with me."

"I... I can't."

"You can."

"How do you know what I can and can't do?"

"I have arranged for the business trip to be scheduled during the easter holidays. There is no reason for it to clash with your studies."

I pull my wrist away out of his hand and place my hands on my lap. "I will need to think about it, Francesco... Will any other colleagues be coming along with us?"

"No."

"What is the business trip for?"

He sighs ever so softly, with a subtle, pissed off expression on his face. "There have been numerous issues concerning the service at some of the branches in my country. My team and I discussed this during the meetings earlier today. We've come to the conclusion that I should schedule meetings with the store managers and overlook workshops with the sales associate teams. I need you there."

I ponder on it in silence, but then accidentally, I whisper aloud, "What about Elian?"

I'm worried that my father will somehow come to London again and expect me to drop everything for his sake. There's no way I plan on informing him of the trip to Italy. He'd probably follow me.

"Sorry, who the fuck is Elian?" Francesco asks.

"That's... that's none of your business."

Quietness instantly creates a very uncomfortable distance between us, and after a while, I think he can sense my disappointment within the air.

He swears under his breath. "Forgive me."

"I want to leave." I sigh, nervous and frustrated all at once. "Take me home, please."

His attention remains so strictly me, but I choose to give him none of mine. Which then brings me to hear him sigh. I say nothing, but watch him in the corner of my eye calling the waitress to pay the bill. Once he pays, he leaves her a large tip. She then thanks him, before proceeding to ask for a few pictures before we leave and head out.

16. Unbelievable

As we're sitting in the car, the ride back home feels much smoother than the morning. The roads are quieter, and the sight of London gleams with a magical glory that glows splendidly throughout the winter evening. I feel much more at peace in Francesco's presence since our dinner, regardless of the little issue that took place toward the end. I've gotten over it already. I always do. I have come to accept that his unpredictable ways may just be something that I will have to get used to. I guess he was right. Tonight is what was needed for us to be better acquainted with each other after all.

"Thanks for such a lovely evening," I whisper. "Although, you really didn't have to do this."

"Do what?" he murmurs.

"Drive me back home. I know that you're a very busy and important man."

"Natalia, I choose what I invest my time into."

"I guess, but this is all new to me."

"*This*?"

"Yeah, being invited to nice places and actually having a social life outside of my family. Since I let go of my life in Carmel, it's as though I've entered a whole new season. A part of life that I never knew that I could ever experience."

"And how have you found adjusting to this new country?"

"Fine," I respond. "Lonely."

"Lonely?"

"Yes."

"Have you not made acquaintances throughout the duration of your studies?"

"You picked the right word. Acquaintances, not friends."

"And your *friend* from this morning?"

"Gideon is wonderful. A true sweetheart."

"Do you miss them?"

"Who?"

"Your family."

"Yeah, I do," I reply, exhaling my sorrow while feeling a bundle of homesickness overflow from within me. "To be honest with you, Francesco, I thought that I'd be okay here. I was so convinced that if I focused enough on working toward becoming an artist, and get my head down to work, then I'd feel less alone. Everyone tends to praise the single and independent career-focused woman, but

I'm realizing how lonely that it can really be if life isn't balanced out with leisure and love. But that's just my opinion, personally. I feel as though my soul is constantly restless, toiling away in survival mode. If I'm not at work, I'm at university. If I'm not at university, I'm working on my art. If I'm not working on my social media, then I'm researching ways how to improve it. Rarely do I ever have a chance to just be still, you know? I miss painting for the pleasure of it. I don't know. Who knew that living in such a massive city would actually make you feel so incredibly solitary?"

My words break, and my sentences are chopped up to the point where I'm unable to speak clearly at this point. It's the pain. It's the pressure of survival, and it's the pressing weight of being away from my loved ones. It's a lot to deal with.

"I'm sorry." I sniffle, with a tear. "I shouldn't be opening up to you like this. You're my boss for goodness sake! You see, that's how you can tell I'm super sad and lonely, it's embarrassing. Ugh, I'm so pathetic sometimes. Honestly, I'm sorry."

"Come here," he says, quietly. "Sit with me."

I blink twice. Worrying and wondering if I've actually heard that correctly. Wondering if it's the sensible, or should I say, professional thing to do. But I long to be held. I yearn to be embraced and comforted. I understand that as a grown woman I am expected to be strong and stable all on my own, but my heart keeps knocking so vigorously upon the walls of my mind, reminding me that I'm human with emotions that matter. I can no longer hide my pain behind my career goals. I miss Julieta, and I miss Diego. I've never felt so alone in my entire life. I try to be careful with Gideon, as I truly don't want to ruin our friendship and break his heart any further, yet it absolutely kills me to try and understand why this business relationship between Francesco and I seem to be appearing out of balance.

I click off my seatbelt anyway, and shuffle up right beside him. "Oh wow, you're so warm!"

"Look, I need you to forgive me."

"Forgive you for what?"

"In regard to earlier. I fear that I'm too harsh with you at times." His deep voice ripples through my skin. "Truth is, politeness is something that I'm still working on."

"I forgive you," I tell him, admiring his grey and lovely eyes that narrow toward mine. "Besides, Elian is only my father. I was just concerned about whether he would need to see me during that time, that's all. But Francesco… I understand that nobody is perfect. Therefore, I don't expect you to be. But it's nice to know that you're acknowledging your weaknesses." I smile at him, but he then stares back at me in silence as though he's trying to make something out. "What is it?"

"You're different to other women," he whispers. His thumb then caresses my face for a moment, and honestly, it surprises me. "You are bewitching, but I don't want to hurt you, Natalia."

"Why... why would you hurt me?"

His gaze falls to my lips then up to my eyes once more. "I can't give you what you need."

"And how do you know what I need?"

He sighs, deeply. "You deserve commitment. Unfortunately, commitment is not in the cards for me."

"Francesco... I'm not asking for commitment from you, because I cannot ask for something that my heart is unable to give right now. My soul is too broken, still healing from so much pain that I've endured over the years. Though one thing I will say, is that something that I've realized is that every second that I'm around you, I only want to be with you more."

He fastens his gaze upon me in silence with pondering eyes, securing me firmer within his arm, which only brings me to mold so effortlessly within his embrace. He then leans in, as though he's utterly decided upon kissing me. So close that I can feel his minty breath on my lips, but then he hesitates.

"You're everything that I want in a woman," he breathes. "But I am not the man that you deserve."

"Help me to understand," I say, softly resting my hand on his shirt.

"Listen." His whisper is the gentlest I've ever heard him. "I'm not good for you, darling."

"I'm no good too... that makes both of us."

I rest my head on his chest, delighting in the manly scent that sits upon his skin. This feels like a haven. Toasting within his warmth, being so passionately bound in his massive arms. I feel safe. Yet his heart begins to drum as my hand rests softly over his shirt. Though still, he doesn't flinch. Just the ardent fire flowing from his eyes are felt all over me, but I don't bring myself to look. I can't just yet. Truly, I'm too shy. My nervousness is bubbling up within me, as though every vein under my skin is close to bursting with lava. Yet suddenly, he tenderly lifts my chin. Naturally bringing my eyes to meet his.

"Natalia," he whispers, softly holding my face, staining my skin with his oud scent. "Tell me, who hurt you?"

"No-one," I lie.

"Then enlighten me, what has convinced you to think such a thing?"

"Myself."

"I don't believe you."

"Why... why does it matter to you anyway?"

"Because you matter to me."

"Francesco, you barely know me."

"Yes," he acknowledges. "I am aware of that. However, I've known you enough to recognize your authenticity. Your pure soul, and unpolluted mind. It is something that is extremely rare for me to come across, and yet, I have never found someone as attractive and fucking beautiful as you. Sei bellissima, Natalia. That man is goddamn lucky to have you."

"W-w-what man?" I whisper.

He releases a husky chuckle without a word. Bashfulness blooms through my cheeks as he snatches my heart away upon tracing his thumb across the edge of my bottom lip. His eyes are screaming with lust as they glue onto my mouth, and everything within me is yearning for more of his touch. Truly, I've never known such intense desire until this moment.

He leans in, lifting me into a whole new dimension as his masculine scent stains upon me with allure. "This is selfish of me," he breathes. "You deserve so much better."

"Better? What is better?"

"Devotion, Natalia. You're the kind of woman who deserves nothing less than that. Regardless of how much I crave to touch you, I can't. You're better than what I can offer you at present."

"Never mind what you think I deserve, have you even considered what I want?"

"Tell me. What do you want, piccola mia?"

He's looking at me with eager eyes, as though he's yearning to grant my request. So I take a deep breath, and tell him, "I want you to kiss me."

"Natalia," he breathes, huskily. "Are you sure that you want this?"

"Why wouldn't I?"

"Because once I do, there is no possibility of us

going back to how things were before. You understand that, don't you?"

"Kiss me, Francesco... please."

Those ice grey eyes blaze intensely over my lips with sultry delight before his lips finally meet mine, and immediately and wholeheartedly, I lose myself entirely within our lust. Ever so beautifully, I soak in every part of his touch, roaming blissfully steady through my hair, taking pleasure in my breasts, embracing his firm hold upon my waist. His touch is intense, ushering the utter depths of my soul to become strongly embedded with a reckless passion for his hands to not slip away.

His lips leave mine, and he gives me this wild look in his eyes that spark an overload of fireworks within my heart. I stare at him as he stares at me, dripping wet while his hands sail over my derrière to tug at my panties. It's overwhelming, this desire that I carry for him. I just want him to make love to me. This yearning that refuses to be tamed simply brings me to lose all sense of self control at this point, so I grab the collar of his shirt, bringing our lips once again to lock. I can't help it. I want Francesco, with all of my heart.

Gracefully with ease, he suddenly sweeps me up in his massive arm just before I straddle him.

"Natalia," he breathes between kisses, "are you still sure about wanting this?"

I nod, feeling all of the heat rushing to my cheeks.

"You can tell me... if you want to stop."

There is a danger in seeing this side to him, I know it. He has me gripped to the core of my very soul. At this point, all my desire remains solely for this man. Our lips refuse to depart as though we're starved lovers, and it literally feels as though it would anguish me to let go of him. He's kissing me as though he's waited so long for this moment, bringing his hands to bite violently into my derrière. I gasp in his mouth, and his teeth tug my lip. His taste is absolutely bittersweet, like the finest red wine and cherries. Every nerve of my lower body comes springs to life as his large, strong hands slip underneath my dress. As light as a rose petal, his fingertips stream so gently across my inner thighs and travel to where I'm wet. He's blazing like fire. I see it in his eyes, I feel it through his clothes. Honestly, how did we get to this point? I feel like I'm evaporating, melting, with every inch of my soul and skin draping over him as though I'm wax being swept over his flaming desire.

His hand grips my waist tight, and with the other, his fingers slip through my lace panties. Such rapture brings my heart to hum out his name as he presses his thumb all over my soaking clit, ardently overwhelmed with grand pleasure and pain as his finger burns blissfully to thunder inside of me. I crave his cock, so badly. And I'm trying my best to be quiet in here, because I don't know whether the partition is up or down, but I'm losing it, failing wholeheartedly to silence my growing desire to have every inch of him to myself. For he lavishes me with the most passionate kisses in the delicate hollow of my neck, pinching me lovingly with his lips down to my chest. It lifts me into a divine euphoria, and I feel my mind running away with every ravenous kiss that he plants on me. I'm going crazy, aren't I? I know it. Letting us come this far is something that I truly may come to regret, but it's him. His ability to ignite every form of desire that exists within me. His voice, his body, the way he makes me feel. The way he's handling me in this moment, gripping tight with such violent love onto my inner thigh, so keen, impassioned, and greatly intense. It truly feels as though he's claiming me as his. It's like ecstasy, his touch. I quiver all over him with the deepest breath of pleasure and relief. My eyes holds his, and they appear absolutely feral and as hungry as ever. He is truly overwhelming to me, I can barely hold myself together.

"Come home with me tonight," he breathes heavily, sweeping his hand through my hair.

"It's too late," I whisper, glancing through the tilted windows. "We've already driven too far."

"It's never too late," he whispers back. "Tell me what you want."

"I know what I want," I tell him, wrapping my arms around his broad shoulders, truly not wanting to depart. "But I... I don't think that means that what we're doing is right, Francesco."

"You're doing it again."

"Doing what?"

"Overthinking."

"But we have work early tomorrow."

Without a word, he inhales deeply with a quiet sort of frustration in his eyes. Then with both hands, he glides my panties all the way down my thighs. "Tell me to turn this car around, Natalia. Let me make love to you, and show you how fucking deeply that I'm enraptured by you. Relieve me of this agony, darling girl. Do not worry about tomorrow."

I spread my legs wider and let him touch me, because deep down I want it, and I can't bring myself to ask him to stop. Ever so rapturously, he slips my clit between his fingers, and I'm honestly unable to quieten my pleasure for much longer. For soon after, one enters me, slow, passionate and deep, thrusting me so powerfully into utter felicity.

He then leans in and kisses my lips before another moan releases from within. "Is this what you want?" he asks.

I peek into his fierce eyes and nod, panting without a word.

"Let me hear you say it."

"Francesco..." I whisper, trying to catch a breath.

He raises me up with the strength of his arm, then carefully positions me down right above his manhood. He's so hard that it shocks me, seeming like at any moment he's going to rip through his clothes. But then he further catches me by surprise as another finger quickens inside of me.

"Are you going to let me make love to you all evening? Or do you want me to fuck you, right here, right now, before your home time? You choose."

His sweet breath warms my breasts before he takes a nipple in his mouth. Moans can't help but leave my body as he devours me.

"Francesco..." I quiver all over his manhood. "I want you," I finally admit. "Take me to yours."

"Shit," he breathes, as eyes light up staring at me in awe. "Despite obtaining all the damn wealth in the world, I have never considered myself lucky as much as I am being in this moment with you."

His sweet words cause me to melt all over him as his fingers thrust deeper within me.

Does he truly feel this way about me?

He is driving me ridiculously insane. Our lips lock then soon depart upon me leaving a path of gentle kisses upon his neck. He moans, and the sound of it resurrects a part of me alight. Like celestial currents, pulling my soul out of the depths with a desire to unveil so much more of this irresistible side to him.

"Peter." I feel his neck buzz. "Change the route at the earliest opportunity and drive back to mine."

"Which one, sir?"

"Belgravia."

"On it, sir. Roads are jammed. Arrival estimated in forty."

Immediately after, Francesco presses a button on his seat nearby without a word, and instantly, I hear the partition coming to a close.

Finally.

I let out a sigh of relief for the privacy, and his face lights up the moment that he catches me.

Before I know it, his hand suddenly finds itself underneath my dress again. He's playing around with my bra strap, looking at me with earnest eyes as though he's awaiting my permission. It feels different. How suddenly the tables have turned, and how truly unexpected all of the power has now shifted into my hands. Witnessing this side to him turns me on so deeply to a point that I've never knew was even possible for me.

I grant him permission, and his fingers ooze out of my river of delight, letting my bra and dress become totally undone in one. I straddle him tighter, feeling all sense of control escape from me as I press down over his cock, giving him all my love on his lips. He moans in my mouth and it makes me feel almost invincible with a guilty kind of pleasure that I find so addictive, because he's my manager, my boss, and I really do not at all comprehend how we've end up here.

All of his desire then flows down to my breasts with heated, brief kisses, unleashing the beast within him that appears to have been imprisoned with a lustful hunger for so long. My eyes follow the tip of his tongue, circling around my nipple, slowly and steadily until it springs hard between his lips.

"Francesco," I moan, "what are we doing?"

He looks up in my eyes. "You're so beautiful."

My inner thighs are absolutely dripping for him, as though every sense within me is fluttering with an inexpressible exhilaration upon being in his fervent possession. A moan escapes me once again as his hands explore my body, traveling over the curves of my derrière and squeezing me tight as he takes my other breast in his mouth.

"Mmmm," he moans, deeply. "Does that little boyfriend of yours touch you like this?"

Oh god.

Words refuse to leave me but moans of delight.

His deep chuckle then seeps under my skin. "I thought so," he murmurs.

He nibbles on my neck with such passion, I'm absolutely certain that it'll leave a love bite.

"Francesco," I breathe, taking in his rich scent. "We shouldn't be doing this."

"Tell me why, Natalia."

"Because…" I can barely breathe, gripping onto his shoulders tight.

"Because what?"

At this point, I'm past caring what the driver thinks. "I told you! It's because… I… umm, I have to get up early for work tomorrow."

"You don't remember who I am. Do you?"

Shyness begins to wave strongly over me for a moment as I think about what he just said.

"Remind me," I tease.

"Shit," he exhales.

I rest my hand firmly around his cock that is bulging so huge through his clothes. "Tell me how much you love to boss me around, Francesco, and I'll never let you forget how weak I can make you at your knees."

"Be careful, Natalia. If you keep that up, I may have to fuck you this instant." He then lifts me firmer by my waist, and presses me down right above his manhood. "Is that something you want?"

"Francesco," I moan. "God, you're driving me crazy."

I undo his belt, listening to his breathing remaining in perfect sync with mine. Heavy, hot and bothered. Truly just ready to have each other.

His huge cock springs out once I let it free. Honestly, he's so big that it's overwhelming. My body flutters with desire at the sight of him. I wrap my hand around him, tugging and yearning for every inch to be inside of me. He's moaning and it's sexy. This is a side to him that barely anyone else gets to see.

"You're so sexy when you let your guard down," I remark, now kneeling down to him.

His eyes are pressing on me. I don't have to look at him to know it, for the heat of his lustful attention is felt all over me as I circle the tip of his cock with my tongue before running it all the way down his shaft. Then finally, I manage to pluck up the courage to look him in the eyes. His gaze is already fixed on me. Hungry and wanting with a desire so strong that it brings me to overwhelm.

"Fucking hell, Natalia," he moans, as I take him in my mouth.

He grabs hold of my hair, wrapping it around his fist while I continue to please him until he comes. Hearing him and seeing him like this alone is enough to make me dripping wet. I've never starved for someone as much as him, and it makes me frightened, for there's a part of me that knows that once the night is over, things will never be the same between us again.

I swallow, then he swiftly scoops me up on his lap and I kiss him. My lips fasten passionately with his as I refuse to let them go. I feel his moans on my lips, and I feel like at any moment I'm going to explode. Words simply cannot describe how madly intoxicated I feel by Francesco Giordano. Our lips eventually part, and we take a breath.

"Is this what you had in mind earlier?" I ask, not being able to help but giggle. "When you said you want us to be better acquainted?"

"No..." he breathes. "Maybe." His eyes then smile. "Natalia, you're fucking unbelievable."

17. California King Bed

His hands thunder all over me the moment that we're alone together. Just one step within his home was all it took for the suppressed desire to unravel between us. There's a sting of shame that masks over me as my mind flickers back to the thought of our behavior during the drive, but this feeling of embarrassment doesn't quite overtake this craving that I'm carrying for Francesco at present.

It's dark within his home, with not a light on in sight. Almost pitch black. I hear his keys dashed aside as our lips refuse to let go of one another. I can't see him, but I can surely feel him, claiming every inch of my body as his. He lifts me up with the strength of both arms, and suddenly I'm floating within the air. I let him take me to wherever we're going without question. Despite my fear and nerves, every cell within my body is telling me to yield myself completely to him throughout this moment.

"Do you want anything?" he asks me, between kisses.

"What?" I giggle, as he opens a door which leads us into a room.

He lifts me up higher as though to adjust me in his arm, while the other switches on a dim light nearby. Everything is still so dark, I can barely see anything but him.

"I asked if you would like anything. A drink, or something to eat?"

"How random." I giggle. "How hospitable of you, Signor Giordano. But, no thank you."

His eyes smile but his lips do not. He then kisses me once more before laying me down gently upon a bed. It's large. Probably a California king size, which is not a surprise, considering his height.

I sink so deeply upon the sheets that it scares me, as though I'm getting swallowed up by the mattress. I gasp, then he laughs, a rare laugh. Hearing it is all that it takes for a wave of desire to pull me back into the depths again. He feels the shift too, I can see it in his eyes.

"Then tell me," he breathes, staring down at me with alluring eyes from the edge of the bed. "What do you want, Natalia?"

"You know what I want," I whisper, catching a cheeky glimpse of his pecs that are bulging through his shirt.

"I want you to tell me."

"Francesco, I want you to fuck me. Now come here, please."

A rare chuckle appears again. "I thought about fucking you since the day I met you," he mumbles. "But now that you're here, I'm not so sure."

"What on earth do you mean by you're no longer sure!" I exclaim, and it's clear that he's amused by it.

"Natalia," he breathes, softly, now with a seriousness about him. "Look at you... how fucking beautiful you are. Laying there, soaking wet. Ready for my cock." He then draws nearer, sinking me further down into the mattress the closer he gets. Our lips are inches away, before he kisses me once. "I don't want to fuck you, Natalia. That would be too quick. Too ordinary. Too typical. You are an extraordinary woman, and I want to treat you as such."

Moans break through from within me as he nibbles upon my chest while taking my dress down with him. It slides off my legs before his fingers fly over the buttons on his shirt. And though the room is dim, the sight of his golden body is all I needed to fuel my arousal further.

Words can't describe how much I want him.

I've never been this turned on in my life.

Why is this even happening?

"What are you saying, Francesco?" I ask, trembling under his touch.

He separates my legs wide to accommodate his

size, leaving trails of kisses up my leg. "Are you going to let me make love to you tonight, without you worrying about tomorrow?"

"I'll try. Though I am afraid," I admit.

He pauses, resting his cheek lightly upon my inner thigh. My skin tickles at the brush of his facial hair. "Tell me, what are you afraid of?"

"I... I've haven't been with anyone in years. I'm shy," I whisper, "let alone being with my boss. It's just a bit overwhelming, you know?"

His eyes soften with a compassion that I've never seen in him before, then with one move, he plants a kiss upon my inner thigh and asks. "What can I do to make you feel more at ease?"

"I... I don't know," I whisper. "But don't stop."

He blinks slowly, beginning to kiss toward where I'm wet. "We'll take it slow," he breathes. "Inform me, Natalia, if and when you want me to stop. I don't want you feeling uncomfortable here with me."

"Okay," I whisper, feeling my heart speed up the closer his mouth gets to the place that yearns for him most.

Before I know it, he takes down my panties along with his pants so effortlessly at once.

Oh god.

"Breathe," he he tells me, calming my nerves as he briefly cradles my face in his hand. "Breathe, Natalia."

I let out a long anxious exhale that has built up

within me. "I'm sorry," I whisper.

"Don't apologize," he says, while his fierce grey eyes stare directly through me. He then kisses me tenderly in the hollow of my neck and asks, "Are you sure that you want this?"

"Yes, Francesco. I am sure. I'm just nervous, that's all. I promise you. Honestly, I swear if you ask me this again—"

He laughs, a quiet laugh. Yet deep enough for the sound waves of his voice to ripple right through my skin. "Tell me, what will you do?"

"I..."

Unexpectedly, pleasure snatches my words away at his touch. His fingers find their way to my clit. He asks me if I like it, I tell him yes. My eyes catch a glimpse of his cock, almost bursting through his underwear and I'm ready to take it. I pull them down and let him free.

"Francesco," I moan, tugging his manhood.

He leans forward to kiss my lips, pressing his cock so firm over my clit. "Not just yet, amore," he says, breathlessly. "Believe me when I tell you, I want to take this slow."

Our lips meet once again, and I wrap my legs tight around his massive torso. Every part of my heart yearns to be as close to him as possible, I don't wish to let him go.

"Fucking hell. Do I make you this wet, darling? I've barely even started."

Before I even utter a response, his lips devour

my breasts, surging me into a sensation of splendor that I've truly never experienced before. A bundle of pleasure and desire, wrapped with flames. I've never desired a man as much as I have Francesco within this moment. I never thought a desire as intense as this was even possible, and it's crazy, because we barely know each other. But every day that we're together, my soul realizes that it can't help but long to be near him. Why?

His facial hair tickles me on his way down to the place that's soaking wet. Soon after, he tastes me, and I'm taken by surprise at the overwhelming passion behind his moan. It's so sexy, that I lose it.

"You will never comprehend how much I am attracted to you," he breathes, ramming his tongue inside of me. "How much I want you."

I moan his name, pressing my thighs on either side of his face, and I can see that he likes it, seemingly as though it has fueled his hunger for more. We then meet eyes as he teases my clit with his tongue, penetrating me intensely with his gaze which only thrusts me deeper into an otherworldly state of aching desire. I feel myself reaching the climax and he knows it.

"Honey," I moan, remembering to breathe deeply.

"Breathe, Natalia." His husky voice vibrates over me. "We're in this together."

I let him bring me to the peak, and he holds my body steady as he devours the most intimate part of me. I feel like a pin underneath his grip. Small and delicate under his touch. He's large and he's strong, knowing exactly what he's doing to me and I like it. I let him. I let him claim me because that's what every cell within me is screaming for.

Suddenly, he lifts me up. Bringing his mouth to mine as he sits me up facing him upon his lap. "I can't get enough of you," he says, breathlessly. "Shit. What are you doing to me?"

"I could ask you the same, boss," I tease, holding in my giggles while leaving no part of him untouched. "This is so unprofessional of you to take me here."

"Fucking hell," he mumbles under his breath, as I touch him where he wants it most. His large hands then follow my curves from my waist to my derrière. His nails dig into my skin so tight as he squeezes me, so much to the point that I feel numb. He spanks me, and I moan. "I love to hear you moan for me, piccola mia."

"Do it again," I beg him.

His eyes darken with desire as he does it once more. I moan louder this time, craving for it again. Why?

"Do you like that, Natalia?" he asks me.

"Yes," I breathe. "Yes, I do."

His eyes lift up and down my body, before he licks his lips and says, "Let's see how you take it on my lap."

Without hesitation, I let him face me down

spread over his lap, with my bare derrière facing him. I watch him, biting his lip as his eyes glue onto it. All my nerves have evaporated by this point, replacing my anxiety with an ungodly amount of lust for this man.

"Your body is fucking perfect," he says, kissing my derrière and kneading it with his hand. "I could worship you all fucking night."

His touch only grows rougher, and I don't stop him because I like it.

"Don't stop," I moan.

He swears under his breath and keeps going. Then to my surprise, he thrusts a finger inside of me while he bites a cheek into heavenly pleasure. It's indescribable, the way he makes me feel, and though my nerves have vanished in this moment, there is a part of me that is worried because I'm not quite sure what will happen between us going forward from tomorrow.

Francesco is right... Why am I really thinking so much about tomorrow?

Suddenly, he spanks me out of my thoughts and into painful pleasure again. I tell him to do it again, and he complies. I tell him to do it harder, and he does.

"You have a way of never failing to surprise me," he mumbles, lifting me up in his arms again.

I smile bashfully as he gazes directly into my eyes. There's a faint smile that appears on his face, and it only makes him more beautiful.

His cock is poking underneath me again, and from the look in his eyes, he can see that I want it.

"Patience, Natalia," he whispers, entering a finger inside of me again. I then moan so deeply as a result of it. "Show me how much you want my cock inside you, darling," he says, now entering a second. "Ride on them."

And in this moment, I just completely let go. Of all the worry, shame and overwhelm that has gathered from tonight, and I delight wholeheartedly in him.

His eyes meet mine, and I can see the immense sensuality that is flooding with abundance from within him.

"I love seeing you like this," he mentions. "Riding on my fingers, desperate for my cock."

"Francesco," I moan. "I want you."

I keep going without any intention to stop, beginning to see an abundance of stars in my eyes. He then guides my hand to his manhood. "Are you sure we're ready for this, Natalia?" he asks.

I nod without a word, but a moan.

"Let me hear it, darling girl. Tell me how much you want it," he breathes heavily, as I take hold of him, yearning for every inch.

"I want you, Francesco," I moan, feeling myself come on his fingers. "Every inch of you inside me, now."

He grunts so heavily that it pulls right from under my skin. Immediately, I'm in the air again as he sifts through a drawer to pop a condom out. He's literally holding me up with one arm as though I weigh nothing, and it's only causing me to be turned on even more.

Once the condom is on, he lays me gently upon the bed. I then sink into the pillows and another smile makes an appearance again.

"I have waited for this moment since the day we met," he breathes. "However, I didn't expect it to come true. What a lucky man I am, for my dreams to become a fucking reality." He chuckles to himself, planting a kiss on my breast.

He sucks me passionately as I feel his body lowering just above me. The heavy weight of his presence is overwhelming with allure. My legs spread wider automatically with yearning. His moans vibrate and spread through my breast, while he pinches my nipple with his lips.

"Honey," I whisper with a moan, gently pulling him nearer by his shoulders.

He sweetly blesses me with a kiss, then he enters me, slow and deep, allowing me to saturate in every movement and every part of him. This is dangerous, because as amazing as this feels, I'm not sure how or if Francesco and I could ever work normally together again. Yet I don't desire to care. I don't wish to fret, for all of my wanting now is for him.

He's fucking me steadily, now beginning to pick up the pace. His breath, his sweat, his scent, his body. Everything about him thrusting me into an arousal that I know I'll never be able to forget. It's the way he makes me feel. This feels more than just a quick fuck, but I don't necessarily know what it means to make love. He doesn't love me. Neither do I love him. So where exactly are him and I going with this?

18. Darling

In the darkness of the night, I'm lying lovingly caged within Francesco's arm as I peer at the clock that reads half six in the morning. I can't help but smile. Because as cliché as it sounds, last night was one of the most magical nights of my life. So passionate and dreamy, in an otherworldly kind of way. It felt more than sex. Almost spiritual, I guess. As though our souls were becoming intertwined together with a sort of intimacy that flows from the divine. I've never felt so present with him before, and it's never felt so wrong, yet so right. We've been intimate, in and out of sleep, had the sweetest pillow talks, only to then restart the whole cycle again. But I need to go home. There's no way I can walk into work with the same outfit as yesterday.

"Where are you going?" he mumbles, still half asleep.

"Home." I try to break free from his arm but his embrace is too strong.

"Stay, Natalia."

"I can't. It's almost seven, Francesco. I have to get ready for work as soon as."

"I am giving you the day off."

"No," I tell him, finally breaking out of his grip. "I want to go to work."

I hear him sighing behind me as I put my clothes on and gather my things together.

"Natalia, it's no trouble at all—"

"Oh no, my phone is dead!" I gasp, trying to revive it without luck. "Do you mind ringing me a cab?"

Steadily he sits up, revealing his grand and golden body. "Are you sure you want to do this?"

"Yeah, please."

"Fine," he sighs, now putting some random clothes on. "But I'm dropping you home myself."

"Why? You need to rest. There are so many meetings scheduled for you this morning—"

"Natalia," he interrupts. "I'm driving you home."

"Okay," I whisper. "If you insist."

He cracks the door open, and leads me down the stairs throughout the dark. It's almost black that I can barely see anything, but like the gentleman he can sometimes be, he holds my hand as we make our way down the steps. He then leads me around the staircase toward the back of the apartment.

Surprisingly, I then find myself in this parking lot full that's so huge and spacious with the most luxury cars that I know would even make Diego envious.

"Goodness, I've never seen so many expensive cars together like this in my life. Do you live near other businessmen too?"

Francesco quickly glances in my direction with his brows creased together. "Excuse me?"

"These cars! Is this like an apartment building for other people who... are like you?"

The corner of his mouth lift in amusement. "Natalia, this is my property. Every car that you see here belongs to me."

"Oh!" Heat pinches the apples of my cheeks. "How lovely."

And that was that.

He picks a sleek black car that I already had my eye on, and then politely, he opens the door for me. Once I pop myself inside, I immediately enjoy the pleasure of taking in that fresh car scent. It's invigorating. It seems as though it's never even been used before. Clean and pristine, vacuumed to citrusy freshness. Unexpectedly, I then hear him chuckle as he takes his seat next to me.

"What's so funny?" I ask him.

"The reaction on your face," he responds, clearing his throat as he starts the powerful engine.

"Oh gosh, what? Does it look silly?" I panic, now looking at the passenger mirror.

"No," he replies, seriously now. "You look perfect."

"Then what is it?"

"You look... impressed."

"I *am* impressed! I've never seen anything like this. It's amazing."

He smiles, a genuine smile. "Tell me your address."

When I do, he enters it into the navigation system and speeds off out the parking lot and into the city.

London looks different at this time of the day. Quieter, and more peaceful than I've ever seen it. There's a serene wonder about it when most people in the city are asleep or just about to wake up. The sky is deep peach, and we zoom off passing by all of the pretty white houses of Belgravia.

"I'll arrange Peter to collect you—"

"No," I blurt, quickly. A little too quickly that it snatches his eyes from the road toward me for a second. "I mean... that would be nice, but I want to take the tube."

"Sorry, the *tube*?" He says it like it's a dirty word.

"Yeah, I want to experience what it's like being a real Londoner."

He laughs, and the sight of him so happy while he is driving is so sexy to me.

"Are you trying to tell me that I am not a real

Londoner? Whatever the fuck that's supposed to mean."

"Well, I should rephrase that. I mean, an average working Londoner?" I respond, shifting down into my chair with embarrassment.

What am I saying?

"If that's preferable to you, it's not a problem. I can see how much this city means to you."

"Thank you," I whisper. "About last night, it was truly wonderful being with you, and becoming, umm, better acquainted with you."

He laughs again. "Yes, last night was fun. Thank you. I cannot promise that it will not happen again, if you allow me."

I clear my throat, trying to buy some time to figure out what to say. "Where do we go from here?"

"What do you mean?"

"Well, do we just pretend like nothing happened from now on, or?"

He glances at me for a moment. "No, I don't want to pretend with you. You're the most real thing that has ever happened to me."

"Francesco, we barely know each other."

"I am aware of that." His jaw locks tight. "But unfortunately, there is a pattern that I've recognized regarding the people that surround me."

"And what's that?"

"The closer that people get, the clearer their intentions become... But you, Natalia, there's something different about you. I discerned it the moment I laid eyes on you."

"Wow, umm, you really have a way of taking my breath away. I... I'm not quite sure what to say to that, but I'm glad that you can feel safe with me. It's important to have someone that you can trust in your life, even though it's a bit awkward now since I'm your employee. I mean, doesn't that feel a bit strange to you?"

"Yes, it does."

"What are you going to do about it? Do you think you'll fire me again?"

"No, I am aware of your financial needs," he says, now parking up. "But if you let me, I will take care of you."

"I don't need taking care of," I whisper.

"But you would want to be taken care of. There's a difference."

How does he know? Surely, he can't read my mind.

"I... I didn't say that."

"You didn't," he responds. "But I don't have to hear the words from you in order to know what you want."

"How do you know that I want to be taken care of?"

"I know you've got a lot of responsibilities to deal with," he says, sweetly. "But tell me, where does your love for art fit in this?"

I sigh. "I'll have to find the time somehow."

"Natalia... let me take care of you."

"You're not my man, Francesco. And even if I did have a man, I'd still feel uncomfortable letting him take care of me."

"Tell me why?"

"I don't really feel safe enough to trust anyone to take care of me. Why would you want to anyway?"

He leans back against his chair. "I have acquired much wealth, yet I never like to be selfish with it."

"But that's a good thing, right? But that doesn't mean you have to help me, honey."

"I want to."

"Why though?"

"You fail to comprehend the difference that you make in my life, don't you? Your presence alone is enough to make me feel human again."

"Ha! Human again? You sound like one of those furniture pieces from *Beauty and The Beast*." I laugh, but Francesco is unamused. "Francesco... is it really that bad?"

"Yes." He sighs. "But you make it less so."

"Umm," I whisper, "I should get going..."

When I grab my purse, suddenly the whole world stops spinning. My keys are absolutely nowhere to be found. I rummage through every area, but they're literally nowhere to be seen.

What terrible luck I have.

"What is the problem?" he asks.

"My keys! Crap, I've lost them. Where could they be? They're probably back at the office as I was clearing out my purse yesterday."

Francesco is silent, and I continue to search through my purse one last time. Though suddenly, the powerful engine begins again, and he starts driving off.

"Wait, what are you doing?" I ask.

He shoots me a perplexed look. "I'm taking you back to mine."

"Why?"

"Where else are you going to go, Natalia?"

"Oh. True, I never thought of that. I'm so sorry. I'll have to ask Gideon collect them at the office for me."

"There's no need for that," he replies, sharply. "I will search for them and give them to you myself."

"But what am I going to do about my clothes? I can't walk into work like this!"

"That's why it would be preferable for you to take the day off. I will get Peter to bring the keys to you at the earliest convenience."

I stare at him for a long, hard moment. I feel confused because he's giving me manager vibes again, but I also can't help but see him romantically too, especially since last night.

"Fine," I mutter. "But no days off after this."

And once again, I'm blessed with his rare smile. "Whatever will make you feel better, darling."

19. Kisses

As I nap bare underneath the most warm and luxurious bedsheets, the pink morning light hits against my eyelids upon waking. My eyes flicker open, only to realize that I'm confined within Francesco's embrace once again. The strength of his arms weighs over me. He is sound asleep as his hand trickles down my spine, stopping at my waist. I'm covered from head to toe in his masculine oud scent. I embrace the serenity, burying my face within his chest. I'd like to lay here forever, but I know that they're expecting him at the office today.

"Francesco, wake up. We're late." I try to lean up to check what time it is, but he murmurs, pulling me tighter toward him. "Ugh! I feel so bad. I don't want to miss work today—"

He kisses me, preventing me saying another word. "Don't worry about it."

"You're not going to go in?"

"Yes." He stretches, revealing that golden body. "Later."

"But what about your meetings?"

"I am rescheduling." His business voice is returning as he begins to wake up properly. "Fucking hell, you are even more beautiful in the morning."

When I look into those mesmerizing eyes, I can see that he means it. Every word that he speaks carries weight. Francesco isn't the kind of man to utter empty words.

I trace his defined jawline with my thumb and admire him. "Thank you, sweetie."

A cheeky smirk appears. "I love when your face flushes like that. It happens quite frequently. Do I make you nervous?"

"Yes, actually. You do."

"Good." He chuckles, while his lips tickle my neck with a kiss. "Mmmm, that scent of yours. I can't get it off my mind since the day we met. Your boyfriend is the luckiest man alive."

Guilt rips me apart to even think of Gideon.

"Francesco, he's not my boyfriend."

"I couldn't care less what it is, Natalia. Either way, I'm not done with you."

He's so serious, he's not even joking. I'm stunned. There's a part of me that wants to tell him that all of this is over, but I know that I would only be deceiving myself. For the longer I spend time with him, the greater my soul yearns to cling on.

"There it is again," he whispers.

"What?"

"You're still blushing," he mentions, brushing his thumb tenderly across my cheek. "Does he have this effect on you too?"

His tongue slips through my lips before I can even answer. Then effortlessly, he picks me up. I wrap my legs around his strong waist as he rises from the bed. I'm up flying high within the air, being carried into another room. The lights switch on automatically. It's a bathroom. I hear the shower beginning to run, now trembling at the sensation of his cock poking stiff right under me. He steps in, and my hair becomes drenched. Every part of us drips wet from the shower head vertically above us from the ceiling. His lips refuse break from mine, thrusting me into the corner, securing me up in his arms. The room begins to steam up, and my vision of him becomes hazy. We take pleasure in each other for so long that I lose track of time every moment we're together.

"Stay here until Peter arrives with your belongings shortly," he commands, walking out from his wardrobe room and fixing his shirt collar.

I watch him from his bed as he puts on his cufflinks while sliding into shoes. It's strange seeing your boss in his business attire versus his vulnerable state. It's something that I'm not sure I'll ever get used to. Let alone be able to forget.

"I can't stay here all while you're at work. I'm sure that Gideon would be fine with collecting the keys for me this morning."

"Natalia, that isn't necessary."

"But I don't see the point in waiting around."

He sighs, now flipping through some cash. "Take this and get yourself what you need," he says, gracefully placing a wad of cash in my hands.

I try to give it back, but he won't receive it.

"Francesco, I don't need this from you."

"Take it, Natalia."

"But I don't need it!" I lie.

"You informed me about the challenges of living here on your own. I want you to have it," he says, planting a kiss on my cheek before striding into another room.

I follow him back into his wardrobe, which is perfectly arranged with luxury pressed suits. He opens a draw, with tons of watches and cufflinks.

"You look so handsome and dreamy in deep blue," I remark. "I love it."

The corner of his lips lift slightly. "Grazie, darling."

I tiptoe to his side and brush a kiss on his cheek. "Gosh, last night was…"

"Perfect," he breathes, rubbing his hands over my backside. "It won't be the last time either."

I see lust all over his eyes, and it stains on me.

"Don't go," I whisper, tugging his shirt.

His eyes fill with a sort of temptation, but suddenly, out of nowhere his phone begins to pulse through his pockets again. It's been ringing all morning.

"Sadly, I can't," he sighs. His hands then sink into my derrière tighter as he gives me one more kiss. "Will you be alright for breakfast? My butler and his team are downstairs. I will inform them of your presence. They will take care of you here."

"I'll be okay, honey. I'll probably get something on the way."

"Ciao." I almost suffocate in his tightened embrace as he kisses me before letting me go.

Once he heads out, I then check my phone again to reply to my texts from Julieta and Diego. I then proceed to respond to Gideon who has replied to my earlier message from this morning regarding picking up my keys. I respond, telling him that the situation is sorted and that all is well. Yet he then asks me if we can meet today, and my heart spirals so frantically into the depths of the darkest shame, dreadfully anticipating what's to come next.

20. Dreaming

The skin on my face feels numb from the harsh chill of the winter frost air. The wind is too strong. I'm shivering cold, feeling sick to my stomach to come face to face with Gideon today. I can see him in the distance already there, waiting on Westminster Bridge. He checks his watch, not once, but three times. He's dressed in dark grey, with a smart winter coat and wooly scarf. It's been one day since I saw him, but why does it feel longer than that?

He catches me in his sight, and a sweet but anxious smile appears on his face. As I'm walking toward him, I'd like to turn back. Back to the time before I made that silly mistake. It was impulsive. Stupid. I wasn't thinking straight. Seeing Gideon's face is all I needed to realize that I was caught in the heat of the moment with Francesco, and not remembering my reality. Deep down I know in my heart that if and when I admit the truth regarding how I'm feeling with Gideon after last night, then nothing between us will ever be the same again.

I simply cannot keep him hanging like this. He deserves so much better. He has treated me with so much care and honesty. It's only right that I do the same to him too, even if the truth does sting.

"Hey," I breathe, watching the cold cloud of air flow from my mouth. He then smiles, hugging me softly without a word. "Are you alright?" I ask.

He stares at me for a moment with a weary expression on his face. "No, not really."

"Why?"

"You had me pretty worried, Natalia. I thought something happened to you."

"Gideon, I was fine."

"Yet you inform me that you can't locate your keys in the early hours of the morning. All sorts of scenarios were plaguing my damn mind, Nat. I was concerned that you were stranded or something of the sort. Where were you during the night if you didn't have your keys?"

I violently wipe the tears away from my cheeks and I know that he saw it. "Gideon, I don't need you to be concerned for me—"

"But Natalia," he says with a sigh, worried, as his eyes grow wider with a sense of perplexity about them. "How can you think that I wouldn't worry about that?"

I ignore him, lost for words.

His jaw tightens as he inhales and looks beyond the river, then back at me again. "Please, tell me what the matter is. What's gotten into you?"

"I told you that this would be a mistake!" I cry, bubbling up with frustration. "I told you that something would happen, that the end of whatever *this* is between us, would be my fault. This is exactly what I was dreading!"

I begin to storm away, but Gideon runs after me and tries to hold me close in his arms, yet I refrain from yielding.

"Hey, hey, hey," he breathes. "Wait—"

I try to shove myself out of his strong arms, but I can't. Eventually I surrender, but I neither hold him back nor meet his eyes.

What have I done?

"Gideon, I've messed up so badly. I know that you won't forgive me, because what I'm about to tell you is going to hurt so much, even though we aren't even together. But I think that you should know because I am aware that you have feelings for me, and I don't want you to keep holding on to me emotionally."

"Talk to me Nat, what is it?"

I take a deep breath. "I... I wasn't home because I spent the night with him."

Gradually Gideon's grip begins to feel much looser, but he doesn't completely let me go.

"I beg your pardon?"

My throat feels clogged with ice at this point

and my lips becoming dry. It takes me a while, but I finally bring myself to look straight into his eyes. "I stayed... No, I mean, I slept with him. With Francesco."

He lets me go.

"Gideon, I'm sorry," I croak, with wholehearted desperation as he takes a step back from me. He's looking at me as though he's in a state of shock, confusion and disbelief all at once. "Please, don't walk away from me."

He exhales. "I'm not walking away. I..."

Silence burns a hole between us. I don't know what more to say, because the more words I speak, the further our hearts separate.

"Gideon."

His eyes flicker to me, then toward the river.

"Talk to me, please," I beg him. "Though I would understand if you don't want to."

"It's not that I don't want to," he replies. "However, I can't find the words to say right now, to be transparent with you."

I can feel his heart drowning, and by watching him alone, my heart is drowning with him. I want to walk away and scream. I despise myself entirely for what I've done.

Irritably, I brush my hair out of my face from the fierce wind. "You hate me now, don't you? Tell me the truth Gideon! Nobody can be nice and perfect all the time, not even you."

He turns toward me and draws nearer. "Natalia,

I could never hate you."

"You're not angry with me?"

"No." He clears his throat. "I'm not angry with you, though hearing this news isn't particularly pleasant for me."

"Why the hell are you not pissed off with me?"

"I have no damn right to be! You have clarified it yourself, Natalia. We aren't officially together, are we? Throughout the duration of the last few months, I have ached so fucking strongly to be with you, but the last thing I ever wanted for you was to feel pressured... I thought it best for us to take things slow, Nat, because you made it abundantly clear to me that you weren't ready—"

"And I still stand by that, Gideon. I'm not ready! But last night with Francesco was a mistake. I feel so wrong and so ashamed telling you this, but I need you to know, Gee. It was so stupid, I know."

He shakes his head, shrugging his shoulders. "I don't know what to say to you."

"Tell me that you forgive me, at least." I go closer to him and tug him closer by his coat, yearning for him to hold me like he normally does. But he doesn't.

"There's no need to forgive you if we aren't together, Natalia."

"But I..."

"But you what?" he whispers, brushing my hair out of my face.

"I really do love you, Gideon. You're my best

friend. But you no longer love me anymore, right?"

His face falls. "I need time."

"Time?"

"Time to get my head around all of this."

"I'm a monster for hurting you, especially in the time you and your family need support the most."

"You're not a monster. You're just human."

"Gideon..."

"I don't expect perfection from you, Natalia. All I want is you."

"What if my heart is so empty that I have nothing left to give?"

He pauses. "Then I'll still be here, for you. If I have to pour my love into you without demanding anything in return, I will. But listen Nat, I have to go. I'm meeting Angelina at the studio in an hour."

He kisses my forehead and takes a few steps back. Disappointment is marked all over his face, but there's something of love that still manages to shine through.

"Alright, speak to you soon."

Gideon blesses me with the faintest smile, then disappears ever so swiftly into the haze and crowd.

The following morning, I send an email resignation to Francesco without any explanation behind my decision. Partly because I'm afraid that maybe someone else in the company also has access to his emails, but also because I can't bring myself to speak about the subject again. Through which, I avoid checking my phone for as long as I can because I'm too afraid of what his reaction will be. Surely, he can't be too surprised. But I just know that after the conversation with Gideon, I realize how dearly I truly love him. I'm concerned that Francesco could be a hinderance to me moving forward with what both Gideon and I want. I know that I need to heal, and I know that I need to learn to open my heart to true love which is what Gideon desires to offer me. Because of that, working for Francesco just isn't the way forward for me.

As I've let go of the job, I have decided to look for new ones instead. I've also been working on setting up new online store to sell some paintings on a professional site. After taking photos of them, I place it up for sale online. After all this mess and heartbreak, I'm praying it'll be a season of change and of renewed hope.

Suddenly, I hear the apartment bell.

Please let this not be Francesco.

When I look at the security footage, I see a delivery man who is holding a huge bouquet of red roses.

"Delivery," he says through the speaker.

"Hello, I believe you have the wrong address."

He knits his brows together as he checks the details of the address. "Miss Natalia Garcia?"

"Yes?"

"It's for you, ma'am."

"Oh," I respond, surprised. "I'll be right there."

I collect the bouquet of roses and can't stop staring at how big and beautiful they are as I head back upstairs. The sweet scent of fresh flowers reminds me of my mother. I smile, thinking of how sweet Gideon is to send me them, but then I open the envelope, and see something totally unexpected.

'*Cara, Natalia.*

I read your email. Let's arrange to meet, and we will speak properly on the matter. I want you to tell me what is troubling you. Not through messages, but in person. Something tells me that you love flowers. I thought these would bring a smile to your face.

With love, Francesco.'

I honestly don't believe what I'm reading right now. It's so unbelievable that I have to read it more than once. I blink, and blink, only to sit down in shock of what's happening.

I keep wondering and thinking whether to ignore it or whether to respond to him. But eventually, I leave it, and rest my mind for a moment, basking in the fresh air and quietness upon my balcony before deciding what to do next.

21. Forbidden

It's one of those grey and gloomy days where I feel to do nothing but rest and snuggle up in bed. I haven't left the apartment today. The duration of the day has been filled with me reading *Emma* and having a pamper day.

I've lost count on the amount of times Francesco has called me over the last couple of days since I received the roses, but I'm not quite sure what he's expecting me to say. I've made my decision, and my resignation is final.

After being reminded about the reality of not having a job yet, I open up my laptop and sign onto my new online store. Suddenly, I get a notification. It's the most excellent news that I've received all week. Finally, I'm getting a glimpse of hope for my greatest dreams coming true. My painting has been purchased! Words can't describe how happy I am, although I am kind of surprised at how quickly it happened.

I check out the buyer's details to write down their address, but then my heart sinks, for I am informed that the collector of my painting is actually named Francesco Giordano, located in Belgravia.

Honestly.

There can't be another Francesco with the same surname and location, really? My eyes roll, and my blood boils. So in frustration, I grab my phone and begin to ring him. It rings for one second and then shuts off. I try again, but I can't get through. Though soon after, I get a call back.

"Bear with me," he snaps.

There are a multitude of voices mumbling within the background. I leave him be. A few minutes pass by, and in the meantime, I make myself a scrumptious cup of hot chocolate with whipped cream, marshmallows and cinnamon.

"Natalia."

"Yes, I'm still here. Why on earth do you sound so moody today?"

"I was occupied in a meeting."

"I'm guessing that you're not pleased with the outcome."

"You guess right."

"Thank you for the flowers, Francesco."

I hear a door slam shut near him. "I want you here, Natalia."

"Francesco, I was only there for one day."

"Yes," he breathes. "But sometimes one day is all it takes for your whole world to change."

"I know," I whisper.

"You do?" His voice sounds flirtatious.

"Francesco, how did you know about my new website? I literally only started recently."

"I have my sources."

"Well, you cannot do that."

"Is that so?"

"Yes."

"Tell me why."

"Well, to be honest, I'd appreciate a real art collector purchasing my work because they actually see the beauty and value in it, and I know that's not your intention for investing in it."

"How do you know what my intentions are?"

"I don't. In fact, I don't understand you at all."

"Where are you?"

"Home. And no, I don't want to go out for dinner."

"Allow me to come to yours, this evening. You have not eaten yet, I presume?"

"Francesco... It's a Friday night. I'm already ready for bed in my pajamas, and apparently, you are a billionaire celebrity. I'm sure that you won't be short of women lining up for you tonight."

"Who said that I want them? I want you."

"But who said that you can have me?"

"I will be at yours shortly."

"Francesco!" I laugh, even though I don't even want to find it funny. "You're the one fooling yourself if you think that you can turn up to my home uninvited!"

"Natalia, your lips tend to say one thing, but your heart wants the other."

"How... how do you know that?"

"It is clear enough. You wear your heart on your sleeve."

"Francesco," I whisper. "I admire you so much but I... I'm just frightened."

"What are you afraid of, darling?" he gently asks me. "Please, grant me permission to see you this evening, and let us speak about the matter in person. I have not stopped thinking of you since the moment that I left you that morning. Relieve me of this excruciation, darling girl. I cannot spend much longer apart from you."

"Okay." I sigh, giving into my desire. "But only for you to collect the painting, nothing more."

"Grazie, bella."

Immediately he hangs up, and once I finish my hot chocolate, I scan around my apartment while quickly brushing through my curls, tightening them up into my cream scrunchy. As I wait for him, I rest outside the balcony to behold the pretty golden hour, which somehow ushers me unexpectedly into a little prayer.

***

I'm startled as the sound of the apartment bell pulses suddenly through my heart. I get up to then see Francesco on the security footage. He's talking with someone on his phone, looking as handsome as ever in his classic white shirt and black pants. I let him into the building. Soon after, my front door knocks. I can hear him still on the phone speaking in Italian, but I open the door anyway.

His eyes fall on me, losing enough words to bring him to hang up the phone without a word.

"What is it?" I ask.

He licks his lips within the blink of an eye before clamping his jaw firmly shut. "When you mentioned pajamas, a t-shirt set came to mind."

I look down to where his eyes are glued. My white babydoll silk dress. One of my many night dresses that I've actually kept for years.

"Is a t-shirt set what you'd prefer?" I tease, walking back into the apartment to pour myself a glass of water.

He doesn't respond. Yet I hear him close the door, then I feel his presence creeping nearer from behind, capturing the lingering and addictive scent of oud.

"I like it," he tells me, whispering into my neck with a kiss.

His hands explore the contours of my body, tempting me to surrender. Thankfully, I gather the strength to break away, refusing to yield to the desire.

"You're wasting your time if that's what you came here for," I tell him, now sitting upon the couch.

He holds up a bag of delicious smelling food that steams beside him with a cloud. "Eat with me."

"Yum, that smells delicious! What did you get?"

"Vietnamese," he murmurs, searching for the plates and cutlery.

"Well, I can see that you've already made yourself at home!" I giggle, hearing him chuckle as I say it.

The couch squeaks underneath his weight as he hands me a plate. "Look, Natalia..."

I sigh upon his seriousness returning. "What is it, Francesco?"

"Tell me the reason behind your resignation."

"Well, isn't it obvious? I resigned because it's impossible for us to work with one another going forward. That night was truly a mistake. It was—"

"It was perfect. Tell me, why the regret?"

I can't take another bite of food. "It hurt him to learn the truth, Francesco! I know it wasn't his business to be informed, but he was worried about where I was that night... and it's so hard for me to lie to him. He's so heartbroken about it. It shouldn't have happened at all."

Francesco puts his plate on the small table in front of us, and I do the same. His eyes then glaze over me with a quiet frustration. "Are you in a relationship with that boy or not?"

"I'm not! But for so long it has felt that way. I mean, we're just friends... but I do love him. That's exactly what I mean, Francesco. It's all been so complicated. It's not as straight forward as you think!"

He doesn't look impressed. "If you love him like you say you do, then why the fuck did you let me make love to you?"

"I don't know." I swallow my nerves. "That's what I don't understand myself."

I feel his stare itching through my skin as we linger within the silence. Tears then inevitably spill out from my eyes, so he sits closer to put his strong arm around me, pulling me tight into his chest. He smells glorious, like men's body wash stained on his skin.

"Tell me what you want."

"I told you what I want," I whisper, blinking up to his eyes from his chest. "I've resigned. We're not good for each other, Francesco. I think that it's best we stay apart."

He shakes his head ever so subtly as he inhales. "I don't believe a word you're saying."

"But honey, just because I want you, that doesn't mean it's right."

"Enlighten me."

"I don't have to explain anything for you to know that this is for the best," I whisper, just before he takes my breath away with kisses in my neck.

His large hand glides down my waist, burning over my hips, to then rests over my bare thigh and caress me. I close my eyes in delight, yielding to his touch without a word, but moans of wanting.

"Convince me that you don't want this, and I'll leave," he tells me.

"Francesco, I know that this is just fun to you, but it would be silly for me to walk away from a kind man who genuinely cares about me—"

"Natalia, he isn't your boyfriend."

"So, what are you implying?"

"I want you to be present with me," he whispers, slipping his hand underneath my dress. His fingers then float over my skin toward where I'm wet.

"Shit," he breathes in surprise, bringing me to remembrance that I'm not wearing any panties.

He touches me where I want it, and I don't tell him to stop. Rather, I fail to withhold my legs from spreading wider once I feel his cock getting hard right underneath me.

"Persuade me to stop this intoxicating madness between us," his husky voice shakes, filling me with a second finger. "And I promise that I won't touch you again."

"Francesco," I moan, breathless. "I…"

"Say the words, Natalia. Tell me to stop, and I will."

His fingers fasten inside me, pushing my body to tremble with a dangerous desire that I don't wish to cease. Moans break out from within me as I lay my arm back to rest my hand upon his glorious face, and when I am finally met with his heavy gaze, there's a lustful weight that falls on me with an indescribable yearning. My heart burns to be with him, no matter how much I try to convince myself that I don't, for the sake of Gideon.

"I don't want you to stop," I admit, staring into his eyes. "I want this... I want you. Take me to the bed."

His face softens as he gently lifts me up from his lap. He then kneels before me on the floor, with earnest eyes that pierce through my soul with longing. "How sure are you, Natalia? The last thing that I want is for you to end up regretting it again. As much as I want to have you all to my fucking self, what you want comes first."

"Yes, I'm sure... I think."

"You need to be clear with me," he says, planting kisses in between my thighs. "Because once I start—"

As much as I tried to fight it, I eventually yield to the lust by bringing our lips to lock. Without hesitation, he lifts me up within the strength of his arms as though I'm as light as a flower bud. So effortless, it's sexy.

With carefulness, he then lays me across the bed and pins me down by the strength of his weight. Merely with just one move, he rips my dress down and my breasts pop out. He's looking at me as though he wants to devour me, with thirsty eyes that drown me into the depths of yearning. I pull him closer by his shirt, undo the buttons, and unbuckle his belt. That glorious body of gold shines right at me. I touch him, and like lightning he shrugs off the shirt and nibbles on my chest with his mouth. Every moan that he breathes buzzes right through me.

"Sei bellissima," he breathes heavily, sitting back as if to admire me. "I can never get enough of you, amore. Your beauty, your presence. It's addictive. You drive me to fucking insanity," he murmurs, lavishing his love all over my breasts. "But you're worth it, Natalia. So fucking worth it."

He makes me feel as though I am the most beautiful girl in the world. It's like somehow his words have a tendency to light a switch in me that I never even knew existed. Through which, I draw him close by his belt, and rub my palm firmly over his cock before ripping down his pants. He grunts into my neck as he steps out of them, now pinching my neck softly with his sweet lips.

"Francesco," I moan with a whisper, ushering his hand to the place where I'm yearning for him most. "See how wet I am for you? No matter how much I try to convince myself that I don't want you, it's so obvious that I do. I try to be good. To be professional and do what's right... but you... you just won't seem to let me. It's like I lose all sense of self control with you, and now I can't help but desire you all to myself. I want you. I want you so much, Francesco."

"Fuck," he breathes, as I slip my hands in his underwear just before sliding them off. His tongue then tickles down between my breasts toward my stomach with every butterfly springing to the surface. "Listen, Natalia... Don't walk away from me because of him, do you understand me?"

"Yes," I moan, as he breaks open my legs and takes my clit his mouth.

"Mmmm," he grunts, so powerfully that it vibrates over me with the strongest of waves. "Good girl."

He penetrates me with his tongue, and I'm beginning to sweat so much with pleasure. I can't catch a breath. The more I moan, the fiercer his touch becomes. Honestly, I feel so weak in his possession. Utterly taken over by his strong and irresistible affection. My nipples spring hard underneath his thumbs, kneading all over my breasts as he devours me as though I'm coated with the finest honey. I moan his name again and again, trembling with desire as I remain pinned under his grip.

He brings me closer to the climax, and it's as though every inch of my body explodes within heavenly exhilaration. With both hands, he secures me by the hips as his lips remain all over my clit, ramming harder and faster within me. I release all my bliss, feeling entirely breathless within the passionate embrace of his steady arms. He then eases up with a face that is absolutely drenched, and after taking out a condom, he places it on.

His perfect body weighs over mine as he kisses me as the bed sinks.

"Tell me that you're mine," he breathes, staring wildly into my eyes.

"Francesco…" I feel his big cock pressing on me, and I'm yearning for it.

"Tell me that you won't lie to me again," his voice crawls all over my skin. He then plants kisses all over my jaw. "I don't like it, Natalia, when you lie to me."

"Francesco," I moan. "I promise that I won't lie to you again… I won't."

"There's my good girl," he breathes, now entering me so slow and deep with his love that I moan louder than I ever have before. "Yes, that's what I love to hear, darling."

His eyes are unwavering from mine as he fucks me, speeding up the pace. A beast rises out of him, and then he goes so wild and so fervent that I can feel this cheap bed rattling, literally close to breaking apart. He thrusts hard until he comes. Then breathless, he lays by my side and I lean in to give him a kiss. His arm locks me in his chest, and brushes his lips softly upon my forehead, ushering me lovingly into sleep.

I wake up the following morning to dark grey skies

and the sound of thunder. Francesco is already awake. I'm still leaning on his scented chest as he tenderly nestles his lips through my hair.

"Good morning."

"Morning." I giggle.

He's so dreamy in the morning, it's unreal.

"Natalia, I have decided that it best for you to remain in one of my spare properties." His sexy morning voice is even huskier than usual. "I'm not comfortable with you living in this place."

"Why not? It's not that bad."

"You deserve better. Something more spacious, with extra security."

"Well, I agree that it is super tiny… But this is all I can afford, Francesco. It's not easy at all living in London alone. I'm sure that I have told you this already."

"Then let me take care of you, Natalia."

"Babe, I can take care of myself."

"I didn't say that you can't."

"But you already pay me enough as my boss," I whisper, completely forgetting that I already handed in my resignation the other day.

"Whether you work for me or not, I want to take care of you."

"And how many other women are you taking care of, Francesco?

"None," he replies, confidently.

"Why me, I don't understand?"

"My darling girl." He gently lifts my face to

bring our eyes to fully meet. "If you bring me to explain the intensity of my feelings toward you, this bed will be broken by noon."

I press my lips against his. "I'll think about it."

"Come back to me," he whispers, caressing my face. "Come back to work, amore."

"Honey... if I do, we'll never be able to get anything done."

"We'll make it work." He kisses me again, and this time we're unable to break apart.

I roll over on top of him and I'm blessed with a sight of him that is so heavenly, it's overwhelming. His eyes alight with full of wonder, and I can't help but give him one more peck on the lips. His body then moves with pleasure under my touch as I take my time kissing my way down to his manhood.

He's already so hard.

I love how much he lusts over me. I can't get enough of him. Through which, I take him deep in my mouth, sucking him with a kind of passion that feels as though my life depends on it. I feel the tip of his huge cock banging against the walls of my throat. Hearing him moaning like this is honestly enough to make me soaking wet. He wraps my hair around his fist, and rocks me with strength back and forth. I feel as though I'm going insane. He's literally become my guilty pleasure that I can't stop indulging in. It feels wrong. It feels forbidden and unprofessional, being with my boss like this, but I want it, and I've lost the strength to fight it. I just hope within my heart that this man won't be the end of me.

22. Cinnamon

On my first day back at work, Gideon asks to meet me on my lunch break since he'll be visiting his studio again. I tell him to meet me at the coffee shop opposite Harrods during the afternoon. He agrees, and there's a huge part of my heart that looks forward to seeing his face.

I'm in the ladies room at the head office, fixing my hair and makeup before starting my shift. I haven't seen Francesco this morning because I was adamant that rather than have a chauffeur, I prefer to take the underground and feel like a normal person again. He wasn't having it at first, but I told him that I would leave my apartment earlier anyway so there's nothing he can do. So here I am, setting my makeup and applying my new red lipstick. I haven't worn red lips for years, but I wanted to try something different today.

I spritz on some vanilla coconut fragrance, with hints of floral gardenia. Though all at once, the ladies room door blasts open.

"What do we have here?" Daisy's heels click against the tiles as she stares at me in the mirror. She's wearing a smart powder blue dress suit with a pretty pearl necklace and earrings. I briefly freeze in shock, feeling the weight of her constant passive aggressive demeanor that scares me. "Miss Garcia, I think the red is a little inappropriate, don't you?"

She stands beside me and smells rich with mint and jasmine fragrance. I then watch her beginning to wash her hands in the corner of my eye. "Umm it's just a color, Ms Smith. If it's such a problem then I'm sure Francesco will let me know?"

Her body turns toward me abruptly. "What gives you the right to call him by his first name? As chief operating officer of this company, I'm ordering you to address him as Mr Giordano from now on, just like everyone else in this company."

"But Francesco, sorry, I mean Mr Giordano and I work together so closely," I reply, almost bursting out laughing upon thinking about that statement. "It's so much easier to communicate with him normally."

"You have become too comfortable with him." She grits her teeth sharply, and every word that she pronounces is so clearly spoken in her polished accent.

"I don't know what you want me to say. Why do you hate me so much?"

She stares at me with teary eyes before leaving the room without a word, then I'm left within an atmosphere so eerily silent, and I can't help but wonder what her problem really is.

I storm into Francesco's office without knocking and sit on the velvet chaise by the library.

"What's the issue?" he murmurs at his desk, typing with quickness on the keyboard, as always.

"Daisy. I mean, Ms Smith!" I sigh, leaning my head back and closing my eyes. "Ugh! She hates me."

Instantly, the keyboard stops. "What happened this time?"

I pop my eyes open to look in his direction. His dark hair is sleek and neat in place, dressed in a pristine all black suit that enriches his golden complexion so handsomely. I flush, because his whole focus is already fastened on me.

God, he's so sexy.

"Well, she randomly ordered me to address you as Mr Giordano from now on, because apparently, I'm getting too comfortable with you. Why does she always look so angry like she's about to cry? She has also expressed her dislike for the way I look today... she just makes me feel so uncomfortable!"

His jaw tightens. "Daisy can be difficult sometimes. Leave it with me, I'll have a word."

"Thanks."

Those grey eyes then sharpen over me. "Come here."

I feel hesitant to walk up to him behind the desk. I've never been behind the desk before. I don't think anyone has. So when I draw nearer, I stand a few feet away from him and wait for his response.

"Natalia, you're looking at me as though I have a disease."

He holds out his hand, and his watch twinkles underneath the sunlight along with his cufflinks. I feel nervous, concerned that at any moment someone could walk through the door. But I comply anyway, since he's the boss, and he gently sits me on his lap.

"I love the red on you. Pay no attention to what she says, you are beautiful. I like this," he assures me, combing his fingers through my freshly curled hair. I spent all morning doing it.

"Aww, thanks! I thought I'd try something new."

"We have a few meetings today," he says, calmly. "I will need you to take minutes. Can you do that for me?"

"Yes," I whisper, struggling to keep the eye contact that he never seems to waver from.

"Good girl," he whispers back, following the curves of my derrière. "I love it when you blush like that for me."

"I can't help it!"

"Do I still make you nervous after all this time we've spent together?"

"Yes... you do."

"Good."

I wonder if he gets butterflies for me too, but I doubt it. I'd like to ask him, yet there's this inner knowing that Francesco is not the sort of man to be phased by anyone or anything at all.

"These," he breathes, irritably, tugging on my thin tights.

I panic. "Oh goodness no, what is it? Do they look terrible? They're new. I can run to Harrods to change them... if it's that bad."

He tries to refrain an amused expression on his face, but clearly fails. "No, but there's a possibility that I'll end up destroying them by the end of the day. Is that what you want?"

Oh god, it's not even nine in the morning yet.

Why on earth are we like this?

His gaze grips upon mine within a brief second of silence as my cheeks heat with ardent wanting for him. Although unexpectedly, the door knocks, and it startles me immensely. Francesco doesn't budge, but rather looks at me with burning eyes as I raise up from his lap. The door then knocks once more while I straighten out my dress upon making my way to my usual seat.

"Enter," he orders.

Darlene pops her head in, happy and cheerful as sunshine. "Good morning Mr Giordano, Miss

Garcia! We're all ready for you now, sir."

"Perfect timing," he murmurs, with a tight smile.

I bite my tongue, holding in my amusement as I gather the things that I need. Francesco is already with Darlene at the door holding it open for me. I get up and hurry out, then he locks the door. Darlene goes before us, leading us through the corridors to the meeting room.

I peek up at Francesco, but all of his attention remains glued upon his phone. I feel my pulse spiraling out of control concerning these meetings because I honestly just want to do my best, and I truly don't desire to disappoint him. He's still my boss at the end of the day.

Though to my surprise, he tugs me closer by the waist. "You look ravishing today," he whispers.

And that's the moment I realize, that hearing him say that alone is enough to calm my nerves for the day.

Lunchtime arrives, and Gideon texts me to say that he's already at the coffee shop. Francesco and I are already walking out of the meeting room, and I'm rehearsing in my mind what I'm going to tell him.

"Giordano, I need a word," Daisy calls from behind.

He doesn't stop walking.

"Can it wait?" he mutters sharply over his shoulder.

"No," she says quietly, with a shaking voice that sounds like it's about to burst into tears. "Please, it's important."

He hesitates, now looking at me like it aches him to depart. "I apologize. Let me deal with this."

I glimpse at her, yet she refuses to detach her eyes from him. "It's okay," I whisper, "I'll see you later."

I head toward the elevator as his eyes follow me, then I glance at Daisy, who's staring right at him. The rims of her eyes appear red, almost swollen. It's concerning. I turn around and focus on what's in front of me, trying to forget the haunting look of deep sorrow upon her face.

Once I step into the coffee shop, I'm hit with the strong aroma of cakes and cinnamon. Immediately, I then recognize Gideon, who is sitting near the front by the window. He gleams with bronze radiance the moment our eyes meet.

"Nat." He grins, greeting me with an embrace. "How are you?"

"I feel great," I reply, as my voice trembles at that familiar citrus and woody scent. "Are you okay?"

Gideon blinks slowly and smiles. "Better, now that I've finally seen your beautiful face."

"I think I'm going to get some lunch, do you want anything?"

"No need." He reveals our table with a hot

beverage, bagel and brownies. "This is for you."

"Aww Gee, you shouldn't have! Bless you!" I joyously exclaim upon sitting down. He's honestly so sweet.

He gently brushes a loose strand of my hair away from my face as I take a bite of the rich chocolate brownie. "That sweet tooth of yours."

"Ha! Yes, you always remember. Thank you so much, sweetie."

"Also, you forgot something at my studio," he tells me, while he takes something out of his pocket. "Your sketchbook."

"I've been looking everywhere for this! Oh my gosh, you're such an angel! Also, I've been meaning to ask how your grandmother and sisters are?"

"They're..." He sighs, shaking his head in defeat. "Kitty has had to finish school early on numerous occasions, due to her anxiety. I think dealing with our grandmother's diagnosis is all just getting too much for her to handle. Phoebe on the other hand, seems quiet these days. Things aren't the best at the moment, but we'll get through."

"I'm so sorry, Gideon." I hold his hand, and he places another over it. "Please tell me if there is anything I can do to be of help?"

He smiles with sadness in his eyes. "Natalia, just seeing you today is enough."

Suddenly my phone vibrates with a text, and I glance at the screen to see that it's from Francesco: *'Where the fuck are you?'*

I cherish this special meeting with Gideon so deeply, therefore I don't bother to respond to the text. Rather, I embrace every moment that I have with him as we continue to catch up about all manner of things regarding our lives.

Moments pass us by, and to my disbelief, I catch Francesco storming nearby the window outside. He then notices us, and words can't fully describe how pissed off he looks. He actually looks disgusted in a way, and I'm beginning to panic internally while I plan what to say. Though luckily, I see a group of girls starting to approach him on the sidewalk. I'm hoping that they will delay him from entering, but instead, he greets them with a firm nod without ceasing his stride. My heart thumps as he steps inside. Instantaneously, he becomes bombarded by a number of his admirers at the door. I discern the deepening pissed off look upon his expression, but politely, he stops to take a picture with one of them.

My attention steers back toward Gideon.

His gorgeous green eyes narrow in Francesco's direction. "Isn't that—"

"Yes," I breathe, taking a sip of my vanilla latte. "I'm so sorry, Gee. I'm not quite sure what he's doing here."

The expression upon Gideon's face now looks just as irritated as Francesco's. There's no mistake of discerning Francesco's frustration that is stabbing right through me. I'm sinking in the chair, wondering what in the world to do.

"Natalia." Francesco's deep voice waves over me. Hesitantly, I bring myself to look at him, and his face is marked with the clearest impatience. "Let's go."

He says it like there's no room for discussion. It stings me, but I can't let him think that he has the right to control the personal matters of my life.

"I'm on my break, Francesco."

"Your break is over."

I check my phone. "No, it's not. I have just under thirty minutes left—"

"Your break is over when I say it is. Now, let's go."

Suddenly, Gideon rises abruptly from his chair in order to step in front of me, now standing before Francesco.

What on earth is going on here?

"Listen, I would appreciate it if you would allow Natalia to have her space. She needs a break in peace."

"Get the fuck out of my way before I do something that I could regret," Francesco mutters quietly, trying to keep his cool in a café full of eyes on him.

"Why is it so hard for you to leave her alone?" Gideon's frustration is evidently rising. "What are your intentions, Francesco? Since you hired her, you've refused to leave her be. I don't trust you."

"Gee…" I whisper, trembling. Yet they both still choose to ignore me.

"Because I want her, it's that fucking simple."

"Yet you refuse to allow her to spend her break alone in peace?"

"She's not alone. She's with you."

"And that bothers you, because?"

"It bothers me because she's mine."

Those last two words brings Gideon to silence, and truly, I can't blame him, for I am taken back a bit myself upon hearing it too. Francesco's eyes fix harshly upon Gideon with refusal to shift without a blink.

"Let me ask you something, Mr Knight," he begins again. "Why can't you take the hint that Natalia does not want you? The only reason that spends time with you is because she does it out of pity—"

"No, Gee," I clarify, now standing up between them. "I promise you that's not true."

"Which part isn't true, Nat?" Gideon asks me gently. "You being his, or you pitying me?"

Francesco sighs impatiently to my side. "Isn't it fucking obvious?"

"Francesco!" I can't help but sigh, wishing he'd just refrain from making the situation worse.

"Are you always this aggressive?" Gideon asks Francesco.

"Are you always this weak?" Francesco fires back.

"You know, I have read the media articles about how shit your behavior can be toward people. I must say, all of the demeaning comments that they have written about you is an understatement."

Francesco exhales. "I could care less about what people think. They still make me billions in my sleep. So tell me, what the fuck is your point?"

"You ought to humble yourself, mate. Having a high net worth doesn't guarantee that you'll always get your way."

"Bullshit. Nothing is out of my reach, including the woman that you claim to want."

"Enough!" I mutter. "Francesco, we're leaving. Not because I necessarily want to depart from Gideon, but because you both can't seem to compose yourself decently with one another! You're like children for goodness sake, stop this nonsense, at once!"

Francesco's jaw ticks. "Let's go."

"I'm sorry, Gee," I say, wrapping him in my arms.

"It's fine, Nat," he replies, giving me a quick peck on the temple.

Francesco's entire demeanor becomes rigid as a result of it. So immediately I storm out, hoping that he'll just let it go and eventually follow. And just as I predicted, it doesn't take long for him to catch up to me with those long legs.

"I leave you for five minutes, and you fucking end up with him," he mutters under his breath, lighting a cigarette to his mouth.

"What has Gideon and I got to do with you? It's

none of your business, Francesco!"

I take a last sip of my latte before dashing it in the nearest bin. I'm fuming, and to make it worse, he's laughing about it.

"You're so cute when you're angry."

The wind directs the smoke toward my face, and it vexes me even more. "Don't."

"Don't what?" he asks flatly.

We walk into the office building and wait for the elevator. "Don't ever tell me what to do again. Francesco, I mean it."

He gives me this daunting look that tells me that I'm going to face consequences for what I just said, but I don't care. I cut my eyes away and step into the elevator. He comes inside, and the doors close. I try not to look at him, but I can see in the corner of my eye that he's pissed. I don't even have to see it in order to feel it, and with every second that passes by in this elevator, the more claustrophobic I'm feeling.

Finally, the door bells open, and Francesco and I stride with speed toward his office. I don't know why I'm walking like I have somewhere to escape from him. He's crawling under my skin, and I'm coming to that place where there's no part of me left that remains unmarked by him.

He opens the office door wide open for me. I'm hesitant, now staring into his ice grey eyes as I step in. The door then slams shut, and with merely one arm, and one move, he pulls me close to him. His rich oud scent clouds over me, and the grip of his strength remains so firm that I know I will fail to shift an inch. He feels like luxury. He exudes abundance. There's a part of me that wants to break free, but I don't. I don't even try to wiggle out of his arms. I just surrender and let him hold me.

"Don't you dare walk away from me like that again." His jaw clamps shut, studying me with serious eyes. "Do you understand me?"

"Or what? You're going to fire me again? I don't need you, Francesco. I really don't!"

I feel myself tripping on my words, because as much as I don't need him, I know that deep down, I very much desire him. I desire Francesco Giordano all for myself.

"Natalia, I want you," he whispers, holding my face in his hand. "I want you all to my fucking self. I can't tolerate another man creeping around you. It fucks with my head."

I lose the words to respond, because deep down that's exactly how I feel about him too.

"How did we get to this point? Francesco, what on earth are you doing to me? Do you realize how frustrating it is to see you with groups of women too? Yet I don't bang on about it and make a big ridiculous fuss! Gideon is my friend. One man—"

"Yes, a boy who clearly wants you. I will not tolerate it, Natalia. I am not sorry for it, either. I won't allow it, darling."

I'm battling.

I keep fighting between frustration and desire. I want to cry, but I'm so angry. Francesco is a giant standing between Gideon and I, and no matter how hard I try, he always seems to push on my buttons of weakness without realizing it.

I feel like I'm suffocating with love and lust, anger and rage, all at once. His grip around me hasn't loosened, and I'm only becoming further immersed within his musky aura of ecstasy.

"What do you want from me, Francesco?" I cling on to his shirt. "Ugh! You're driving me so mad right now, like you always do for goodness sake!"

He kisses me once, and says nothing more. I then grab him by the collar to kiss him again.

"I don't understand this," I whisper. "You say you don't want commitment, yet you want me all to yourself. Did you mean what you said back there... about me being yours? It doesn't make any sense. Francesco, we can't continue like this. What is it that you want from me? How can we move forward from here? Tell me, please! This is getting really overwhelming for me, it truly is."

I wait for his response as he remains still and silent, staring at me without a word. Yet his lust digs so deeply through to my skin. I sense the intensity of his yearning without him having to even utter a word. Therefore, I bring my hand to make its way down to touch him how he likes it.

"Is this what you want?" I ask.

Instantly, he grunts.

"Tell me that you want me all to yourself again," I breathe, guiding his hand over my breast. "Tell me that I'm yours once more, Francesco. You make me feel so wanted and beautiful. I like it, honey, when my boss claims me as his. But deep down, I love it even more when you order me around. I find it so funny because you're not in control as much as you think. I carry the power to drive you so fucking crazy. Don't I, honey? And there's absolutely nothing that you can do about it."

His jaw tightens. "For fuck's sake. Get on your knees, Natalia. Let me fuck that smart mouth of yours."

I exhale deeply with strong wanting to obey, restraining every temptation within me to comply.

"Why should I?" I tease. "I'd love to take your cock in my throat right now, Francesco, but you're so used to getting your own way. Not with me, honey. Especially not today."

"Fucking hell," he moans deeply, as I lead him backward into a corner, refusing to let go of his cock.

"Be careful," I tease. "Your other employees will hear you."

He growls with passion and swears under his breath as he lifts me up before I even realize that I'm off the ground. I lock my legs around him just before he thrusts me with violent lust against the wall. His cock is rubbing hard against me, and I can't help but make it known how much I want it.

"What do you want, darling? Tell me."

"Firstly, I want you to understand that you have absolutely no control over me."

"And secondly?"

"I want you to fuck me before the next meeting in ten. I need you, Francesco. I need you inside of me," I moan under his touch.

"Fucking hell, you make me so weak," he breathes, keeping me lifted in the air while taking my dress, tights and panties down all in one. I hear the tights tearing apart as he does.

"And you make me reckless," I breathe heavily as my bra pops off. "Doing things I shouldn't be doing at work. I feel so terrible for it. Yet here I am, always wanting more of you."

"Why do you feel terrible for it, Natalia?"

"Because I feel as though I'm not doing my job right."

"It's only your second day."

"And look where we are," I respond, glancing down at my bare body pressed against his suit.

"Shit," he whispers.

"I don't want us to stop," I whisper, holding him tight. "But I'm just worried as to how this will end."

"Be present with me, amore. Don't worry about tomorrow."

"But it's so difficult for me to not worry. I've

already got so much on my plate as it is."

"I know," he says, brushing my tear away. "But I won't allow you to struggle, piccola mia. Whether you work for me or not, I'll take care of you, if you let me. I have never felt this way about a woman before. Let me help you and take those burdens away, darling girl."

When I look into his eyes, I watch the lust turn into something else. Something softer, deeper and more genuine at heart.

"Okay," I whisper, reaching up to kiss him.

Sweetly, his lips tugs their way down to my chest, breaking ravenous all over my breasts with no intention of slowing down. He's carrying me across the office, now laying me face down, bent over his desk.

"Honey," I moan, catching the time on the clock. "They'll be here in..." Pleasure suddenly snatches my words away as he digs his nails into my backside, squeezing them apart.

Oh god, the door isn't even locked.

My heart skips the moment I hear a knock on the door much earlier than expected. I wonder if Francesco will stop, but he doesn't. He only sucks my clit harder as though he's starved. I want to laugh and cry and hide at the same time. So I bite my lip, forcing silence as the door continues to knock. It's definitely not locked, but at this point, I don't think he cares anymore. Neither do I.

Eventually the door stops knocking, and I feel

him get up. He then tears open a condom, and places it on.

"Francesco, look at us... honey, what are we even doing? We really shouldn't be doing this here."

"Darling, you forget don't you?" he mumbles quietly. I then suddenly feel his cock pressing on my clit as he leans in to whisper, "I warned you of this, when I mentioned that you would have an effect on my work. Did you think that I was joking?"

"Francesco," I moan, as he pulls on my hair.

"You're so beautiful, it's addictive. What will it take for me to let you go?" he mumbles. "I don't know."

He leaves kisses down my spine before entering me, and I moan with no choice but to grasp on to the edge of the desk. He penetrates me so deep that I'm burning with fire and delight. It's all too much, the affect that he has on me. It's deceptive, for I feel as though I'm just falling deeper and deeper into something, but into what? Because it can't be love. I am afraid because I have no idea what this is between us. Yet I continue anyway, because I'm utterly obsessed and I truly can't get enough.

We hit the peak and I melt all over his desk. Then with one scoop, he brings me up in his arms to sit down on his lap on my usual chair in front of the desk.

"I want you," he whispers, brushing his fingers through my curls. "I don't like to play games, Natalia. Let me be clear, I want you to be mine. I fucking adore you." I kiss him and then lock eyes with his passionate gaze. "Your lips often taste like cinnamon and sugar," his eyes smile as he says it. "It's those drinks that you love so much. So beautiful, my gorgeous girl."

As he nibbles down toward my chest, I see my painting hung on the wall, which I didn't realize until now. It brings tears to my eyes. I can almost say that it only causes me to fall further into the trap of calling my feelings love.

"Tell me that you're mine, amore," he whispers softly. And just when I thought I couldn't get enough, he thrusts his finger inside of me. Surprisingly, I moan so loud that I'm scared someone may have heard me. Though still, his gaze remains striking over me with cool grey eyes that anticipate an answer. "Tell me, darling girl. Let me hear it from your lips."

I brush my fingers through his hair, and plant a kiss on his lips. "Honey, there's no longer any doubt about it. I am wholeheartedly, yours."

23. Positano

As the winter blooms into spring, Gideon and I eventually learn to love each other from a distance. Words cannot describe how greatly it has hurt me. For deep down, I know that I still love him. Yet still, it's been months last since I saw him. The recent death of his grandmother had left him no choice but to return to the Cotswolds on a permanent basis in order to raise his twin sisters in their family home. At just fifteen years old, they only have their brother in the picture from now on. As much as this has been breaking my heart, the acceptance of this new chapter between Gideon and I is something that I'm trying my best to believe that all things work out a certain way for a reason.

The last few weeks traveling throughout Italy with Francesco have flown by much faster than I expected. Although, I'm not quite sure whether it's because of Francesco's super busy schedule, or if it's due to my heart becoming deeply saturated in a whole different sphere of admiration for him. Truly, it's as though I completely lose track of time when we're together. For even as the days softly transition into night, my soul seems forever set on him. He has become my sun and my moon, the absolute light of my life. After so many years of living in a state of anxiety and darkness, it's like I've finally caught of a glimpse of brightness and bliss. For whenever I'm in his presence, it's as though he carries an ability to lift my soul out of anxiety and settle me rapturously into a dreamy state of escape.

He's been spoiling me, and I like it. He takes me everywhere and anywhere that I wish to go. He never tells me no. He even took me to the most stunning art galleries throughout Rome. I asked him to take me to the Trevi Fountain, Sistine Chapel, St. Peter's Basilica and the Colosseum. He did so, without delay. He cancelled his work plans to take me shopping in Milan, and he sweetly blessed me all of the diamonds, dresses and art pieces that I wanted. It's addictive.

When he's supposed to be at work, he's fucking me. When I desire him to finish a virtual meeting early, all I have to do is take his cock in my mouth to get what I want. I like his attention on me, and me only. For I have come to understand that there's a certain power that I have over him, yet there's also a different kind of hold that he has over me.

I really can't grasp the madness between us, yet this man can't help but be my greatest escape.

We had pizza and gelato in Naples earlier today, and he held my hand in his, telling me that he'll take care of me while I work toward my dreams of becoming an artist. It's only now that I'm starting to realize how much I want this. I feel bad for it.

This isn't what I expected at all to come out of this relationship between us, but I'm loving it. For no man on earth has ever cared for me nor made love to me as passionately as he does. I'm utterly enraptured, for in his arms I can't help but feel the most beautiful, safe and wanted than I've ever felt. He has chosen me. Despite the endless amount of women that he could truly be with, he still claims me as his, and it makes me feel special and more wonderful than I've ever been in my existence.

I know that I shouldn't have to wait for a man to validate me and make me feel better about myself, but I can't help what I feel.

Francesco has become medicine for my anxiety. It's non-existent when I'm with him. It's literally as though every curse that my father has ever spoken over me is finally void. I feel free to dream, to live, and learn to fall in love with myself again with the most wonderful man on the earth by my side.

His heart is the land of my dreams that I've always wished to escape my troubles from. And finally, he's here. Radiant in the form of the sexiest man whose soul is impossible to fail to adore.

It's indescribable the amount of security that I feel with him. I know that nothing can hurt me, and with him, lack is never present.

My father no longer intimidates me whenever he rings, because with Francesco, I feel invincible. Nothing can break me, not with my absolute rock by my side. I thought that what I felt for him was lust, but the safer that he makes me feel, the more my heart grows strong.

Since we arrived in Italy, there's never been a moment when we aren't together, and that scares me, because I know that once we return to London, things will never be the same between us again.

"Umm, where are we going?" I ask him, noticing that our chauffeur is driving the wrong way to the airport. Today is our last day in Italy, and we're supposed to be scheduled to fly back to England this evening.

He rests his hand on my thigh and squeezes me softly. "I have something planned for us."

"Really?" I gasp. "Can you tell me what it is?"

"No."

I catch myself frowning. "Why not?"

"Patience, Natalia."

I drink in the sight of him, losing myself entirely at the glory of his golden skin, kissed to bronze by the sun. Those dazzling cool grey eyes contrast beautifully. He looks ravishing today. Striking, like a heavenly being that roams like a god upon the earth. His shirt is the color of the sky, with ivory pants that look absolutely dashing on him. Our fingers interlock together, and he secures my hand in his. The spring Italian air is warm and humid. His masculine scent consumes me so heavily with desire. I listen to the beating sound of his heart softly tapping against his chest, clutching him closer, as his hand plays with the frilled hem of my mini dress, and as the car speeds toward our destination, I bask in the serenity and my soul enters into rest.

"Honey, pinch me!" I gasp, almost trembling as my eyes remain attached to the deluxe yacht near the coastline. "Where on earth are we going?"

He chuckles, deeply. "Positano, darling."

"But... but what about all of your meetings scheduled back in London, baby? Will I need to write up some new emails?"

"I'll handle it."

A worker on the yacht randomly calls out to Francesco, and they converse for a brief few moments in Italian.

"Let's go," he says, taking my hand in his.

Our hands mold together as though they were formed for each other, and as we enter the yacht, everyone is as sweet and friendly as ever.

The perfect bright sky deepens blue with hints of lilac as Francesco and I have a glass of wine.

"Who keeps ringing you?" he asks me, glancing at my phone that sits upon a nearby table.

I ignore it. "Oh, nobody."

"Natalia," he responds, irritably. "Don't lie to me."

"I'm not lying to you!"

"Then tell me, who is it that keeps calling you?"

"Francesco, you don't need to worry about it."

His gaze holds mine. "I need you to be abundantly clear with me—"

"I am!" I exclaim, close to tears.

"Are you fucking around with that boy again?" he mutters, striding toward the table as though he's about to pick up my phone.

"Stop it!" I tell him, grabbing it out of his hands. "I'm telling the truth... I'm not seeing Gideon. As I told you before, I haven't seen him in months!"

He looks unconvinced.

"I promise you, honey. This is nothing for you to worry about, at all. I'm not seeing anyone else."

His jaw hardens like rock under my touch.

"Why don't I believe you?" he whispers.

"Honey, please..."

He stares at me for one last moment before striding away elsewhere.

I follow him. "Francesco..."

"What?" he mutters, leaning over the railing preparing to light a cigar.

I snatch it out of his hands. "Don't ever accuse me of that nonsense again, I mean it."

"If you fucking told me the truth, Natalia, then

I wouldn't in the first place."

"But I am telling you the truth! It's my father! Okay? You happy now? For heaven's sake—"

"What does he want with you?"

"Nothing. He's just... I really don't know how to explain it you. But I assure you, all is truly well."

He chuckles, humorlessly.

"Francesco," I whisper. "It's fine, I promise!"

"Is there a reason why he keeps ringing you?"

"We're just close that's all," I lie.

From the look on his face, I can clearly tell that he doesn't believe me at all. "Natalia," he breathes, "I don't appreciate dishonesty."

"Well, neither do I!"

"Expand."

"You've been avoiding your family since we've arrived here. Yet whenever I ask you to tell me why, you never explain the reason."

"Listen." He sighs, pulling me in tenderly by my waist. "My personal matters do not concern you, and let's not make this about me. I want to know what the fuck your father wants. Natalia, he rings you several times a day. What's his deal?"

"Well, I could also say the same thing to you too. My personal matters don't concern you, do they?"

"Don't start this shit with me. This is different."

"No, it's not! How can you truly expect me to be open with you if you refuse to share things with me. That's not fair, is it? Don't you think that it's time we start being vulnerable with each other, baby?"

A deep breath leaves him. "No."

"Why not?"

"It's not necessary, Natalia."

"But it is!"

He's losing his patience. "Why is it?"

"Because I…" I bite my lip to shut, battling to withhold myself from using the word love and you in one sentence.

His grip loosens. "No… don't say it."

"Don't say what?"

His eyes darken without a word.

My whole soul fills with so much frustration and sorrow that this point that I attempt to walk away, but his grip around my waist keeps me steadfast in the same place.

Sometimes I get so fucking tired of his ways.

"Let me go," I tell him.

"Wait, I'm not done with you yet."

"Francesco…" I lose the words to release, and let the tears fall out instead. This is the first time that he has seen me this heartbroken and angry in tears. He feels tense. I can sense it in his body, and the way he's currently holding me.

"Natalia," his voice breaks.

"Was all of this just a mistake?" I ask him.

I lift my eyes in an attempt to meet his, yet his face hardens completely like stone. There are no words coming out of his mouth, just thick silence magnifying between us. It hurts.

"Natalia, I mean it when I tell you that I love being with you…"

"I love being with you too. You make me so happy, honey. These past two weeks have been heaven for me. I honestly can't imagine being without you."

"My darling," he whispers, ever so sorrowfully as though he's in pain. "Look, you're beautiful, Natalia. But… fucking hell, I can't give you what you want, princess. Not right now."

"If you can't commit to me then explain to me why on earth are you wasting my time, Francesco?"

"Have I not made myself clear enough on how much I want you? Dammit, Natalia. Give me time."

"Time for what? It's not fair that you're so inconsistent regarding where we stand with one another. I'm falling for you, baby. Please tell me, what are we?"

"I'm not ready to discuss this with you."

My heart breaks. "But why?"

"I will lose you, if I do."

"How are you so sure of that?" I whisper.

He stares at me in silence as though he's already decided there's no more room left for discussion. But it hurts. It hurts that he won't open up to me and tell me what the matter is. What is he hiding? I don't know whether it's something serious, or whether it's something that he's most likely overreacting about. He's so strong, always carrying armor of steel over his heart, so much to the point that I can tell he never lets anyone in. It's bothering me, knowing that there's something between us that's hindering our love. It also bothers me that I'm not able to be open and honest with him about my father. All of this overwhelms me, immensely. All I want is for us to be happy. Never do I ever want to let him go. Through which, I hug him tighter, allowing my heart to fall deeper and deeper into the unknown.

Positano is stunning at night. The village lights up as though the cliffs are beautifully encrusted with billions of specks of gold. The scent of lemons and sun lotion leave a soft stain throughout the shore breeze. Music travels quietly through the narrow streets. The sound of children's laughter and various conversations are everywhere. Tanned skin and ice cream is seen on every corner. The delicious aroma of freshly made pizza teases my tastebuds with its scent while Francesco and I pass by the restaurants. There are couples blissfully breezing through the village on vespas, families overjoyed inside the pizzerias, and children within the streets that scream so loudly with joy as they sit high upon their father's shoulders. This is heaven.

"Are you hungry?" he asks me.

"No thank you, honey."

He glances at me for a quick second. "Are you certain?"

"Yes." I giggle. "That pizzeria in Naples was a dream. I've been full ever since!"

He smiles, taking out some keys as we stop before a building. It's night with blackened skies, so I can't see all of the outside clearly, but there are beautiful little red and pink flowers adorning the terracotta building, climbing so stunningly around the front door.

"It's so pretty here. Where are we?" I ask him.

"One of my villas," he responds, pushing the door open for me.

I step in and gasp, almost dropping my purse to the floor. It's the most gorgeous Italian villa in the world. Lovely stone walls, with beautiful pots of colorful plants and pretty tiled patterns of white and blue on the floor. The rooms are stunning. I can even see a grand dining table outside beside the lemon trees, and a pretty pool area that comes with the most wonderful view of the sea.

"Francesco! This is..." Suddenly, he snatches the words from my mouth as he pulls me in for a kiss.

"Natalia," he breathes softly, lifting my face in his hand with sweet gentleness. "I need you to forgive me, regarding earlier. I do not take pleasure in seeing you upset due to my actions."

His words take me by surprise. "Oh, umm, it's okay. I forgive you, honey. No worries!"

Surprisingly, he then kneels before me, and cups the back of my thighs with each hand. "Tell me what you want," he begs me, looking eagerly into my eyes. "Tell me how I can make you happy, Natalia, and it's yours."

"Babe, you've already done so much for me. I'm happy here with you! That's all I want, honey, truly. I don't know how I'll bear to be apart from you when we go back to England."

His lips plant a kiss right above my knee.

"Then stay with me, amore mio," he breathes.

"Sweetie, I already am staying here with you! And I'm enjoying every moment of it."

"No. I am asking you to move in with me, once we return to London."

"What, are you really serious?"

"Yes."

My heart is pounding with excitement, but I'm honestly so afraid that it may be too good to be true.

"Are you sure about this? I don't want you to feel rushed, baby. Neither do I want to be a burden."

He rises from his knees, now towering over me once again. "Yes, I am certain. You are no burden to me, Natalia. I was serious when I said that I want you, and if I can take financial pressure off you, all the better."

God. I'm falling for him, so deeply.

Without an utterance between us, his lips lovingly hold mine, tenderly flowing down to my neck as he raises me up in the air. He's taking me somewhere. As he does, a wave of longing brings me to unbutton his shirt while his fingers unlock my dress so effortlessly tender, I can never get enough of him touching me.

The heat of his soul spills over into mine, burning with a blazing fire that flames over his skin to mine. His moans, his lust. It taints me with a dangerous desire for him that I know I'll never be delivered from, because no matter how much of him I receive, I will always yearn for so much more. Regardless how hard I try to let him go, I always end up running back to him. I know it. For he's my ecstasy, and my safe place. Every inch of this man intoxicates me to the core. I sink into the sheets, and I'm drowning in his love, suffocating with his fervent desire that constantly overwhelms me to more wanting.

His strong body weighs down on mine with a kiss, then the next moment I find myself completely on top of him. I ease myself down on his cock as I'm filled with the greatest delight. Every part of him envelops me deeper in his lock of ardent rapture, as we make love together underneath the Italian stars.

24. Mrs Giordano

Our first morning in Positano has to be the most marvelous breakfast that I've ever had. Such a stunning sea view graces my vision with picturesque bliss, vibrant with tones of turquoise and powder blue. The sun rays over the Mediterranean sizzles with heat through the layers of my skin. It's shining golden, glistening over the crystal clear sea as it dominates the sky. The village that surrounds us lights up with such magnificent splendor and luminosity. The fragrance of flowers and citrus trees refresh me, being just as invigorating as my ice-cold orange juice while I sink in the view of the horizon.

"Does your sister know that you're here? I know how close you are to her," I say, admiring Francesco's darkening complexion opposite the grand dining table. His white shirt and beige pants remind me of my first day at work with him.

"No, she doesn't."

"Maybe you could ask to meet her here, if you don't want to go back to Tuscany right now?"

"Preferably not."

There's irritation in his voice, and he only further confirms it by snapping out a lighter and cigarette. A gush of smoke flows through his lips as his gaze fixes sharply upon the horizon.

"Honey, it's too early for that." I release a sigh while rising from my burning hot chair upon walking toward him. "What's the matter? You seem so agitated this morning. Talk to me, sweetie."

His jaw clenches firm against my cheek. "It's fine."

"No, it's not fine. I can tell. You may not be a man of many words, but I discern something in your eyes. You're so great at putting this mask on with everyone else around you, but you doesn't work with me, baby. I see right through you… just as you can with me."

He ignores me.

"When will you let me in?" I ask him, kissing the space between his brows to soften his frown.

"In where?" he asks.

"Into your heart."

He pauses. "We spoke about this, darling."

"But you can trust me, Francesco."

"It is not as straight forward as you think."

"But love never gives up… and I'm not giving up on you, baby."

"Natalia…"
"Yeah?"

His eyes refuse to steer from mine, as though he's searching for a shooting star. Patiently, I wait for his words, but nothing comes.

"What is it?" I ask him, softly.

His focus flickers from my eyes to my lips. "Never mind, darling," he says, blinking his gaze away. "Let's go for a drive."

I slide on my white mini dress and heels with a spritz of vanilla coconut fragrance. Francesco is waiting for me in the entrance, and the moment I draw close, I briefly catch his gaze sail steadily across the curves of my hips just before my lips touch his.

"What are the plans for today?" I ask, super excited.

"Tell me what you want, and it's yours."

"Hmmm, well I certainly wish to go to the beach, and then maybe see around the village if you're up to it too? Do you know any good restaurants around here?"

A small smile appears. "Of course I do."

He takes my hand and opens the door, leaving me utterly astonished at the breathtaking car that is parked up outside. It's one of those vintage classic convertibles in a perfect shade of cream, adorned with dark rust colored interior. All at once, it feels as though I'm transported back into the early twentieth century. For just by looking at it alone, I'm reminded of old Hollywood glamour and the glory of romance within Europe.

I hear Francesco laughing quietly under his breath nearby. "Are you ready, darling?"

"Francesco, I…"

"What's the matter, princess?" he asks.

"I'm… honestly so lost for words right now, this is perfect! It's almost like a dream come true. Sometimes I feel like this is too perfect though, like at any moment I'm about to wake up."

He strides toward me and wraps an arm around my waist. "Natalia, this is real."

His facial hair prickles against my thumbs as I behold his handsome face. Truly, I'm so deeply in awe of his soul. He takes up so much of my world and my heart, in one. Yet my soul also fully comprehends that the longer that he stays, the deeper his spirit will remain embedded within mine. He has marked me, in every possible way. For he is everything that I've ever wanted, but there's a part of me that is also afraid that something bad will happen, because good things don't happen to women like me. I'm so used to pain that I genuinely don't know how to be free. Whether this thing with Francesco is temporary or not, I hope that I'll be able to learn the art of living freely, without doubt nor fear.

We drive through the narrow roads of Positano.

Vibrant pink flowers and rays of sunshine are everywhere. There's not a cloud in sight upon the canvas of the clearest blue sky. The higher we drive upon the cliffs, the greater I admire the breathtaking view of the sea. It reminds me of home so dearly. Traditional Italian music is playing quietly through the vintage speakers in the car. Soft enough that I can still hear the roaring waves of the wild shore. I close my eyes, delighting in the orange light of the sun peeking through my lids. I breathe in the warm air, brushing both hands through my hair as I glimpse at him in the corner of my eye. He's brilliant, and utterly divine. Shining in this moment with the brightest countenance that I have seen in him since the day we met. His watch dazzles golden, just like his complexion, with a ruddy flush of color spreading beautifully over his face. He looks free, as though he comprehends that this is his home, where he belongs. But there's a fear that is rising within me, for I never knew that one could find a home within a person, until I fell in love with him.

Francesco has taken me to a romantic restaurant that feels like it's floating in the sky. We're sitting on a beautiful table on a balcony that towers over the glorious village with the perfect sea view. He's having red wine, and I drink rosé, delighting in the scrumptious meal that we had just finished. It's been a perfect day with him. Serenity is spread all over his face, until a couple randomly appears beside us.

"Ciao, Giordano." A man's voice pops out from nowhere.

There's a lady with him, whom I presume is his wife. They're both wearing rings, glowing with tanned skin and bright white smiles that look perfectly polished. She looks at me, and I smile. She then smiles back, and greets Francesco too.

"Giovanni," Francesco responds, now rising to greet the affluent-looking couple. "Come stai?"

"Bene, bene, grazie…" Giovanni's focus then speeds in my direction with a look of anticipation.

"Mrs Giordano, it's a pleasure!" he rejoices, suddenly shaking my hand with an unusual amount of enthusiasm that instantly thrusts me into a state of shock.

I'm too speechless to say anything, so I find myself freezing stiff as the lady shakes my hand too. But Francesco speaks up, immediately interrupting the situation by saying something in Italian that's too quick for me to even grasp.

I feel embarrassed. There's a sense of perplexed disappointment that I can feel from the couple. The lady, I can tell, is trying so hard not to look at me, but I can feel her attention creeping in my direction so strongly.

Giovanni responds in Italian this time, and they both converse in the language long enough to let my heart sink into the depths of despair.

There's a long pause of silence, before Giovanni

then asks him, "Francesco, dov'è lei?"

I have no idea at all what that is supposed to mean. I just stare at Francesco, who is now seemingly as pissed off as ever that it scares me. I haven't seen him this disturbed since we both saw Gideon that lunchtime.

"Look," he begins, rather harshly. "It was a pleasure seeing you both, but Natalia and I must leave."

"Of course," the lady speaks up, quickly filling in the gap for her speechless husband. "Arrivederci, Francesco, Natalia."

There's a false smile upon her face as Francesco leaves cash on the table before grabbing my hand to lead the way out. There's a part of me that's wants to kick myself for not knowing the Italian language. I don't understand what was said at all, but I wish I did.

The drive back home is eerily silent. I hear nothing but the car breezing through the warm air, and the enjoyment of families throughout the streets as we drive by. I want to ask him who the couple was, and I'd like to learn why Giovanni appeared to be so unsettled as we left the restaurant. I'd like to understand why he was so quick in presuming I'm Francesco's wife.

Francesco mentioned once that he grew up in a strict catholic family, I'm not sure if that has anything to do with it. I'm just so eager to get home and kick off these heels that have been burning my soles all day, because honestly, I want to finally rest and reflect on what just happened.

Once we return to the villa, I kick off my heels and rest upon the sun lounger beside the pool.

"Honey," I call out, as Francesco steps outside, to smoke another a cigar. "What was that about... back there at the restaurant?"

His eyes fly in my direction for a brief moment. "What?" he murmurs.

"Who is that couple that we met?"

"Family friends."

"Seemed like a pretty awkward reunion to me. Was it my fault? I'm so stupid, I'm ever so sorry that I haven't made much of an effort to learn your language yet."

"Natalia..." He sighs, dropping to his knees beside my sun lounger and tenderly takes hold of my hands. "None of that was your fault."

"Then why did Giovanni seem so disappointed? Especially when he learned that I'm not your wife. Is he super religious like your family?"

There's a look of sadness in his eyes before he kisses my hand. "Look," he whispers, with a hint of frustration. "Don't worry about it, darling."

I stare into his eyes, and gently take the cigar out of his hands. I feel his body releasing all tension as he surrenders, watching me let it rest on the ashtray.

"You know how I feel about this habit of yours. Take a swim with me instead. It'll be so much fun! When was the last time you had fun?"

"No, thank you."

"Why?"

All he does is shrug with a faint smile. "It's been decades."

"Well, let's change that today!"

I kiss him on the cheek and run into the bedroom to put my pretty white bathing suit on. Once I head back out, I enter the pool and float upon the refreshing water.

"Come on in, honey. It's so lovely in here!"

"You are so beautiful, amore," he tells me. "However, I would much prefer to watch you enjoy yourself from here."

"Nope, I won't allow it! Come here, baby."

From the look on his face, I can see that my words are tempting him. "I can't darling. I haven't brought—"

"Who said you have to wear anything? There's nobody around here, just me!" I wink at him, having a party of a time in this refreshing water. "Otherwise, I'll have to come and get you myself!"

He doesn't look convinced, at all.

"I'd like to see you try, Natalia."

Without hesitation, I leap up from the pool and sit on top of him, with my legs spread on either side.

"Francesco please, come inside with me. See,

you're wet now, anyway! You'll have to take those clothes off sooner or later. I just want to see you have fun, honey. You never have fun anymore."

His sweet pink lips spread into the most gorgeous smile. "You're so cute."

"Let me enjoy my time with you, as much as I can," I whisper. "Before I wake up from this dream. Things aren't always this perfect forever. Let's make the most of our time here together."

"Oh, my darling girl." His cool mint breath breezes softly over my lips. "I will do everything in my power to make you happy. You understand that, don't you?"

"Yes," I reply, wrapping my arms over his large shoulders. I feel the tears beginning to prickle my eyes as I do. "But I don't want this to end. I never want to lose you, Francesco."

"Tell me," he whispers, "why are you so fearful, amore?"

"I don't want to be abandoned or hurt again."

"Natalia, I am going to ask you again. Who hurt you, darling? Talk to me."

"I don't want to talk about it," I whisper. "Not right now, but I will soon... I promise. I just want to enjoy my time with you. You're one of the rare few people that actually make me happy, honey. For once, I just want to be happy without fear or a care in this world."

"Amore," he whispers, with softening eyes that rest lovingly upon mine. "I won't let anything hurt you. That's my promise to you."

His eager hands follow the contours of my derrière, slipping underneath my wet suit. I can't get enough. Our lips touch, bringing them to lock. My fingers play with his buttons, undoing every one upon his shirt. His golden body drips with sweat and water from my bathing suit soaking over him as he lifts me up with one arm the moment that I release him from his pants. He's carrying me, now heading toward the water.

"Ha! See, I told you it's wonderful in here!"

He hugs me from behind to plant a kiss in the hollow of my neck. I then then turn to him, tiptoeing to kiss him once more, but I fail to reach him.

He laughs with clear enjoyment spread all over him as he leans down to pick me up. I surrender my body to him, wrap my legs around his torso upon becoming fascinated at the way that he's staring into my eyes. It feels as though he's sharing a silent serenade, for I sense the intensity of his longing without a word. He moves with an effortless ease as he gently takes me into a corner. Every part of me wants to melt within his arms, right here and right now. I can feel him getting hard through the thin layer of my bathing suit, driving me to insanity right in between my legs.

"Come to bed." His facial hair tickles me as his lips nibble into my chest. "I don't have anything out here on me, darling."

"Honey, I brought the pill with me. It's fine, I promise you."

He pauses, gazing into my eyes. "Are you sure?"

"Yes, wholeheartedly."

His gorgeous grin illuminates the night, then his kisses rise above passion and into another world. I lose myself so beautifully in this divine intimacy called love. It's the way he touches me. It's the way my body, soul and spirit moves in perfect rhythm with his. Every time that we make love, it feels different. It tugs me further into an indescribable attachment that I'm afraid will ruin me if we ever depart. The closer I feel to him, the more sensitive my heart becomes to his. It's like our souls are merging together, and it's almost impossible to imagine my life without him.

25. Masterpiece

It's our last morning staying at this spectacular Italian haven, and the heat of the sun lounge pinches my skin as I create a quick impression of Francesco in my sketchbook. He's carrying out his video call meetings, sitting at the table underneath the lemon tree for shade. The sun shines its love over him through the cracks of the tree leaves, saturating luminous light over his skin which highlights the inhumane beauty that so potently immerses him.

My sketchbook is progressing nicely, with pretty works of flowers and various places within this beautiful country that I've visited so far. But today, I thought I would try something different. I guess it's a way for me to carry memories with me everywhere. I don't ever want to forget this perfect trip away with the man that I love.

"What is it that you have there, princess?" he asks, now shutting his laptop.

"Oh, nothing much, really! How did the meetings go, honey?"

I put away my sketchbook just before he heads near to kneel beside me. Yet clumsily, I cause my pencils to end up scattering as they fall to the ground. He then sweetly gathers them, and places them aside back in the case for me.

He smiles with love in his eyes. "Are you not going to show me what you've been working on?"

I bite my cheek and try to fight the insecurity, but I never can. "I'd love to show you, but I can't."

"Why not?"

"Because..." I sigh. "This one is not to the standard I would like. It's not perfect."

"Natalia, I appreciate anything that you create."

I have a long think about it before I show him the drawing that I created of him. Though once I do, I'm unable to look at his expression nor the artwork itself. I'm extremely embarrassed. There's this long and strange pause of silence that only deepens my discomfort. I want to look at him, but I refuse to. I simply can't bear the shame to see the disappointment in his eyes.

"What do you think?" I ask him, nervously.

He clears his throat. "I have not had anyone create such a skilled piece of artwork like this of me for a while. Particularly, not since..."

"Since?"

He clears a wave of sadness from his eyes and then kisses me. "Never mind," he breathes. "This is perfect."

"You're too kind."

"Tell me, what is the reason behind you being too hard on yourself?"

I think about that for a moment. While I do, he gently lifts me from the lounge, then he sits himself right on it in order to place me on his lap. He enwraps me tightly within his arms, and the scent of fresh, laundered cotton from his shirt brings me calm and comfort.

"All I've known is discouragement. It's like I'm in the process of unlearning all that I have ever known in my life."

"Talk to me about it," he whispers, kissing the crown of my head. "Tell me what is causing you to be hurt. Who hurt you, Natalia?"

Suddenly his phone begins to ring, and instantly I lift up from his chest, anticipating him to answer it.

"Umm, you're not answering?"

"No," he murmurs, declining the call without hesitation. "This conversation is more important."

"No it's not, baby. Besides, we can always talk about this later."

"Natalia, you are my priority now."

"Francesco," I whisper, trying to mask my pleasure at what he just said. "What if it's an urgent call? Please, you don't have to worry about me! So many employees and partners look to you to keep various businesses afloat. Honestly, I truly don't mind, baby. I understand."

"These investments mean nothing compared to how I feel about you."

"You don't mean that," I whisper.

His eyes narrow. "Do you doubt me?"

"No, not at all." My breath quickens. "I just never thought that someone like you could love someone like me."

"What do you mean someone like me?"

"Francesco, you're so honored and admired by all who know you. You're a very distinguished man, and you know it… but I cannot help but feel so insignificant. Not just regarding us, but I mean in this world in general. I feel so small and unworthy. I guess that's why it bothers me so much when you put me before your businesses, because it's like… what do you really see in me?"

"My achievements mean nothing compared to what I've found in you," he replies, with an undertone of hurt magnified within his voice.

"What? Honey…"

"To be clear with you, I never once thought that I was capable of falling for someone until I met you."

"Francesco…"

"I mean it," he says quietly, caressing my face. "I'm enraptured by who you are. I was convinced that it was not possible for me to feel the way I do about you. I thought love was all bullshit. Yet as cute and cheeky as you are, you tame me. You put me in my place like no other human being would fucking dare. Yet here I remain, every single day, willing and eager to give you more of myself."

"Oh, honey! You're the sweetest."

He stares heavily into my eyes, as though a weight of love floods through from his gaze to mine.

"I'm truly so happy being with you," I whisper, letting him wipe my tears away.

I watch the rims of his eyes darken crimson red as we hold each other's gaze in silence. "Shit, what are you doing to me?" he asks, pained and perplexed. "You make me feel…"

"What, baby?"

He hesitates. "Weak."

"How so?" I whisper.

"I'm falling in love with you, Natalia, and it's frightening," he begins, withholding a blink as he stares thoughtfully into my eyes. "Because the more time that we spend together, the greater I gain an understanding of my willingness to give up the entire damn world for you. For your well-being, your safety, and your general peace of mind. I'd be willing to sacrifice anything for you, amore. I fear it, because I know full fucking well that there is no limit as to how far I would be willing to go in order to keep you happy and safe. This is an experience that is foreign to me. You're making me soft, I sense it. It goes against my pride and drive for control. But with you, I fail to compose myself. You humble me, and shrink my ego to nothing. Brutally soft in areas that I was determined to hide from this fucked up world and the people within it. I have fought strenuously throughout the duration of my years to keep a soul of stone, in order to shut out everyone's bullshit and focus on my work. But fuck it. I love you, baby."

I've never felt this strongly before about anyone in the world. I feel his passion in the way he holds me, and the way he looks at me as though I'm the brightest star that shines within all the galaxy. I've never yearned for a man's heart much as him. There's a mighty release that I feel blossoming between us. The magnitude of his feelings and my own, finally released to where they belong. I no longer carry the heaviness of not telling the man that I love how I truly feel about him. Indeed, I am shocked to hear how fervently his soul burns likewise. But honestly, I am at liberty. No longer caged to hide the intense reality of love that keeps pounding unto my soul for this man. Mere words can't describe the bliss as we've finally come to confirmation of how firmly intertwined his heart is entwined with mine.

We scrapped our plans to go on excursions the moment that we declared our love for one another. Since making love, we've not left the villa at all, let alone the bed. I no longer feel homesick for Carmel, for I have come to find my home is within Francesco's arms, and this day was the most perfect day of them all during our time in Italy. It's been out of this world. I'll always treasure it.

Do you think I'm falling too fast?

"Everything about this trip was perfect," I whisper into his bare chest. "Being here in this beautiful country with you."

His lips nestle through my hair. "You are perfect for me, amore."

"I wish I could see what you see, honey."

"It concerns me to hear you talk about yourself in this manner so frequently," he tells me.

"Really? I'm sorry. I... I'm just so used to being belittled and overlooked, so much to the point where I've come to view myself that way as well."

Softly, he lifts my chin with love. "Who could ever belittle you?"

"My father," I whisper, breaking our gaze. I hold on to Francesco tighter, feeling the chill of fear as my remembrance of my father comes to mind.

I can tell that his soul immediately discerns the discomfort that's rising within mine. There's something in the air that's become so cold and unsettling. I can sense his perplexity, but he still wraps me closer into his chest anyway.

"Your father?" There's a pause before he begins again. "Talk to me, darling. What did he do?"

I look into Francesco's eyes and fear what his

reaction would be. This powerful man knows no limit. I don't think he would ever do anything inappropriate regarding my father, but I can just see from the look in his face that what I'm about to tell him, he won't take lightly.

"Honey, umm I'm kinda worried to tell you…" I wait for his response, but he says nothing. He's just looking at me with a serious gaze that's full of anticipation for anything. So I hold his hand and draw nearer to him. "Well, my father hurt me recently. Umm, he hit me down the stairs… then strangled me the night before I left to leave Carmel." I feel as though my throat is breaking down into pieces, so I refrain from expanding, and rather release such silent and painful tears instead.

"Excuse me?" he mutters. Shocked, disgusted and pissed all at once. "What the fuck are you telling me, Natalia?"

"He… he can be violent and controlling at times," I whisper, with drying lips. "He always has been, really. That's partly why he's also been calling me a lot. Since I left for London, he hasn't left me alone. It's so hard… it's been so terribly hard. Back when I lived at home with Julieta, I had Joseph, who is her husband, as well as Diego to keep our father in his place. We all made an agreement that he wasn't allowed to see Julieta, Maria or myself without Diego around, because he can be so unpredictable and so aggressive at times. I regret it. I regret going to say goodbye to him all alone. But there was a part of me that thought everything would be okay. I guess that I was wrong. Though now... what hurts me is that he randomly decides to turn up to London whenever he wants, demanding that I see him. There always has to be some kind of threat that he gives me if I'm not compliant. God, I can't deal with this anymore! Diego isn't even here with me!" I cry out. "I can't live in peace, honey. I'm so scared."

"Shit," he breathes. "Baby... Why didn't you share this with me sooner? Help me to understand. What the fuck brought your father to put his hands on you like that?"

"He didn't want me to leave," I reply quickly in a shudder, feeling super afraid upon sensing the anger within Francesco's aura. "He believes that I should remain in Carmel... and pursue something that is more realistic, I guess. Something that I've noticed with my father is that he tends to desire control over everything, especially with women. It's sickening. Sometimes I think that remind him of mamá. She was an artist with such an ambitious spirit that desired independence from him. He was violent with her a lot. But... honey, I really don't want to get into that right now. I can't. All I can tell you is that night when I announced to him that I was leaving Carmel... Francesco, it still haunts me to this day. I've been so scared to tell you, or anyone else for that matter, because I don't want to be a burden, honey. I really don't. I understand that you're so busy with work so I... I just keep it to myself. He's never been so violent with me like that before. It almost felt like I caught glimpses of what mamá had to deal with constantly on a daily basis. There's honestly no wonder at all why she attempted to leave him... before doing what she did."

"Natalia, let me make this abundantly clear. You're no burden to me, darling. You can tell me anything. You have no reason to be afraid to share things with me. You understand that, don't you?"

"I'm trying..." I sniffle.

"Is your family aware of the situation that took place before you left?"

"No," I whisper, shuddering at the pissed off tone in his voice. "I haven't shared this with them."

His jaw clenches so tight that I can hear it.

"Francesco, I can't let them know about this."

"Why can't you? Tell me."

"Because it will only break us as a family even more. There's so much to the story that you don't know. It's truly not as clear and straight forward as you think!"

"Well then I need you to inform me all about it, Natalia. Help me to understand all of this bullshit that's gone down with your father, before I end up doing something that I could regret."

"I hate speaking about it so much, because it only resurrects the painful of memories... But as you know, my mother passed away when I was five.

She took her own life on Christmas morning. Ever since that day, my father turned into something so much more unpleasant toward my siblings and I. I felt like he was this monstrous demon that kept my siblings and I locked in his dungeon of pain. If not physically, then emotionally. The house was like the darkest prison after my mother died. I lost my light, my angel, only to then be left abandoned in a nightmare.

My siblings and I stuck together throughout those years of growing up. Diego took on the role of our guardian, and Julieta shared such motherly love with her nurturing spirit. My father is a very successful restauranteur, so he was barely ever home. Therefore, we had to learn how to look after ourselves from such a young age. But whenever my father would be home, it was like the worst and most torturing dream that you could never wake up from.

He would return drunk and high, with a new woman in his arms every single night. He makes me sick. It's been hard to forgive him. My siblings and I were so broken, so confused about our mother's place in his heart. We wondered where we truly belonged. We felt lost. Lost without a mother. Lost without a father. Orphans, with nothing but each other. All of my siblings know that my father despises me the most. I do not know why. They don't know why either, but we have a feeling that it's due to me being so similar to mamá.

Honey, I can't describe how deep it cuts to have a parent who only speaks curses over you, rather than love and admiration. It's truly like this constant feeling of unworthiness and abandonment, and it truly never goes away. I've carried it for years. I don't know what it's going to take for me to heal from it."

"Fucking hell, Natalia... I'm so sorry darling," he whispers, while pressing my tears away. I can't help but notice how my pain is so potently reflected within his gaze. "Remind me what his name is, darling. Or his company name, at least. Let me deal with this."

"No, honey! I don't need you to deal with anything! I really do believe you when you say that you may end up doing something that you'll regret. I've forgiven him, Francesco. I have! Well, I am trying to every single day. Promise me that you won't do or say anything, for me?"

"Natalia, your father is a criminal. If you don't inform me about his details, believe me, I will find them elsewhere." The deepest hurt screams through his eyes. "Baby, do you really think that I can keep living comfortably... knowing that he is still out there roaming free after what he did to you?"

"I know, honey... but he's my dad. Literally the only parent my siblings and I have left. I'd rather shrug it under the rug in order to keep peace."

"For fuck's sake, that's bullshit. As long as he is not facing the consequences of what he did to you, there is no such damn thing as peace as far as I'm concerned."

"Francesco!" I tear up even more as he holds me tighter. "Please don't. I'm fine. I'm used to it. I'm used to the pain."

He says nothing, but he truly doesn't have to say anything at all for me to see the frustration in his eyes.

"Honey, you're honestly going to have to restrain yourself about this matter. Retribution truly won't solve anything in this case, I know that it'll only make things worse for my family."

He holds my eyes for a long moment. "If you ever decide otherwise, then please, inform me."

"But what would you do?"

"I'd like to break his fucking neck, thinking that he can put his hands on you, but that would be the easy way out for him. Natalia, I would not be satisfied until seeing him suffer considerably. That's why it would be preferable to learn the name of his company, since I can shut it down by morning with a few calls. What is it, baby?"

"No... I'm not telling you. Promise me that you won't do anything!"

"I'm not making any promises," he murmurs.

"Honey." I hug him.

"Fucking hell, you didn't deserve this."

"I know." I tear up again, and he presses them away with his hands. "It hurts so bad."

"You kept this all to yourself... for this long?

Oh, my darling." Sorrow steals his words for a moment, so he kisses me through my hair. "Is there anyone else outside of your family who is aware of how fucked up your father is?"

"Yeah, Gideon is."

Francesco's chest lifts and expands as he takes the deepest breath. "And his reaction was?"

"He comforted me and encouraged me."

"Encouragement." He chuckles, without humor. "Shit, I could tell he was weak."

"Baby, please please please promise me that you won't do anything!"

"Natalia..." He sighs. "The thought of anyone putting their fucking dirty hands on someone as pure and beautiful as you. I don't think I can let this go, darling."

I cry, hugging him close. "His words haunt me every day. I'm so scared of my future, honey. Because it's as though after all this suffering I've lost hope to believe that good things can happen to me."

"Whatever he has said or done to you is a clear reflection of how fucked up he is."

"He says that I'm going to fail, that my dreams are childish and immature. He says he's so certain that things won't work out for me, and that I'll always need him and his money, in the end. And this is why I'm so adamant that I'd like to be independent, honey. Because I want to prove to not only him, but to myself that I can actually do well and prosper as I pursue the desires of my heart."

"I understand your concerns, but you have not endured through all this bullshit for nothing. I will do everything within my power to support you."

"I love you so much," I whisper. "Thank you for listening to my heart.

"Ti amo, darling," he breathes, muzzling through my skin as he starts kissing my neck. His hands to float gracefully over my body, down toward my inner thighs where I'm getting wet. Those sweet, soft lips begin to sweep down my curves, tasting the most intimate part of me. "With everything within me, amore."

26. Famiglia

I wake up from an afternoon nap to a husky whisper calling my name. Francesco's facial hair lightly scratches against my face while his lips cushion upon my cheek. I stretch deeply, wakening to the brightness of the sun fluttering my eyes open. He's sitting at the edge of my side of the bed, fully clothed in his usual smart attire. But there's this dark expression of dread all over his face. Just by looking at him alone I can clearly tell that there's something deeply wrong.

"Natalia," he whispers. "We need to leave."

"What's going on, honey?"

"I received a call."

"A call?"

His sharp eyes glance at me before snatching away. "Yes, from my mother."

Immediately I sit up at this unexpected news to

embrace him, but his stiffened body feels utterly cold to the touch. So tense and clearly discomforted that I notice his fingers becoming formed into loose fists. Through which, I place my hand over his, and ever so slightly he softens while a grave sigh leaves him.

"What did she say?"

"Giovanni fucking pisses me off," he mutters, gently breaking out of my embrace to pace steadily throughout the room. "He notified my family that I am home, and now that my mother is aware, she has requested a visit."

"But babe, isn't this kind of a good thing? She's your mother. Of course she'd want to see you! If I'm honest, I'm not surprised at all that she called. She loves you, dearly."

"Look, seeing my mother today is not going to be a positive experience," he responds, with quiet frustration. "You do not know my family, Natalia."

His words capture my voice for a moment. "I know that, honey. I just thought that since you're barely ever here, it seems like a perfect opportunity to see your family, you know? Do you not get along with your mother?"

"I do," he whispers. "Very much so."

"Then what's the problem, Francesco? Please tell me." I walk over to him and slip my arms under his to hold him. "There's something that you're not telling me."

Tenderly, he tugs me close, staring into my gaze so intensely with deep thought. "There's no time, darling. We must prepare to leave within the next quarter of an hour."

His huge arms gently let me go as he steps aside, but I clutch his hand before he leaves.

"Promise me that you will tell me. If not now, then at least when this trip is over."

His brows knit together. "And what if I cannot tell you, Natalia?"

"But why couldn't you, baby?"

Slowly, he begins to draw nearer again, though with the darkest countenance that masks the entire room with unease. "Believe me, it is much more complex than you could think."

Tuscany is everything that I truly ever envisioned it would be. The pictures that you see online truly don't fully capture the splendid beauty that's so deeply admired as one of the most stunning places in the world. Francesco and I drive in another vintage convertible throughout the breadth of the Italian countryside. The gorgeous hills of Val d'Orcia are absolutely mesmerizing. The greenery is as pretty as a painting, and as we pass by numerous farmhouses, every sense within me springs to life as the scent of grass and citrus invigorates me.

My skin soaks up the much needed vitamin d, bronzing underneath the Tuscan heat. Francesco gleams utterly angelically, dressed in a white shirt and cream pants that compliment his darkening complexion. He's driving very quietly today, with the most haunting silence as his gaze remains fixed unwavering from the road ahead. There's something in his eye that screams dread. Not once has he smiled today, which is rare since our time away from London. I'm wholeheartedly hoping that he's just overreacting, and that visiting his family won't be as bad as he anticipates. For I can see that his unsettling weight of nerves are crippling him with tension so uncomfortably thick that I feel his anxiety twisting on my veins. His hands are gripped tight on the steering wheel. Those large, strong knuckles look as though they're about to burst through his skin. In the space of a few hours, he's only said a handful of words. No conversation, absolutely nothing at all but an unsettling dread that I'm so eager for us to be set free from.

"This is it." His jaw locks, nodding toward a neoclassical estate in the distance.

I look ahead and almost gape at the glory of it all. The ivory estate is surrounded by the largest, well-kept garden I have ever seen, with mesmerizing sculptures and classic water fountains plotted throughout. Neat flower beds are planted so beautifully outside the entrance, complimenting the long row of towering Italian cypress trees which reign so perfectly on each side of the road toward the drive.

Finally, Francesco parks up. He then gets out

and slams his door shut, but instantly, I sense his anxiety beginning to avalanche heavily on me.

"Baby, please tell me matter," I beg him, worrying to death about what's troubling the man that I love.

"I'm sorry," he murmurs, brushing his hand anxiously through his hair.

"What are you apologizing for?"

"For being so unpleasant with you today," he responds, while taking a quick glance at the front door. "I have not been here since…"

"Since when?"

His ice grey eyes hold mine for a second, before ripping them away as the front door opens.

"Francesco!" His sister, Valentina, suddenly pops out the entrance and leaps happily into his arms. He has shown me a picture of her before, and she looks exactly the same in person. Tan and tall with the darkest hair, just like her brother. They speak joyfully together, just before he introduces me to her.

Suddenly, another voice emerges from the door. "Francesco…" It's deep, quiet and shaky, bringing Valentina's laughter to cease immediately.

Everyone's focus shifts toward the direction of the ghostly voice, and I'm met with a frail looking mature lady, whose cold grey eyes have such a striking resemblance of Francesco's. She looks at me and I smile, but she does not. Rather, her eyes zip toward her son once more.

"Dov'è tua moglie?" she asks him, loud and sharp.

He just stares at her. "Mamma, per favore."

All hell breaks loose when his mother begins raising her voice so rapidly in Italian that I can't keep up. Her warm complexion deepens red in exasperation, and ever so calmly, Francesco ushers her to the side.

Is it my fault?

I watch Valentina whispering something to Francesco. He then glances at me, saying something back to her just before leading his mother inside the house.

"I am sorry," Valentina apologizes. "My English is not so very good. I know little. My mother was an English teacher, you see."

"Aww please don't apologize. It is fine."

"Ah. Francesco has gone to talk to our mamma in private. You can come inside. Sit with me, if you like to do that."

"Thank you, that's so kind of you."

She smiles, awkwardly, while leading me inside to the old estate. It's a spectacular sight. Classic neutral decor that stands timeless with breathtaking beauty, but it looks empty. Something about it seems haunting in a way. Silence takes over the building, with the quiet conversation between Francesco and his mother somewhere far away in the distance.

The sound of my heels slowly clack against the

hard flooring. It echoes eerily throughout the hallway. I find myself drawn to the artwork and historical looking portraits that hang upon walls. There are photographs of Francesco and his family back in the day. I smile, admiring the cuteness of Francesco as a young boy, but that smile instantly fades the moment I catch an odd family picture. The one with the father's face scratched completely off. And that's precisely when I notice that every family photo I've seen in here is not only Francesco, Valentina and the parents, but there's also a little boy in the pictures too. It's strange. Francesco has not mentioned another person in the family before. I feel very tempted to ask Valentina about it, but there's something that is telling me to hold my tongue.

"Natalia Garcia is your name?" she asks, as we both sit down together in what looks like a living room.

"Yes," I reply.

"Ah. Francesco told me about you. He has love for you, very much so!"

I giggle, speechless at what to say. It's strange to hear that Francesco could possibly tell someone else that he admires me. I guess for so long I have grown used to him being someone that isn't so clear with his feelings and intentions, but this trip away from London has changed our world entirely.

"I'm shocked to hear it," I whisper, without even thinking first. It's only been a matter of days since Francesco declared his love for me. My heart hasn't absorbed that reality just yet.

"I am also not very surprised that you are shocked."

"You're not?"

"No." She shrugs quickly, with her lips turned downward as she speaks. "I did not think that my brother could have love for someone again... after what happened."

"Again?"

"Oh," she whispers, as horror waves over her cat eyes. "I am sorry. I didn't know. Umm, do you want a glass of water?"

She shoots up from her chair and leaves the room before I can even say something. My heart beats so vigorously with desperation for clarity, yet I'm itching with discomfort and fear. Creepiness fills the home. What happened here? Everything about it screams bad energy, and I can't understand why.

Suddenly, Valentina enters once again with two glasses of water in her hands. "So," she breathes nervously, as she sits down beside me. "How old are you?"

"I'm twenty-four."

"Same as me! You are so pretty."

"Aww! Thank you, so are you! What are your dreams or your plans for the future?"

"I am not so sure yet," she responds, sulking. "Francesco thinks I should not rush to look for work. I do not need the money. He thinks that I should go traveling first instead."

"That would be absolutely lovely! Hmmm, would you consider working within your father's business?"

"No, I definitely do not want that. I do not know how Francesco still does it. Not after what happened."

"What do you mean?" I ask her.

Unexpectedly, we both jump as Francesco and his mother startles us upon barging through the large squeaky door. Something has changed. Her demeanor is much softer than it was, though still, intimidatingly unsettling. She's staring at me with wide and wet eyes with tightly shut lips. Francesco introduces us. I say hello, but for a long while, she just looks at me without a word to say. Until unexpectedly, at the most awkward moment, she speaks up.

"Natalia." Her ghostly voice peels off every layer of my skin. "Please, what do you want with my son?"

"Mamma!" Francesco and Valentina interrupt.

"You're only with him for the money, aren't you? That's all everyone wants from this family."

Francesco's impatience becomes more evident, but I can see that he's trying his best to hold it together.

Valentina wastes no time to quickly lead me outside into the hallway. Though Francesco stays behind, quietening down his mother while tears begin to shed from her eyes.

Seeing that alone also brings me to cry.

"Please do not cry, Natalia. I am sorry. So very sorry!" Valentina's voice trembles with worry as she looks at me with concern in her eyes.

"It's okay." I sniffle. "It's not your fault. Umm, do you mind telling me where the bathroom is?"

"It is on the first floor to your left."

"Thank you," I reply, heading up the stairs.

"Call out if you need me... or if you get lost."

"I will."

I sweep through the lifeless hallway and find myself upstairs in the bathroom. Then after having moments of quiet and deep thought to myself, I fix my makeup and head my way back. Throughout the hallway there are several rooms. Some doors are open, and some are shut. But there's an open room that has caught my eye. One with an easel that is situated in what looks like a child's room. The door is decorated with colorful letters of the name 'Roberto' hanging at the front of the door. Nosily, I peek in further, which brings me to see car toys, a dusty old television that looks as though it's from the last century, as well as lots of books with another little easel in the corner of the room. There are immaculate sketches pinned on to the wall. One of Valentina and one of Francesco, but they look much younger. I gasp, only to be frightened further at the unexpected sound of Francesco shouting my name. I freeze in place, absolutely overwhelmed by everything that's happening all at once. Eventually, I see him striding up the staircase with distress.

"Darling," he approaches, breathlessly, "I'm so fucking sorry for my mother's behavior..." Almost instantly, he then notices the room that I'm standing outside of, and I watch his throat stiffen as though he's swallowed a fist of blades. "What are you doing here?" he asks, darkly.

"Nothing," I whisper.

Without a word he takes me by the hand.

"Where are we going?" I ask him, trying not to trip as he hurries us down the stairs.

Suddenly, I hear the echo of a nearby door slam so loudly that it causes the walls to shake.

"This was a mistake," he mutters under his breath, as we breeze through the hallway. "We're leaving."

"Already? Shouldn't we say goodbye first?"

Once we're at the front door, Valentina pops up out of nowhere behind us.

"I am so very sorry. I hope to meet again, Natalia."

"Me too, it was lovely to meet you."

Francesco kisses Valentina on her head before he pulls open the front door. He then holds the car door out for me, and I put on my seatbelt as he breezes toward his side of the car.

"Francesco," Valentina calls as he starts the engine.

"Sì, Vale?"

"Ti amo," she tells him, with water in her eyes.

The rims of his dry eyes transition into red, then he clears his throat with a tight smile. "Ti amo, Vale."

And just like that, before I know it, we speed miles away from his childhood home. Not a word is uttered between us, but I know that he will talk about it when he's ready. For I can't help but feel his pain surging right through my heart, and it hurts. I glance at him in the corner of my eye, only to see a single tear escaping his. My soul overtakes me with distress as I see it. So I put my hand on his, and I tell him how much I love him, absorbing every moment as we make our way back home underneath the peachy, Tuscan sunset.

27. Belgravia

Upon arriving back to London, I immediately move in with Francesco. His property located within Belgravia is one of the most exquisite homes that honestly deserve to belong within an interior design magazine. It gleams with luxury and sophistication, thoughtfully decorated with neoclassical interior style upon a rich palette of honey, cream and gold. Walls stand tall with golden frames that hang captivating artwork throughout the home. Dark wooden floors sparkle to absolute perfection. Ivory colored furniture and marble fireplaces fill almost every room with coziness and charm. I've never been in a home that reflects such a strong character before. I can't believe that I actually live here now.

A day has passed since we returned to England. But still, no conversation has taken place regarding what happened in Tuscany at his family home. For so long I have waited patiently for him to bring it up, but the longer I wait, the more I'm beginning to grow frustrated.

"Francesco, we need to talk about it," I whisper, staring at him across the dining table.

He stares irritably at Ben, his butler, while he carefully pours us a glass of wine as we eat dinner. "There's nothing to talk about."

"Oh honey, you know there is. There's so much for us to talk about. You're hiding something from me, I know it. It's so obvious!"

"It's for your own protection."

"What? For my own protection!" I exclaim, with an overwhelming despair sizzling from deep within. Instantly, the butler excuses himself, and I wait for him to close the dining room door before I speak again. "Francesco, who even said that I want protection? Protection from what?"

"Natalia, you need to trust me."

"Well, I don't! Not if you're going to continue hiding things from me, Francesco. It's not right! How on earth is this relationship going to work if there's a huge barrier of deception between us?"

"I'm not deceiving you, for fuck's sake."

"Well, it feels like you are!"

Suddenly, his business phone begins to ring, and without a word he reaches for it.

"Honey," I whisper, just before he answers the call. "Who is really calling you at this time? It's not your working hours. You shouldn't feel obliged to answer right now, let them leave you a message."

"It's important."

"But I'm not done with this conversation, with *our* conversation."

"Sorry, darling," he replies quietly, rising from the table.

He leaves the room, marking me stunned. I'm left to eat within an uncomfortable silence that penetrates my heart with an indescribable anxiety. Perhaps I am just overreacting? I don't know how to navigate through this. I don't know how to deal with his denial, and I don't know what in the world he could be trying to protect me from. It's such a shame because we've come so far. However, now that I've moved in, I feel as though it's too late to go back or slow down at this point. He said to trust him, and I'm trying. Yet I can't help but feel stupid and perplexed, not knowing what to do next. Therefore, I guess I'll just wait for him to open up when he is ready. Like always, I will wait.

The next morning, there's a knock on the bathroom door as I step outside of the shower.

"Natalia?" Francesco's voice calls out.

"Come in, honey."

He steps in the room full of steam, smartly dressed in a dark grey suit that is just a few shades darker than his eyes. He then kisses me and greets me with a good morning.

"Babe, I thought that we don't return to work

until tomorrow... Why are you dressed like that?"

"There are urgent matters I need to deal with."

"Oh, honey. Then I'll come with—"

"I have something else for you in mind."

"Really, what is it?"

He kisses me once more upon my lips. "Get ready first, then I will show you."

Once I'm finally ready and refreshed for the day, I meet Francesco downstairs in the hallway. He's currently engaged in conversation with two of the housekeepers, something that I've noticed happens every morning.

"You look beautiful," he tells me, shortly after dismissing the housekeepers to their duties.

"Thanks, baby. So... What is it? What is this this thing that you have in mind for me?"

"Come here," he whispers, softly taking my hand in his.

He leads me downstairs toward the lower ground, a place within the home that I've never been to before. All this time I thought it was empty or just a place that nobody tended to go to, but it looks just as normal and well-kept as every other floor in the house.

He stops outside of a room, and searches through his keys to locate the right one.

"Honey, what are we doing here?"

He glances down toward me, just before the door cracks open. "Close your eyes first."

"What, why?"

"It's a surprise."

I sigh with a giggle as he steps behind to wrap his arms around me, resting his chin in the hollow of my neck. He leads us forward, and my eyes are flickering so much as I try my best to keep them shut.

Finally, I hear the door close, and I sense the warm window light seeping through my eyelids. It smells like something familiar in here. A scent that I can't put my finger on.

"Open, piccola mia."

My eyes spring open, only to see the most glorious, most wonderful art studio that I could ever dream of in my life! It is literally painted in blush pink, my favorite color, and filled with an innumerable amount of white and pink roses. Real, fresh roses. Bouquets and vases, with pretty plants everywhere. There are five large easels. Along with shelves and cupboards full of paint, both acrylic and oil. He then turns on the studio light, which is perfect and bright. Truly, just what I needed!

There are also the most feminine fairy lights hanging so beautifully around throughout. I even gasp when I see my new collection of luxury paintbrushes gathered so beautifully in stunning pots right beside the bright and open windows. It's so beautiful, it's unreal! It's a dream that I never expected to receive! I don't think anyone has done something so kind and generous for me before. It's so touching that I begin crying. Instantaneously, I feel Francesco's warm and massive arms enveloping me with love.

"Amore, you deserve this."

"Thank you so so much, baby! Francesco, this is perfect! So perfect!" I tighten my grip around him and squeeze as hard as I can, taking in that manly scent that I love so much.

"I am pleased to see you happy with it."

I look at his eyes through my tears. "When did you do this?"

The corner of his lips spring up slightly. "I arranged this when we were in Positano."

No words leave me. Nothing but love.

After a pause, I hug him once more. "Thank you."

"Look, we need to talk," he tells me.

"About your mother?"

His jaw stiffens. "No."

"Oh, what then?"

He brings a chair aside for me to sit down. "I'm releasing you from your position as my assistant."

"Wait, what?" My heart sinks. "No! Why on earth would you do that? I can't believe you've now fired me twice! How am I going to get good work references when I need them?"

"Baby," he breathes, in a way that is merged with amusement and impatience. "Let me make this abundantly clear to you, I want to commit to take care of you as my girl, not my employee."

"But... what about money?"

His brows grip together. "What about it?"

"I need an income of my own, Francesco."

"That's not for you to worry about. You will never lack with me, Natalia. Just tell me what you want, princess. It's yours. There is no limit as to what I am willing to give you."

I blink a few times, desperate to find some words to flow out of me. "I really don't know about this, honey. It feels... I'm worried. Especially after what your mother said. I don't want to give the impression that I'm here to live off you."

He holds both of my hands in his. "I know you, Natalia."

"But *they* don't."

"Who the fuck is they?"

"Your mother! Maybe your sister too, and also everyone else who knows you."

"Look, what is between us is none of their business."

I sigh, staring around the beautiful new studio that I'm falling in love with so deeply. "Words can't express my gratitude to you, honey. It means the absolute world, truly. I can't wait to get started on some pieces."

He rises from his chair and straightens out his suit, then leans down to kiss me tenderly before leaving. "I look forward to seeing them."

"Where are you going?" I ask, clinging on to his hand to stop him.

He lets me. "The office."
"I'll miss you."
"I love you."
"I love you too."
He smiles at me once more before striding out of the studio. "I'll call you later."

His words echo through the hallway, shortly before I hear him proceeding to take what sounds like another business call. I smile at the sight of this haven of a studio, sinking in the heaps of blank canvases that I'm so excited to paint on. Without delay, I'm eager to begin. So I pull my curls back in my scrunchy, and plan to spend the rest of the morning getting familiar with my favorite new dwelling place.

After lunch, I decide to head into Francesco's library and look for a new book to escape into. His library is enchanting, resembling the Beast's library from *Beauty and The Beast*. The shelves are so high and absolutely full, golden ladders and a pretty chandelier instantly bloom the room to life. It looks regal yet still so homely.

I end up reading a few of *Shakespeare's Sonnets*, and after a while, I continue to browse through the shelves, opening books to see which novel I'd like to read next. But then something surprises me. A pink colored letter that has just fallen out of one of the books as I opened it. I pick it up, and strangely it has the word 'Honeybun' written so beautifully in calligraphy. It's so stunning, I'm struggling not to open it.

I wonder if it's for me?

But Francesco has never called me that before.

I'm hesitant. Yet there is something in me can't help but want to see what it is. Through which, I open it and it reads:

My dearest honeybun,

I understand that we are going forward with this for the sake of convenience. You have your reasons, and I have mine. We can both agree that there is no such thing as love in matters such as this. We have come from families that prove that love is fickle, as false as fiction. Love cannot hold a marriage together, but devotion and focus, will. I am determined to do whatever it takes to make this work for us.

There is money to be made, and there is no doubt in my mind that you are the perfect man to do this with. You are unmatched, my sweet. There is no man in all of England that can surpass all that you are, and all that you have achieved. You must hold on to the belief that regardless of what life brings, I will always remain by your side as your devoted wife.

I promise you, honey bun, that I will do anything for you and I as we build our legacy together.

Yours, D.

All at once, I'm startled by the sound of a loud thud against the floor as I accidentally drop the book.

"Miss Garcia?" One of the housekeepers call out and knock before entering the library. "Is everything okay, ma'am?"

She stares at me, now locking her eyes upon the pink letter with horror.

"Yes, Dahlia. Everything is fine."

Her eyes remain glued on the letter, which is only feeding my distress. Through which, I put it back in the book and put it where it initially was.

"Would you like a cup of tea, ma'am?" she asks.

"No," I respond in sheer frustration, only to then feel sorry for being so harsh. "I'm sorry, Dahlia. You just startled me... I'll be fine, thank you. I think I will return to my studio now."

"Yes, ma'am."

Quickly, I hurry down to the lower ground and shut the studio door behind me. Holding my hand upon my heart, I try my best to calm myself as it thuds to pieces. It's beating so loud that I can hear it within my ears.

Suddenly, my phone begins to buzz, and with all my heart, I am hoping that it's not my father. Luckily, it's not. To be honest, I'm finding it strange, for I haven't heard from him in a while since I was back in Italy. Rather, I see that it's Francesco who is calling. So I take a deep breath, and answer to see how he is.

28. Wife

I jump out of a dream to the haunting sound of glass shattering in the middle of the night. Peeking at the time, I notice that almost two in the morning, yet Francesco is nowhere to be seen at all.

That's odd.

A high-pitched scream suddenly lifts out of nowhere. "Where is your new pretty little wife? You're bloody replacing me with a younger woman already? You fucking creep! I hate you, Francesco. I fucking hate you for what you did to me!"

It's pitch black in the home that I can barely see a thing, but I can hear the familiar voice traveling throughout the house from downstairs. I can't quite make out where I've heard the voice before.

I hear Francesco demanding her to leave as I quietly tip toe my way toward the sound of their voices.

Who is this?
An obsessed fan, I hope, and nothing more.
Should I ring the cops?

I'm at the top of staircase, and I can feel their presence not far away. Literally at the bottom of the stairs, I think. I can barely see anything. So I stop, and listen. Not merely out of worry, but genuine curiosity. I hear absolutely no urgency in the sound of Francesco's voice at all, which tells me that something about this encounter is not a case of emergency. All I hear is the woman crying. Sniffling and swearing uncontrollably under her breath. Something about her tells me that she's drunk, I can tell.

"Is she going to give you what you really want? Since I am incapable of doing it for you?"

Francesco asks her, "Fucking hell, how much have you had to drink?"

"Why would you care?" she slurs. "Why would you bloody care about little old me... now that you have that young girl? It's all over the internet!" she cries. "You and her. You and that girl. What about us, honeybun? You can't do this to me!"

"How many more times must I clarify this to you, there is no us, and there never will be. For fuck's sake," he complains, bringing goosebumps all over my skin.

"But there was! You forget, don't you?"

He sighs. "Look—"

"No, don't tell me anything further," she says,

clearly losing it now. "Tell me that we can make our marriage work again, and I will put all of this to rest."

Francesco pauses. "You're deluded," he mutters. "Listen very closely to me, because I'm not going to tell you again. Get the fuck out, now—"

"Or what?" she hisses. "Your employees are bloody stupid for leaving your back door unlocked tonight. Did you know that I've been trying to visit every night since you returned here with her?" She laughs, frighteningly. "Yes, do you want to know the reason why?" Francesco doesn't respond, yet she continues anyway. "Because I'd love to get my hands on her, and wipe her fucking clean off the face of this damn earth! You have no understanding of how much I fucking love you... do you, honeybun? Because you're mine, Francesco! You. Are. Mine."

She laughs hysterically again as though we're in some sort of horror movie. All I can do is rush back upstairs in panic mode and bury myself underneath the covers. What is going on, truly? I genuinely don't know what to do at this point. Am I going to confront Francesco about this tomorrow morning? Absolutely. Yet there's a part of me that is afraid, because he's become my whole world. If anything at all crumbles between me and him, then truly, I've got nothing, and I'm left alone and broken-hearted, all over again.

29. Secrets

The next morning blooms with a quiet heaviness that lingers throughout the home. Surprisingly, I find Francesco rummaging through his study before he leaves out for work. This is very strange and unusual to see, for other than yesterday, the study is usually locked for some reason I do not know. Though since the door is left wide open, I head in to see what's going on.

"Honey," I whisper, staring at the tall black shelves that are stacked with books. "Is everything alright?"

"Yes. All is well, darling."

That's odd. He's acting like nothing happened.

"What are you looking for?" I ask him.

"Nothing for you to worry about, piccola mia."

"But you look worried."

"Is that so?" he murmurs, still hunting around.

"Francesco, we need to talk."

He then gives up searching for whatever he's looking for, and ceases flipping through his draws. "I can't right now, darling," he replies, very sharply under his breath. "But listen…"

"Yeah?"

"I don't want you coming in here."

"Wait, what are you saying?"

"This study is out of bounds."

"Out of bounds? You're treating me like some employee now, are you?"

"Don't start with this shit with me, Natalia."

"But you invited me here to move in, how can you then tell me that I'm not allowed to enter one of the rooms? What's in here?"

"That's not for you to concern yourself with."

"Fine," I mutter, with tears welling in my eyes as I head out. "I'll be in my studio."

"Natalia!" his authoritative voice calls out with such dominance that it masks me with the most dreadful anxiety, but I don't bother to look back.

I hurry down the lower ground to my studio and quickly shut the door behind me. Heartbroken, perplexed and worried, flowing out an abundance of tears all at once.

While Francesco is out at work, I sneak to his study in the afternoon to see if I can find anything else suspicious. However, when I try and open the door, I realize that it's locked.

Damn.

"May I help you with something, Miss Garcia?" A quiet and frail voice asks, while of one of the older housekeepers startles me as she passes by.

"Yes, Betty. You can actually. I would like the keys to Francesco's study please."

A weary look spreads all over her wrinkled face. "Oh, Miss Garcia, I'm awfully sorry, but I'm afraid that I'm not authorized—"

"Francesco just told me that he needs me to find something in there quickly. It's urgent! Betty, please hand over the keys."

I feel extremely bad for lying to her, but this is important.

Ever so swiftly, she springs out the keys from her pocket. I thank her, then she's gone. Afterward I pop through door and close it half shut behind me.

Francesco's study gives me the creeps. Don't get me wrong, it's luxury and modern, yet there's a dark and eerie presence about it. It gives me a similar vibe compared to his family home back in Tuscany. Everything just cries out gloom as though it's desperate to be used. It seems vacant and barely ever occupied. I can't help but think to myself what the purpose of this study is if Francesco is always out at work anyway.

Curiosity overcomes me. Therefore, I start to scan across the study, not knowing where to start.

Gosh, am I losing my mind?

I'm beginning to think to myself whether I

should just turn away and get back to working on some art downstairs, but there's a strong pulling within my soul that tells me something is wrong. Therefore, I begin sifting in between the shelves, then I search through the draws, but nothing is here. I try to log on to his computer, but it's locked and in need of a password to sign on. So eventually, I give up, resting myself against the chair that smells so strongly like him. Though something suddenly catches my eye. A draw that is partially open. I peep inside and discover my absolute worst nightmare.

A sonogram.

There's an ultrasound scan of a baby right in front of me. I genuinely can't believe what I'm seeing. Frantically, I look for the date, only to find that it's dated a few years back. It's so odd that I'm wholeheartedly struggling with disbelief. Francesco has never mentioned anything about having a child, but then again, maybe I'm getting too far ahead of myself. This baby scan probably isn't even his, but perhaps a friend of his?

For goodness sake.

I hold myself still as though I'm a little deer in headlights, utterly stunned at what is before my eyes right now. Though shock pulses right through me upon my phone ringing so unexpectedly. I then take it out of my dress pocket to see that it's Diego.

"Diego," I breathe, with relief. "It's quite early for you to be calling me. Are you okay?"

"Yeah, Nat. We're all really good here. Actually,

it's my day off, and our morning bird of a sister persuaded me to ring you now since it's a good time over there, right? How's it going over there?"

"Hello, Natty dearest. We're missing you so so so much, my love!" Julieta squeals.

Diego switches the audio call to video call, but before I accept the request, I'm trying to head out to lock the door to Francesco's study first.

"Nat, what's going on?"

"Oh, umm. Nothing. Wait one sec."

Finally I manage to lock it, and once I accept the video call, I speed into the living room for refuge. Although, I then instantly notice Diego and Julieta's brows scrunching tightly together as though clearly perplexed about something.

"Oh, Natty, you didn't tell us that you moved? Where in heaven's name is that place? Goodness, that looks nothing like the apartment!"

"Oh yeah, I was waiting to tell you. But I—"

Unexpectedly, Betty appears out of nowhere like a ghostlike spirit, standing right beside the couch.

"Miss Garcia, do you mind giving me the key back please? Mr Giordano wouldn't be too happy if he learned that I misplaced it."

"Oh, of course. Thank you, Betty."

I quickly give her back the keys, then she leaves the room as quick as she came.

"Miss Garcia?" Julieta bursts out giggling.

Diego looks uncomfortable. "Nat, what's going on?"

"Umm, I don't know how to tell you this."

"Come on, Natty. We're your best friends—"

"No, I'm her big brother. There's a difference."

"Alright, alright..." I sigh. "The reason why I haven't told you guys is because I feel—"

"Oh no, what did you do now, Natty?"

I pause and take a deep breath. "Francesco and I are, umm, living together."

"What? How wonderful!" Julieta rejoices, right next to Diego's straight face.

"Hold up. Francesco Giordano?" he asks, then I nod. "I thought he was just your boss, Nat? You know, there are articles of you online—"

"See, Dee! I told you that it was more than just a working relationship!" Julieta happily interrupts. "You looked rather romantic, Natty, in those Italy photographs that we saw. Oh, it's so lovely to hear this news dearest! What is he like? I heard that he can be quite rude sometimes... but he isn't rude to you, is he sweetie? He treats you so lovely, doesn't he?"

"He is certainly treating me well. Everything is perfect," I lie. "He even blessed me with a dreamy art studio! He's so wonderful and supportive of my dreams, I couldn't be more grateful."

Julieta gasps while beginning to tear up. "What a generous gentleman!"

"That explains why it was so hard to video call you," Diego speaks up. "What happened to that artist you told us about? What's his name again?"

"Gideon!" Julieta remembers.

"Yeah, him?"

"Well, I told you both from the beginning that we were just friends," I breathe, trying to balance out my voice from shaking. "He's fine, I think."

"You think?" Diego raises a brow.

"Yeah."

"Tell us everything about Francesco, Natty! Tell us, this instant!"

The next thing I know, I hear keys pushing through the front door.

"Umm, guys. I have to go! It's urgent."

"But why, Natty? It's not even been ten minutes into our call yet!"

I glance quickly at Diego, whose face appears to be quite unconvinced about something.

"I know, but I have to go," I tell them. The front door then slams shut, followed by Francesco's footsteps drawing closer. "Francesco has returned home, and I'd rather introduce you properly, not over video call like this. Especially not so soon. It's been lovely catching up with you both, though. I love you so much! I promise I'll check in later."

I hang up immediately, just in time as Francesco passes the living room. He strides throughout the hallway appearing as polished in his suit as he did before he left this morning.

"Francesco," I call out. "We need to talk."

"What is it?"

"I heard you last night."

His eyes widen in horror for a moment, before he blinks the shock away. "Excuse me?"

"You heard what I said, Francesco. Who came here last night?"

"Nothing for you to concern yourself with," he dismisses, proceeding to walk away from me.

"Wait!" I command him, but he doesn't comply. "Slow down! Francesco, for goodness sake... I'm speaking to you—"

Suddenly, he turns around. "What do you want, Natalia?"

"Francesco, I'm afraid for my life! I heard what the lady said about wanting to hurt me."

"I'm handling it."

"Who is she?"

"Why the fuck is that your concern?"

"Why are you being so defensive with me?" I ask him, crying now. "Francesco, I'm just scared!"

He softens. "Fucking hell. I'm sorry, darling."

"Who is she, baby?" I ask him again.

"An ex."

"You're not married with children, are you?"

"Why would you assume such bullshit?"

"Are you seriously asking me that? Francesco, I heard the whole damn conversation!"

"She's deluded, Natalia. Trust me on this, she's not well. I'm handling the situation."

"But how?"

"We'll be introducing 24/7 security."

Instantly, I breathe out a sigh of relief. "Well, I

mean, that's certainly helpful... but what if I want to go out in public? I need my space, Francesco. Are you sure that we shouldn't we get legal advice about this?"

"I've sorted it."

"Well then tell me exactly what you have done to ensure that she will never come close to me or this house again?"

"Do you doubt me?" he mutters.

"Yes, entirely."

"Why?"

"I know that you're hiding something from me, Francesco. I found a pink love letter in the library, and a sonogram in your study."

He steps closer. "Who the fuck authorized you to enter my study?"

I dismiss it. "Are you hiding a family from me or not? Tell me the damn truth!"

"Don't you think the whole damn world would know if I had a fucking family?"

True, he is right about that.

"Well then, explain to me who the pink love letter was from, and why you have a sonogram in this house!"

He looks me dead in the eyes. "That letter was from a decade ago when I was in my twenties. I forgot I even had it. Dammit, Natalia."

"And the sonogram?"

He breaks his gaze from mine. "I can't discuss that with you."

"What do you mean?" My voice trembles as he strides away from me. "Francesco?"

I follow him with so much adrenaline rushing through me as we speed quickly upstairs and into the master bedroom. Instantly after, he snaps out a cigarette upon the balcony.

"Is there a child in your life or not?" I ask him.

He looks at me, once. "There was."

"W-w-what?"

"SIDS. End of story."

"I... I'm so sorry, honey."

He exhales a cloud of smoke without meeting my eyes. "It's fine," he murmurs. Yet I can feel the pain in his voice, and hit hurts me more than I can describe.

"Why didn't you just tell me about this before?"

"I don't know," his voice breaks.

I wrap my arms around him and let him hold me. "If I would have known, honey... I'm so sorry. When was this?"

"Few years back," he breathes.

I look into his eyes that are bloodshot red around the rims. This hurts me to hear this as much as this hurts him telling me this.

"And your ex... is she the mother... the one who came here last night?" I ask, then he nods. "Gosh, I'm sorry. She must be hurting so deeply too. But what does she want with me, Francesco? I'm so concerned."

"I won't let her hurt you."

"How can you be so sure?"

"We're moving tomorrow."

"Where?"

"One of my other properties in Mayfair."

"And if I want to go out?"

"We'll have security with us 24/7 from tonight. Which means, Natalia, a member of the team will have to be alongside you wherever you go from now on."

"Francesco, I don't like this. I need my space."

"I need to be sure."

"Sure of what?"

He pauses. "Just trust me, Natalia."

I'm trying to. But why does it hurt?

"Promise me that everything will be okay," I tell him, crying into his chest. "If I hear it from your lips, I'll believe it."

He exhales, deeply. "I won't let anything cause you harm. You understand that, don't you?"

"I love you," I tell him, searching into his tired eyes. "Thank you for telling me the truth."

"I love you too, princess."

30. Mayfair

By the first morning of May, I am notified by my period cycle tracker that I am approximately five days late. I actually think nothing of it. In fact, I simply ignore it, and carry on about my day. Worry fails to overcome me concerning the matter as I tend to suffer with irregular cycles now and again. It will start sooner or later, I tell myself, then I get on with the rest of my morning.

Francesco and I have finally moved location from Belgravia to an affluent area called Mayfair that I'm not at all familiar with. It seems to be much busier in comparison to where we used to live. Which is fine, I keep telling myself. For I'd rather be here than reside in fear back where we used to be.

He tells me that he's working on a new studio for me in our new home. I tell him that it's fine, and that there's no rush at all. Yet I still feel like an intruder, lingering through his beautiful home with neoclassical decor that blooms with neutral shades with hints of gold. I feel like I should be back at my apartment. The little rundown one in Maida Vale. He has transferred six figures into my account. To play with, he says. I feel like I'm a gold-digger, even though I know that I'm not. His mother's words sail through my mind over and over again. It's a cycle, the guilt and discomfort that I'm experiencing, for I want to be independent, and be able to stand on my own to feet. I'd like to prove my father wrong, yet I know that if and when he finds out about Francesco and I, I'll just end up as a ridiculous joke to him. I comprehend that other people's opinions shouldn't matter to me at all, but I so desperately wanted to prove to my father that I was right, showing him that actually, I am able to prosper on my own while doing the things that I love.

"All settled?" Francesco asks me, striding into the fresh grand living room as I stare at the cherry blossom tree outside our living room window.

"Yes," I reply with a smile. "Very much so."

He doesn't smile back at me. "Everything will be alright."

"Okay. I trust you... but there's a part of me that knows how much I'm going to miss my freedom, Francesco. This situation won't go on for too long... Will it?"

He ignores me. "Look, I need to get going," he

murmurs, suddenly distracted by his phone.

"Where are you off to? It's a Saturday."

"Nothing for you to concern yourself with, darling."

Before I answer, he kisses me then speeds out. It's frustrating and perplexing to me all at once. I know that I haven't made a mistake moving in with Francesco, and I believe every word that he says. But why are things between us weirdly becoming strange?

A full week has passed, and my period still hasn't arrived. I try not to stress myself out about the situation and try to relax in the meantime, but I can't. I cannot rest knowing that there's possibly a baby living inside me. Through which, I hurry to get ready and make haste to the nearest convenience store.

"Where do you think you're going?" Xavier, the new head of security asks me.

I lose my words as he stands before the front door with large crossed arms and a stern looking face that stares down at me as though I'm some sort of convict.

"Out," I tell him.

"Not without me, you're not."

"Xavier, I'll be fine."

"Giordano's orders."

For goodness sake.

"Fine," I mutter, a bit too harshly.

I catch a smirk on Xavier's face. He reminds me of Gideon, but a taller, larger and tougher version that scares the living daylights out of me.

"Do you need a driver?" he asks me.

"No," I respond. "But I do need you to show me to the nearest convenience store, since you're coming along with me today."

He nods a firm goodbye to the several security guards that are plotted throughout the property. "Course," he responds, withholding a laugh. "And, try not to look so scared, Miss Garcia. I'm only here to keep you safe."

The tests came back positive. I never in a million years thought that this would happen to me so soon and unexpectedly like this. My periods have been so inconsistent over the years, there was a hint of belief within me that I was barely ovulating at all. My heart is so full, yet breaking all at once. For I have always desired to be a mother, yet I always envisioned myself married and settled once that happens. I'm just about to finish with my studies, and I'm only starting to begin with my career. It's overwhelming.

Am I even capable of being a good mother during this time in my life? And Francesco, good heavens, what is he going to say or think about this? His ex girlfriend, what about her?

There is absolutely no money to my name, and I'm entirely dependent on Francesco financially. I don't like it. What would happen if him and I were to break up? I understand that provision would be there, but I want to be so much more than to just be a billionaire's babymother.

My heart is aching, because this is not what I dreamed of when I first came to London, at all. I have not even sold one painting since I arrived, other than the one to Francesco, and I'm terribly ashamed. I have nothing to show to my father nor my siblings regarding the progress that I have made over here. I'm not happy. I'm petrified. Because as much as I do love and want this child, I'm not sure if Francesco and I are ready to be the emotionally stable parents that the baby needs. This is far from a healthy and safe environment. I can't even exit this building without a security guard breathing down my neck because a woman is out to kill me.

I can't help but wonder if bringing a child into this situation is something that is the right thing to do. My heart truly does not have the capacity to make this into a beautiful surprise for Francesco. I need to tell him, urgently. I'm so scared that I can't be bothered with decorations or gifts. All I want to tell him is the truth, because it's killing me so deeply, knowing what we've got ourselves into.

The moment Francesco arrives home is the moment that I rush toward him through the hallway.

"What is it, darling?" he asks me, with concern in his eyes.

"We need to talk," I tell him, leading him aside into the library.

I shut the door behind us for privacy from the housekeepers and security about. It's suffocating. I can't breathe. I'm so awfully nervous to tell him. He's looking at me with fire-filled eyes that scream an earnest anticipation.

"What is the matter, Natalia?" he asks me, a bit too harshly with impatience this time. "Baby, speak. You're concerning me—"

"I'm pregnant!" I squeak, now covering my lips. "Francesco, I'm pregnant. I literally only just found out today. I'm so sorry honey that I couldn't make this a special announcement for you, but I… didn't know how you'd feel about this."

Silence.

"Honey, I'm scared." I tell him, teary-eyed.

For a long moment, nothing departs from his mouth as his gaze fixes firmly onto mine. "Are you absolutely positive about this?" he finally asks me.

"Yes," I breathe. "I took three tests… they're all in our room. My period is almost two weeks late."

I start pacing about the library as his lack of response is making me utterly anxious to the core.

My strength fails me as I release the bundle of distress that have so long bubbled up within me. I literally almost drop to the floor in tears, yet he swiftly catches me, holding me steadfast in his arms.

"Natalia," he breathes, leading me to a nearby chair. "You don't need to be afraid. Talk to me, me, darling. Tell me about your concerns. What are you scared of?" he asks, unusually gently.

"This isn't what I wanted, Francesco," I admit. "I mean, I've always wanted to be a mother, but I didn't expect it to be now. I wanted to work on my dreams first. To be honest with you, I feel as though we aren't ready for this... you and I. Far from it."

His softening eyes search through my soul with just one word. "Expand for me."

"Honey, our relationship has been so rocky ever since we returned from Italy. You're always so busy going in and out of work, or to other places that you won't tell me about. You're not cheating on me, are you?"

"No," he responds, firmly. "There's no-one that I want but you."

"Well then tell me what's going on, honey. Please!" I cry, begging him for relief. I just need to know the truth. "You always tell me that it's nothing to concern myself with... but there's now a child is involved, Francesco. Please don't keep me in the dark anymore, this is important."

He pauses, still embracing me. "Alright, look. I'm juggling work and dealing with legal issues regarding all this bullshit that's gone on."

"What?" I panic. "Oh god, this is exactly what I'm talking about, baby! Are we ready for this? I don't feel safe or secure at all."

"Listen, amore. I will support whatever decision you make, but please rest assured that I will devote myself to secure everything within my power to keep you both safe."

"You will?"

He nods, but I can tell that something is wrong. There's a barrier that he's trying to keep up between us, yet I can still see right through it.

"What's the matter, honey?"

He pauses. "Do you want this child?"

"Yeah," I whisper. "Absolutely, I do. I've always wanted to be a mother. I'm only concerned for the child's safety and well-being. That's all it is, honey. I'm concerned whether we're ready to provide a stable and safe environment for the baby... Why do you ask? Do you want to go ahead with this?"

"Ultimately, the decision is yours. But to answer your question, yes, I do."

"Wow, I never thought you were a family man."

"This child is a blessing, darling. And it's ours."

I burst into tears. "I really want this too," I tell him, leaning deeply into his chest.

"What's troubling you, princess?"

"I don't want this child to go through what my siblings and I went through, at all. An emotionally unstable artist mother, and a father in business who is barely ever present. The thought of it kills me."

He pauses for so long that I question whether he even heard me.

"Amore, we can make this work."

"Promise me, and I'll believe you."

His thumb presses my tear away. "I promise,"

he breathes. "Natalia, I will do better."

"I want us to be healthy and emotionally stable if we're going to become a family. I want to feel safe and continue following my dreams even when I have this baby. I want you, honey. I want this, but the uncertainty is killing me."

"No lack or harm will come near you," he tells me so confidently, while holding my gaze with such fervent conviction that flows though his heart to mine.

"No more secrets between us?" I ask him.

"None," he responds, firmly.

"Tell me that you'll be the father that this baby needs, and my mind will finally be at rest. Not just financially or physically… but emotionally, honey."

"I promise," he whispers, planting a kiss on the crown of my head.

Those two words were all I needed to usher me into the deepest sleep. For the waterfall of my tears carry me swiftly away, into the most blissful and calmest state.

31. Mine

As spring blossoms closer to the summer season, morning sickness begins to torment me immensely. Today, I've found myself so tired and unwell that I don't feel like doing anything at all. Through which, I'm resting within the bed, trying to get much needed sleep. Though out of nowhere, my phone disturbs me. I check it immediately to see if it's from Francesco, as he not long left for work. But to my surprise, it's a sweet text from someone totally unexpected.

Gideon: Morning, Nat. It's been a while.

Me: Hey, Gee! How are you?

Gideon: Not too bad. Missing you.

Me: Awww, Gideon... how are the girls?

Gideon: Phoebe is quieter these days. Kitty on the other hand requires much more support, which is understandable. We're getting there.

Me: I'm keeping you and the family in my prayers, Gideon. I know this isn't easy to lose such a dear family member. I'm so sorry that I haven't been present to support you during this difficult time. If you ever need anything, please let me know. You've been such a good friend to me. I really want to be there for you too.

Gideon: It's alright, Nat. I understand that you have other priorities. How are your studies?

Me: Finished by the end of this month!

Gideon: Did you get your graduate visa sorted?

Me: Yeah, thankfully! I'm so happy that I can stay here longer. I've fallen in love with the city.

Gideon: The girls are on a school trip this week. I could pop by Maida Vale sometime to see you, if you're around?

Me: Gideon…

Gideon: What's up, Nat?

Me: I moved early in the spring. I no longer live in Maida Vale, as I'm currently residing in Mayfair with Francesco now.

Two long minutes have passed by, and he doesn't respond. I just watch him typing, only to come to a stop. It's frustrating to me, yet it's all just so saddening. I feel so bad. But honesty is the best thing that I can possibly give him right now rather than build up any hope.

Gideon: Oh, I see.

Oh no, is that all he's going to say?

Me: How are things with you, Gee? Any new exhibitions coming up soon? I'd love to check them out and support.

Gideon: Unfortunately, I've had to take some time off with work over the last few months since my grandmother passed. It's challenging, juggling it all with the girls now. I may to return to it soon, hopefully.

Me: I understand. Yes, I hope you do.

Gideon: It was a pleasure catching up with you again though, Natalia. I didn't expect for you to respond as quick as you did.

Me: Ha! I'm unwell in bed that's why.

Gideon: Sorry to hear that. I hope that you are able to recover soon.

Me: Thanks, Gee. You're a sweetie.

He takes longer to reply this time.

Gideon: Maybe we'll catch up someday. Take good care of yourself xx

I don't reply with words, but rather respond with a heart upon his last message. It's difficult. My soul longs to see Gideon, but with the way things are going between Francesco and I, I just don't think it's wise.

On the last Saturday of June, Francesco decided to

take me out for dinner to celebrate me finally completing my master's degree. It's been a splendid evening. As I step out of the shower and prepare to hop into bed with him, my phone buzzes out of nowhere.

"Who is texting you this time of night?" he asks in a humorous way, though I can tell deep down that he's unsettled by it.

I brush my curls into my scrunchy in front of the mirror. "I don't know," I breathe. "Julieta, maybe... or my dad."

The next thing I know, he reaches across to my side of the bed and picks my phone out of the charger.

His face tells it all.

"Who is it, honey?" I ask him, worried now.

"You're still in contact with this pest?"

I feel my eyes widen with horror as I rush toward him on the bed. "What?" I ask, panicking. I try to grab my phone out of his hands, but he won't let me retrieve it.

"He has asked how you are."

Francesco's direct stare is beginning to make me feel uncomfortable. There's a soft flush of red that spreads over his golden complexion, and honestly, it's scaring me.

"Francesco—"

"Have you been fucking him all this time?"

"What?" I mutter. "Of course not! How could I anyway, when I'm not even allowed to step out this damn house without an annoying security guard following me around!"

"The child... isn't his, is it?"

I stare at him, long and hard. "Don't you dare ask me such a hurtful question ever again."

"Answer me."

My heart annoyingly refrains from holding in the tears, and I break down in front of him.

How on earth could he doubt me like this?

"Gideon and I haven't seen each other for months. We haven't even shared a kiss, yet you're asking me such a ridiculous question if this baby is his! You know how much I love you, don't you? I would never do such a thing to you."

He doesn't even react to my tears. He just swears under his breath, throws my phone onto the bed, and walks out.

"Where are you going?" I ask him, following him through the hallway. "Honey, come to bed. Let's not fight, baby. There's no need to be mean."

"I need my fucking space."

"But where are you going?"

He ignores me.

"Francesco!" I raise my voice as high as I can, yet he doesn't even flinch. I'm ignored once again.

I leave him to it, because I refuse to be treated like this. So I turn back to the bedroom, switch off the lights and take refuge in bed.

I wake up to my phone missing, completely gone

and out of sight. It's not plugged in the charger, neither is it on the bed or anywhere beside it. It's strange, because in the middle of the night I could have sworn that I saw three missed calls and a few angry texts from my father.

What on earth is going on?

I rush downstairs to find Francesco casually sitting in the kitchen, currently in conversation with Giuseppe, our chef, who is cooking breakfast.

"Good morning," I greet them.

Giuseppe, as always, responds to me with a warm welcome, but Francesco ignores me as though I'm not here at all.

"Honey, can I have a word privately with you please?" I ask him, boiling with frustration at this point.

"Can it wait?" he mutters, sharply.

"No," I respond, firmly.

He apologizes to Giuseppe as I lead us out toward the main room and shut the door behind us.

"Where is my phone?" I ask him.

"Gone," he tells me.

Sweat and fire is prickling at my fingertips as a spike of nerves hit me to the core. "What do you mean by this, honey?"

"I got rid of it," he replies, utterly unbothered. "Natalia, do you honestly think that I'm going to let your father and that so called friend of yours fuck up our family?"

He's stepping closer toward me with something

sinister in his eyes that it's concerning me.

"Honey," I whisper, beginning to tremble upon not recognizing the man that I love in front of me. "This... this isn't you."

"You don't know what I'm capable of, Natalia. If he puts his dirty hands on you again, I'll fucking kill him myself."

"Baby, you're tired..." I croak, holding back the tears. "I can see that you've been working so hard recently. You're restless, honey."

Then that's when I'm realized that I'm cornered, having absolutely nowhere to go.

"You don't realize how much you mean to me, do you, darling? I fucking meant it when I told you that you're mine... that I'd do anything to protect you."

"Francesco, you're scaring me..."

He traces his thumb over my lip, attaching his gaze onto it. "Do you honestly think that I will let a bastard like your father threaten the safety of our family?" he whispers.

"You don't need to worry about him."

"And what about your friend?"

"Gideon is not a threat, Francesco."

"Natalia." He sighs, deeply. "Are you telling me that you're oblivious to his feelings toward you?"

"I'm not," I clarify. "But I'm also certain that nothing will ever happen between us. I love you, honey. Not him. You are the man that I love and want, so much. You're the man that I truly can't imagine living without! So I really need you to stop worrying and overthinking about Gideon!"

His gaze over me softens for a mere moment as my eyes overflow with what feels like an unending amount of silent tears. "Shit," he breathes in distress, before stepping back to give me some space. "Forgive me, Natalia... I keep fucking up here."

"Francesco..." I sniffle. "What is going on with you? This isn't what I wanted for the baby. This is exactly what I have feared!"

"Look, I'm so sorry, princess... but I can't stand them around you. Your father, in particular."

"Well then I won't speak to them again, honey. Truly, I promise! I'll inform Gideon of it too. I just want to do what is right for this family now. Truly, I do."

"Alright," he breathes. "Promise me—"

"I promise, honey."

"No, promise me that the kid is mine."

"Francesco!" I cry. "I don't understand why are you being like this. What has caused you to doubt me? I would never do such a thing to you!"

He sighs deeply, pulling me tenderly within his arms as I cry my heart out into his chest. He doesn't respond to my question, but I wish with all of my soul that he did.

"There's honestly no-one else that I want but you, honey," I tell him. "You're my everything. My absolute heart."

His lips press upon my forehead, and he tells me that he's sorry. "Natalia," he breathes, with worry in his eyes. "You're the most priceless treasure that I've ever had. It fucks with my head to even think about losing you or seeing you hurt."

"But you're not losing me," I whisper, holding his handsome face. "I'm right here... we're right here," I assure him, bringing his hand to my stomach.

Tears well within his eyes, yet they don't fall. "I'm so fucking sorry. I don't take pleasure seeing you cry."

"It's okay." I sniffle, trying to calm my anxiety back down. "But tell me... what are you afraid of?"

He pauses. "I'm... concerned about making the same mistakes, and seeing the same bullshit happen again."

"Same mistakes?" I ask him, intrigued. "Like what, honey?"

He holds my eyes without a word. Yet his jaw clamps shut. "Here," he breathes, taking my phone out of his pockets. "Forgive me."

After one last kiss, he strides away. Leaving me with nothing but confusion and utter heartache.

32. *Summertime*

The midst of July welcomes me with a heatwave and a death threat. Upon finishing my most recent painting within my studio, my jaw drops upon seeing the sight of it on my social media. For not only has my following grown ever since the news about Francesco and I got out, but I have also found that I've been drawing more and more attention that is rather mean and heartbreaking to me. As much as I try to ignore the comments, I fail to do so as my curiosity pulls me deeper into the pit of despair. Social media has a way of making you feel worse than you initially felt before you signed on, and the comment section on my recent post brings me to become absolutely sick to my stomach.

@mrsdgiordano: This home-wrecker deserves to die after what she did. Natalia, if you're reading this, I will find you. You cannot escape your fate.

@sunflowerlover: What did she do?

@mrsdgiordano: She stole my husband.

@artbyambroise: Who, Francesco Giordano?

@mrsdgiordano: Yes.

@sunflowerlover: But he's never been married.

@mrsdgiordano: You don't know the truth.

@sarahlisa: Francesco can get any woman he wants, yet he chooses this girl. Can someone explain what's so special about her?

@jessicaaaathomas: I think she's really pretty.

@sunflowerlover: She's obviously stunning, but I bet you she's only with him for his money.

@breanna3657: Why do you say that? Is there a reliable source who has provided that information?

@sunflowerlover: No, but everyone knows how much of a dick Francesco Giordano can be. Why would anyone love and tolerate someone like him?

@sherri_king: I'm going to end up killing myself if he marries her. I wanted it to be me.

@mrsdgiordano: You don't know him like I do.

@latoyabeauty: Does anyone know if she got a BBL? Who is her doctor?

@sarahlisa: If you look very closely, you can see two little zits on her forehead. It makes me sick. Does she not wash her face?

@barbara_: Why are her dresses always tight and revealing? Doesn't she know how to cover up?

@emilylove: Does anyone know where she actually met Francesco?

@ilovefrancesco2: I heard she's from Carmel-by-the-sea, apparently. How did she manage to get someone like our Francesco? She does not deserve him!

@mrsdgiordano: Does anyone here know her address? She has siblings, doesn't she? I'll find them too.

@francescogiordanofanpage: I agree that she has a nice body, but she's short. Is Francesco obsessed with petite women with doll faces now? Why can't he be with a real woman like me?

@standforbiblicalfemininity: She needs to repent and give her life to Jesus Christ before she ends up in hell! You all do.

@francescoandnatalia4eva: Hi Natalia! I'm your biggest fan!

@mrsdgiordano: She doesn't deserve to live.

@francescofanatics: Natalia might be a witch who put a spell on Francesco, because why has Francesco all of a sudden got into a relationship? We all know, as his fans, that he doesn't believe in love. He never has for years. So why now?

@reginarossi: I want Francesco to be my hubby.

@pritichauhan_5: Well I can see why Francesco is with her. Like… look at her. It's not fair. Why can't I look pretty like that? She makes me feel ugly.

@mrsdgiordano: I'm watching you, Natalia.

Immediately, I delete that particular post, but my comment section then begins to blow up even more on the previous one. It all reminds me of my father. The constant harsh words and negativity. It's painful. So terribly heartbreaking. Honestly, I'm not sure what to do about it. I feel so confused. Though to my shock, Diego begins to ring.

"Hi, Dee."

"Nat?" he breathes, sounding different. "What's up, you don't sound yourself today?"

"Neither do you," I respond.

He clears his throat. "Man, umm. I got some pretty bad news."

"Oh no. What is it?" I whisper, hearing the anguish creeping forward in his voice. "Diego?"

Suddenly, I hear the sound of Maria wailing in the background, and it's frightening me.

"Maria's home?" I ask for clarification.

Diego sighs. "Something has come up."

"What is it? Please please please don't tell me that it's something to do with Julieta."

"Oh no, dearest," I hear her quiet voice rise somewhere in the background. "I'm here."

I let out a huge sigh of relief before I compose myself again. "Then what's the issue?" I ask, getting impatient. I'm so scared because I worry if it has anything to do with that particular social media user who keeps sending me creepy messages.

"It's dad," Diego tells me.
Oh no.
"W-w-what about him?"
"He... he passed. Last night."
I don't believe it. "Excuse me?"
"Some things came up over the last few weeks. You haven't heard about it?" Diego asks me.
"No, what sort of things?"
"Oh dearest," Julieta steps in. "Terrible things! Accusations were piling up against him during the last month or so, about the restaurants and his personal life. Employees have come forward, young girls, about his... his... his behavior!" Julieta bursts into tears and it numbs me.

I haven't heard her cry like this since mamá passed.

"Is any of this true?" I ask them.

It takes while for Diego to respond. "We aren't certain, Nat. But it fucked dad up for sure. We don't know if this is what's caused his death in the first place. He just dropped down dead as they were arresting him. Shit, imagine if I was on duty."

"We didn't even get a chance to say goodbye!" I hear Maria crying out. "Who could do such a thing?"

"What do you mean, Maria? Surely, nobody would be behind this. If things got out... then things got out. Maybe the employees all decided to finally come together and wanted to speak up on the issues. Those poor young girls were so brave and courageous to do this. It must have been hard."

"But the accusations, dearest, about the chain of papá's restaurants..."

"What about them?"

"Rumors regarding various bad practices and such throughout the establishment and tolerated by papá, not just within the kitchens, but the company itself. Serving food that was out of date, and cooking vegan dishes within dirty equipment that were used for meat."

"That's so damn disgusting!" I sigh, extremely disappointed to hear it.

How could he do that, really?

"It's fucking embarrassing." Diego sighs. "The shit that we have to deal with as his kids now."

"What are we going to do?" I whisper. "I've heard nothing of this in England."

"Thankfully, papá's restaurants aren't popular over there. It's just mainly in Spain and the US, dearest."

"I'm sorting it, Tally," Diego tells me. "Man, I'm sorry I had to tell you this over the phone, but I'd rather be the one to inform you, instead of you having to find out elsewhere online."

"It's okay," I whisper, but no tears leave me.

Why am I not upset about his death?

In fact, why am I relieved to hear this news?

Julieta sniffles. "We've got to go, dearest," she tells me. "We have so much to sort out and plan."

Maria's crying softens to eventually cease. "Will

you be attending the funeral?" she asks me, sharply.

"Actually, can I get back to you all about that later?" I respond, truly not wanting to get into a disagreement right now.

"Sure," Diego replies. "Speak later, Tally."

"Bye, Natty," Julieta breathes softly.

I hang up. Only to be startled by the deep sound of Francesco clearing his throat behind me.

"Oh my goodness! What on earth? How long have you been standing there, honey?"

"About a second or two," he responds with a chuckle. "How is my girl today?"

I rise to greet him. I'm so relieved that he's here right now. "Thank God you're home early! I have received the most terrible news."

"What's the matter, amore?"

"My father passed," I whisper, burying my face into his chest. "Some news came out about the running of his business. Poor young girls have come forward about his abusive ways. Baby, it's awful."

He pauses for such a long time that it becomes awkward. Eventually, it brings forward my memory of the moment we had in Positano. That time in the villa, when I specifically begged him to not act out in retribution.

"Shit, I'm really sorry to hear this," he breathes, nestling his lips into my hair. He then kisses me, but something doesn't feel right.

I look up to meet his eyes. "You didn't know anything about this... did you, honey?"

He grips my eyes in silence. "Natalia."

"Oh my... don't tell me..."

"Look, I was aware of his downfall regarding the company. However, I wasn't made aware of his passing."

"Did you do this?" I ask him, utterly shocked at this point. "Was it you who got the stories out?"

I loosen my arms from our embrace, but his arm secures me firmly. "Natalia, those girls deserved to be free and speak their truth."

"And the lies, about the business itself?"

"Those weren't lies," he tells me, locking his jaw shut. "If you do enough digging, you'll always find something eventually."

"This doesn't make any sense. How on earth did you gather this information?" I ask him, with tears dripping down my cheeks.

"I have my sources," he breathes, pressing the wetness away from my face. "Look. I'm so fucking sorry, amore. I didn't expect for him to die. I just wanted to see him suffer for what he did to you—"

I just kiss him, passionately. Wholeheartedly touched by what he's done. I understand that part of it is wrong, but knowing that my father is no longer guarded by lies helps me to accept the truth for what it is. There's a freedom in knowing that those young girls are no longer crippled by their secrets too. If it wasn't for Francesco, I'm not sure if this would have gotten out at all. And yes, it is heartbreaking that my father has lost his life. It also hurts me to know that he last conversation that I had with him wasn't a healthy one. But finally, I am free. No longer will I have to walk with the weight of the universe upon my shoulders, treading throughout the earth as though I'm walking on eggshells. I feel terrible for it. How someone's lack of existence in my life has ushered me into a place of safety and relief. I feel heartache. For I know that my father claimed to love me, but how he showed that love was something that always ignited a dreaded fear within me. My heart aches to learn that he has passed, although, I can't say that I'm sad. For to be honest, he was always dead to me. Always has been, and always will be.

33. Ours

The following week I spend all my time practicing abstract work, filling my canvas with flourishing flowers that are embellished with thick textures of pink. This is my happy place. My haven and new home where I'm able to express freely without restrictions.

As difficult as it's been, I try to not give my father a thought at all, unless Julieta or Diego calls to update me on certain matters. There's part of me that still can't believe that he's gone. It feels unreal to me. The funeral is also coming up within a week, and I really can't decide whether to stay or go. Francesco has been wonderfully supportive, but my heart simply longs for us to move on from all the discomfort and turbulence that has gone on over the last few weeks, especially in preparation of this sweet baby of ours that will soon come.

I feel bare. Utterly free, yet constricted all at once. For I comprehend that my father is gone, but my worst fear is that he will still find a way to haunt me. There are times when I still expect him to call me. There are also moments when I'm afraid that I'll suddenly see him around some corner of a random road.

Recovering from a controlling relationship isn't an overnight thing, not for me. Even if you're absolutely positive deep down that they no longer have access to you, you can't help but live in a place of constant worry. It's draining the life out of me. The distress and anxiety. It withholds my body to get some good sleep. I often wonder why he had to die the way he did. So quick and so sudden.

Francesco and I are not to blame, are we?

I've had to disable the comments on every picture of my social media pages from now on, because it's all becoming a little too much. That @mrsdgiordano account continues to threaten me, yet when I click on her page, it's set to private without a picture up or a clear name. I've had to block her and tell Francesco everything concerning the matter. He said he'll take care of it, and he has assured me time and time again that no harm will ever come near me or the baby, but I can't help but worry if something will end up happening to him too.

The day has blooms smoothly, and all is going tremendously well as I finish off my most recent art piece, only until the core of my stomach shifts abruptly into an indescribable discomfort that brings me to shriek. It's as though something has just churned so painfully inside of me, absolutely unexpected.

It hurts too much.

Is this normal?

I decide that it's best to cease painting for a moment, and wait for the sting of anguish to subside. Finally, it does. But soon after, it returns, so much more vigorously this time, as though a ball of fire is blazing with an evil aggression from within me. An unsettling feeling hovers over my spirit so heavily that I honestly have no choice but to put my paintbrush down.

The excruciation is killing me. All at once, everything around me starts to blur hazy. I can't see. My utter discomfort from the cramps pulls me immediately to my knees, banging so harshly upon the wooden floor that it hurts so bad. My whole world has stopped spinning completely. It's like every layer of my skin is stiffening tight and completely numb, yet I still feel the prickling hot tears that are leaking from my eyes.

I can't think straight. I can barely stand up.

My heart is pulsing out of control, and my mind feels like it's seriously on fire at this point. It's hell.

What kind torture is this?

I rest my hands upon my stomach, and my body really can't help but tremble back and forth as an involuntary response. Why can't I stop shaking? I have never known a pain like this before in my life.

Is the baby okay?

It's like lava, trapped within me trying to come out, burning and ripping through my insides apart as it does. I try to reach for my phone on the studio table, but there's no strength within me to grasp it. I feel so terribly weak right now that I truly can't bring myself to get up. So I wait here, in agony, before attempting to try again. I let a moment pass, and decide to give it one more shot. So I rise from the ground and manage to grab the phone in order to attempt to ring our private doctor. It rings and rings, over and over again, but I fail to get an answer.

My palms are thickening with sweat as I clutch on to the device, absolutely desperate for him to pick up. But I feel myself slipping away. I can sense it. At any moment I'm about to black out, I know it, but I'm trying my best to hold on. Despite my fear and despite this confusion, I'm trying and fighting to stand, refusing to let this hurtful attack take me out. But things can't get any worse, just as my phone slips out of my hand while my body drops lifelessly across the ground. Words can't describe the way I'm feeling right now. It's so painful that I've lost the will to keep ringing. I'm curled up like a ball, wishing and waiting for the pain to just leave me. I try to call out to the housekeepers and security, but my words are barely a breath. I then try once more to reach out for my phone, but it's too far for me to reach this time. I whisper a prayer to God for mercy, to protect my baby, and let the pain depart and go away. But the excruciation is dragging on too much, I can't even bear it much longer. So I just surrender, and lie here within a pool of suffering, letting the darkness usher me into sleep.

I jolt up to the sound of a door slamming loudly nearby. I then hear my name being called as the echoes follow, yet my body continues to gravitate toward the ground. I hear random doors through the hallway downstairs swing open, followed by Francesco's frantic voice repeat my name again and again. The sound of heavy footsteps sweep up the staircase right near my studio, while I gather my thoughts and rub the soreness from my eyes away.

Instantly, the door bursts open, and the sudden waves of movement that travels through the room only causes me to tremble with fear even more. I look up into his eyes, feeling extremely confused and perplexed.

"Natalia," his voice breaks, as he falls to his knees beside me. He swears under his breath, and I hear every bit of fear and urgency behind his voice.

Every ounce of strength is entirely drained from within me. I am empty, and all I can do is cling on to him. I capture the sorrow in his eyes as he stares at the floor, and upon following his gaze, I find us surrounded in a pool of blood. His beige suit, now stained red. I'm in so much pain. Emotionally, physically and mentally, it's like I've forgotten how to breathe.

He is saying something to me, but his voice is so unclear that I barely can make out his words at all. I'm tired, slipping away, drained completely to an indescribable amount of exhaustion. I let him do what needs to be done. For not a word can be ushered out of my mouth at present, just tears of anguish that ruptures from my heart.

When the doctor announced that I lost the baby, I believe that he announced the beginning of the end for me. Francesco has not spoken a word. But with one look from me, his rims darken bloodshot red with a weighty mask of distress. Tears fill up and refuse to escape his tired eyes, and his body only stiffens up beside me as he holds me tight. Then suddenly, he breaks.

I've finally lost what little mental and emotional strength I have left, seeing the man that I love in this state. For never have I ever seen someone so broken and distraught as he is in this moment. This is the man who is known to carry a soul of steel, whose spirit is now crumbling to pieces, breaking down in desolation right in front of me. He adored our baby, deeply. It was so clear that he was looking forward to being a father, but I can't help but feel like I have let him down. I hate to see him upset. It hurts that we both have to go through something like this.

Why us? Why does life have to be so damn painful? Why does it feel like I attract so much bad luck? Why didn't God protect my baby after all those nights I prayed for him to protect us? I wish with all of my heart that I wasn't alive right now, for I keep losing those who matter the most to me. There are times when I'm afraid to continue living if disappointment delights to torment my life. I don't ever want to experience a loss like this again. Words cannot describe the intensity of grieving a child. I don't care how small the baby was, it was still mine. It was ours. That child was my first, and I'll never forget him or her.

The following morning weighs with heaviness upon my heart. The bright sunlight pierces my eyes through the bedroom windows, glowing directly onto Francesco's golden skin. He lies there next to me, typing away on his business phone, catching my eye as I met his.

"Natalia," he whispers quietly, beginning to brush his fingers softly through my hair. "Can I get you anything?"

"Aren't you supposed to be at the office today?" I ask, perplexed.

His jaw tightens. "I have taken time off. I'm not leaving you like this."

"I'll be fine," I lie.

He sighs. "Nothing about this is fine. Do you honestly think this hasn't affected me too?"

I think about that for a minute, only to realize that what he is saying was true. Just because he didn't feel the physical pain of losing our baby, it doesn't mean he didn't feel anything at all. I am so used to him being so unbothered and unmoved by many things. This chapter is all new to me.

I've lost such a huge chunk of my heart, and all of a sudden, it's like I don't know how to keep living.

"I'm sorry," I whisper. "Why... why did this have to happen to us? Why, honey?"

He inhales sharply, blinking his eyes dry. "I do not know why this had to happen, darling."

"I'm scared, Francesco!" I cry, cuddling up nearer to his chest.

"I'm here," his voice breaks. "Tell me how I can support you through this, please."

"I don't know." I sniffle. "I truly don't know how I'm going to overcome this. We were going to have a family... our baby... just taken away from us like that. Our sweet baby. How am I ever going to cope with this? How are we going to handle this?"

Words can't leave him. He looks speechless and absolutely broken, hushing me tenderly in his firm embrace. It's hard seeing him like this. I wrap my arm around him tighter and cry into his chest. And for long, we just dwell here in silence, resting underneath the bedsheets as I listen to the soft beat of his broken heart.

I have spent the last week in my bed after losing our baby. I have no energy nor the capacity to create any paintings or do anything else. Through which, I have just remained at home with Francesco by my side. He has been extremely supportive, but I know that he's just as broken. I have even lost my appetite. Any thought of eating right now makes my stomach turn. I have lost my child. And now, I have lost myself.

"Amore," Francesco softly whispers, as I hear the bedroom door creak open. "Please eat, darling. Look, I am not the best chef in the world, but I cooked up some prawn linguine for you. I heard that it's one of your favorite dishes."

I stare at him standing in the doorway with his eyes narrowed with desperation to see me well. He looks more shattered than I have ever seen him before. No longer clean-cut and polished as he always was. He looks absolutely defeated, in every possible way.

"What happened to Giuseppe? You're so sweet, baby. Thanks… but I'm fine for now."

He sits beside me on the bed. "I thought it would be best to give the team a few days off from today… we need our fucking space around here. Have you informed your family yet about the news?"

"No," I whisper. "They didn't even know I was pregnant. I can't share this news of a miscarriage with them. My siblings and I have been through enough, it would only further their heartache and disappointment. I had to make up a random lie as an excuse for not attending the funeral. I've already caused so much trouble, honey."

He cradles my face with his warm hands. "You're no trouble, darling. They care about you. What about your sister? The one you are close to."

"The news would break her even more, honey," I say. "I can't do that to her, especially not now."

"Alright," he breathes, leaning in to give me a kiss. "Do not hesitate to give me a shout if you need anything."

"Wait," I call out in a whisper as he arises, heading toward the door. "Honey... how are you feeling?"

He glances in my direction with a brief and faint smile. But then softly, it drops. "I'm alright, darling," he says quietly, before shutting the door gently behind him.

34. Her

It has taken me just over a month to start getting out of bed. The harsh chill of fall returns to England once again, and Francesco is so sweet to take me out for dinner this evening. It's been a while since left the house together, and this time, I can tell a difference. For as we exit the restaurant building, the photographers are absolutely ruthless, blocking our entry to head into Peter's car. Xavier is with us, along with two other members of the security team who create a safe distance between the cameras and Francesco's fans about us. I've never felt so insecure as much as I do right now. Flashing lights, screaming voices, the scent of smoke and alcohol while Francesco tenses up beside me only heightens my nervousness. He dislikes the attention, I can tell. Yet he puts his guard up so well, holding my hand firmly within his and presses his lips against my cheek for the sweetest kiss as Xavier proceeds to open the door for us.

Suddenly, someone swiftly barges through the surrounding crowd. Security immediately withholds the mysterious man from coming any closer.

"Oi Francesco, I know you haven't seen me in some time, but it's urgent. I need a private word," the man says. His bright blue eyes then quickly glance at mine. "It's about *her*."

Francesco doesn't delay to murmur something to Xavier, and instantaneously, security comply to whatever he has said.

"Alright Miss Garcia," Xavier strictly directs to me. "Get in."

The open door to Peter's car awaits me, yet I'm confused as to why Francesco won't come in.

"Honey?" I ask him.

"I'll be with you shortly, darling."

Xavier gives me no room to respond as he shuts my door so firm that I almost shudder.

What on earth is going on?

I try to peer out the window to see what Francesco is doing, but I can barely see as Xavier and his team completely block all entries to the doors.

Then all at once, my phone rings.

"Hello?" I breathe.

"Natalia, it's me."

That voice.

"Daisy?"

"Listen attentively to me, Natalia. Try not to draw attention to yourself during this call, and under no circumstances inform Francesco—"

"What?" I mutter, questioning why on earth she is even calling me. "Where did you get my number? And what will happen if I do tell him?"

"There's a man outside speaking to him right now, isn't there?"

"Yes," I whisper. "How do you know that?"

"Natalia, if you're going to be difficult with me, I will bloody command the orders to shoot Francesco dead this minute. Have I made myself clear enough?"

This isn't real. I'm dreaming. I have to be.

"Daisy what the hell do you want?" I beg her, in anguished tears at this point. "What the actual fuck? How dare you threaten me and my man!"

"He's my bloody husband! You fucking home-wrecker! You're lucky that I'm not there to kill you myself, but I wanted to give you a chance."

She's lying. She has to be.

"You are not married to Francesco!"

"Are you telling me that you've been living with him for all these months, yet you've found no trace of our marriage in the home?"

"Daisy, this isn't a good prank at all! In fact, it's extremely distasteful! Why are you joking around like this? When Francesco finds out—"

"I've been watching you since you walked in for the interview that day!" she cries. "You consume my mind, all day and night! All I want is for you to be wiped off the face of this damned earth so that Francesco and I can have a chance together once again. You're ruining my life, Natalia! You're in the way of my husband and I giving it one more shot again. I'm begging you, earnestly, to leave my husband alone."

"I... I..." I lose the words to speak. For there's this tempting feeling to knock on the walls of the window and warn Xavier of the matter. But I just cannot take that risk. I feel like she's watching me. In fact, I know she is.

And everything that she's saying actually adds up.

"What exactly do you want me to do, Daisy?"

"I beg you, Natalia," she pleads in anguish, "leave my husband, and I'll let you both live."

A huge cluster of pins form in my throat as she says it. Why would she want to kill the man that she claims to love?

"Okay," I whisper, signaling to Peter to get his phone out. I know that she won't be able to see this as out windows are tinted. Immediately, Peter complies.

"How long have you been married to Francesco, Daisy?" I ask her, while pressing the record button on Peter's phone. I put mine on loud speaker, silently telling Peter to stay silent and trust me.

"We've been married for ten years!" she cries harder. "Although, we've been separated five. Shit, it's my fault."

"Why is it your fault?"

"Because I... I made a mistake and left him while taking a huge chunk of his money to run away to Ibiza with Sebastian."

"Who is Sebastian?"

"The man outside who Francesco is having a conversation with right now as we speak."

"Oh, I had a feeling Francesco knew him."

"I can't believe that I am doing this to him," she says, starting to wail in such a way that brings horror to my soul. "I blackmailed Sebastian into doing this, but that's how desperate I am to get Francesco back to me."

"Blackmailed? How so?"

"I told him to shoot if you refused to agree to leave my husband. But you agree, Natalia. Don't you?"

"Yes, I will leave him," I tell her. "But why is Sebastian so willing to get arrested if he were to get caught?"

"Because there are things that I know about Sebastian, that you don't. Such things that can send him to prison, and I will get him locked up either way if I don't get what I want from him... and I always get what I want, Natalia."

"Oh god."

"I need you to know that I'm sorry that it has to be this way." She sniffles. "But I didn't know what else to bloody do. I warned you, didn't I? On your first day... but you wouldn't listen."

"But Daisy, I had no idea that you were married to him! If I had known earlier—"

"I was unsure whether to tell you."

"Why?"

"Nobody but his family and small circle of friends are aware of the situation back in Italy. It is not yet out in the public news. Francesco and I agreed for it to not be so."

"And the reason for that is?"

"I wanted my privacy. Look at you, Natalia. Have you not despised how drastically your life has altered since being with him? You can't even walk down the street in peace. On top of that, I see your following online has blown up too. That is the kind of life that I dread to live."

"But Daisy, if Francesco and I agree to stay together..."

"Then sadly, I will have to get rid of you both."

"Even Francesco? Isn't he supposed to be the man that you love? How could you even consider such a thing? This isn't right, Daisy."

"But if I can't have him, nobody else should."

"Love doesn't work like that..."

"I no longer believe in selfless love, Natalia," she responds, very tearfully. "Certainly not since Francesco and I lost our children."

"Children?"

I thought there was only one.

"Our poor Emmy passed away due to SIDS!" she cries louder, losing it this time. "And Liam, our second son, was stillborn. Francesco wasn't this hard and cold man that the world sees today. No, my husband was so much different, but life… life broke him, as it broke me."

"I'm so sorry Daisy. Truly, I mean it with all of my heart. What you experienced must have been such a terrible thing to go through."

"It's my fault, isn't it?" Her voice crackles. "I'm so incapable of being a good mother. I've failed them, and I've failed Francesco. I'm a monster. An absolute hopeless wreck! Ever since my children lost their lives, all I want is to end the lives of those who get in my way. Because if my children didn't get to live… as pure and special as they are. Why should you?"

"Daisy… you're not well. I'm so sorry that you're going through this. This is trauma that you're dealing with. Please, allow Francesco and I to get you the help that you need."

"If you're so sorry then you'll leave him, won't you? For both your lives' sake."

"Yes." I sigh, possibly lying once again. "I will."

I honestly have no idea what I'm going to do yet.

"Good," she whispers. "I will send the signal to Sebastian that all is well then. And I'm warning you, that if you ever change your mind, I can bloody promise you that I will find a way to get rid of you."

I take a deep breath. "Okay…"

"And Natalia?"
"Yes?"
"I'm sorry things had to turn out this way."

35. *Fervent*

I remain silent on the entire way home, and I ask Peter quietly to forward me the recording as I step out the car. Francesco gives me this concerned look as though he can't quite make out what is going on. The anxiety is breaking me, immensely. I'm not going to utter a word until we're both inside and safe.

"I feel so damn sorry for her," I murmur to myself.

Instantly, he looks at me as though I'm speaking another language. "Forgive me. Who?"

"Daisy," I mutter. "Your wife! How on earth could you keep something like that from me? Daisy. Out of all people, it was her!"

Irritably, he runs his hand through his hair while firing curse words under his breath. "Look, Natalia—"

"Don't come closer to me!" I tell him, creating distance between us. "Don't touch me, Francesco."

I can't stop crying.

"How the fuck did you find out?"

"How on earth could you hide this from me?"

"Natalia, listen. I was trying to protect you—"

"Protect me?" I exclaim. "While you were out speaking to Sebastian tonight, she phoned me and threatened to get you killed if I don't comply to her wishes. Sebastian is in on this too, Francesco. I do not know what he said to you, but Daisy is mentally unwell. She's battling with trauma. Why the fuck have you not provided the professional support that she needs?"

"I've been handling it, Natalia. For fuck's sake."

"Clearly not well enough!"

I play him the recording that Peter forwarded to me. His face is as stiff as rock. Straight and poker-faced, with no expression at all that gives hint of any emotion.

"Well?" I mutter, growing impatient for a decent reaction to come from him. "Honey, please explain everything. I feel so damn sick to my stomach! As heartbreaking as this is to hear such difficult times that you and Daisy have experienced, I can't help but feel betrayed that you withheld such important information from me. I genuinely thought that this madness over the last few months was all due to an ex girlfriend, but to hear that you still have a wife… this isn't making sense!"

"Look." He sighs. "You have all the right to be angry with me, Natalia. I've fucked up, bad. I know that."

"But baby, you clearly told me that you're not married. I believed you because I trusted you. This makes things so much more difficult for us now."

"Daisy and I have been separated for five years. There have been various complications regarding moving forward with the divorce due to her fucking up my finances. It's bullshit. I was so damn certain that we'd be divorced by now. I withheld this information from you darling because I was afraid of losing you."

"But honestly… that shouldn't come at the cost of deceiving me, Francesco. Honey, this isn't what love is about!"

He takes an irritated, deep sigh, now sitting upon the couch. "Fucking hell," he breathes. "I'm filing a restraining order first thing tomorrow."

"What have you been doing all this time?"

"I can't recall how many occasions I've been in discussions with the police about her bullshit."

"What have they been saying?" I ask, taking a seat right next to him.

"They aren't taking it as serious as I'd like," he tells me. "They initially suggested to tighten up on my security team, and that's what I've done. But don't worry about this, darling. I'll sort this."

"How can you tell me to not worry when she almost got you killed tonight? I'm so angry with how you've been handling this. Who is Sebastian anyway?"

His jaw clenches as he pauses, letting his gaze fall to the ground. "An old friend of ours who persuaded her to run off to some other country with him before we separated. Clearly, they didn't last."

"You have mutual friends?"

"Yes, we were introduced when I first moved here."

"Were you in love with each other?"

"No."

"Really? But then why did you get married? This nonsense isn't making any sense to me, at all. A couple has to love each other in order to get married. Shouldn't they?"

He chuckles, almost humorlessly. "Piccola mia, you're so young," he breathes. "But no... not every married couple marries for love."

"What was your reason for marrying her then?"

"We agreed it was to be for convenience sake," he replies. "But in the first few years of marriage, I suppose the nature of our relationship developed into something different."

"Honey," I whisper, in utter disbelief. "Why on earth would you get into a marriage of convenience so young?"

"I had no choice," he murmurs, breaking eye contact with me now. "A lot of bullshit went down back home in Italy. It was expected of me to redeem and uphold the Giordano name after the family's reputation got fucked up by my father."

"Oh... What did he do?"

He searches into my eyes ever so quietly. "I can't do this," he dismisses, shaking gently out of my arms to walk some place elsewhere.

I follow him into the kitchen where he now pours himself a glass of wine. "Tell me, baby."

He ignores me.

"Please. I know it's hard opening up about the past... believe me, I've been there. But honey, let me be there for you as you've been there for me."

I feel his entire body tensing up under my touch, so much that it honestly is beginning to concern me.

Is he really this afraid of opening up?

"Can we talk about this later, darling?" he asks.

"No. You and I been keeping secrets long enough. Vulnerability is crucial, Francesco, if we are to move forward from this point. Truly, I really don't want anything at all to be kept between us anymore."

He sighs as though exhausted, while brushing my tears away. "Alright. Luigi Giordano murdered my brother, Roberto, at the age of eleven. It was my fucking fault, Natalia. If I were there to protect him..."

He stops speaking, and I wait patiently for him to start again. "It's... it's okay baby... Take your time. I'm listening."

I hug him as tight as I can, yet I can hear the swift beating of his heart. He's panicking inside. Yet on the outside, he's as standing as strong, firm and unmoving as ever. There's a part of me that feels deeply for this side of him. For it's as though he believes he can't be vulnerable with the world, let alone with me.

"Natalia." He sighs. "I can't talk about this."

"You can, honey," I assure him, now holding his handsome face in my hands. "I promise you that you can be open with me."

He pauses, taking a deep breath. "July 27th, I took Valentina out for a walk of fresh air. Mamma was sick, and Roberto decided to stay behind to look after her while my father was at home. That's where I fucked up by letting them out of my sight. Fucking hell, why didn't I think? I should have been there to protect them.

Yet when Vale and I returned, all my mind keeps replaying is that damn memory of Roberto's body being dragged across the ground by my father," he tells me, clearly breaking now. "I called for medical assistance, as well as the police. But like always, the police can be fucking hopeless when you need them. They failed to come in time in order to stop all of my father's bullshit.

I took it upon myself to restrain my father from taking Roberto's body away. But I failed. All I remember was beating the crap out of him, only to end up blacking out on the ground. Vale was only around five or six for fuck's sake, and she stood there, watching every fucking detail of what went on in this family. And yes, I was only sixteen at the time, but I should have known better. I should have taken them with me. I knew full fucking well about my father's abusive bullshit ways, but I didn't think any attack would play out during that short hour of being out. Fucking hell. It's haunted mamma every damn day since it happened. She can't stop going on and on about Roberto protecting her while my father attempted to attack her. It should have been me that got killed, not him. It is my job and responsibility to protect my family. It's that same fucking house that we went to in Tuscany that all of the bullshit went down. I hate going there, darling. I fucking hate it, but mamma refuses to let it go."

"I... I'm so sorry to hear this baby... but why, honey? Why can't your mom let the house go?"

"Much of our wealth is inherited by her side of the family. My father established the business successfully throughout the country through her initial financial support. Everyone in Italy praises the Giordano name, yet they remain so fucking ignorant of the sacrifices my mother has had to make."

"W-w-what happened to Roberto's body?"

"A search team found him months too late."

"And... your father?"

He sighs. "My father was on the run for a while before eventually getting caught. He died in prison a year later by suicide... Since then, the Giordano name has been infamous back in Italy for obvious reasons. It was necessary for me to leave the country in order to get away from all the bullshit. Mamma was insistent on me having to redeem the name through charitable works, various business investments, positive press and a respectable marriage. But fucking hell, that damned marriage with Daisy only made things worse for me."

"I can't believe what I'm hearing... truly, I had no idea at all that you experienced such pain like this, baby. It all makes sense now. All of it... But that still doesn't explain why is Daisy the chief operating officer of your company?"

"She *was* the chief operating officer of the company, not anymore. Initially, she helped build the business here with me in the UK over twelve years ago. We met through some friends at business conference in our early twenties."

"*Was?*"

He sighs. "Yes, I released her from her position the moment she started threatening you. I refuse to tolerate that bullshit, Natalia. Darling, I can't go through it again."

"Go through what again, honey?"

"Losing someone that I love... due to my failure to protect them," he breathes, holding his gaze with mine. "I won't let anything hurt you, amore. I can assure you that."

"I..." I'm honestly at lost for words to say. All I can do is hold him so tight as he enwraps his arms around me. "Thank you for telling me," I whisper.

"You're not pissed off with me?"

"Yeah, absolutely. Of course I am, regarding the Daisy situation... but I understand why you did it. I certainly don't agree with how you handled it, but I love you too much at this point to just give up on us now. I can't... but I am afraid of what she'll do now."

He sighs softly. "We're filing the restraining order first thing tomorrow, and we'll take it from there."

"She said she'll kill us," I whisper, trembling.

"I'm not going to allow anything to happen to you, Natalia," he tells me, with a dark seriousness about him. "I will fucking die for you if I have to."

"What? Baby—"

"My love for you is fervent, Natalia. I mean it darling, I'm yours."

36. Beautifully

We officially have a restraining order against Daisy Smith. Words cannot describe how relieved that I feel right now, and as I finish off my new series of paintings, I receive a knock on my studio door.

"Come in," I call out.

Unexpectedly, I'm surprised by Claudia, one of the lovely housekeepers, as she appears in my studio. Honestly, she's one of the sweetest ladies that you'd ever meet. Though today, there's an expression on her face that tells me something is deeply wrong.

"What's the matter, Claudia?" I ask her.

"Forgive me, ma'am. I really don't wish to be a disturbance. I wanted to ask if you have any sanitary pads," she says quietly, now clearing her throat. "Or tampons, please. I've started a few days too early."

"Awww, of course! Please don't worry, it's no trouble at all," I assure her. "I'm always happy to help."

I quickly lead her into the bathroom upstairs and hand her what she needs. "Hmm, you don't need any painkillers do you?"

Her face immediately darkens red. "Actually, now that you mention it..."

We both laugh as I hand her a box full of them.

"Thank you," she whispers, before rushing off out the room into the distance.

But then something switches in me. A thought that hasn't crossed my mind for weeks.

Oh goodness, no.

My period is late.

I stare at the three positive tests that are all placed across the edge of the bath.

"Are we ready for this?" I ask him.

Francesco stares at them in silence before fixing his focus straight onto me again. "We're ready for anything."

"I'm scared," I whisper.

"Darling, it's alright to be scared," he tells me.

I close my eyes into his chest as he carries me next door to the bed. "What if it happens again?"

"Amore..." He sighs, gently. "Let's not predict such things. Look, I understand that you have concerns about welcoming a child into the world, so do I."

"Why?" I whisper, as he places me on the bed.

"More responsibility," he breathes. He then sits beside me, and stares deeply into my heart. "But I'm willing to do whatever it takes to keep you both happy and safe."

A single tear escapes me.

He's softens around me so beautifully.

"I want to be happy about this, I really do. But I'm scared of getting my hopes up again. Honey, don't you feel the same way too? After losing…"

"Yes," he breathes, sorrowfully. "I do… but I don't wish to lose hope, darling. Neither should you."

"Francesco?" I whisper.

"Yes, princess?" he whispers back.

"What are we going to do?"

He takes hold of my hand and plants a kiss on it. "Do what we've always done. Take one day at a time."

"I want to be a mother," I tell him. "A good mother. One who is present emotionally, and supportive to our child's needs. But do you think I'll be good at it? I'm worried that I'll fail at it."

Quietness fills the room for a moment, before he lifts my face tenderly to meet his eyes. "Listen, I mean it when I tell you this… I couldn't have chosen a more loving and courageous woman than you to be the mother of my child."

Rivers instantly flow from my eyes. "Thank you so much, honey. Oh god, that's one of the sweetest things I've ever heard in my life. It's so comforting to hear that."

He pauses. "How would you feel about us going to therapy for a short period of time?"

"Really, like couples therapy?"

"Yes," he confirms. "To prepare for the baby."

"I'd love to! That's such a good idea, honey."

"We've been through... tough times. Haven't we, darling? All of the bullshit with our families and such. I think that this is the right step for us to take."

"You're right. I don't want to carry any baggage in this new chapter of our lives."

"Likewise." He smiles, a genuine smile.

I cry, because I can't help but think of the first day that I met him. How beautifully things can change in such a short amount of time.

"I love you," he whispers.

I bask deeply within his embrace and saturate in his sandalwood and oud scent. "I love you too."

37. Fortress

When I held my daughter in my arms for the first time last week, I knew that I would never be the same woman again. Nothing else mattered to me from that moment but her well-being and safety, even before my own. Sofia Rosalia Giordano became the treasure of my existence, and when I looked into her eyes, suddenly all at once, my priorities shifted. I know it's to be expected, but if you were to ask me a week ago that one day I would go a week without picking up a paintbrush, I wouldn't believe you. It's strange, really. A blessing such as this coming to me in a way that I least imagined. The sacrificial love that my heart holds for this precious girl is beyond expression. I'm willing to do anything, and give up anything, solely for the best interest of my daughter.

Watching Francesco's journey to fatherhood has

touched me so deeply beyond that I could ever describe. He's a perfect father. The divorce has finally been finalized, and thankfully, the prenup came in handy. Smoking is no longer present in our house, neither in Francesco's life altogether. I couldn't be happier. We now even have a fluffy white rag doll cat named Lily as another new addition to our family! She's so cute, and only around a few months old, but I know that Sofia will love her as they both grow older.

I've never felt more blessed as I am in this moment.

Rosalia was my mother's name. I sometimes wonder if she's with us and watching over this family. Would she be proud of me? I hope that she would. My heart aches to think about the fact that she'll never meet her granddaughter in this life, but I also eagerly await to tell Sofia when she's older about all of the wonderful things about her grandmother.

Sofia is currently sleeping in Francesco's arms as we all rest in the living room. He always likes to be with her. She could sleep in his arms for hours and he would never complain. I love him, and I'm falling in love with him so deeper by the second. My old life seems completely alien to me now. For I can't imagine a life without Sofia, and without Francesco too.

Suddenly, the doorbell rings.

Sofia flinches, and Francesco hesitates.

"Don't worry, honey," I tell him, remembering that our butler and the housekeeping team left for the evening. "I'll get it."

"No, please hold her," he orders me, sternly. The doorbell then rings again. "Where the fuck is security?" he murmurs under his breath. "Baby, let me take care of it."

"Honey, it's fine. You're already holding her."

The doorbell then pulses through the entire property so loudly that Sofia wakes up and begins to cry.

"Take her, Natalia," he repeats quietly, yet clearly pissed off now.

He hands her gently to me and then strides irritably through the hallway to the front door. I peek through to watch him fling open the door from afar with Sofia still in my arms.

"Francesco," the soft familiar voice speaks.

All I see is blonde hair to make out who it is.

She can't be here. Not with Sofia around.

"Daisy?" A sound of urgency vibrates through his voice. "What are you doing here… and how did you find out our address? How the fuck did you get through security?"

Immediately, he closes the door a bit more, only leaving me a slither of a crack to see Daisy.

"I heard that you'll be on paternity leave for a few weeks." I hear her sniffle. "From a source of mine."

He crosses his massive arms. "Who provided

you with that information?"

"Why didn't you tell me? Why didn't I know you were... having... a b-b-baby with her? She's just a girl, Francesco. You know that s-s-she's nothing compared to me, compared to *us*. What about our children? Our precious little sons."

"Natalia is twenty five," he corrects her, vexed now. "You're breaching the restraining order, Daisy. I'll be reporting this—"

"You haven't answered my question, Francesco. What about *our* babies? Have you forgotten about them? Or are you just going to move on now like our children never existed? You fucking little prick! I hate you. I hate you!" she cries louder, beginning to hit him. As a result, Sofia wakes up crying hysterically and it causes something to switch in me.

"Get your hands off my man!" I raise my voice at Daisy, feeling my footsteps storming like fire on the floor tiles. "You're upsetting my daughter, and you've disrupted her sleep. I request that you leave this property and refrain from troubling my family again or else I will get the cops involved this instant. Do you understand me?"

Her sapphire eyes bulge out as they stare at me in disgust. "You sound just like him. Who do you think you are?" she roars, almost charging at me before Francesco's arm hinders her from coming forward. "Who the fuck do you think you are? You're fucking little home-wrecking whore! I'm going to ruin you! You took my husband away—"

"Daisy." Francesco's loud and authoritative voice silences her hysterical tears with immediate effect, and without fail, it sends chills down my skin. Instantly afterward, he then gives me one look. "Natalia, I need you to take Sofia somewhere quiet. I will not have this going on around our child."

Before he even finishes the sentence, I'm already walking down the hallway anyway. But then something in me brings me to halt. "Daisy, I never took Francesco away from you. He left you long before all of this! In fact, the moment you took off with another man with *his* money, was the precise moment his heart left you! It just took you too long to realize that you'd never have him again."

I turn back toward the hallway and then walk back into the living room, letting the deepest sigh leave me as I apologize to Sofia and hold her close. I hear Daisy breaking down so scarily in the background. I hear her hitting him, again and again. I'm trying to comfort my baby, but I'm panicking if Francesco's alright. It sounds like a right mess out there. I'm sick of it all. So I just pick the phone up, and ring the cops. I refuse to crumble, and I refuse to break down. Because my whole world is right in my arms, and there's nothing more that I am dedicated to do than to devote myself to be her fortress.

38. Regrets

"Ideally, Sofia could do with some fresh air today," Francesco murmurs, while his eyes become focused on the balcony window that reveals the stunning weather of June.

The light and refreshing air flows through the crack of the window, hitting against the fresh cotton laundry that Dahlia and I have just finished folding.

"Hyde Park is just a fifteen minute walk from here, darling." His gaze meets mine, with a certain warmth simmering in his countenance.

"Hmmm. You're right," I breathe airily, trying my best to brush aside my deep fear of seeing Daisy again after what happened a week ago. The court issued her a warning, but I can't help but continue looking over my shoulder. "Honey, I'm scared. Especially because we no longer have security."

"I won't let anything or anyone hurt you or Sofia, darling. You are aware of that, aren't you?"

"Yes," I whisper. "I just… didn't expect you to fire the security team so suddenly."

He cuts his eye as he shakes his head subtly. "What the fuck do they expect, Natalia? Jason fucks around on duty to sleep around with one of our neighbors, while the other one left sick to go home early without my authorization. What sort of security team jeopardizes my family's safety?"

"Xavier didn't seem very happy." I sigh.

"I don't pay him and his team to fuck around."

"Give him a second chance," I beg him.

"No, darling. I'll find someone else. A team that is competent to carry out their work."

"Okay," I breathe. "I'll get Sofia ready."

Once Sofia is ready and settled, we take a cute family stroll to the park. It's a beautiful experience that I've never had before. The sweet feeling of being a family, having my own to love and care for. It's so rewarding and precious. It's these treasured memories that I will cherish so much. Like Sofia's sweet little face as she rides softly within the stroller. Her priceless expression as she stares in wonder at the beauty of the sky. She's learning so many new things. Discovering a whole new world, and it's so wonderful to me. Motherhood can be super challenging, but moments like these I truly adore.

When we walk through the park, I intentionally avoid the rose garden. Because every time I see it, I gain an uncomfortable twisting sensation within the depths of my stomach. Memories of Gideon resurrect to haunt me. They torture me, truly. I sometimes wonder what life would be like if he were still close to me. They say friendships and romantic relationships are never truly the same after you have a baby. And though Francesco and I have had our challenges, I can't help but think about Gideon from time to time.

There are moments when I miss him, and then there are moments when I don't. Life has grown too busy for me to keep dwelling on what was, and what could have been. Every day I try to make that choice to focus on what's in front of me, and this darling bundle of joy that I hold in my arms always grounds me in peace.

We stop underneath a large floral tree, where a bench was layered with lots of fine lilac flower petals. I sit down to breastfeed Sofia, and as Francesco sits beside us. Half an hour then passes by, and I feel someone's eyes on me.

"Nat?" I hear a very familiar voice in the distance. "Natalia, is that you?" Gideon calls out.

"Gideon!" I breathe out my nerves. I'd like to get up to greet him properly, but I don't want to disturb Sofia.

He notices. "It's... been a while."

"Yes," I agree, realizing that he's keeping his distance. "This is my... I mean, *our*, daughter..."

"Gideon." Francesco nods, firmly.

Gideon returns the gesture. "Congratulations to you both. She's beautiful."

He's always so lovely to me. I thank him, despite the uncomfortable feeling that spreads rapidly about us.

"Angelina informed me of your first exhibition in October," he tells me, smiling sweetly.

"Yeah, I had a lot of time to create some pieces during the pregnancy. I look forward to sharing them with the world. Gee, I wouldn't have got this far without you. It was you who truly encouraged me, just over there in the rose garden. I'm so grateful, Gideon."

"You deserve, it," he says, with a shimmer in his eye. It twinkles to the point where I have to ask myself if it's a tear.

Sofia begins to make her little noises as she finishes her feed. I apologize as I settle her down, and Gideon tells me it's fine, revealing those sweet dimples of his as he looks at her. "Wow, Nat. She looks just like you—"

"Yes, she does." Francesco fires out of nowhere. "Unfortunately, Gideon, it's time for us to leave."

I can't help but stare at Francesco with a hint of disappointment in me. Because as much as I know that they're not fond of each other, Francesco knows that Gideon is one of the best people I have ever met. He knows how dearly I have held him close to my heart.

"I'm sorry," I direct to Gideon.

He shakes his head ever so subtly. "Don't be."

Francesco shoots me a look. "Are you ready?"

"Yes," I reply, weirdly unable to break away from Gideon's eyes as Francesco settles Sofia in her stroller.

I swallow the hard ball in my throat. "Bye, Gideon. It was lovely seeing you again.

"It was great seeing you today too, Nat, and your daughter." He smiles so serenely as we walk away from him. It hurts to say goodbye again.

I wave once more before looking forward, feeling Francesco's intense attention on me. But then suddenly, I hear Gideon calling out my name.

I look back quickly in uneasy anticipation, only to be met with a bright grin spread across Gideon's face. "What is your daughter's name?"

I hear Francesco losing his patience next to me, swearing under his breath.

"Her name is Sofia!" I respond. And for some strange reason, I can't stop grinning.

Gideon smiles with a nod. "She has a very beautiful name. Take care of yourself, Natalia."

"You too!" I wave.

I wait for him to walk away before I look away, but he doesn't.

I keep on walking and watching, seeing him become smaller as our distance grows bigger. He is waving, I am waving. I feel happy. I don't want to take eyes off him, my best friend, the person I genuinely deeply care about. Even though this is most certainly the last time I will see him now, I feel utterly sad and utterly happy at the same time. Because I am grateful that fate gave me one last chance to look into the eyes of a man I genuinely admire.

"Natalia," Francesco snaps, to get my attention.

"Yes, honey?" I ask airily, turning my focus toward Sofia with a face that can't help but smile.

He looks at me without a word, but then breaks our eye contact once Sofia begins to cry. His attention is immediately glued on to her again, and in that last second, I check back to see if Gideon is still there, but he's gone. It's within that moment when I feel my heart beginning to drown within the greatest ache, yearning to see him more often than we do now, like old times.

39. Family

In the midst of fall, my family arrive in London from Carmel just a few days before my first ever art exhibition. Julieta's husband, Joseph, and their children, Rosa, Carlos and Gabriella, will also be coming along to visit us in Mayfair. I actually look forward to seeing Maria today. Since our father's passing, we managed to finally have a private heart to heart conversation which lasted much longer than I expected, and shockingly, it enabled me to understand why she acted the way she did.

I was completely unaware throughout all these years that that my father had discouraged her from pursuing a career as a make-up artist in the movie industry. I'll never forget when she told me that she lived solely to please our father by getting a law degree, and to her, it only discouraged her further from being herself.

She mentioned that she saw mamá in me, and understandably, that was something that she found triggering. An artist, a dreamer. Someone that my father had a habit of taking out his anger upon, and to be honest, the thought of it still hurts.

I'm coming to a place of acceptance that I'll never really get full closure in regard to my father, but my heart feels closer to rest now that Maria and I are at a better place again.

Suddenly, the doorbell rings.

"Are you ready, honey?" I ask Francesco, as we take steps together toward our front door, hand in hand.

I decided to give Ben, Giuseppe, and the girls a day off today. Therefore, I've been cooking dinner and dessert with Francesco today.

"Hurry up Nat, we don't have all day!" Maria's impatience causes me to burst into laughter as I finally get round to opening the door.

Ever so wonderfully, I'm finally met with the whole family greeting us with a huge roar of excitement. Upon exchanging hugs, kisses and sweet greetings with one another, they all say hello to Francesco, and he seems pretty relaxed! I know that this is a big step for him, because he isn't so used to family gatherings or social environments outside of business matters. Because of that, I'm proud to see how far he has come. It's an exceedingly great delight to watch him finally meet Diego, and honestly, it's an interesting sight to see.

Joseph is super friendly, as always. Maria seems different, for the better. After greeting me she also gives Francesco a quick hug before darting toward me to say that he looks the same in person as he does in the photos.

The cutest thing that I have seen in a while is seeing Francesco kneel down to speak to my little nieces and nephew as they play with Lily. Other than Sofia, I have never seen him interact with young children before, ever! It melts my heart, deeply.

We all enter the living room, and everyone sits down, other than Julieta. Her eyes are scanning all around the room with a sort of eager anticipation.

"Excuse me, dearest, but I would really like to see Sofia now. I cannot sit down yet without seeing her beautiful face in person—"

"Yeah, she's been going on about this moment throughout the whole plane journey, and every second since we landed." Joseph chuckles as he sits Rosa on his lap.

Diego's loud and booming laugh instantly makes its appearance as he leans back on the couch. "Yep, you got that right Joe. Where's she at, Nat?"

"Oh come on guys, seriously? If she's not here then she is obviously sleeping. She's only a baby! Remember? Wait for her to wake up, and we'll be able to see her then. If I see her now, I may accidentally wake her up with all of my cuddles!" Maria exclaims.

"Yeah, Maria's right. Sofia is sleeping at the moment," I tell them. I then glance at Francesco, whose eyes are already fixed on me. He looks so amused, though in the most subtle way possible, as I would be the only person to see that he's hiding it deeply in his expression.

"Would anyone care for a drink?" Francesco asks, rising from the couch.

"Oh, yes please Fran!" Maria responds ever so casually. I chuckle at his new nickname after seeing gentle change of expression upon his face. "I'll have lemonade, if you have any!"

Just as I expected, Julieta quietly clears her throat as if to say something.

"I mean, I'll have a lemonade if you have any, *please.*" Maria smiles.

"Of course." Francesco nods, sweetly. "Joseph? How about yourself and the children?"

"Nah, I'm good you know man. But the kids like fruit juice if that's possible please, Francesco."

Diego rises up from the couch and unexpectedly strides beside Francesco. "I'll come with you, if you don't mind. Pleasure to be a help."

Oh god.

"Sure," Francesco responds, not phased at the slightest. His attention then switches to Julieta.

"Oh, sweetheart don't worry about me please," Julieta assures him before grabbing hold of my hand, interlocking her fingers in mine. "I would like to see my beautiful niece, even if she is sleeping... if that's okay with you both?"

"Sure," I reply, leading her the way.

Francesco and Diego then head to the kitchen, and Julieta and I make our way to Sofia's nursery.

"Natty, you didn't tell me that your new home is so glorious! Good for you, sweetie," she whispers in my ear. "How has Francesco been with you, and how is he as a new daddy?"

That question honestly seems like a tiny pin being stabbed in an old wound. Sure, Francesco has been wonderful, but it would be impossible to erase our darkest moments away from my heart so quickly. The last few months have been torture and bliss all at once, but I shrug it off anyway as we enter the nursery.

"Well, he's been wonderful, Jules," I tell her. "Such a perfect, devoted father."

Once Julieta finishes admiring Sofia while she sleeps, I close the nursery door behind us. Suddenly, I then hear an unfamiliar laugh that booms from the kitchen, but it's not Diego's. It sounds much deeper. I hurry to the kitchen, eager to see what was happening, but to my surprise, I see Francesco howling in laughter almost on the floor! Diego is laughing too, with tears in his spilling from his eyes. I pinch myself to double check if I was dreaming, but it is very much a reality!

What on earth is going on here?

"Oh my goodness, what a sight! The two most serious men in my life are having a laughing fit, pinch me!" I exclaim.

Instantaneously, I am pricked with a random pinch. Maria draws near to step beside me, looking at me with an apologetic expression on her face.

"You said to pinch you!" she says with a shrug, walking toward the counter to help herself with another drink.

"Ummm, anyone like to inform me on what's so funny?" I ask, trying to figure out what Francesco and Diego are now murmuring about among each other.

Francesco gradually composes himself, then puts his arm around me to give me a quick kiss on my head. "Nothing, darling—"

"We were just talking about soccer. I showed Francesco the old video of you back when you were like nine years old trying to make a goal, but you ended up slipping on a snail." Diego folds his huge arms and chuckles underneath his breath.

I can feel my cheeks heating up as more laughter from everyone else begins roaring around me, including Julieta and Joseph.

How embarrassing.

"How did you guys get round to talking about that anyway?" I ask, trying to hold my head high despite the shame that I'm immersed in right now.

Diego takes a huge sip of his beer. "Francesco and I have something in common. Sports." His eyes shoot to Francesco with a friendly nod.

"Yes," Francesco begins. He then looks at me and says, "You know how much I love it, darling. I didn't know that your brother was into it until we got talking."

I close my eyes upon being stung with greater shame. "Diego! Tell me why on earth did you have to show him—"

"We've all seen it Natalia." Maria laughs. "You know you would be famous on social media if that video was uploaded? It would go viral."

"Okay, okay. Don't go and get yourself any ideas," I mutter, failing to hide my amusement.

Francesco's warm hand tenderly rubs my arm. "Don't worry, darling. I'm pleased to see it."

"Oh, Francesco sweetheart. Has our Natty showed you her baby photos? I have them all saved on my phone for us to look at this evening to see if she looks like our darling Sofia! I don't mind sending them over to your phone too! Keep them and print them! Show the little one when she gets older!" Julieta proceeds to get out her phone.

Oh gosh. I can't help but sigh quietly to myself at the thought of it. There's a mix of embarrassment and felicity of having all of my family here, happy together. I'm intrigued in the fact that I'm already seeing a different side to Francesco. This is a side to him that brings utter bliss to my soul. It's lovely to see.

As I watch Julieta showing Francesco the

photos, the rest of the family begin to surround them. Ever so cutely, Francesco's eyes dart between me and the phone with such a joyous serenity, that it spreads the most gorgeous smile that I've ever seen on his face.

The whole family are absolutely in love with Sofia! We spend the rest of the evening chatting away and watching movies after dinner. Julieta desires to leave in the early evening due to the children's bedtime coming up. Therefore, the time comes where we all hug each other goodbye, while Francesco and my siblings exchange numbers.

I'm happy to say that Diego has been super engaged in conversation with Francesco throughout the entire evening! Words can't describe how lovely that is, for I can see that Francesco has made a new friend. It's been a splendid time, and we've taken plenty of photographs that I plan on printing to put into a new photo album.

Once everyone has left for the evening, I put Sofia to sleep and hop into bed. Francesco enters in, and snuggles in warmly beside me. I lie on my side facing toward him, feeling at bliss as his big arm brings me closer.

"I enjoyed myself today," he says, beaming with radiant his light grey eyes.

"Me too," I whisper. "You looked so incredibly happy, honey!"

His brows shift as he smiles. "The truth is... I've

always been intrigued to know what it's like to have a big family. Particularly one that is happy and healthy."

My heart fills with so much compassion for him upon hearing that. "Well, my family are now your family, honey. Always remember that, and they love you too! Even Diego!"

He kisses the back of my hands, not once, but twice. I watch his lashes flickering as he studies my face. "You are a gift to me, Natalia."

"I love you, honey." I kiss his sweet lips. "Each day, you grow more handsome to me."

He chuckles so deeply that I feel it underneath my skin. And there, I fall fast asleep, dreaming of how ardently that I'm becoming enraptured by him.

40. Flowers

Julieta's tears wet my face as she embraces me with all of her strength at my first exhibition opening. "Oh Natty, I am so so proud of you, my dearest. Mamá would be delighted to see this!"

"I'm so proud of you too, Tally." Diego beams, standing proudly next to Francesco. "Come here," he says, giving me one of those brotherly bear hugs which squeeze the tears right out of me.

The bright white flash from Maria's phone almost blinds my eyes as she takes a picture of Diego squishing me in his arms.

"Your work is beautiful, Natalia." Maria takes hold of my hand. "They remind me of mamá's work, full of flowers! I'm sorry for all of those times that I doubted you. I know that you're going to go so far, isn't she Fran?"

Francesco's eyes light up in amusement, which I

guess is due to his annoying new nickname. "Yes, she will."

"Even the kids are inspired by you," Joseph begins. "Little Rosa is always getting her paints out saying she wants to be you when she grows up."

"What! Really?" I ask, now thinking of Sofia and the rest of the kids back home. I hope they are okay with the new babysitter. This is my first time away from Sofia, and I feel terrible for it.

"Oh yes, dearest!" Julieta confirms. "Bless them, my sweethearts."

I sometimes wonder what my father's reaction would be if he were actually here to see this.

Would he apologize?

It stings me to think that there's a part of me that wishes he was here. Not necessarily because I miss him, but because I have yearned so long to prove him wrong.

"We love you, Nat. We'll always support you, remember that." Diego winks at me. Unexpectedly, he then put his large arm around Francesco in such a rough, boisterous and brotherly manner. "And you know what, I'm pleased you have this one by your side to support you with this."

The room illuminates with Diego's white grin as we all burst out in laughter. Francesco included. Something then draws Joseph's attention, which brings them all to discuss light matters that I can now barely hear as my attention is fully absorbed in the surroundings of the exhibition.

This is utterly crazy!

My dreams have actually truly bloomed to fruition! It's so beautifully unreal, I want to cherish this moment forever.

I journey throughout the gallery again, which brings me to come across one of my favorite pieces. I stop to admire it, but then I feel taken back by the memories that it carries. Isn't it funny how one picture can resurrect memories that you buried long ago? It's a painting of a flower that I took of a photograph of in the rose garden, the very same day I met Gideon. Tears stab my eyes, before I blink them away again.

"This is an excellent piece," a familiar voice speaks beside me.

"Thank you," I reply, but not a second passes, before I realize who it is. "Gee?"

My heart bursts out of my chest as I turn to see Gideon standing beside me. His demeanor, calm and collected as his passionate eyes dance over my painting. He's wearing the messy bun that I love so much, with a white collar shirt, khaki pants and brown loafers. Honestly, I'm overwhelmed by what I'm seeing right now. Never in a million years would I have expected to see Gideon again so soon.

"Hello Nat," he says, almost grinning. A thin film of water cover his eyes. "Look at this, look at *you*! You did it, Natalia. I always knew you could."

I blink many times as fast as I can, not only to confirm that I'm not just seeing things, but to also blink the rising tears away. I wrap my arms joyfully around him and hold him tight as much as I can.

"Gideon, I truly wouldn't be here without you. I would have never made it this far, without you. You have been a massive help, my constant support... the most wonderful friend that I have ever had." I wipe my tears away with the back of my hand before they drop on his shirt.

"Nat," his voice wobbles.

I gently let go of him and step back to look into his wet eyes. "What is it Gee?"

"Gideon? Gideon Knight? Wow, you're here!" Maria gasps loudly with excitement and leaps into Gideon's arms. He hugs her back, and his eyes glisten as they glide over her.

"Maria," he greets her, politely. "It's brilliant to see you. How are you doing?"

"Great, thanks!" she exclaims, leaving her hand lingering within his for a second too long.

I clear my throat. "Ummm, you both know each other?"

"Oh gosh, yeah!" Maria grins widely with genuine happiness. "Do you remember when I had to go abroad for one year during college? Well, Gideon and I met here in London through some good friends of ours. It's been so long, Gideon! What, like eight years now?"

How can a dream quickly turn into a nightmare?

Gideon's cheeks become blossom with red. "Yes. It's been a while, Maria."

"You know, we should meet up over the next few days if you're free? I'm leaving in a week."

An awkward silence creates an uncomfortable distance between us and I'm panicking. I'm not quite sure whether to stay or walk elsewhere. My eyes travel throughout the exhibition to see if Francesco has caught on that Gideon's here, but he still seems thoroughly engaged in conversation with Diego.

Thank God.

I miss Gideon's response as Maria hugs him one last time and suddenly dashes off toward Julieta.

"Why didn't you tell me that you knew my sister?" I ask him.

"I didn't know that Maria was your sister, Nat. How could I have possibly known that? You've never shown me a photograph of her before."

"I guess so…" I breathe. "Gideon, can we talk somewhere privately? I feel I must apologize to you over how things unfolded between us…"

"Nat, trust me. It's alright. We don't have to talk about it. This is your day, and I came here to celebrate you."

"But Gee, I have to speak to you. I need to! I don't know when I will get this chance again."

His eyes fall to the ground as he releases the quietest sigh. Then upon looking at the painting again, he meets eyes with me. "Alright. I'll be waiting outside the entrance."

I stride toward Francesco and Diego who both seemed entirely engrossed within their conversation to even realize that I'm standing with them for a moment.

"How are you, piccola mia?" Francesco asks me. "You look startled."

"What's up?" Diego asks with a slightly lifted chin. Whenever Diego does that, it usually indicates that he suspects something is off. "Everything alright?"

I let out a deep breath to try and regulate my crazy heart rate. "Yes... no. No, I'm not alright. Well, I am. Gideon's here."

"Excuse me?" Francesco's sharp eyes narrow in disbelief.

"Yeah! I know, right? And I only just found out that he is an acquaintance or friend or whatever you want to call it of Maria!"

"That artist dude?" Diego laughs humorlessly under his breath. "Oh, Lord. This will be good."

"What's the matter dearest?" Julieta comes around after hearing what Diego had just said.

Diego raises his brows and sighs but says nothing at all. Francesco's jaw ticks, and Julieta's eyes hold mine with an uneasy look that can tell what's going down.

"Gideon is here. He came to support me, which is a lovely surprise! But I just came to let you guys know that if you're looking for me, I'll be outside having a catch up with him."

I keep my eyes firmly locked on Francesco for his reaction, but he refuses make eye contact with me.

Julieta is frozen speechless, and Diego for some reason looks silently amused yet not surprised.

"Alright," Francesco breathes. He then glances at his watch before directing his attention back at me. "If he doesn't bring you back within ten minutes, I'll come out and meet you myself."

"Fine," I mutter, as I turn to hurry outside. For I don't want another second to lose.

Quickly, I step outside, eagerly looking around for Gideon through the congested city. but he's nowhere to be seen.

My heart rate boosts up a notch as a result.

Did he leave?

"Hello," he whispers smoothly from behind me. He's leaning against the wall by the entrance, with his hands in his pockets and the most beautiful smile spread across his face. "You look worried."

"I was afraid that you left!"

His chocolate brows briefly tug together before resting again. "I would never leave you like that."

"Shall we go for a walk?" I ask, wanting to get away from the entrance as much as possible.

We begin walking, though no words leave our lips throughout the the first minute or so.

"Gideon, can you pinch me please?"

His head rears back slightly as he chuckles. "You're not dreaming, Nat."

"How did you know what I was thinking?"

"Because I know you."

His words bring me to an abrupt stop in the middle of the street. He's right, he does know me, because he's my most treasured friend. I would have never made it this far without him.

"Gideon," I begin, staring wholeheartedly into his eyes, "I am so terribly sorry that I neglected our friendship the way we did. Even the way that I treated you… it wasn't the best way to handle it. Every day I carry this weight of regret. I didn't want what we had to end that way."

"Natalia, I would never want you to carry any kind of heaviness because of me."

"But I do!" I tear up. "It's not your fault, though. It's mine. I should've handled it better. I feel the pain of it every time we speak or meet, and I wish I didn't have to feel it so bad. It haunts me, Gee."

His face becomes stained with the deepest defeat. "What can I do to make it better?"

"I don't know…" I croak. "There's a part of me that wants you to hold me, and tell me that you've forgiven me and that we can be friends again. But I know that can't happen."

"Natalia…"

"So… we can't be close friends again?"

"That can't happen, Nat. I don't think it's a wise decision for us to make."

"Why?" I sob, quietly.

A quick, gentle sigh escapes his mouth. "I liked you more than a friend would, Natalia. I always have, and I am convinced that there will always be a part of me that cares about you. Because of that, we have to do what is sensible."

"But Gideon... are you sure that we can't keep in contact more often? We never speak anymore, at all."

Silence bleeds so deeply into my heart as we just stand there, absolutely still. He has said his part, and I have said mine. And from here, I don't know what else to say.

"Nat, I'm still here. You understand that I'm always a phone call away. However, I believe that going forward it's probably better for us to refrain from being as we once were. I only came today to celebrate your achievements. Your joy is my joy. Though my intentions, I assure you, were not to make you upset upon me being here. I fully comprehend that this exhibition means a lot you."

"You really think that distance is best for us?" I croak, stepping nearer to close the gap between us.

"Yes," he says, decisively. "I believe that boundaries are necessary."

"Gideon." I tremble with tears, almost feeling my knees shake. I can barely stand. Through which, I hold on to him and bury my face in his chest as he wraps me close. "I'm so sorry."

"Hey, don't apologize," he says gently with such comfort.

"Gee?" I whisper.

"Yeah?"

"Will I ever see you again?" I ask him, as we stop back outside the entrance door.

He looks at me silently with weary eyes, before the door suddenly bursts open.

"Time's up," Francesco mutters in a way that fails to mask his frustration. He strides with poise toward me, nodding at Gideon as a greeting without a word.

I feel as though my skin is being ripped apart from me and it's painful, because I hold Gideon so close. It's utterly heartbreaking to walk away from a man that I found such a loving friendship in.

I have no choice but to force the tears away. "Later, Gee. Thanks for coming."

Francesco puts his arm around me as if to shield me from Gideon, as well as guide me quickly inside.

At the last second I hear Gideon respond, "Bye, Nat. I'm so proud of you."

I try to tip toe to peek back at him just above Francesco's arm, but I fail to see his face as he disappears into the distance. Instantly afterward, I'm met with the exhibition hall being filled with much more people than earlier. Francesco is quick to lead me back to my happy family, who continue to remain celebrating exceedingly over my new accomplishments. But for the rest of the night, I know that I won't be able to help but think about Gideon.

41. Exhibit

Besides the bittersweet encounter with Gideon, the exhibition opening is going as splendid as I could ever dream. The turnout is wonderful, Angelina and the gallery managers are literally as happy as I am. I never thought that I could be this overjoyed in my life, ever. Neither did I envision my dreams to be fulfilled this way at all, for the path that I desired was much different to what I expected. Being a mother and in a serious relationship was not on my to do list, but regardless, I wouldn't have it any other way. This is all perfect.

The gallery is beginning to get busier, with so much traffic of art lovers and collectors spread throughout, gazing with wonder upon my artwork. There are oceans of sounds all about. From roars of sweet laughter to conversations, and the scent of champagne filling the air.

ARDENT

Though suddenly, all hell breaks loose.

"You fucking home-wrecker!" I hear a female voice crying out near the entrance.

Silence breaks through the gallery, with every head turning uneasily in the direction of the voice. The female voice then shouts the same thing again, and this time, lots of people draw toward the scene.

"She's still fucking my husband!" The feminine voice appears again, and so many people begin to take out their phones to record whatever is going on near the doors.

"Honey," I whisper, grabbing on to Francesco with concern. "Please don't tell me that it's her."

"Come, darling." Francesco's large hand holds my mine firmly like a glove as his eyes narrow toward the direction of the chaos. "Let me take you to your family. I will take care of this."

We swiftly stride toward my family who seem to have absolutely no fear regarding the situation, other than Julieta. Francesco leaves us, then squeezes his way through the crowd. Diego puts his arm around me and tells me not to worry. Julieta's arm is linking through Joseph's, and Maria's focus is still glued to her phone.

"What in the world going on?" I think aloud.

All at once, I see two gentlemen from security rushing through the dense crowds. I hear screaming and gasps that pinch my anxiety to heighten even more. Automatically, I move forward toward the crowd, but Diego gently tugs me back.

"Natalia, you little whore! I'm addressing you!" Daisy's voice haunts me so terribly at this point that all of the blood within my body feels as though it has frozen cold.

What is she doing here?

Lots of heads within the crowd glance back toward me, sticking their wide eyes onto the surface of my skin. It's uncomfortable, I feel horribly sick to the core.

Where on earth is Francesco?

I need to go home to Sofia.

Multitudes of whisperings are going on, and even pictures and videos being taken. I feel the utter sting of embarrassment, refusing to leave me while I remain the focus of many people's attention. I keep my eyes forward, looking out for any sign of Francesco, desperate to tell him that I need to go home. But there's also a part of me that can't bear to look behind me in the face of my siblings. Even Diego who is standing right next to me. I can feel his attention on me so strongly, but I don't yield.

I'm so ashamed by all of this.

I swallow in panic, not knowing what to do. But then something takes over me. I rip myself out of Diego's arm and speed straight through the tight crowd of what feels like a pack of sardines. Then that's when I see her, fighting and growling with a large knife in her hands, refusing to submit to the authority of the security guards. Francesco is helping them with the situation, but he looks pissed off as ever. Although, I feel like the sight of him here is only making Daisy react worse. Her eyes then immediately grab me, and she cries out hysterically.

Diego, Joseph, Julieta and Maria are quick to hurry by my side, barely making it through the commotion within the crowd behind us.

"You're a disgraceful woman!" Daisy cries, so hard that her fair skin turns crimson. "Why won't you let my husband and I be together? You little shit! Francesco and I belong together, but you ruined it, you ruined our family. You had a baby with *my* husband, you devilish woman. I hate you. I hate you! I will end you for this! I. Will. End. You!"

She's not even married to him anymore. And yes, I've seen the divorce papers. I've also met with Francesco's legal team myself during this process. So why on earth is Daisy still so damn delusional about all of this? I want to scream at her and tell her that Francesco is no longer her husband, yet every cell in my body is hardened like ice. I feel so numb at this point I can't even shed a tear. Nothing is coming out.

"Natty?" Julieta whispers, softly.

"Nat!" Maria's sharp voice cuts right through me.

Diego is silent, and I'm glad that he is, because I know that any word that comes out of his mouth at this point will have enough power to make me cry.

Literally all I can do is just stand here, stunned, feeling utterly stupid and hopeless while watching

Francesco on the phone to what seems like the cops. The guards struggle as they remove her and her swiping knife from the building. All I can think about is how much I really need to get home to my daughter, immediately.

The gallery seems to be much quieter after Daisy was finally arrested. Too quiet, in fact. The crowd begins to dissipate, and people start to leave as soon as. Out of nowhere, I then catch the glimpse of the gallery manager who's staring at me in shock. Disappointment marks her face, which brings me to notice the sparkle of a ring on her marriage finger. She's looking at me like what just happened hit close to home.

"Natty," Julieta whispers, placing both hands over my shoulders. "Natty... who was that lady?"

"Natalia, please tell us that all she said wasn't true," Maria says, sharply.

When I look at my Joseph and my sisters' faces, their expression on their faces says it all. Immense disappointment, but they don't know the full story. It's not my fault. Yet that's when I notice that Diego is no longer here.

"Wait, where is Diego?" I ask them.

Julieta and Maria look at me with an awkward look on their face. "Outside," they say.

"Outside doing what?" I tremble.

Julieta's eyes fill with a sting of pain. "He's having a word Francesco... he's not happy, Natty."

I almost fall to my knees, but my sisters hold me up. Phone cameras are being pointed at me, left right and center.

"Right," Maria snaps. "Natalia, we're taking you home."

It's crazy how a blissful dream can easily turn into a nightmare. Like lightning, within the blink of an eye, it will surprise you out of nowhere. I knew that it was all too good to be true. How stupid I feel for believing that yesterday would have gone smoothly.

This morning I have even more issues to deal with. For upon waking up, I instantly receive several notifications from the news app, informing me with heartbreaking headlines:

'Natalia Garcia, failed artist turned Francesco Giordano's mistress.'

'Unfaithful husband, Francesco Giordano, has a baby girl with 25 year old artist, Natalia Garcia.'

'Francesco Giordano has a child with sugar baby, Natalia Garcia.'

Before I even have a chance to sink further into despair, I hear Francesco in another room, arguing so loudly with someone over the phone in Italian. I can't even be bothered to get up and see what's happening, because I've honestly just lost all the strength within me to keep fighting. But then my phone pings with a text notification, and then again, and once more after that. I check to see who it is, and it's Gideon. He's asking me if I'm alright, and he's asking if I can give him a call as he's worried about me, but I just don't have it in me right now.

Sofia's voice then muffles with soft cries through the baby monitor, and my head only feels more pressured with anxiety in this moment. I manage to shrug it off anyway, forcing myself to put my issues behind me to focus on my daughter. Through which, I burst out of the bedroom door and make my way to the nursery.

"Natalia," Francesco breathes, striding fast toward me in the hallway. He tries to hug me but I step back. "My darling, I am sorry. I am so fucking sorry—"

"I didn't want this!" I cry. "I didn't want to be known to be a home-wrecker, sugar baby, gold digger or whatever other horrible things they're saying about me!"

I let him hold me. "I know, Natalia. I know—"

"Francesco, my dreams are fucking shattered! The exhibition turned out to be a complete mess!"

"We will recover from this, Natalia."

"How are you so certain?"

"My publicist is working on it, and the legal team and I are looking to press charges. We have one of the most efficient lawyers in the country behind us, darling. He's working on the case."

"That's great, honey, but that doesn't take away the fact that I'm marked forever as some kind of money hungry home-wrecker! What is your mother going to think about all of this? Gosh, thinking of her reaction makes me feel even more nervous."

Sofia is crying even louder now, and every nerve within me is reaching overload.

"I'll take care of Sofia," he says.

I gaze into Francesco's eyes and come to notice that he is also absolutely shattered too.

"What did Diego say to you last night? You didn't come home until late."

He sighs. "I told him the truth, Natalia."

"I bet you he was really pissed. I feel so bad!"

"You are not to blame concerning this matter."

"But honestly, how are we going to move forward from this, honey? The whole world hates us, even my brother."

"He doesn't hate you, baby. I will do everything in my power to sort this shit out. I'm sorry that you're having to deal with this mess. I'll fix this and deal with the issue at hand."

"I trust you." I sniffle, crying into his chest.

"Let me take care of Sofia. Get some rest."

He kisses me once with a passionate embrace, then strides swiftly toward the nursery.

There are only a few days left before my family are due to return home. So this evening, Francesco and I invite them over for dinner. They agree, and as the time swiftly approaches, I spend the late afternoon adorning the dining room as beautifully and presentable as I can. Betty, who I guess you could say has found much joy in becoming a new nanny, is playing with Sofia in the living room, while Claudia and I position the polished plates and cutlery neatly across the table.

I enjoy helping out in the house, actually feeling as though I am contributing to the household. I've also found that through this, my relationship with the team here is improving significantly.

After checking over the dining room, I check in with Giuseppe regarding the food choices for the meal. Everything is going smoothly so far. I just hope that when my siblings come, all will be well.

The doorbell rings, and I hear Ben open it. He greets them, and they return the gesture. I hear them saying hello to Sofia and Betty in the living room on their way to the dining room. Sofia's cute little noises in the distance ushers away my anxiety for a moment.

"Are you ready?" Francesco leans against the kitchen door.

"Yes," I respond, straightening out my dress.

I hold his hand as we make our way to the dining room. I feel so bad for him. He looks just as tired as I am right now.

"Hello..." I greet my siblings who are sitting ready at the table, Francesco does the same.

An awkward silence follows.

"Hello dearests" Julieta's airy voice speaks up, nervously. "Joe and the kids are quite tired after their day at Madam Tussauds."

"Aww! No worries, Jules!"

Silence hits again.

"Hey," Maria breathes.

"How you keeping?" Diego finally asks me.

"Not too bad," I reply, while Francesco pushes my chair in for me.

He then sits down. "Thank you for coming."

"Anything for Nat," Diego says, flatly.

Ben and Dahlia then begin serving the steaming hot dinner.

"Alright, I'm sorry that I didn't tell you guys," I begin, just wanting to get it all over and done with. "I was afraid that if I did, you would not only see me differently, but Francesco too. I love this man with all my heart."

"But you're not still married now, right?" Maria asks.

"No," Francesco confirms.

She takes a mouthful of broccoli. "Gideon is pissed."

"Why on earth should he be?" I mutter. "He's got nothing to do with this, at all! And why are you in contact with him all of a sudden?"

"Obviously he's concerned because he is your best friend, Nat," she replies.

"Well, fine! I find it uncomfortable that you're talking to him already. Who messaged who first?"

"I did! Gosh, Nat... what's up with you all of a sudden? I haven't said anything to hurt you, have I?"

"Whatever!" I snap.

Diego leans forward. "Come on, Nat—"

"No, I don't understand why Maria is speaking to Gideon? Like, what are your intentions, Maria? Seriously? You saw him after eight years, that's fine! But I don't understand why you want to catch up with him—"

"If you must know, Natalia, I wanted to see how he is. But now I'm helping him find somewhere to live in LA."

"LA? What the hell for?"

I can sense that Francesco is getting frustrated right beside me, but I honestly don't care.

"There's a possible career opportunity at one of the movie studios in LA. Someone on the art team found about his work, and apparently they loved him. It's so exciting, I'd be happy to live closer to him. He's so lonely, he needs company—"

Julieta quickly rests her hand softly behind Maria's shoulder as though to quieten her down. "Maria, that's enough dearest. Don't you think?"

"Well, sorry." She sighs with a sad yet confused expression. "But then again, why should I be? Nat, Gee is your friend. You don't want him out there all alone, do you? I can help him too."

"Honestly, Maria, do whatever you want. I've got so much on my plate as it is."

"Nat, you're gonna get through this," Diego assures me. "What steps will you be taking to resolve the issue, Francesco?"

"We are pressing charges against Daisy Smith. My publicist and I are still in discussion about what steps to take regarding the media."

"As long as you make it abundantly clear," Diego's loud voice takes over the room, "that Natalia had no part in this bullshit—"

"Of course," Francesco responds, laying his hand tenderly over mine.

"But honey... are you really sure about going to the media about this? I thought we wanted to keep your marriage and everything that happened within it, private. It's painful what you went through, it's not fair for the whole world to know about this."

"It's necessary, darling."

"I commend you, Francesco dearest, for doing what is *right* rather than what is comfortable," Julieta speaks, while her hands clutch tightly on to the cutlery.

"I would do anything for Natalia," he breathes, staring lovingly into my eyes.

"So no more secrets?" Diego speaks up. "No more bullshit we need to be aware of?"

"None," he responds, firmly.

"Glad to hear it," Diego finishes his plate and leans against the chair. "Nat you're not alone in this. I'm with you. We're all with you on this."

"Thank you, Dee," I whisper.

Suddenly, he rises from his chair. "Now," he breathes. "Where's my beautiful niece? Let me give her some cuddles."

42. Piccadilly

As days pass, the news about Francesco and I within the media only end up getting worse. I've never felt so caged before, like a hamster, running on that dreadful wheel over and over tirelessly, getting absolutely nowhere. This is exactly how my heart feels recently, because looking back on the last year or so, I've often questioned myself if I've truly worked hard toward my dream of becoming an artist for nothing.

There's another text from Gideon that pops up on my phone, asking me to meet at Piccadilly Circus for seven. I ask him why. He says it's a surprise, and that it will be good for me.

I haven't been out of the house for a week now, besides going for walks in the park for Sofia. But getting fresh air this evening will do me good. Besides, I have so many questions for Gideon.

"Honey," I begin, looking at Francesco sitting at the couch from across the living room. "Umm, would you mind if I pop out for the evening?"

I've never had to ask Francesco this before.

Instantly, his brows grip together, while Sofia lays adorably on his chest. "Out? Out with who?"

"Gideon."

It only takes a second for his demeanor to switch. "I thought we dealt with this."

"We have! Francesco, I just need a break. I need to have some fresh air. Some time to myself. Just for a few hours for goodness sake, please!"

"I don't want you seeing him."

"But I'll probably never see him again. You do realize that he's moving across the world soon? Please, baby. Don't act like this."

"What the fuck do you want me to tell you? Yeah, just go and spend an evening with your little ex boyfriend while I stay in and take care of our daughter? Natalia, this is bullshit—"

"You need to watch your language around Sofia! I'm serious, Francesco."

He rolls his eyes. "Look, I'm sorry. But baby, I'm not comfortable with this."

"Francesco please let me go! Just for tonight."

"No, stop this. Don't beg me. I'm not your father, Natalia. You're free to make your own choices."

"So you're saying that I can go?"

"Do whatever the fuck you want," he murmurs.

"Honey, don't be like this. This might be my last chance to see him before he moves... but I'm also just desperate for some fresh air tonight. I barely have a social life! Please, I just need to get out the house."

His jaw ticks. "On the basis that this will be your last time seeing him, then fine. What time can I expect you home approximately?"

"Francesco... do you not trust me?"

"I do, amore. It's him that I don't trust."

"Have you not heard the conversation between Maria and I at the dinner table the other day? It clearly seems to me as though his interest has settled elsewhere! And that's a good thing, isn't it, honey? You have absolutely nothing to worry about. Just trust me, baby."

He pauses. "Where will you be meeting? He can't meet you here."

"Piccadilly Circus."

"To go where, exactly?"

"I don't know, he said it's a surprise."

Francesco rears his head back slightly as though overwhelmed. "Natalia—"

"I'll try and be back by ten, the latest."

"What time is he expecting you?"

"Seven."

"Peter is on annual leave," he murmurs. "I will take you. Betty will have to watch Sofia."

"No, honey! I promise you that I'm fine. I want to just go out by myself for once. And you know, take the tube? It's so quick and convenient—"

"Natalia, tell me you're not that stupid."

"Why should I be stupid for wanting to feel human again?" I whisper, not wanting to wake Sofia.

"You forget that the whole damn world is not only watching me, but they're now also watching you too, as my girl, and the mother of my daughter. Some of these people within the public are severely unstable. Brutal, even. I'm not comfortable with you going out alone."

Silence grips me for a while. "I honestly don't care. I know I'll be fine, Francesco."

His eyes squint toward me. "You don't care? Do you have any idea what could happen to you going out all by yourself?"

"I'm going to get ready." I sigh, leaving the room.

"You could've at least informed me beforehand, for security purposes."

Instantly, I halt at the doorway. "I don't need a bodyguard, Francesco. As we've both learned, they can be truly useless anyway! Besides, I need to feel normal again!"

He cuts his eye at me, then immediately calls Betty. Within a minute she enters the room.

"Yes, good evening," her elderly, wobbly voice shakes. "May I help you sir?"

"Yes, please," he gives her a polite smile, but I know he's pissed deep down. "Unfortunately, Betty, something urgent has come up. I'll need to take Natalia somewhere shortly. Would you mind watching Sofia, please?"

"Of course, Mr Giordano. I'll take the lovely little angel." Betty takes Sofia in her arms and instantly heads toward the nursery.

Francesco waits until he hears the door shut, then he takes steady steps toward me. "Natalia, nothing about *us* or this family will ever be normal. When will you understand that?"

"But why not? I know you're this celebrity billionaire business mogul that everyone worships, but it can't hold us back from living, Francesco!"

"Listen very carefully to me, you are not taking the tube. I am driving you instead."

I have no words to respond to him, because it's like whatever I say completely goes over his head. Through which, I leave the living room and just get ready, eager to speak to Gideon and find out what's going on with him.

Francesco takes me by the hand as we walk from the car to Piccadilly Circus. It pains me to say that he was right. Staring eyes and pointed fingers surround us from every angle. Cameras flash and a couple of women scream Francesco's name in the distance.

"Honey, will you be okay getting back to the car by yourself?" I ask him.

"Natalia, don't worry about me."

"I'm so sorry," I whisper. "I never thought it would be this bad. I've never really had this much attention before."

"Never mind, darling. It's done now."

Piccadilly Circus comes into full view, and it doesn't take me long to see Gideon standing there in his classic sage button-down shirt with dark pants. He looks at me and waves, but his face looks as pale as a ghost the moment his eyes become attached to Francesco.

"Gideon," I greet him. "It's so lovely to see you again."

I want to hug him, but I can't. Not with Francesco still holding my hand so firmly. Not with all these people staring at all of us.

"You too, Nat… I didn't know we were having an additional person to the party."

"No," Francesco mutters. "I am here to ensure Natalia gets to you safely. Be here by ten, I'll need to collect her."

"Actually, it'll best if you come before then."

"What time, approximately?"

"Nine, if possible."

"Done."

"Wait… Gideon, two hours? That's not enough! Can't we spend a bit more time with each other?"

"I can't unfortunately, Nat."

"Why ever not?"

"I… I have to meet someone later on."

"Your sisters? Are they in the city?" I ask.

Francesco chuckles without humor beside me. "I think he's talking about Maria, darling."

I glance at Francesco who seems subtly amused. "Gideon..."

"Look, I don't like to leave Sofia alone without us for too long. I'll get going," Francesco tells me, now planting a kiss on my forehead. "Gideon, be here with Natalia by nine. Don't make me wait."

"Of course," Gideon responds, looking irritable.

I watch Francesco walk away in the distance as he remains the center of almost every woman's attention on the street.

"We need to talk," I whisper, now staring into Gideon's soft emerald eyes. "But first, where are we going? What's this surprise?"

"Jazz bar." His dimples show. "Something to uplift up your spirit after a hard few days. You'll love it, Nat. I'll lead the way."

The jazz bar is tremendously lively, filled with vibrance and splendor, so loud that I even heard it from across the street before we entered. Gideon and I are sitting at the table, admiring the artists play their masterpiece. There's an audience all around, and luckily, I'm not being stared at in here. Everyone is so relaxed and so at ease. The music is invigorating, and my soul feels refreshed. This is exactly what I needed.

When the music softens with smooth jazz piano, I lean in closer to Gideon. "I recently heard that there's a possibility of you moving to LA?"

"Maria told you?" he asks, staring at me with confusion marked all over his face. "I'm sorry, Nat. Part of the reason why I invited you out here tonight is because I wanted to inform you myself."

"Gee, I thought you would remain settled in the Cotswolds? I also assumed that traveling wasn't your preference right now as your sisters are your priority."

"Indeed, they still are absolutely my priority," he clarifies, now clearing his throat. "But there's an opportunity for me to work in the art department for a well-known film studio. It's a big deal, and I think it would help me find more financial stability for my family."

"But what about your house at the Cotswolds? And what about your sisters, what are their thoughts on this?"

"It will always be there. I can't give that up, it's been in my family for generations. My sisters and I will return here hopefully a couple of times a year during the holiday breaks. Kitty is pleased to go. You know how she can be very open minded. Phoebe, however, is taking her time getting used to change. I know it will work out though, Nat. It's the best thing, for all of us."

"Well," I exhale. "I'm proud of you, Gee."

"Natalia," he breathes. "There's something else that I need to tell you."

"What? I hate when you say this, it makes me

so scared! It's rare that you need to tell me things."

"Don't be scared, Nat. But you really should be informed that Maria will be helping me look for homes in America. Do you mind?"

"Umm... of course I don't mind," I lie.

He releases a breath of release. "Thanks. I appreciate any help that I can get in order for the girls and I to get settled. Maria has been supportive over the last few days."

A pause lifts between us, and my heart can't help but want to speak about what I've always wondered.

"Gee..."

"Yes, Nat?"

"I know that I keep repeating myself, but I genuinely don't understand why all of this has happened. Those beautiful encounters we had, all for our friendship to just... end up apart? I know we spoke about this previously, so I'm sorry if I'm getting irritating, but I think I'm finding it hard to let go."

"Nat..." He sighs, sorrowfully. "As hard as it is, letting go is part of life. We know this, don't we? Losing our loved ones... Sometimes, we have to trust that we meet people for a reason, even if it's just for a season, you know? How can I make this process easier for you?"

"You can't, Gee." I sniffle. "You can't make it better, but I also don't want you to feel bad or pressured in any way because all this time you have given me the choice to do what I desired to do. You never forced me to choose you, and you never stopped me when I chose Francesco. It's only right that you have the freedom to make your own choices too, even if it's uncomfortable for me. I love you, Gideon. You're my best friend. I'm convinced that you're absolutely heaven sent."

"I care about you, Nat. But things can't be how they used to be between us... you know that, right? With family and children involved, I think it's sensible for us to establish boundaries going forward. Don't you?"

"Yes..." My voice croaks. "I do."

"I wanted to take you out here tonight to not only inform you of the news, but to also remind you that you're not alone in this current situation that you're facing. All those lies within the media, they don't know you. But I do, your family does, and we all love you to pieces. I hope being here and experiencing this jazz bar helped a little."

"It did, Gee. I needed it!"

"Thank you for coming," he says, smiling.

"I'm so glad I met you," I whisper through my tears. "I'm going to miss you when you leave."

I rest my head on his shoulder, blinking away the tears, enjoying one of the last few and rare moments that we will ever share with each other alone.

As Gideon and I quietly head back to Piccadilly

Circus, Francesco is already waiting there. He's swamped with a group of women who are taking pictures with him and bombarding him with conversation.

"Do you ever get tired of this?" Gideon asks.

"Yep, always. It's not often Francesco and I go out in public, and this is the reason why."

Finally, Francesco breaks free. "You're late," he directs to Gideon.

Gideon glances at his watch. "It's what, three minutes past nine?"

Francesco pays him no mind and looks at me. "Are you alright, Natalia?"

"Yeah, why wouldn't I be?"

"I'm just making sure, darling."

"Where are you off to now, Gee?"

"A late dinner—"

"With Natalia's sister," Francesco puts bluntly.

A fair wash of pink covers Gideon's cheeks.

"Well," I start, wanting to avoid a scene. "Have a lovely night, Gee. I need to be with Sofia... so we better get going, right honey?"

"Right," Francesco mutters under his breath.

"See you, Nat." Gideon gives me an embrace like it may be the last one for a long time. I hug him back, and when I come to step back I see horror marked all over Francesco's face. "Thanks for coming out tonight. I hope it helped in someway."

"No, thank you! It was just what I needed. I feel so much better since this evening. Bye, Gee! Tell

Maria that I said hi. She's leaving tomorrow, isn't she?"

"Yes, I believe so."

"We need to get going," Francesco murmurs, as greater crowds begin to recognize him.

"Of course, honey," I tell him.

"Is this it then?" he then randomly mutters to Gideon. "You're finally going to leave us be and move elsewhere?"

Gideon clears his throat. "An opportunity has come forward in the United States, so yes, I will be relocating."

"Perfect." Francesco's lips spread thinly into an insincere smile. "Pleased to hear it. You understand the importance of boundaries, don't you? I can't have anyone else fucking with my family."

Gideon makes it clear that he understands, but Francesco seems unconvinced. To avoid a scene, I quickly say my goodbyes to Gideon one more. As I do, I just watch those serene, emerald eyes becoming stained with such sorrow. It hurts, but I'm also glad that we've settled into boundaries and how we'll be moving forward in our friendship. It only confirms to me what I have always believed all along. Love alone is not always enough to sustain certain relationships, but I'm hoping this new beginning will be the start of something better, not only beneficial for the both of us, but also our families too.

43. Union

On the first Sunday of November, I wake up early to get Sofia and I ready for church. I haven't stepped foot in a church for over twenty years since my mother passed, but at this point in my life, I feel like I've reached an all time low and I'm in need of some hope.

"Where are you going?" Francesco mumbles in the doorway, rubbing his eyes and still waking up from his sleep while I get Sofia ready in the nursery.

"St Margaret's. Service starts at ten and I don't want to be late, so I figured that I'd get us ready extra early. And no, don't worry, this won't be happening every week. Just today."

His brows tug together. "You did not think to inform me of this?"

"No."

"Tell me why."

"Well..." I huff softly. "I know that you have a difficult relationship with religion, because of your family and all. I didn't want to pressure you into coming. I only thought of it last night anyway."

"I'm not comfortable with you making decisions like this without me."

"What do you mean by decisions like this?"

"Planning to leave the property without myself or security. Introducing faith into Sofia's life without even discussing that with me first. Natalia, you are aware of my concerns about these matters."

"I'm sorry... I didn't know that you'd be that annoyed about me bringing Sofia to such a short service!"

"It's not about the duration of whatever fucking service it is, Natalia. It's about her safety and clarity of mind if you decide to keep bringing her to a church as she gets older. I don't trust some of the religious people out there—"

"Baby, I understand the reason why you feel the way you do. I mean... what your father did... he twisted scripture for his selfish reasons. That was a reflection of him, not God."

"Fucking hell, we could debate about this all day," he complains, rubbing his tired eyes.

"Give it a chance, honey," I whisper. "I promise you that not all religious people are like your father... do you trust me?" I ask him, resting my palm on his cheek.

"Yes," he whispers, gazing into my eyes. "I do,

baby. But I have reasons for my concerns."

"I know you do," I whisper. "It's trauma that you're dealing with, honey. I can't force you to come because I'd understand if you don't want to, but please consider trying. It's only just this week that I want to visit. After all that's gone on recently, I want to go somewhere that stands for peace... and then I won't feel so alone. Please come with me, Francesco."

He pauses. "Alright, baby... just this time."

"Really?" I brighten, and he nods. "Honey, this is perfect. We can go together as a family!"

"Yes, princess." He kisses my forehead, and Sofia's too. "Have you both eaten?"

"Yeah, I fed her first thing. You know how she can be." I giggle. "Can't keep our little madam for too long."

He chuckles. "Alright, I will get ready."

"Okay, I'll pack Sofia's bag in the meantime while she watches *Peppa Pig*. Thank you so much honey, for coming with us."

"We're a family now," he breathes. "You come first." He softly brushes Sofia's chubby cheek with his thumb before leaving.

I switch on the television and sit Sofia in her little wiggly chair. Lily instantly sits in a loaf beside her with a loud and adorable purr. Upon getting her bag out, I mentally tick off my list of essentials. Wipes, diapers, blankets. The list is endless, really.

But Sofia makes me feel a way I've never felt before. She could keep me busy all day, not having a minute of opportunity to focus on my art and I would never complain, because I live for her now. To love her, care for her and protect her. There's a new sense of purpose that flourishes within you when becoming a mother, and I know that ever since I have been given this gift of a child, I will never be the same again.

St Margaret's church is even more glorious in person than I thought it to be. The moment I step in, I'm honestly overwhelmed with an immediate wave of serenity and quietness to the soul. There is an abundance of heavenly beauty and splendor that exudes throughout the church. The architecture is absolutely outstanding, clearly striking divine. Tall ceilings, beautiful sculptures and stained-glass windows of the most mesmerizing religious art is utterly breathtaking.

Once service starts, it passes by so quickly that I don't wish for it to end. After an hour of singing peaceful hymns and listening to a lovely sermon by the reverend, the service is over. Being here is truly so refreshing to me.

Francesco, Sofia and I head toward the exit, passing by the reverend who is expressing his thanks to the visitors just by the exit.

"God bless you, thank you for coming," he tells us, shaking Francesco's hand.

"It was... an interesting service," Francesco replies, sternly.

"Yes, it was," I happily add. "And what you mentioned about the importance of forgiveness really touched my heart. Thank you, reverend."

"It's a pleasure," he responds, politely. "And what have we here?" He smiles, now gesturing to Sofia. "What a beautiful little one! A gift from heaven."

"Yes, she is." Francesco rejoices over Sofia like a proud father, and I can't stop grinning about it.

"May your family and your union be blessed, in Christ's name." The reverend nods and shakes our hands once more. "Grow in grace."

Once we say our goodbyes, we step outside into the fresh air and sun.

"Wow! That was wonderful, wasn't it honey? I haven't been to a church in years! I completely forgot what it was like. Did you notice that we weren't being stared at like crazy in there?"

"Yes, I noticed," he responds.

"How are you feeling?"

"Perfect, with you. How are you, amore?"

"Serene."

He holds me close and kisses Sofia and I. "That's all I could ask for."

Since it's Giuseppe's day off on Sundays, I decide to cook Francesco and I some seafood paella. He loves it. He loves it so much that he requested for me to cook it again next Sunday! There's something different about today. The cozy atmosphere of our home, and our relationship in general. Truly, there is so much peace. A heavenly kind of serenity we haven't felt in such a long time.

Later in the evening, I decide to relax for a while after putting Sofia to bed. I've been reading *Sense and Sensibility* within the library, and as hours pass by, I realize that Francesco hasn't even watched sports today, like he does most Sundays.

That's very strange.

I get up and search for him to find out what he's doing, only to find him in the new study with his head down in his computer.

"Sweetie," I greet him, massaging his shoulders.

"How are you, piccola mia?"

I lean in and kiss his neck that smells perfect with oud. "What are you up to, honey?"

"I wrote something," he responds, now clearing his throat. "A statement, regarding all the shit that's gone on the last week."

"A statement? Why a statement?"

"My team advised me to get someone to write it up from scratch, but I'd rather do the draft and they can polish it from there. We think it's the best way to start sharing the truth."

"Actually, that makes sense. May I read it?"

"Of course. You're just in time, darling."

His eyes glisten over me as I sit on his lap to

read what he's written. It reads:

'Over the course of this past week, a woman's false and repulsive claims have severely altered the lives of not only my family, but also those around us whom we love.

Daisy Smith's claims concerning Natalia Garcia are false, yet complex. It is my aim within this public statement to share with you the truth regarding the status of my relationship with Ms Daisy Smith, and reveal to you my clear intentions moving forward with my partner, Natalia Garcia.

First, it is imperative for me to clarify that I am no longer married to Ms Daisy Smith. As Natalia and I initially entered into a relationship, I kept all things pertaining to my relationship history hidden out of fear of losing her as the woman that I love.

Natalia had no knowledge of any matters between myself and Daisy Smith. For that, I, Francesco Giordano, take full responsibility in admitting that I was entirely in the wrong.

Secondly, my marriage with Daisy Smith had deteriorated over five years ago. We separated due to personal matters that I don't deem necessary to share. Over the course of the last few years, Ms Smith and I have gone back and forth regarding settling a divorce. It has been my aim to part ways with Daisy for a matter of years, but working with her on a daily basis did not made it easy to navigate through.

When Natalia entered my life, I fell in love with her more fervent than I have ever known before. The passion that I carry for her is something that I never knew was possible, and the thought of me losing her over the disputes with Daisy troubled me.

It was only months into my relationship with Natalia that Daisy Smith sought to inform her that we were still legally married. Once again, I'd like to make it abundantly clear that Natalia obtained no knowledge of my marriage with Ms Smith beforehand. In this difficult situation, I accept the blame for not being honest with the woman I love. This situation has enabled me to learn from this and move forward as I aim to grow in maturity.

Natalia and I welcomed our daughter in June, and my partner has been the most devoted mother that anyone can ask for. I love this woman with all my being, and she is the most honorable and resilient person that I have ever known. It has been thoroughly displeasing to hear about the appalling news about my partner that is spiraling through the media. I accept that there may be opinions concerning this matter, due to my faults. But Natalia has no part in this, nor should any blame be placed on her. All who have known her are aware that she is a woman of dignity, integrity, kindness and grace, who deserves to live just as freely and peacefully as anyone else does. Therefore, I write this statement, to clarify any misunderstandings regarding the upsetting headlines that are affecting my family.

Once again, I take full responsibility for my actions,

and it is my aim to learn from my faults and improve as a human being.

Francesco Giordano.'

I read over the statement twice with tears flowing out from my eyes. Every word that he writes is filled with such conviction and sincerity. Despite the mistakes that he has made over this past year, I'm so proud to call him my man.

"Francesco, this is perfect. It's beautiful, the way you speak of me. You write well, honey! I do hope that one day you would consider writing a book of some sort. A memoir... perhaps?"

He chuckles in response. "I love you, Natalia."

"I love you too, baby!" I cry, molding myself in his embrace. "I have good feeling that we'll be moving forward from here."

He gazes lovingly into my eyes. "I won't rest until you and Sofia can abide in peace."

"And you too, honey. You deserve peace too!"

His eyes detach in deep thought. "Today I've seen a glimpse of what that looks like, darling. It was perfect."

"Well, I hope that you'll experience many more days like this." I kiss him. "I love you."

44. *Amore*

During the holidays, I've been spending most of my time either homemaking, volunteering at the local homeless shelter, or working on a new collection of paintings while keeping Sofia wrapped around my chest. I feel like an octopus, constantly multi-tasking with my focus jumping back and forward all over the place. But I am happy, because Sofia is happy. She's become the absolute joy of my world. Every morning regardless of how tired I may be, I remain surged with strength because I know that Sofia is my reason to keep going every day.

However, today will be different. Valentina and Francesco's mamma will be visiting us. They're eager to meet Sofia, and apparently, Francesco's mamma wishes to make amends.

I settle Sofia down in our bedroom on the play mat next to Lily while I get ready to freshen up before they arrive. Though, out of nowhere, I hear the doorbell ring.

"Honey," I call out to the hallway, popping my head out of the bedroom door.

Francesco springs out of his study, almost bumping into Ben. Lily gets scared and suddenly runs toward me rather startled, so I pick her up and give her a sweet kiss for comfort.

"I'll get the door, sir," Ben says.

"Grazie, grazie."

Francesco strides toward me, looking a bit concerned about something as he shuts the door behind him.

"What's the matter, sweetie?" I ask.

He picks up Sofia in his arms and gives her a kiss. "Nothing, darling."

"I'm just going to freshen up and get changed, I'll meet you and the family in a sec."

"Alright, baby." He rubs his hand softly over my shoulder before leaving with Sofia.

Soon after, I hear very loud greetings in Italian, all of which I can tell is due to meeting Sofia. I smile at the thought of it, but I'm also feeling unsettled myself. How will Signora Giordano behave around me this time? This time Francesco and I have nowhere to run, nowhere to leave at all, because this is our home.

For a quick moment I pray to God that all will work out well, then I leave and head toward the living room.

Peppa Pig is still playing on the television from earlier, but the volume has quietened down. The noise between the family softens immensely as I enter the room. Valentina and Signora Giordano's eyes zoom straight toward me.

"Ciao, Natalia! Come stai?" Valentina leaps up from the couch to greet me with a kiss on each cheek.

"Erm, *bene*... grazie," I reply quietly, trying to remember the little Italian Francesco taught me.

Signora Giordano steadily rises robotically from the couch, with blank eyes but a soft smile. "Hello."

"Hello, Signora Giordano. How are you this lovely afternoon? I hope that your flight went very smoothly for you."

"Please." She steps forward, taking both of my hands in hers. "You may call me, mamma."

Immediately I catch Francesco's face in the distance light up as she says it.

"Mamma," I breathe, smiling. A bittersweet sting fills within me as I think of my own mamá.

"I have such a beautiful niece!" Valentina exclaims, now pinching Sofia out of Francesco's arms. He tells her to be careful, she rolls her eyes and continues to cuddle Sofia.

"I have always waited for this day." Mamma releases quiet sigh of relief as she sits back down so elegantly upon the couch. "The day that God graces me with the opportunity to meet my beloved grandchild. A blessing, indeed."

I feel sorry for her as she says it, for I was made aware that she didn't have the chance to meet Daisy and Francesco's sons.

"Would you ladies care for any tea?" I ask, shortly afterward.

Mamma, Valentina and Francesco look at each other with subtle amusement, but Valentina is the first to laugh and say, "Mamma hates tea. I do too."

"Oh, goodness! I apologize—"

"There is no need to apologize, darling." Francesco smiles peacefully. He then directs to his mother and sister, "Volete l'acqua?"

"Sì, grazie," mamma responds, and Valentina also agrees while she plays with Sofia.

"Do you want anything, darling?" he asks me.

"I'm okay thank you, honey."

Once he leaves the room, I immediately feel the lack of his presence. I'm not really the best at surface level conversations, but I still make the effort anyway. Therefore, I try to quickly think of something to say as I sit down on the couch. But then suddenly, mamma surprises me and beats me to it.

"Natalia, allow me to express my apologies for the way I treated you last spring."

"Aww, it's okay. No worries at all!"

"The Giordano name carries weight." She sighs.

"We all have had our challenges, when it comes to choosing the right mate. Haven't we, Vale?"

"Sì, mamma," Valentina replies. "I have had plenty of men that were only interested in me for the wrong reasons. Even before Francesco left all those years ago for England, he had a girlfriend who admitted to one of my best friends that she was only in it for what we have too. So yes, it is hard, mamma. But Natalia is not like that."

"I promise you, mamma, I love Francesco for who he is. With all my heart, I do!"

"Yes, I am aware." She smiles, softly. "We had a conversation, my son and I, about you."

I feel myself blushing. "Aww, what did he say?"

She sits up straight. "I hear that you have many ambitions of your own."

"Yep, that would be me!"

"An artist, how marvelous."

"Thanks, although it's hard with the little one. I can't paint as much these days."

"That is understandable," Valentina says. "But mamma, maybe we could ask Natalia to do some paintings for us one day? Our house is looking too dull. So very dull."

"Yes," mamma agrees, engaged in deep thought. "I agree, Vale."

"What are you speaking of?" Francesco now enters with their glasses of water.

"We need a change," Valentina begins. "I am tired of seeing those dusty, ancient paintings of people we haven't met hanging on our walls."

"Vale," mamma speaks in an authoritative tone. "Those portraits are dated as far back as the renaissance period."

"Sì, I am aware of that. But can't we put them in the attic? We need something new, something bright for once."

"I am sure that Natalia can help you with that. She's a spectacular artist." Francesco's eyes smile at me.

"Will you, Nat?" Valentina asks.

"If mamma is happy for me to do so, then of course! I don't see why not."

Mamma smiles at me so sweetly. "Sì, it would be a pleasure."

"Fra," Valentina directs to Francesco. "When are you taking Sofia to come and see home?"

"Soon."

"Do not delay, Francesco," mamma orders, while taking a sip of her water. "It is important that Sofia is aware of her background. Her immersion within our culture is imperative."

"Yes, I will keep that in mind."

"And you, Natalia, dear? Remind me of where you are from?" she asks me.

"Well, I was born in the US, but my family are from Spain."

"A beautiful country." She nods firmly.

"It is, though I haven't had the opportunity to see it."

"Oh, what a shame," she responds. "Fra, ensure to take your family to Spain as soon as you are able."

"Yes, I will do. It's been on my to-do list for a while."

Francesco's eyes meet mine and I've never felt such felicity that flows from him. This is what he's wanted for so long. A family at rest. In peace and tranquility. It makes me happy to know that he's serene in this moment. That's all I want for him. It's all I want for all of us.

45. Grace

Francesco reads Sofia a bedtime story as I hold her in my arms. God, he's so sexy when he does this. What happened to him? What happened to the grumpy man that I met in the coffee shop? If only you could see him right now, you'd see his radiance and fatherly love beaming right through him. He's so beautiful, I love him.

Lily snuggles up in a loaf next to our feet while it's happening. This is heavenly. There are moments where Sofia will just look at him and smile, revealing that cute gummy grin that I adore so much. The way he looks at her is out of this world. No words can fully describe the ardent love that he has for our daughter. I feel it, every time that we're all together.

Eventually she falls asleep, and the moment we leave, he scoops me close to him with one arm.

"I have news to tell you," he tells me.

"So do I, I have news for you too!"

"Tell me. What is it, darling?"

"Well, Angelina contacted me today and told me that I'll finally be having a solo exhibition in one of the galleries within Chelsea! I'm so happy about it!"

His hands grip me tighter with excitement to then lift me in the air and spin me around like a child. I can't help but laugh!

"Oh, amore. You deserve this!" he rejoices.

"Thank you, honey!" I giggle, as he gently puts me down. "Now tell me! What's your news?"

"Well," he begins, taking my hand as we walk through the hallway. "I have had much thought about certain things. Watching you pursue your dreams has sparked something inside of me. You inspire me, darling."

"Aww! Thank you so much, honey. I'm so happy to hear that! What is it? Have you decided to start a new business?"

He chuckles. "Baby, I'm always working on new businesses. No, what I'm talking about here in particular is that I've decided to write a book."

"A book!"

"Yes." He laughs softly at my response.

I forget that my mouth is still hanging open. "What kind of book, baby?"

"A memoir," he replies. "Reflecting on grief as a brother... and father. I have a reputation for being cold, but no-one knows what shit I've endured."

"Wow, oh my goodness honey. That's so powerful and it is also much needed! I feel as though many men don't share their story about the pain they've been through when losing a child. As well as Roberto's story, it will touch so many hearts. I know that it will!"

"Grazie... I just hope that I'm able to deliver the memoir in a way that is effective."

"I have faith in you, sweetheart," I say, lifting up to press my lips to his strong jaw. "I believe in you. This was your childhood dream, remember? To be a writer! And now you are one, honey."

He stops walking and looks at me with such deep love within his eyes. "Where the fuck would I be without you?" he breathes, as his facial hair tickles my neck.

"I mean this when I tell you that I can't imagine life without you, Francesco. You've become a part of me. Something that no-one will ever be able to uproot, because you're so deeply embedded within me. I'm so sure, honey, that I'll adore you until I take my last breath."

"My darling love," he whispers in the hollow of my neck while he kisses me softly. "You don't comprehend how greatly that I'm enraptured by you... Come with me, baby. I have something I'd like to show you."

Ever so sweetly, he takes hold of my hand and leads me into the main family room. As he does, all I suddenly begin to hear is soft classical music sailing so lightly throughout the home. I don't understand what is happening, but my cheeks are tingling with spice, and my skin is burning up at this unexpected moment.

What is going on?

There are an abundance of sparkling tea light candles that illuminate the dimmed hallway so prettily. It's so wonderfully stunning. I can tell so much love, thought and effort has been put in this.

How and when did he manage to do this?
Was it the Ben and the girls?

"Honey, what's going on?" I ask him.

Suddenly, I find myself positively and beautifully overwhelmed by the magnificent splendor of the living room. Face to face with an innumerable amount of massive red rose bouquets so perfectly throughout. There are red rose petals everywhere, scattered beautifully upon the ground, and clusters of flowers upon the wall that spell, *'Marry me.'*

I lose my breath at the glory of it all, only for my heart to intensify the moment I see Francesco now kneeling behind me.

"Natalia," he whispers.

I suck in a deep breath, automatically placing my hand on my chest at the sensation of my heart pounding so vigorously. "Francesco..."

His loving grey eyes flood with water, then presses his lips so tenderly upon my hand.

"Natalia, believe me when I tell you that I am

enamored with who you are. Your presence alone has set me free in a magnitude of ways. For decades I carried the belief that love, *real* love, was not destined for a heartless fool like me. I was certain of it, amore. I did not think that I was ever capable of giving my myself away to someone else. But amore, I have found my heart when I found you. And if you would have me, Natalia, I wish to remain fully committed to you until death, we part. I cannot pass through life without you by my side. Even with all the fucking wealth and the fame in the world, baby, it means nothing to me without you. If I lack your presence, I lack everything. You are my laughter and my joy, my glory and my crown. Amore, I would not be the man that I am today without you."

"Honey..." I can barely stand with my face soaked with a waterfall of indescribable bliss. But I search into his eyes to see the most sincere soul, and it makes me love him even more.

"Natalia Garcia," he breathes, with a hint of nerves. "Will you marry me?"

He opens the ring box, and it shines like the moon encrusted with all of the stars of the galaxy.

"Yes!" I cry, falling to my knees to kiss him. "Yes, absolutely yes! Yes, honey! I will!"

There's not a second that passes by before he places the beautiful ring on my finger, and as he holds me in his arms, his face is gleaming like the sunrise on a summers day. It's like my long lost dream, blooming to reality. I bask in this glorious moment, and saturate the richness of his oud scent as we embrace. He is my home now.

"I love you," he whispers.

I tell him that I love him too, while gazing into his ice grey eyes that immerse me into a dimension of love, lust and wonderment all at once. I've fallen for this man so deeply. It's the way he has changed, softened for the better. Whole and healthy, yet still the Francesco Giordano that I know, deeply adore and passionately admire. I love him with a passion more than any man on this earth. There's a fire and desire that burns within me for him, and it lingers on and on with no force in this world having the ability to put it out. Being in this moment with him is all I need to further confirm that I have wholeheartedly fallen for the right man that has been destined for me. Francesco is mine, and I am his. It's clear that Gideon and I were never meant to be. Friends, we were. But true lovers, we were not. And I've come to a place where I am at peace with it all. For I am a firm believer in that everything happens for a reason, and my absolute source of bliss pours out from the man that stands in front of me. A gift from heaven, he truly is. As well as our daughter, I can't think of anything that I appreciate more in my existence.

Ever so romantically, he swiftly swoops me up in his massive arms, carrying me toward our nearest bedroom. I love when he holds me up in the air. It feels like I'm floating in a cloud of fervent love and felicity. It's the way he holds me. The firm grip of his arms that secure me tight. The strength of his muscles, caging me in and pressing me against him. I feel safe and desired. I feel wanted. Nobody has ever made me feel as sexy and as special as he does.

We enter the room, and he releases me softly, laying me on the bed. "I never knew that this was possible for me," he whispers in between our kisses. "That I could feel something as intense as this. Fuck," he breathes. "You're the reason why I believe there's a God out there. That a love this fervent exists. Because what I feel for you, darling, is out of this world."

Gosh, I love this man so much.

"Oh honey." I let the tears and moans flow out from within me as his lips kiss my breasts. I'm panting so strong that I can barely even get a sentence out. He touches me in ways that make me feel so beautiful. I'm wholeheartedly enthralled by him.

My fingers fly over the buttons of his shirt, saturating the glory of his body. He shrugs it off, then brings my knees over his large shoulders, and presses his solid cock right over me through our clothes. His whole body weight rocks back and forth on my clit as we kiss, and just when I feel like I can't take much more, he picks me up and presses me down with strong arms over his manhood.

"See how hard I am for you?" he breathes, violently. "Darling, this is what you do to me. I can't get enough. You're my fucking ecstasy. My oxygen, my sun. Everything good that I am is because of you, baby. Life is so much better with you in it."

His lips lavish me with love between my breasts, bringing my head to tilt back in delight as he pulls on my hair.

There's a wanting within his eyes that I can tell only I will satisfy. I tell him that I love him, moaning greatly at the overwhelming pleasure of his fingers inside of me.

"I can't wait to marry you, amore. Finally, we'll be official, with no-one fucking between us this time. Just me and you, darling. I'll say my vows before God concerning how fervently I devote myself to you."

I climax into another world, potent with pleasure in every sense. His love is my heart and my entire universe, through him I've found a steadfast joy that remains utterly endless.

"I look forward to being your wife," I say in a breath. "To sharing the rest of my life with you."

"Is it even possible for me to get enough of you?" He leans in, taking me further up the bed as he holds me on his lap. "Natalia, I'll always love you. Every part of you, darling. Both the good and the things that you try to hide from me. I adore you. All of you, baby."

With one hand he cradles my face so tenderly, forcing our eyes to lock with the deepest love. I watch his pupils dilate, completely ridding those eyes of the coolest shade of grey. They're almost black. Utterly wild. Penetrating me with love that cannot be uttered in mere words.

"Nat," Francesco breathes. "I'm yours."

God, my heart.

He lays me down lovingly, with the sweetest kisses that follow throughout. Tears spill over my temples as he enters me with a slow, deep thrust. He does it again, and my breathing then starts matching his. Violent, and heavy, utterly mirroring our devotion to each other. He's taken my heart into a whole new dimension. It belongs to him, and I know that I'll never get it back. For he is my love, my soon to be husband, and the father of my child. God knows that even beyond my very last breath, my heart will always belong to him.

46. Ardent

Heavy winter rain begins to shower on and off over the flowers as I speed toward the rose garden. Now is not an ideal time to meet Gideon, but since his move has been finalized, today is my last chance to say goodbye before moves to LA tomorrow.

I feel hot and cold, both in body and spirit. My hair is soaking wet, drenched in the magnitude of raindrops that are soaking through my clothes. I see Gideon there, waiting for me underneath the arch of flowers, finding shelter from the rain.

"Hey!" I hurry toward him, catching a breath. "Sorry I'm late, I was busy taking care of Sofia."

"It's fine, Nat," he replies, smiling as raindrops make their way down his curls. "My apologies, I should have chosen somewhere more suitable. If I had known it would be raining—"

"It's alright! I also never knew too. I should've

checked the weather app. But I mean, I still find it strange when it rains here so much during the summer. One minute it's sunny, then the next there's a thunderstorm!"

"That's British weather for you," he says in a chuckle, revealing his sweet dimples. "How is the situation with that lady... Daisy, is it?"

I nod. "Yeah, umm, sadly she will remain in a psychiatric hospital for a while. Apparently, rather than remain in prison, it was a better option for her to receive the help she needs elsewhere... which is understandable. I feel sorry for her. She haunts me, Gee. Just like my father does."

"Come here, Nat," he breathes, giving me a hug. "I'm sorry for all of the pain you've endured throughout these last couple of years. But my hope is that you'll soar from here and make the most of life with the blessings you've got right here, right now. That's all we can do, Nat. Take one day at a time. You're never alone. You comprehend that truth, don't you? You are so loved."

I look at his face, and I look at the garden that surrounds us. So many memories of when I first met him. So much heartache we've both experienced since we first encountered one another. I swallow the hardest pill, and whisper, "Yes... I'm going to really miss you, Gideon."

He blinks the wetness in his eyes away. "I will miss you too, Natalia. More than you know."

"I hope that you will find everything that you need and desire there. Are you sure that you'll be okay?"

"Of course," he breathes. "I have to be, for them."

"But your sisters need you to be okay for you too, Gideon. You matter too, you know that, don't you?"

"Nat," he responds, with a gentle sigh. "Even if that were true, I am not in the position to consider myself first anymore. Kitty and Phoebe come first. Everything that I do now, it's all for them. I'm hoping that America is the best choice for them."

"I'll be praying for you, Gee. Things have to get better for you and your family from here. The darkest of seasons always come to light eventually, don't they?"

"Nat, if that's true, it's been an arduous season for me and the girls. Long enough to make me wonder if this is all that's it for us. But you know, I have always loved something particular about you…"

"Really! What is it?"

"You have a spirit full of hope. Since the day that I met you, I could see it in your eyes and hear the passion within your voice. That's something not many people have. Where did you get that from?"

I smile. "My mother."

"A strong woman." He smiles back.

"Are you really sure that you're going to be alright, Gideon? I can't imagine you living across the world from me. What will you do when Phoebe and Kitty eventually go to college? The day will come when they will live their lives independently from you... I just can't bear the thought of you out there all alone!"

"Don't worry about me," he says, hugging me close. "I'll be fine, Nat. I always have been."

"Gee, you're not an island. You matter—"

I begin crying uncontrollably, and he hushes me softly to comfort in his arms. "Hey, it's going to be alright, Natalia. I promise."

"Ugh, there you go again." I croak. "Always promising me with comforting words about things that aren't even certain."

"There's no benefit in worrying though, Nat."

"I feel as though I think of you more than you think of yourself."

"That's probably right."

"But it's wrong," I breathe. "For the past how many years you've been taking care of other people. When will you ever look after yourself?"

"My guess is, that when the girls do eventually leave for university, I most likely will have plenty of time on my hands to start again and focus more on me."

"Start again? But what does that look like for you?"

I feel him shrug ever so softly. "Try everything

that I've had on my bucket list since I was a teenager, before my grandmother fell ill... before my parents got into the accident."

"Tell me some of the stuff that's on your list," I say, looking up into his emerald eyes.

"Well, maybe start an art school for kids on the weekends," he responds with a shy smile on his face. "Travel to Dominican Republic, to see the country my mother was from," he continues, blushing. "Maybe even travel to Thailand for a few months."

"Aww! That truly sounds lovely, Gee."

"Don't forget I'm just a call away if you need anything."

"The same to you too, Gee." I sniffle. "I know that I've failed you in the past, and I'm sorry. But I'll never forget how such a good friend you are in my life. I want to support you too, wherever I can. You're my angel, Gideon. You always will be such a massive treasure of my destiny. Without you, I wouldn't have made it this far, nor obtained the strength I needed to keep... living and pursue my dreams. You mean the world to me, Gee. I'm just so sorry that I've failed to show it in the way you truly deserved."

His eyes deepen red, and I kiss him on the cheek. The rain lightens up and the sun begins to peak out again.

"Hey," he whispers. "Don't worry about it. I'm glad we met, Nat. I look forward to seeing what more great things will unfold for you."

"You too, Gee."

He smiles. "We better get going, before the rain gets heavy again," he says, glancing up to the sky. "Where are you off to now... back home?"

"Yeah, how about you?"

"Me too." He smiles. "But I have a brief meeting to attend with Angelina before I head home... are you going to be alright?"

"Yeah, I will Gee. Go ahead, I'll be alright getting to the underground station."

He smiles softly after he gives me one last hug. "Take care, Nat."

He doesn't wait for me to say anything before he begins walking away.

"I adore you, Gideon. Always and forever, I will," I tell him.

It stops him in his tracks, and he turns round to look at me one last time with water filled within his eyes. He says no words, but one last smile. Then strides through the floral archways to his next destination, just before the sky begins to reveal its thunder.

47. Love

When I paint with Sofia, I have memories of mamá. She once had a studio, and she used to wrap me over her chest while she painted. I still remember her scent. Coconut and vanilla. Her chocolate hair with stands of honey always brought me comfort whenever I laid my head to rest with her. Sofia does the same.

She tugs on my hair and stares at me in wonder with her grey doe eyes. I wonder what she will be when she grows up one day. I envision her being free. Completely at liberty to pursue whatever her heart desires. I will tell her that anything is possible, and that there is beauty within life, despite the ups and downs. Because it's filled with an abundance of precious, little things. The simple things. The light of hope in her little heart. For as long as she dreams, wondrous things are possible to obtain within her reach. I don't wish to limit her. I don't desire for her to lose sight of pursuing the things that matter to her. Because life is about living, and not merely clinging on to what makes sense to us. She has a father who loves her affectionately, and that's something not many people have been able to experience nor comprehend. She has a mother who is devoted to her, and that's something not many people are truly able to say. I want to be present in her life, and give her the love that she deserves, that I may show her how precious and cherished she is, especially before a man could ever validate that for her.

I'd like to teach her to count her blessings, while still reaching for the stars beyond her most glorious imagination. I'd like her father to teach her that no amount of money could never buy true happiness, and I'd like to remind her that true love and belief in oneself doesn't come from others, it comes from within. Then when I'm old and grey, I will rest within my heart, knowing that despite the trials and tribulations, I have persevered with all of my strength to keep on living with an ardent love, that overflows with passion for life.

Epilogue

Just Over One Year Later

It's officially the holidays, and the glorious festive spirit overflows cheerfully throughout our new home in the Cotswolds. My wedding band sparkles beautifully underneath the colorful Christmas lights that mamma and I carefully decorated throughout the house. Valentina, Kitty and Phoebe are making a snowman in the front garden with Carlos, Gabby and Rosa.

Julieta is baking with mamma in the kitchen. The scrumptious aroma of warm vanilla Christmas cookies blooms absolutely mouthwatering. Diego's booming laugh explodes from the living room, and honestly, it is much louder than the Christmas movies that are actually playing in the background. I quickly peek through the door, to see Francesco, Gideon and Joseph with him chilling beside the grand fireplace. They're all watching Maria being silly as they all play a game of charades.

Suddenly, I hear Sofia's voice as I step inside.

"Dada!" she calls, taking cute little steps toward Francesco and into his arms. He then lifts her in the air, and she squeals in excitement as she holds on tight to her favorite teddy bear.

"Oh yeah, Francesco..." Phoebe quickly steps in, hopping onto the couch. "I forgot to tell you that I read your memoir in one sitting! It's been number one on the bestseller list for weeks now. I had to get it!"

"Grazie mille!" He grins so beautifully. "We also are very much looking forward to reading one of your works someday too, Phoebe."

"Absolutely we do, dearest." Julieta pops in with mamma as they both hold trays of Christmas sugar cookies and gingerbread men with jelly tots buttons. "I must say Phoebe, my love, you're getting me into reading books again! Maria and I love being part of your book club online!"

Phoebe blushes and thanks Julieta as she takes a cookie, and suddenly I feel something spark so wonderfully within me that it causes me to gasp.

"My goodness! The baby just kicked for the first time!" I squeal in excitement.

My sweet son.

Everyone gasps, and Francesco is the first to draw nearer with Sofia.

"Your little brother is saying hello, piccolina!" he rejoices, kissing her on the cheek. His hand moves Sofia's over my stomach ever so gently as I guide him to where the baby is kicking.

"He is going to love you, my sweet angel," I tell her. She then smiles at me and clings on to her daddy.

Mamma takes a seat on the couch as Valentina and Kitty join her. "Glory to God," she whispers, patting her tears away.

"Oh, mamma," Valentina breathes in delight, hugging her mother.

Diego puts his arm around me and kisses me on my head. "So proud of you, Nat."

"Yeah," Maria smiles, as she sits next to Gideon, joining her hand in his. "Mamá would be so proud of you."

"She'd be proud of *all* of us," I tell them.

Julieta wipes a tear away and sits on the carpet next to the fire. Gabby, Rosa and Carlos then leap over her with a sea of happy cuddles and kisses.

"Ah, Gee," Joseph calls Gideon as he switches through the television channels. "What's the one to watch some game?"

Gideon laughs. "I'm not quite sure why you're asking me, Joe. I'm not into sports as much as Francesco or Diego."

"401," Francesco responds, trying to hide his amusement. "But I doubt there will be any live matches on Christmas Day, Joseph."

"What's on then? Better be good." Diego heads toward the couch and plants himself on it.

Kitty jumps before the television. "I know! Let's watch a *Disney Princess* film!"

All of the adults begin to sigh with laughter.

Sofia is smiling, revealing her little teeth coming through. Francesco grins with so much happiness and tickles her chubby cheek with another kiss.

"Hmmm," I wonder aloud. "I think maybe another Christmas film would be better."

"Nat's right," Maria agrees.

"*A Christmas Carol?*" Phoebe suggests. "It's one of Charles Dickens well-known stories."

"That's too scary for us!" Carlos exclaims, then everyone chuckles. "It has ghosts in it!"

"Okay, well… everyone have a think on it. I'm going to get some matches from the kitchen to light my new vanilla candles!" I tell them.

Not long after I head into the kitchen, I hear someone behind me, stepping closer through the dark.

"Gee!" I gasp. "My goodness, you scared me!"

"Sorry, Nat," he apologizes. "I just came to tell you that the matches were already beside us on one of the shelves. We tried calling you, but—"

"My goodness, I don't think I heard! I've been in my own little world."

He chuckles. "No worries."

"Ah! Well, now that you're here, I have a lovely

gift that I'd like to share with you."

"What is it?" he asks, surprised.

I take out a little red envelope from one of the draws that has his name on it. "Open it."

When he sees what it is, he looks absolutely stunned. "Wow! Tickets to the Vincent Van Gogh Live Exhibition?"

"I never forgot, Gee. When we were in the gallery admiring one of his pieces. You adore him just as much as I do."

He says nothing but gives me the loveliest and most sincere hug. "Thank you, Nat."

"You and Maria can go before you leave back to LA, hopefully?"

"Indeed, hopefully we can," he replies, sweetly.

Suddenly, we hear the family calling us from the living room. Once we head back together to the living room, we see that they're all watching *The Grinch*.

"Oooh! I love this movie so much!" I beam with happiness, sitting next to Francesco and Sofia.

She's looking at me as she rests on her father's lap. "Mama!" she squeaks, blessing my heart so beautifully.

I give her a kiss, then lean into Francesco's chest as Lily loafs adorably on my lap.

"This day is perfect," he whispers into my ear.

"I pray that there will be many more for us to come, honey," I whisper back. "Though I must say,

I've found it difficult to find a gift for someone who has almost everything."

He stares silently into my eyes, before finally saying, "Look, Natalia... all of the wealth of the earth can't compare to what I've found in you. You're my greatest treasure, amore mio."

I look into his gorgeous grey eyes, utterly lost in his blissful smile and sweetest love. To say that I'm happy is an understatement. For though life may not always be picture perfect, I have found strength in pushing through the hard times. Only three years ago, I was genuinely convinced that I would be dead by this point, but I can wholeheartedly say that it was my art that kept me alive. My passion. It anchored me into believing for something more, something greater beyond what I could see, while holding wholeheartedly onto gratitude for the simple things that matter most to me. My loved ones.

I have come to accept that in life we may lose many things. Like my mother and father, whom I thought as a child that they would always remain with me. But as time blooms on, I try to hold on to the positive memories. Forgiving what was, while looking forward to beautiful possibilities to come. I'm learning to comprehend what that true love is. It's selfless and patient, far from mirroring what my father claimed it to be. But in order to receive love, I've had no choice but to learn to love myself, despite my past and deepest heartaches. I've grown in understanding that faith for better days to come is the kind of hope that encourages the human spirit to keep going. But through that journey, I found it necessary to be gentle with myself. For though people may come and go, I will always be my home. And falling in love with oneself is one of the most beautiful experiences to cherish and grow. Despite the uncertainty, and regardless of what happens within my destiny, I let go of my need to control and be so hard on myself. Rather, I keep my eyes fixed toward the heavens, grateful for the breath in my lungs and the resilience that is birthed through ups and downs of the life. For with all my heart, I truly know, that ardent love that has carried me through it all.

Acknowledgements

I decided to write Ardent after I dreamt about two artist friends named Natalia and Gideon who lived in a city. They would visit art galleries together, and they both seemed really happy to be around one another. Francesco didn't enter the scene until later, and from there I could tell that something about his presence instantly became a hinderance to Natalia and Gideon's relationship. Initially, I thought it was just a random dream at the time so I ignored for a while, but after months passed, I couldn't help but think about the characters. I often wondered who those people were and I was intrigued to learn about their story regarding how they had come to have such a strong passion for art. Through which, I decided to just start writing about it just for fun, but that fun turned into almost four years of wonderment for the story that eventually came to fruition. I couldn't let the story go. It was truly so odd to me at first because I carried no desire at all to write a novel, but there's now a part of my heart that flows so deeply with gratitude upon being discovering Natalia's story. It's been a beautiful and life-changing journey for me, and I've fallen utterly in love with the characters, yet I wouldn't have been able to do this without the support of many loved ones in my life.

Rayarna, words can't describe how much you've been an absolute blessing in my life. I feel as though the way Natalia feels about Gideon in regard to believing that he's an angel who encouraged her to pursue her dreams, even when she didn't believe in herself, very much mirrors how I feel about you. You're an amazing friend that I'm convinced has been sent to me from heaven. Your constant support and encouragement through this journey has helped me to keep believing in the beauty of Ardent during moments of discouragement. I wouldn't have made it this far without you. I'm so truly grateful to have you as my best friend. You deserve the world and more.

My parents, whose support means a lot to me. Since I've embarked on my journey to pursue my dreams, you've helped me in ways that many other parents wouldn't, even during those times when you didn't understand. For that, I'm extremely grateful. Thank you for believing in me.

Vanessa, thank you so much for always being absolutely amazing and creating the most beautiful cover ever for Ardent. I can always rely on you to make the most stunning covers for me. You're a star!

Thank you to all my close friends for being the sweetest throughout this wonderful journey.

Kieran, I wouldn't have come this far without your constant encouragement.

Marisa, Ardent wouldn't be what it is today if it wasn't for your kind encouragement and feedback. Thank you for seeing potential in my writing.

Jessica, I'm so deeply grateful for all that you've helped me with as I've embarked on this new path in writing! You have shared so much of your wisdom with me that I very much treasure and appreciate. Thank you so much.

My readers, who have been with me through my journey of writing throughout the years, thank you so much for being super sweet and encouraging about my poetry. Although Ardent is much different to my poetry collections, I hope that you adored reading my first novel! I'm so grateful for your constant support and lovely messages.

I'm a huge believer that nothing is impossible with God, and I'm so thankful that I've been given the grace to receive such a beautiful opportunity to follow my heart, and pursue my dreams.

Printed in Great Britain
by Amazon